RED AT NIGHT

JERRY FARNHAM

Published by the author
Edited by Pat Cole
Cover Art by Bryan Soeres
Interior Design by Eric H. Bowen
Body Text set in TeX Gyre Pagella 10 point

ISBN: 979-8-218-12793-0

This book is dedicated to all those who were told they couldn't, shouldn't or wouldn't. I had people in my life call me stupid, saying that I wouldn't get anywhere. Yet here I am with my book before your eyes. Don't listen to the naysayers. Be brave. Step up. Be the person in the arena.

"It is not the critic who counts; not the man who points out how the strong man stumbles, or where the doer of deeds could have done them better. The credit belongs to the man who is actually in the arena, whose face is marred by dust and sweat and blood; who strives valiantly; who errs, who comes up short again and again, because there is no effort without error and shortcoming; but who does actually strive to do the deeds; who knows great enthusiasms, the great devotions; who spends himself in a worthy cause; who at the best knows in the end the triumph of high achievement, and who at the worst, if he fails, at least fails while daring greatly, so that his place shall never be with those cold and timid souls who neither know victory nor defeat." - Theodore Roosevelt

Acknowledgments

I have had this book in my head since I was 16 (1994). In 2016 I met the person who I would use for Tommy Macintye. I started writing that day. This book would have never happened without the support and patience of my wife and good friends. My wife kept me motivated and was there to bounce ideas off. My friend Severre St. John fueled my ambition by asking me when the next chapter would be done. Will Murphy did my editing for me and had me do minor….and major tweaks here and there. Other friends Chris and Lexi Bergy, Laura East, Dave and Bev Sutherland, Shonn Moulton and his wife, Diane Wescott, Greg Jbara, the Kanney's and all of you on Facebook who encouraged me, thank you all.

Credit for the cover art goes to Bryan Soeres. I sent him a picture of my dad's 38 Young Brothers and the color scheme I wanted. I would say he nailed it! I sent the raw image that Bryan gave me to Jamie and Ruth Lowell at Time Bouys to finish the cover and format it. The chart work was done by my wife Marty Farnham.

Shortly after the book came out a gentleman approached me about how much he enjoyed the book. We met over a beer at my old workplace. He said the book was great but needed some.... polishing to get it to the next level. Andy Roberts got in touch with Pat Cole and did a great final edit. Andy has the patience of a saint dealing with my busy work and life schedule and Mrs. Cole did a great job editing without bruising my ego. Thank you to the following people who took part in my pre-purchase campaign that funded my printing costs. Without you all, this book would have never hit paper: Colin Stokes, Kent Colby, Vickie Colby, Betsy Lowe, Fred Farnham, Michelle Farnham, Erin Burr, Logan Vail, Clive Farrin, Elise Cundy, Eric and Jen Reiter, Tom Fogarty, Jeff and Kristy Douglas, Kevin Street, Shonn Moulton, Rachel Fecteau and Sherri Hersom.

About the Author

I was raised in Boothbay Harbor, the son of a lobsterman. I grew up on a lobster boat going sternman every summer from age six until I left to serve my country in the US Navy. I returned to civilian life in 2007 taking several jobs and going back to School before settling in Gorham Maine with my wife and 2 kids. I enjoy writing, unprofessionally, for www.DowneastBoatForum.com, archery, working on my boat *Tip Jar*, or my Jeep named MeatLug, and most of all I love being a husband and father.

Connect with me online:

http://www.jerryfarnham.com/

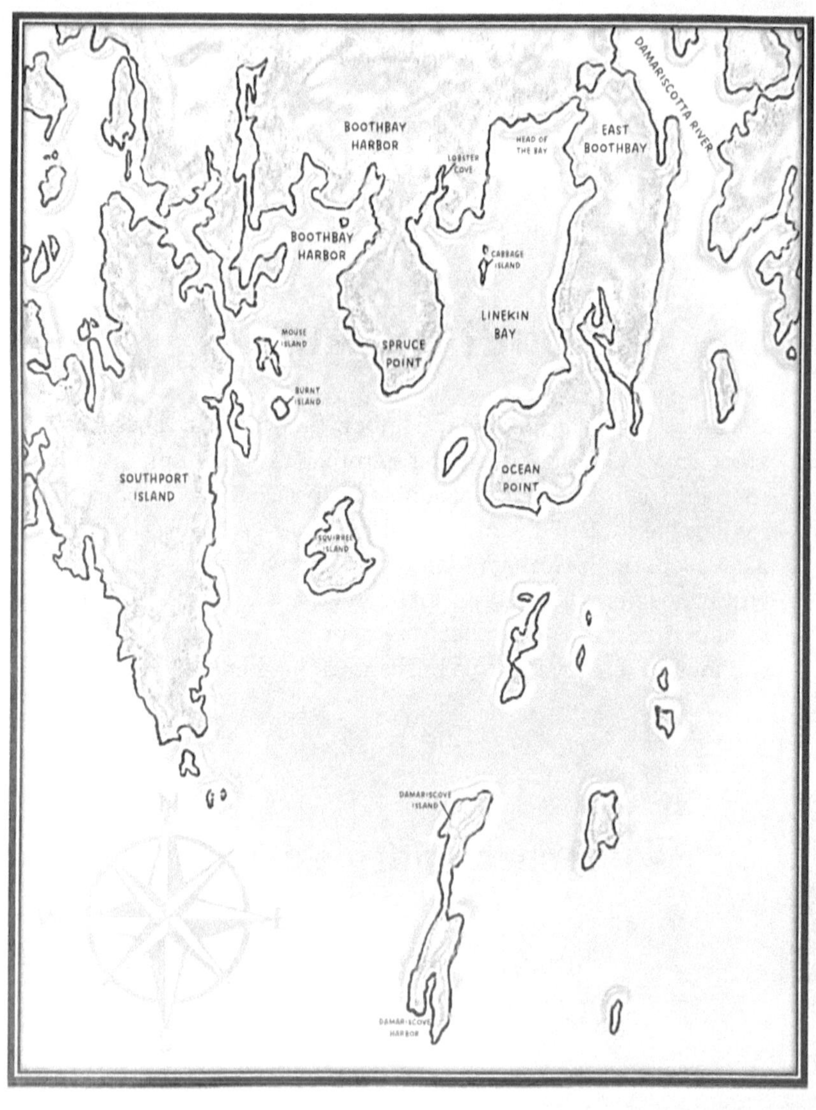

DAMARISCOTTA RIVER
BOOTHBAY HARBOR
HEAD OF THE BAY
EAST BOOTHBAY
LOBSTER COVE
BOOTHBAY HARBOR
CABBAGE ISLAND
LINEKIN BAY
MOUSE ISLAND
SPRUCE POINT
BURNT ISLAND
OCEAN POINT
SOUTHPORT ISLAND
SQUIRREL ISLAND
DAMARISCOVE ISLAND
DAMARISCOVE HARBOR

Chapter 1

The sun was just peaking up onto the horizon, setting the glass smooth water on fire with reds, oranges, and pinks. It was just the type of morning that Jack Finn lived for. With one hand on the throttle and one hand on the wheel he looked over the bow of the Red at Night and took a long deep breath of the ocean air. His heart got heavy and a tear rolled down his cheek as he passed Barret's Park. His reminiscence was interrupted by a familiar voice on the radio.

"Red at Night, are you on, boy?" the VHF radio blasted over the sound of the humming diesel.

"Go ahead Dad," Jack replied, his voice cracking a bit.

"Where you headed today, boy?" Jack's father replied.

"Hauling the bay today. Then after I sell, I am gonna wash up and head over to the co-op for a couple beers. What you up to?"

"I am setting a handful over to Ocean Point then haul the eastside of the bay and the ledges."

"Well then, maybe we can grab a cup of coffee and a sandwich later."

"Alrighty then boy, have a large day."

"Talk at you later, Dad."

Jack pushed the throttle up to 1600 rpms and the Red at Night planed off and made way to the tip of Spruce Point.

The Red at Night was the typical Maine lobster boat derived from early sail boats and slowly mutated over the course of time to fit the needs of the lobstering industry. The Maine lobster boat, often called "Downeast" where most of the modifications came from simple sailing vessels to steam, then to small gas, and now to bigger diesel engines. The hulls grew, longer and wider. Some designers kept the deeper sailboat like bottom which is referred to as built-down. Other designers wanted to meet the needs of lobstermen fishing shallower waters and started reducing the bottom making the skeg-built design. The sailing vessels of old were limited to 7 or 8 knots while the fastest modern lobster boat can achieve 40 to 45 knots. The materials changed with time as well. Wooden boats are a thing of the past. Some still used them, but fiberglass was much more efficient and easier to take care of. Jack's boat, a 38 Young Brothers, had been his dream boat since he first laid eyes on one back when he was just a boy. Designed by Ernest Libby Jr. for Arvid, Arvin, and Colby Young, the Young Brothers is a skeg-built hull with a flat smooth bottom known to be a fast hull. Jack had started out fishing in a 12-foot skiff he had bought from his father. When he graduated high school he had saved enough money to buy a used 30 Repco that had a small 4-cylinder Diesel engine. The Repco had the reputation of being a good starter boat, small and efficient but not the most seaworthy. All the while Jack kept his eye on the few 38 Young Brothers in Boothbay Harbor. Fred Farnham had one that was built kind of heavy. It had a 12-liter 490 horsepower Lugger diesel in it. It went pretty good but Jack wanted faster. Billy Hallinan had one that was built light. It had a 700 hp Detroit Diesel in it. Billy often had the engine "bumped up" to as much as 900hp for racing on the weekends. Jack wanted his to be in between those two. After years of saving money, patching together his Repco to keep it going, and help from the bank, he ordered a 38 Young Brothers. These fiberglass boats could be ordered in any stage of completion that the owner wanted. Jack had ordered just the hull to keep the cost down. He and his father would place the engine, build the deck and topsides, and make any other finishing touches Jack wanted. The hull came cherry red with a bare white bottom. Jack planned on white topsides, smoke gray bottom paint, and a black boot stripe one inch above the waterline. She would be powered by a 13-liter 675 horsepower Scania Diesel engine. Jack had fished these waters all his life. He started going sternman with his father during the summer when he was just six, before fishing his own traps in his own boat when he turned twelve. This was his calling. Being his own boss out on the water. He slowed the boat down and gaffed up the first buoy. It would just be singles, one trap per buoy, and pairs, two traps per buoy today. He flipped the rope up around the snatch block then the pot hauler. Then he pushed the handle to the hauler forward and started hauling the traps off the bottom. The first trap had two keepers in it and the second had one.

"Not bad—Not bad at all," Jack thought to himself.

The day continued on with idle chatter over the VHF. He kept up to the rhythm of the music he had playing over the radio. He was lost in his little world of counting lobsters, running the boat, and hauling traps, one after another. To most people it may seem monotonous, but to the Maine lobstermen it was freedom, a way of life and food on the table.

Melissa Andrews rolled over in her bed to look out the window. It was the same red boat she had seen almost every morning. She wondered what required getting up so early. She could barely make out the figure running the boat. He was a man… that was it. She could tell this man was methodical. His boat went by at the same time if, it went by. Sometimes if it was too foggy, she wouldn't hear him go by. If he didn't go by in the morning, sometimes he would go by later with his traps neatly stacked on his boat with the…, what were they called?... Buoys painted white with a Newport green top, and a pink shaft called a spindle through the middle of it carefully placed on top. She could only assume there was a strategy to the trap and buoy placement from how organized it was. She had caught the name, Red at Night, which she Googled out of curiosity. The name came from an old maritime rhyme.

Red at Night, Sailors delight. Red in the Morning, Sailors take warning.

She had gone down to the dock one morning when there was a black boat close to the dock. She watched the old man grab a buoy and take in all the rope until a green cage-like thing came out of the water. The young teenage boy aided in taking lobsters out and putting dead fish in. Again searching the internet to find out what was going on, she found a few YouTube videos explaining everything. For some reason she found herself drawn to the red boat. She wanted to see the man running it closer. At first she was annoyed by them going by in the morning, but it had grown to a curiosity.

She had to keep her distance from people. She had come here to hide. Get away from Hollywood and it's turncoat media. One minute they are putting you on a pedestal, the next you are fodder for their next big story. She was hurt and angry. Coming here to Maine in this little town would hopefully help give her some perspective. "Boothbay Harbor", she said to herself out loud as she took a deep breath of the morning sea air. When the press started rolling its half-baked stories of drug overdose she started looking for an escape. She wanted to get as far away from Hollywood as she possibly could. She considered leaving the country, but instead went to the opposite side of it. She wanted to hide some place remote, but she needed the benefits of civilization. She had an interest in the ocean so she thought it should be something by the water. She started looking at coastal towns up the east coast. Soon she found Boothbay Harbor. She looked at the images of the little shops and stores. She started looking at rental houses and found a small rental cabin perched on a hill overlooking Linekin Bay. It had a community access dock and a small beach. She knew she could hide herself pretty well in a place like that. No makeup, a hat and sunglasses. Rent a small compact car. Avoid eye contact and small talk. She finished her thoughts as the sound from the mysterious red boat faded. Then she planned her day. Normally her days were planned for her. She had input, and some say in her schedule, but for the most part her agent set up her day. Here in Boothbay Harbor, away from her agent and all the Hollywood fluff that filled up her day, she had complete control. There were small shops to explore and shore front to be walked. She looked down towards the dock at the kayaks and paddle boards available to renters like herself. "Maybe go out in a kayak to see if I can find that mystery boat," she thought to herself.

She had never kayaked before but figured it couldn't be too hard. She had to learn to surf for one of her movies.

It was about noon when Jack spied his father just ahead of him setting back a pair of traps. Setting back traps was an art form in and of itself. You have to watch the fathometer, some call it sonar. It sends sound waves to the bottom of the ocean. Using the echo of those sound waves, it projects a picture on the screen to show the dept and shape of ocean floor. When the type of bottom and depth that the lobsterman is looking for is found he then has to calculate, using his instincts, the strength and direction of the tide (underwater current). If wrong, the trap could drift while falling through the water away from where the lobsterman had wants to set it. Jack watched his father push the first trap over. Rope trailed over the side while the boat idled forward. Jack's father volleyed his eyes from looking where he was going and watching the rope flow over the side. Watching the rope go over the side was important for two reasons: making sure there were no tangles, and for the safety of the sternman. If the got sternman tangled in the rope he or she would be pulled over the side of the boat and underwater. The rope pulled tight and pulled the second trap off the stern. When the second trap was completely clear, Jack idled alongside and shut the boat down. He grabbed his cooler and took a seat on the wash rail.

"How you making out today, Dad?"

"Doesn't matter how fuckin well we did. The god damn price just dropped a quarter…A fucking quarter!"

"What the hell is up with that? Tom said that he wouldn't drop the price until Monday."

"Well you know Tom, he will tell you one thing and then turn around and do something the opposite."

"At least I'm catching something. I nailed them over to the Cove, Seal Rocks and Cabbage, and I am doing at least a pound to a trap here at the ledges, but the head of the bay was naked."

"We're gonna finish hauling here and head in for a cheeseburger. I am so pissed I could spit nails."

Jack turned to his father's Sternman and said, "How ya liking it so far, Josh? He ain't slapped you with a bait bag yet, has he?"

"No, but he threatened to eat my lunch if I lost count on the lobsters again" The 14-year-old said with half a grin on his face.

"Just make a number up, that's what I used to do."

"Yeah, the asshole tried to tell me we caught 46 lobsters out of 7 pair," Jack's father chimed in.

They shared a good laugh and finished their lunches. Russell watched his son head to his next buoy. Sometimes he just liked to watch his son. He was proud of his son. Jack was a successful lobsterman, something not easy to be. Russell knew the moment Jack stepped onto his skiff when he was six years old, he was going to do something on the water. It is a tough life. Your pay is based on the catch. No catch, no pay. There are always issues with the price, bait, and fuel. Then you have to deal with the weather. These hot summer days were nice but come winter, you had to pick your days. Winds were stronger and the air was much colder. Ice could build up on the boat to the point it would become top heavy and unstable. The water temp was so cold that you only had minutes (if not seconds) before you would drown. Even in early summer the water temp is in the low sixties. Russell and Jack fished year round. When things slowed down in the winter they would finish off a boat for somebody just like they finished off Jack's boat.

Melissa had managed to find the mysterious red boat. She was completely exhausted having paddled across Linekin bay. She realized just how small she and the kayak were compared to the boats out on the water. When looking down on the bay from her cabin the bay and the boats looked smaller. Now being in the bay amongst the boats her perspective had changed immensely. She reflected on how at one point in life everything can seem small and manageable and how that can change on you quickly. Now the waves from the boat traffic had started to rock her kayak more; her arms felt like noodles. She started thinking about paddling to the closest shore. Just then a white lobster boat went by pulling a large wake. Melissa could not get the kayak turned into the wake fast enough. The wake hit hard and fast. The kayak rolled, dumping her into the water. The water was cold…so cold it shocked Melissa. She came up to the surface and grabbed the kayak. She had no strength left, and the kayak was full of water. The wetsuit did very little to hold any of her body heat in. Her fingertips were numb, and it was creeping up to her hands. "This is it" she thought to herself. The small waves splashing her face like water torture. She felt like just letting go and ending it all. Then just as her hands started to slip off the kayak, hope arrived. It came in the shape of the mysterious red boat and the man that piloted it.

"Hi, I am going to throw you this bumper." Melisa could see a large orange ball shape with a rope tied to it.

"I want you to sit in it like a tire swing. Then I am going to haul you up and get you on board. I will get your kayak after you are onboard and safe."

The mystery man gave the commands like an EMT speaking to a patient. Demanding, but with a tone of assurance that everything would be alright. He swung the bumper to her; she did just as he said. As she got closer, she could see more of her savior. She started to get a little nervous.

"What if he recognizes me?" she thought to herself. She looked on as he ran the trap hauler to get her up out of the water being careful not to get her hands caught in the snatch block. He put one arm down under her bottom and the other around her back and in a swift movement swung her on to her feet on the deck of the Red at Night. She watched him reach down and grab the kayak and place it across the stern. Jack now took a second and looked at the young woman who was now standing, shivering on his boat. The wet suit she was wearing complemented her athletic figure. Her wet, partially blonde, hair reminded him of the girls on the swimsuit calendars. His trance was broken when he remembered he had just pulled her out of the cold Maine water. Jack grabbed a hooded sweatshirt he had onboard and offered it to her. As he passed it to her, he looked at her face a little closer. He had seen that face before, but where? She took it and put it on. He could tell by the twitch of her nose that the hoody smelled like bait.

"Sorry about the smell, it's all I got to get you warm. You can sit up here on the engine box if you like, it's pretty warm. I have some Gatorade and some saltine crackers if you want them. Where would you like me to take you back to?"

Melissa sat up on the engine box relieved it was nice and warm, and even though the hoodie smelled like nothing she had smelled before, it felt quite cozy. "I am renting a small cabin on Spruce Point. There is a dock that all the cabins there use…. I don't remember what it looks like though. Thank you for saving me. With the waves and the cold water there was no way I could get back into the kayak. I was getting so cold I could hardly move," she responded gratefully. She was wondering if he would ever figure out who she was.

That voice… Jack had heard it before. It was coming to him now.

"I know where the Spruce Point dock is, I just hauled through there this morning. Are you who I think you are?"

"Maybe," she paused nervously. "I am Melissa Andrews."

The minute Jack heard her name he remembered who she was. Melissa Andrews was an actress. She had starred in a few big hits. Jack decided not to make a big deal of it. Figured she was embarrassed enough already.

"Well nice to meet you. Welcome aboard the Red at Night. What are you doing here in Boothbay Harbor?"

She was surprised there was no fanfare when she said who she was, but happy not to have to deal with that. "I am getting away from work, and life for a little bit. I am surprised that the water is so cold this time of year." Melissa wanted to change the subject.

"The water is sixty-five, out here in the middle of the bay. If you go to Barret's Park by Lobster Cove it will be a bit warmer."

Melissa listened carefully to every word. The Maine accent took a bit to understand, but she loved it. R's at the middle or end of words were rounded with an "ah" sound. Syllable's often broken while other words seemed merged together. She found herself liking this stranger too. He seemed confident and secure. He looked at her when he talked to her. Looked in her eyes. She felt his words as well as heard them. She was almost nervous trying to think of what to say next to keep this odd conversation going. "What is your name?"

"I am sorry, my name is Jack, Jack Finn."

"Hello, Jack Finn." She liked saying his name. It had a ring to it. "Have you lived here all your life?"

"Don't know. Haven't lived it all yet." Jack paused to see Melissa grin at the slight of humor. "Born and raised right here in Boothbay

Harbor. Right up in Lobster Cove actually. How long have you been in Boothbay Harbor?"

"About a week."

"Wow Melissa Andrews has been in Boothbay Harbor for a week and nobody knows. That is crazy."

"Jack…. I would like to keep it that way, please."

"Yessah."

"What……."

"Ha ha sorry…yes"

Melissa again was trying to keep the conversation going. It was nice to have someone to talk to for a change. She liked Jack so far. He was cute, funny, and confident. "What are your plans for the rest of the day, Jack?" She asked, hoping it didn't sound too forward.

Jack had to pause a bit. Melissa Andrews, the Hollywood "A" lister, seemed to be asking him out. "No", he thought to himself, "she is just chatting".

"Well, Friday nights we all hang out and have burgers, beer, and music at the co-op."

Melissa really wanted to spend more time getting to know this new stranger. He was attractive, but not only that, came a genuine glow of kindness and goodness. Much different from what she was used to. It was new and refreshing. She knew she could disguise herself well enough that nobody would know who she was. She only had to drop enough of a hint to get him to invite her. "That sounds like fun. Are there a lot of people?"

"Yeah, my folks, my sister and her boyfriend. Sometimes my buddy, Michael, shows up with his wife and kids. A few of the lobstermen that fish for the Co-op. A few locals pop in, along with select summer people."

Melissa was getting frustrated that Jack didn't take the hint. She wanted to learn more about this man. What was he like? Why was she so drawn to him?

"Hey, you want to go?" Jack asked, then almost instantly regretted it. He wasn't ready for this. Melissa was so easy to talk to.

She was also very pretty. The blue eyes, full lips, and the warm smile. Her hair was still so pretty and sexy half wet. He thought to himself, "Please say no. I can't do this."

"I thought you would never ask. Burgers, beer and music sound better than sipping wine in an overpriced dress and acting like you're having a good time while a producer is checking out your tits." Melissa was shocked at herself. What had she just said? Where did it come from?

Jack was stumped. With no clue what to say. Had he been staring? This was one of those awkward moments in life where you just wish someone would change the subject. He thought quickly.

"We should probably think up an alias for you. I mean looking like Melissa Andrews is one thing. Having the same name would be hard to play off," said Jack, trying to get away from his thoughts.

"Good idea…you got any ideas?"

He thought for a minute and said, "Madison Adams".

"I like it, how did you think of it?"

"Madison was your character's name in "Beach Days", and Adam was your boyfriend."

"Clever, very clever. Jack, does everyone here talk like you?"

He laughed heartily. "You think my accent is bad? You should hear my dad."

"Bad, no I like it. It's cute."

"Melissa, I have a question. In your last movie, who did the singing for you?"

"I did, I have always done my own singing. Did you like the movie? It is one of my favorite characters I have ever played. It was neat to play someone that really lived, not some fake character."

Melissa was feeling much warmer now. She got up from the engine box and walked toward the back of the boat. Jack glanced back to watch her walk towards the stern. The hooded sweatshirt hung down past much of her bottom, but the wet suit showed off her legs. Jack was caught in a bit of a trance until she turned around to catch him checking her out. He snapped his head around to play it off and then turned the wheel to avoid running over a buoy. He looked back again to see Melissa looking at him with a girlish grin. Jack was at a loss for words. The Melissa Andrews was on his boat and had agreed to go out for a date. "No", he thought to himself. "It is not a date. It's just two people going out for a drink. I am not ready for this, but how do I explain that. What am I making such a fuss about. She just wants to have a few beers, maybe a burger. She just wants to be normal for a little while. Jack pulled the boat into the dock and helped Melissa out.

"Ok then… Um…I will pick you up here around six?"

"Ok, Jack this may seem like a foolish question, but what is the atmosphere, what do I wear, what are these people like?

"Atmosphere? At the Co-op? Loud lobstermen, fisherman and dock grunts talking about boats. Bitching about the price of lobster, fuel or bait. All solving the world's problems with simple solutions. Lots of swearing, but good people, damn good people. As far as a "dress code" T-shirt and jeans or shorts."

The minute he said good people it put her mind at ease. This wouldn't be one of those Hollywood "get-togethers" where everyone is fake and just telling you what you want to hear. These would be honest people, real people. She was thankful for him saving her, but also thankful for his whole demeanor. A lot of people freak out when they meet a celebrity. Instantly getting a selfie and posting them. Not even asking if it is ok. Jack didn't seem phased by it. He was obviously a fan because he asked about the singing. As far as him checking her out, she didn't feel as violated as she would have in other circumstances. Producers, directors, and other men had looked at her as a piece of meat, like a centerfold in a porn magazine. She didn't get that vibe from him. Jack pulled the boat alongside the dock. Before getting out of the boat she gave him a hug. Jack tensed up at first as if it was unwelcome or unwanted. She was about to let go and take a step back when she felt his muscles ease and return the gesture. She stepped out of the boat and turned and watched him leave. "See you soon."

Jack pulled away from the dock and throttled up. He ran the boat a little faster than usual. He didn't want to take a chance of being late. He unloaded his catch and listened to Tom MacIntyre give every excuse ever heard about the drop in price. Jack's mind was elsewhere. He cruised the Red at Night back to Lobster Cove. His father was already in and tied up. Once his boat was tied up he walked up the hill to his house. Jack's house was on family property. The property had been in the family for three generations. He jumped into the shower with his mind spinning. He hadn't gone on a date for years. Five years to be exact. "This isn't a date" he reminded himself. "This is just two people going out for a beer. Wait, does she even drink beer?" He finished his shower and put on some clean clothes. His typical white t-shirt and blue jeans. He grabbed two beers out of the fridge and headed down to the boat. His mother and father were just outside talking.

"Two beers to get to the Co-op. Jack, you looking to tie one on tonight boy?" Russelll said giving Jack a hard time.

"Nope, I am picking someone up on the way over. You guys did teach me to share."

Jack's mother chimed in with her curiosity. "Who are you picking up?"

"Just a friend, no big deal. I will see you at the Co-op."

"Ma," Russell said, to his wife, "I think that boy had cologne on"

Jack felt like a teenager hopping into the boat. He calmed himself down and headed off to the Spruce Point dock. He could see her there. She had a blue, Red Sox baseball hat on, small oval sunglasses, a white "Boothbay Harbor" spaghetti string tank top and cut off shorts. Topping off the "normal" look, drug store flip flops. She held his hoodie in her hand. She stepped aboard and took a seat on the engine box. She smelled good. She looked better. Melissa Andrews was on his boat. He had seen her on the red carpet wearing a fancy dress, but here and now, she looked the best to him.

"I washed your sweatshirt, but I shrunk it…I am sorry. I will gladly get you another one. It has been a while since I had to do my own laundry."

"That's ok, I have hundreds of them. You can keep it as a souvenir. I brought you a beer if you want one."

"Beer…I haven't had one in a long time. Let me try it."

Jack popped the top on the glass bottle and passed it to Melissa. "That beer is a microbrew made right here in Boothbay Harbor at the Footbridge Brewery. There is even a hole in the floor in the brew pub from the old rum-runner days"

Melissa took a small sip, it was bitter at first with a pine like finish. She took another sip. "Well, it's not Dom Perignon, but I like it. "She smiled back at Jack and they tapped bottle necks together.

"Here is to new friends."

"New friends," Melissa responded. She already knew the answer to the question she had in her head. It seemed obvious but she wanted to be sure. "So, is there a Mrs. Finn?"

"Sure is," Jack responded quickly.

Melissa was in shock. Then what was going on here. She was confused and upset. Then Jack spoke again.

"Yup, she is my mothah," he said pouring in a little extra Maine accent.

"Ha ha ha, are you married, do you have a girlfriend?"

Jack wanted to make another joke, to stop this conversation from going too deep. "Nope, I'm single."

"Handsome guy like you single...why?"

"The bait smell...major turn off." Jack again was using humor to deflect any emotion.

Melissa could tell there was something he wasn't saying or something he was hiding. She decided not to pry.

As the boat made its way around Spruce Point and into Boothbay Harbor, they talked and got to know each other better. Melissa loved the stories Jack had about growing up in this little town. He had an enormous pride in his town and family. Melissa had been with other men before, but none like Jack. He was fresh. She only had known him a couple of hours but felt like she could trust him with her life...her soul. Jack interrupted her thoughts.

"Want to be the first Hollywood actress that has run a lobster boat?"

"Yeah… are you sure?"

"Yup, I figure you make enough to pay for anything that breaks."

Melissa took the wheel. Jack stood behind her pointing out what direction to go. The boat took a small roll of a wave. She stumbled a bit and felt like she was going to fall, but Jack grabbed her by her waist and stood her back up and steadied her. The feel of his hands on her sent a tingle up her spine. She was a little disappointed when he took his hands off her. He could have kept them there and she wouldn't have minded.

"You see the short lever right there?" Jack pointed.

"Yes" Melissa answered.

"Slowly push it forward."

Melissa pushed the lever forward. The engine got louder, the bow got higher then slowly came down a bit as the boat gained speed. She felt scared and thrilled at the same time. Even though the boat felt solid under her feet, there was still a feeling of raised inertia. Almost as if hovering on thickened air. Her left leg was against the engine box and it started to feel warmer as the engine worked harder. The whistle of the engine grew louder the faster the boat went. The air coming through the open window felt like a constant cool breeze. She hardly noticed she was leaning completely back on Jack now.

"32 knots…" Jack said proudly "Slow down hotrod, you're coming into the harbor. Just pull back on that lever slowly"

"Jack are there any lobster…. women?" Melissa asked as she looked over the bow. Getting the feel for running the boat.

"Yes, here in Boothbay Harbor we have Heather Thompson, she runs the Gold Digger. Her sister goes sternman or woman for her. There are other women up and down the coast that go lobstering or go sternwoman."

"What is that…sternman?"

"A sternman helps the captain. Different boats do it differently. Some captains help out and take the lobster out of the traps and measure them while some have the sternman do everything even pick up the buoy."

"I have watched a black boat that comes close to where I am staying. It looks like hard work. I think the name on the back is "Old Smoke.""

"Old Smoke is my dad's boat. It is hard work, but you are your own boss and you never know what the day will bring…I mean case in point," said Jack as he gestured towards Melissa.

Melissa smiled back at Jack. She liked the sound of being her own boss. These days it seemed she had too many bosses. Agents, directors, producers, media, her fans and the list went on. Jack took the wheel and brought the boat into the dock. There was a big sign saying "MacIntyre Lobster". Jack could see a small crowd had already gathered at the Co-op. A few heads turned to see him coming in. When they saw he wasn't alone, Jack could tell they had become the focal point. He tied up the boat and helped Melissa out. All eyes were on them now. Melissa turned toward Jack and spoke.

"Did you tell them about me already?" her tone was agitated.

"No, I didn't. They're probably shocked to see me with someone..." Jack hesitated a bit trying to figure out what to say. "It's a long story."

Melissa was now feeling a bit nervous as she walked up the ramp to where everybody was standing. Everybody was looking at her and whispering amongst themselves. She started thinking this was a bad idea. Jack came up behind her and spoke to the group.

"Christ people, ain't you ever seen a woman before? This is my new friend Madison. She fell out of a kayak and I picked her up. She wanted to meet some of the locals, but if you guys are going to just point and stare we'll find another party to crash."

The group slowly introduced themselves to Melissa. With the hat and glasses no one seemed to really know who she was. She was not famous. For once she was just an average person hanging out with average people.

"Are you hungry?" Jack asked her. "I am about to order some burgers and get a beer. What would you like?"

"A hot dog… wait. Two hot dogs with everything on them, and a beer please."

"Everything… even sauerkraut?"

"YES!"

"Ok… be right back."

As soon as Jack went to order, a young woman broke away from her male companion and came to Melissa. Her steps were quick and with a purpose and she looked directly at Melissa as she walked up. Melissa felt a bit of tension as this woman walked up. "Hiyuh, I'm Lucy. Jack's sistah." The tall young woman spoke with a thick Maine accent. She was taller than Melissa with a bigger build, but still attractive.

"Hi, nice to meet you." It was all Melissa could think to say. She knew she was about to be interrogated.

"So you're here with my little brothah. Is this a date? How come I haven't met you? Are you from around here? You look familiar, but I know everybody in Boothbay Harbah."

Melissa felt more nervous than she felt on any set with any director. Lucy fired off questions faster than she could answer them. This was Jack's sister so she had to be nice. "Jack found me when I fell out of my kayak. He scooped me up and brought me to the dock and invited me here so I could take in the local scene."

"That's fine. I am just keeping an eye on my little brothah. It is strange that he hasn't been on a date in five years then shows up here with you."

It caught Melissa a bit off guard. Why had Jack been single for five years? What was wrong? "Well like I said, it's not a date really. Just friends hanging out."

Just then their conversation was interrupted by another member of the Finn family.

"Just friends, but Jack has cologne on and he skipped down to his boat like a teenager. Hi, I'm Russell, Jack's father. Lucy, try to be nice, would ya. Jack is a big boy, he can take care of himself. Now Madison, I have permission from my wife to get one dance with you. Strictly for reconnaissance purposes. I am in no way to have a good time." Russell had a huge smile. He stuck out his hand to guide her to the dance floor.

"Well, I don't know how much information I have, but I would love to dance." Melissa took the rough working hand of the old fishermen and let him lead her to the dance floor where the local band was just starting "Hotel California".

"You have to forgive Lucy. She has always been super protective of Jack," he told Melissa as they danced.

"She is fine. It's kind of cute." She wanted to ask about why Jack hadn't been on a date in five years but was afraid of overstepping. "I have been spying on you actually. I have been watching you and your sternman haul your traps. I can see you from my cabin on the Sprucefull shore."

"Ah yes, me and Josh, the dynamic duo. Just don't go telling Jack what we catch. We have a little hot spot right there."

"Your secret is safe with me, Russell."

"So where are you from, Madison? And what do you do?"

"California," Melissa stumbled a bit to think of a job. "I am a teacher."

Russell and Melissa chatted more. Melissa was elated to be having normal conversation with normal people. It was refreshing. While dancing with Russell another older woman was watching carefully. If she had to guess, it was Jack's mother. Lucy and her male companion were standing with her. She didn't mind though. She admired the protective nature of Jack's family. She didn't have that. The only one who looked out for her was her. Jack had come back from getting food and drinks as the song ended and she walked back to him. He had a beer in his hand, a mustard stain on his shirt and a smile that made her warm.

"So who have you met, other than my dad?"

"Your sister."

"Oohhh, how did that go?"

"Not bad, I don't know if she likes me or not."

"To be honest, probably not. For now. She takes the big sister role too far sometimes."

"I am guessing that is your mom over there, too."

"Yep."

"Should I introduce myself?"

"No…she is probably your second biggest fan here in Boothbay Harbor. Not to mention she has a built in lie detector."

"Really?"

"Yep, it sucked growing up. I couldn't get away with anything."

"You were probably an angel growing up."

Jack had a grin on his face that said otherwise. As they talked, Melissa took in her environment. She was sitting on a picnic table out in the open. The section she was sitting in was a "locals only section" which she thought was funny. When she went out to eat in Beverly Hills, she normally sat in a section reserved for the Hollywood elite. She was eating hotdogs off a plastic tray with a cardboard liner and drinking beer out of the bottle. Every so often someone would come up and talk to Jack and say hi to her. Everybody seemed nice and kind, asking how she liked the town. Nobody knew who she really was and she loved it. No pressure, no cameras, no pushy fans, or nosey reporters. She felt like she had never felt before. She never wanted to go back to Hollywood. In a matter of hours she was in love with this little town and the people. Then there was Jack. She hardly knew him. She really didn't know him at all, but she wanted to. He was handsome, tall, strong and funny. Then there was the mystery behind why he was single for so long.

"After we finish eating we usually go for a boat ride around the harbor. Do you want to come, or run you back to the Sprucefull Shore dock?" asked Jack.

"I would love to go. Just make sure your sister doesn't throw me overboard."

"You betcha."

As they walked down to the boat Russell and his wife followed, trailed by Lucy and her male friend. They all got in Jack's boat and he untied from the dock and pulled away. She decided to ignore Jack's warning and went to his mother to introduce herself. Jack's mother was tall and skinny. With black curly hair with streaks of grayish white. Her eyes were such a dark brown they almost seemed black. It seemed like she was staring through Melissa as she approached. She had an air of confidence that surrounded her like a forcefield. It was intimidating.

"Hello…Mrs. Finn," said Melissa.

"Yes, hello…you may call me, Anne." Jack's mom replied. Her tone was nice but challenging.

"Nice to meet you Anne, my name is…"

"Don't tell me your name is Madison…. whatever. Your name is Melissa Andrews."

Everybody in the boat turned and looked. They all were shocked. Shocked that they hadn't noticed, and shocked that THE Melissa Andrews was on a boat with them. Except for Jack, he was trying to figure out what to do or say next.

"Yes, I am Melissa Andrews." Her secret was out. First only Jack knew, now everybody on this boat knew.

"Don't panic. Your secret is safe with us," Anne quipped.

"Holy shit I am on a boat with a movie star and… Shit hell, I danced with a movie star and nobody told me," Russell beamed in.

"My brother is dating Melissa Andrews… The Melissa Andrews!" Lucy said.

"Wait just a minute here. We are not dating. We just met. She came to Boothbay Harbor to get away from all the flu fla Hollywood drama. So we are not going to be making any onboard Red at Night". Jack paused and looked at Melissa, then he turned to the group saying "Nobody on this boat is going to tell anybody who you are or that you are here. Right?!" Jack spoke as if he was Melissa's security guard. The group all nodded in agreement that nobody would disclose who Melissa was.

After that she stood beside Jack in the boat while the Finn family talked about their hometown. They gave her a tour of the harbor talking about the rich history in every nook and cranny. She admired their pride. They knew every inch of that harbor. Often Russell would take the opportunity to tell a story about Jack, his sister or his wife. He was the kind of father Melissa wished she had. She never knew her father, he was never in the picture. Just she and her mother bouncing from one hotel to the next. Sometimes living in her car. Her mother would get hired to be an extra or shoot a commercial, but nothing permanent or big. She had managed to land a small role in a movie. She had Melissa take her through her lines every night and every night she promised Melissa that things would get better. She brought Melissa on set on the day they were filming her part, sat her in a chair and told her to stay out of the way. When action was called Melissa decided to act out the lines just as she had with her mother. The director happened to catch Melissa and started watching her. The eight-year-old girl stole the scene. He asked to put Melissa in another movie he was working on. You would think a mother would be proud of her daughter landing a role in a movie, but Melissa's mother hated her for it. She thought it was Melissa's fault she never got a part and never treated her the same. Melissa got even more movie contracts over the years. Melissa left her mother when she was 16-years old. She had plenty of money from all the contracts she got and put herself through college. She bought cars, jewelry and eventually a mansion, but that didn't fix the hurt of not being loved by the people that were supposed to love you most. The one comfort she had was her career. She was an incredible actress. She could sing and dance, often being compared to Julie Andrews or Judy Garland. The press recently had not been on her side though. She was at a party drinking more than she should have when her agent offered her a pill. Next thing she knew she was waking up in the back seat of her car. A reporter with a camera had his head up her dress. She lashed out and hit him and he pressed charges. The only witnesses were other media types and since he hadn't got the chance to take the picture, the media twisted the story. Before she knew it was on the cover of every tabloid. The picture of her hitting the reporter, and the headline painted her as a closet pill popping lunatic. That is what brought her here to Boothbay Harbor. To get away. She wanted some privacy, and time to think. Now out on a lobster boat with common normal people, she felt so alive.

"Jack, how did you become a lobsterman?" Melissa asked to get away from her thoughts.

"Oh, that's my favorite story to tell," piped in Russell. "You mind, Jack?"

"Go ahead Dad, the floor is yours as usual."

"Jack told me one day when he was six he wanted a dirt bike. I told him we would work on getting him one tomorrow at four o'clock in the morning. He looked at me kinda puzzled. The next morning he found himself on my boat stuffing bait bags. I paid him ten dollars a day and by the end of summer he had saved enough for that dirt bike"

"That is incredible. You had to work for it. Every bit of it" Melissa was impressed.

"My kids have had to work for anything they ever wanted. My wife and I gave them what they needed, but anything extra they had to earn it."

"That is enough about us, what about you, Melissa? What brings you to Boothbay Harbor?" asked Anne.

"Well as you can tell from the tabloids, I am kind of waiting for things to blow over. I am not that person. It was a bad night. I don't do drugs." Melissa started to feel worried again. She liked these people and wanted them to like her.

"You owe us no explanation," said Anne. "We don't judge people on what other people say. Your actions define you, not tabloid gossip."

Melissa loved the way Anne talked. She liked the way they all talked. These people lived by a code. An unwritten law. It made her feel safe and secure amongst them. They were strangers but in a few short hours she already felt she knew them. Overcome with emotions she couldn't think of anything to say. She felt she owed them something, but what could she do? She took a deep breath and started singing "Over the Rainbow". She had been singing it over and over for her last movie so she knew she could do it. With Anne being a big fan, it only seemed right. The words and harmony poured from her filling the air with a sweet tune. When the song ended there was a round of applause from everyone on the boat, and even some of the boats nearby. Jack stood there in shear awe of Melissa. She wasn't a Hollywood actress. Not right now. She was a feeling he had not felt in a long time. He wanted to take her hand. He wanted to hold her. Hell, he wanted to kiss her. He was scared, happy, anxious and sad at the same time. He almost started to shed a tear until he caught his mother watching him.

The boat pulled up to the co-op dock and the family got out and said their goodbyes. Jack pulled away from the dock and started making his way back to Melissa's dock. She was sitting on the stern. Her blonde hair was being tossed by the slow summer breeze. Her blue eyes were taking in the red sunset and hypnotic wake. She looked content, as if all the world's problems had just disappeared. As the boat sped up and made its way out of the protected harbor the breeze got a little chillier. Melissa came up into the cockpit and stood behind Jack. She wrapped her left arm around his waist. He was slightly startled at first, then took his right arm and wrapped it around her shoulders. She felt warm almost instantly. He felt like he was doing something right and wrong at the same time.

"What are you doing tomorrow, Jack?" Melissa asked, hoping he wasn't going to be busy.

"I gotta run out of town to grab parts for this thing in the morning, then at high tide I am going to load ten strings on and set them over to Damariscove, and bring in fifty or sixty traps that stayed in all winter over where I found you this morning."

"Wow… Sounds like a busy day… you want company?" She was hoping with all her heart he would say yes.

"Sure, I'll pick you up at 7."

"Seven! In the morning?!"

"I can get you at six and you can come down to the dock with me for coffee?"

"Nope…seven will work, but you better have some coffee and breakfast."

"Now the Hollywood comes out."

After dropping Melissa off, Jack took his boat back to the family dock and walked up the hill to his house. His mother was out on her porch reading the local paper and drinking tea. He knew she was waiting up to talk to him. He also knew his mother could read him like he was the Boothbay Register.

"She is a nice girl, Jack," his mother said peering over the paper with her glasses on the end of her nose.

"Yes, she is, Mom, not what you would expect from a Hollywood type."

"Jack…" Anne took a deep breath. "I have been waiting for you to take this step, but you're getting into something more complicated than you can fathom. What are you going to do when she goes back to Hollywood?"

"Mom we are just friends, and…"

"You can't pull the wool over my eyes, Jack Bryon Finn." Anne interrupted. "Jack, I saw the way you looked at her tonight. I have only seen you look at one other person like that."

"Don't bring her into this, and you're right. I felt so good with her, then I feel guilty for feeling good. Even though she is rich and famous she doesn't act like it. I like her a lot… and I think she likes me"

"No… there is no think about it. She is falling for you, but is she falling for you because she loves you? Are you falling for her because you love her? Don't feel guilty, son. You lost Stephanie five years ago, and you haven't let her go yet. You two had a magical kind of love. I know, I watched it. She is gone now. Let her rest."

"Thanks, Mom. Good night."

"Goodnight, Jack".

Jack walked into his house, went up to his bedroom and got ready for bed. He thought about what his mother had said. Stephanie had been gone five years, but he still felt her. He felt her in the house, in the boat and in his truck. He did not feel her when he was around Melissa. The minute he got her onboard Red at Night he felt better than he had in a long time. Now the guilt of feeling better started to weigh on him.

He went to sleep looking at a picture of him and Stephanie and remembered the day the picture was taken. A week before he had driven up to Brunswick and bought an engagement ring. He thought all week long about how to pop the question. He ran it through his head a thousand times. Then that night sitting on the cabin of his boat with Stephanie sitting next to him, he reached into his pocket, and "Damn" he thought to himself. He had left it in his truck. He would have to wait until tomorrow, but tomorrow never came for her. When they got back to the dock that night Jack asked to take her home. She insisted she was fine to drive and had to work the next day. Jack told her he loved her and to drive safe. That was the last time he saw her alive.

Melissa opened her eyes and looked at the alarm clock, it was five thirty. She had time to meet Jack down at the dock, she thought to herself. She had the best night's sleep she had had in a long time. She felt rested, and ready to go. She got herself ready, going easy on the makeup and putting on a t-shirt, jeans, and Jack's hoodie that had now became hers. She put her feet in her sandals and went out to the car. The rental she had gotten was far different from the Mercedes she was used to. She didn't care, not right now. She didn't know where MacIntyre's was, but she knew she could see the big Catholic church from the dock last night. She had seen that same church when arriving here. She drove to the corner where the church was and looked in the direction, she thought the dock was.

"Where is it?" She asked herself.

Then she was startled by a loud horn behind her. She looked back and saw an old pick-up truck. The truck idled around beside her. She was a bit nervous at first, but a familiar face came into view.

"What did you do, wet the bed?" Russell asked practically yelling over the sound of his beat up Chevrolet.

She didn't know how to answer such a question.

"Sorry, that's an old lobstermen's way of asking- "why are you up so early?"

"I really don't know, I had the best sleep I have had in a long time. I was hoping to surprise Jack at the dock. Are you headed there?"

"No, I got to talk to somebody, just take this left and as soon as you start down the hill you will see the sign for MacIntyre Lobster just behind those lilac bushes. Jack's truck is the black Ford. He should be there by now."

"Thank you, Russell"

"No problem. Melissa, can you do me a favor?"

"Sure, Russell." She wondered what Russell could need from her.

"Be good to my boy."

With no need for explanation or any discussion of what was or wasn't going on between her and Jack, she spoke true.

"I will, Russell." She felt warm saying that. Something she hadn't felt in years.

"Good day." And with that Russell and his old beat-up Chevrolet idled down Atlantic Ave.

Russell was headed to talk to somebody. He was going to talk to Stephanie Ann Turner. He was going to talk to her grave. After seeing his son so happy last night and overhearing the conversation between Anne and Jack last night, he felt the need to speak to her.

He pulled the truck up by the grave. The sound of his squeaky door sounded louder in this quiet, peaceful place. He walked up to the head stone and rubbed the engraving. Almost as if reading Braille.

Stephanie Anne Turner

October 16, 1982 – July 4, 2012

Taken too young

"Hey, Steph." He paused to take a long breath.

"Sorry I haven't been here in a while, but it doesn't look like you have had a lack of visitors." He paused again and looked at the fresh flowers. "Steph, this ain't easy, and it certainly ain't my sort of thing, but you got to help me here."

Russell removed his hat, almost upset with himself he hadn't done it sooner.

"Steph, Jack met someone yesterday…a woman someone. I know what you're thinking- about damn time right? At least that is what I hope you're thinking. Ann tried to talk to him last night. She mentioned "letting you rest" and that hit me harder than anything I have had to deal with these past five years. I loved you. I loved you like you were my own daughter. I used to daydream about the grandkids you and Jack would bring into this world. Now I have accepted the fact that ain't going to happen, but, and I hate to put this on you, but you got to help Jack. He feels guilty about you. He feels he should have not let you drive that night. Now he feels guilty about feeling good around another woman. You were the only one that could ever get into his head. Maybe you can do something on your end. I will keep trying on mine. I feel kind of shitty asking you to do this, but you always put Jack before yourself." His throat got tight, and his eyes welled up. "Alright, Kiddo" the old lobsterman's voice cracked a bit. "I got to get my ass in gear. Talk at you latah." The old man stood up. Dried his eyes with his handkerchief. Walked backwards away from the grave a couple steps. While getting back into his truck a warm breeze swept through the graveyard. Russell smiled and gave a small chuckle. "I knew you were listening".

At MacIntyre Lobster, Jack was sitting on a wooden lobster crate sipping a black coffee. Tom MacIntyre and a few of the lobstermen were there as well. The subject today was the sudden drop in price of lobster. One bearded old lobsterman was doing the majority of the talking. He had on his boots and rubberized bib overalls called "oilskins". Underneath the oilskins was a hooded sweatshirt with the sleeves cut off and the neck cut to make the opening a bit bigger. He spoke with authority, and even with his deep Maine accent, his college education showed.

"Tommy, you sat on that very crate where Jack is sitting right now. You sat there and told us the price wouldn't drop until Monday. Yesterday while hauling along, I get a text from Russell saying that you dropped the price while we are all out hauling…and you didn't even tell us. We had to hear it by word of mouth. Tommy, I have known you since you were a kid sitting in a cardboard box making engine noises with your mouth pretending to haul traps. This is not pretending any more. Real men with real families, with real bills depend on your word." Clive Farrin, the bold bearded lobsterman finished with his finger inches from Tommy's chest.

The group was silent, waiting to see how Tommy was going to slither out of this. Until an unfamiliar voice broke the silence.

"Hello?" Melissa called, she was unsure about interrupting the conversation.

Jack hopped up so fast he nearly spilled his coffee.

"Me…Madison…what are you doing here? I would have come got you."

"I know, I woke up early and figured I would surprise you."

"Well, I am, very surprised," Jack said happily.

By this time Clive had taken a step back and Tommy started breathing again. All the men on the dock turned to take a look at the gorgeous figure before them. There was a bit of an awkward silence as everybody took in the sight of Melissa and Jack.

"Christ. Jack," growled Clive "I know your parents raised you better than that. Are you going to introduce us or what?" said Clive.

"Oh…yeah. This is my friend Madison, some of you met her last night." Jack went on to introducing her to the group of lobstermen. As old and salty as these men were, they got up off their perches to shake the lady's hand. Not one of them could tell who she was. With her baseball hat and no makeup, she didn't stand out. Jack showed her around the place.

"Who is that girl over there?" Melissa pointed to a teenage girl counting lobsters from the tank into a crate.

"I would introduce her to you but remember me saying my mother was your second biggest fan, well that is your first. Her name is Elizabeth, we call her Lizzy. Her brother goes sternman with my father. Two of the hardest working kids you could ever meet," Jack explained.

"Wow, I want to introduce myself so badly, but I don't want to blow my cover. It sounded like I walked into a serious conversation. I am sorry I walked in when I did, Jack."

"No biggie, Clive had Tommy in the hot seat long enough. I don't think he will be pulling any more shenanigans."

"What did he do?"

"Well, let's put it this way. When you sign your movie contracts you know what you're going to get paid, right?"

"Yes."

"Now let's say half way though the movie they decide to cut a little from what they agreed to pay you, but they don't tell you until the end."

"Ooh, not good."

"Now yesterday when I left this dock the price was $3.35 a pound. Tommy dropped the price without telling us during the day. It's really messed up for a couple reasons. First he told us the price was going to hold all weekend and second he didn't give us a chance to come in and sell what we had at the higher price. Now twenty five cents a pound may not sound like much, but put that over 600lb and that is hunnerd and fifty bucks. That could buy a barrel of bait, or pay a sternman."

"I have a lawyer to handle my contracts, don't you guys have someone to watch this stuff?"

"Yeah… sort of. We have each other. We can go on strike, we can go to another retailer, or" Jack paused a bit and looked at Melissa. Wondering if he could trust her so soon. Of course he could. She was already trusting him and his family with a secret "or we can save our money, and hopefully buy Tommy out."

"Wow, Jack…Is that your plan?

"Yup, me, my dad, and Elizabeth's dad. Only we…and you know about it."

"Would you keep lobstering?"

"Yup, we all would. Elizabeth's dad, Michael, would operate his mechanic business out of here as well."

Melissa was beside herself. To her Jack was perfect…so far. He was handsome, smart, and he had dreams. He didn't seem to care about her Hollywood background. Her lips and fingertips felt numb. She began to speak more honestly and sincerely than she ever had.

"Jack, I haven't even known you for a full day yet, but... I really like you. Maybe even more. Jack, I love saying your name, Jack. I have no clue what to do, or what to…"

At that moment Jack put his right hand gently on her cheek and kissed her lips and held her tight to him. He had wanted to do that since the first moment he saw her. They stood there in that embrace, both of them feeling numb and warm until they were interrupted by a familiar voice.

"Are you two stuck?... I could go get a pry bar if you need it," Russell interrupted with a huge grin that went from ear to ear.

"Damn it dad… Don't you know how to knock?"

"On what door, you're standing in the middle of a lobstah house. Not exactly private…or romantic."

The two took a step away from each other, both feeling hot in the face but grinning as much as Russell.

"We got to get going up to Brunswick and get parts. Dad, you need anything?

"Yeah… a barf bag from watching you play sucky face."

"Christ, dad. Alright then, call if you think of something. See ya latah."

"Have a good one, boy"

As Jack and Melissa walked away, Russell tipped his head, looked up and said, "That was quick" with a grin so big his pipe almost fell out.

Jack and Melissa walked out to Jack's truck. Jack was still a little numb. His mind was racing as fast his heart. What…Why…How did he do that? It felt good to him. His mind was reeling so fast that he couldn't think straight. He felt Melissa's hand slide into his. He turned to look at her. She was smiling like a teenage girl who just gotten asked to the prom. She stopped walking and gave his arm a small tug to get him to turn and face her. She reached up and put her hands on his shoulders, leaned in and kissed him. His arms wrapped around her and held her tight and secure. An eternity passed in that minute. They slowly let go of their embrace.

"What do we do now?" Jack asked.

"We take it slow. This is going to be complicated, and I don't want to mess this up," Melissa answered.

"Yes definitely slow, definitely complicated."

They smiled at each other.

Chapter 2

MacIntyre Lobster was first opened as a Co-Op back in the 1900's. A group of fishermen ran the place and as one fisherman left, they would vote another in. That was until Tommy's grandfather passed away and left Tommy's father a bunch of money. Rather than investing into the co-op Tommy's father bought up half of the fisherman's shares and ran the place himself. Eventually the business passed completely to Tommy, and it started to change. He started charging interest on charge accounts then raised bait and fuel prices. Some fisherman tried to leave but other retailers had a limited capacity. Recently there had been some strange people coming and going at odd hours. Most of Tommy's workers would hang out and talk to the fisherman, but his newest truck drivers didn't hang out and nobody knew them. Certain rooms had become off limits and were padlocked.

Tommy MacIntyre stood all of 150 lbs soaking wet and 5 foot 10. His greasy black hair, with strands of white mixed in, went past his ear lobes, but the length of his hair didn't cover his bald spot on the top of his head. It looked like an old mop turned upside down. His face looked sunken into itself like his skin had been shrunk wrapped onto his skull. His clothes were always dirty and full of holes. He never wore shorts even on the hottest of summer days. He always had a cigarette in his mouth unless he was drinking his cheap vodka or doing some other vice. His other vices were at first just for him, but was now a major cash cow. It brought in two or three times as much as the lobster business. His dealer was in Boston. There was a dealer in Portland but Tommy wanted to skip over him to get more profit. Crates of lobster would go down with one of his newest drivers who was also carrying cash. The truck normally would come back with empty crates, but now was coming back with cocaine, heroin and other drugs. Tommy would distribute to local dealers and keep a little to himself. All this while he was keeping the appearance of a typical lobster retailer with a restaurant. Tommy thought he had the perfect operation with the perfect cover.

Russell walked down the ramp puffing on his pipe and humming a happy tune. Clive Farrin was sitting on his boat stuffing bait bags. These two had been friends since they came into the world. They were next to each other in the maternity ward at St. Andrews and had grown up together.

"What's got you all chipper this morning? And why are you so late getting down here? I had Tommy in a corner this morning," Clive said while stuffing a handful of herring into a bait bag.

"Life, Clive…Life is why I am so happy and life is why I am late." Russell said with an air of lightness.

"Christ…did Anne let you have some last night? You need to come back to reality, we got shit to tend to. Who is that girl that came down here for Jack?" Clive snarled at his old friend.

"What is the matter, Clive, nobody allowed to be happy?"

"No! Tommy has his head up his ass, you got your head up yours, and Jack seems to have his head up her ass. Meanwhile I'm the only one seems to care about our price."

"If I had known you were going to put the heat to Tommy I would have been here. I had something to take care of. As for Jack, you know as well as I do he needs to take this step. To me this is more important than the damn price. The girl's name is Madison, she is from away. Don't you worry, there ain't a fisherman here that ain't concerned with the price. Now get your head out of your ass and tell me what went on this morning."

"Well, I had my finger to his chest asking for an explanation about what happened with the price change when she showed up. She kind of distracted everybody."

"Yuuupp," He chuckled. "She sure has that ability. No matter about Tommy he would have just lied to you anyway. I am kind of tempted to ask Lizzy if she knows anything. She is smart, honest and Tommy has been letting her handle some of the paperwork. Just the other day she was asking about the shipping receipts. I just don't know how I feel about putting her in that position."

"What we need to do is have a meeting. You, me, Jack and all the rest of the fisherman that fish for that snake. That way we know where everybody else is at."

"Good idea, I'll get Michael Williams to come too."

"Why him? He's not a lobsterman!"

"Well, if we are going to ask Elizabeth anything we should speak to her father first. Also, he has roots here, remember."

"Yup…You think you can get Jack here or will he be… busy?"

"Well I think that Anne needs to have some "girl time" with Melissa. I think it would make her feel better about that."

"By that you mean Jack and Madison. It is good to see that boy smile again. Shit, the whole time I was putting the irons to Tommy he had a goofy ass grin on his face. When she came on the dock he came to attention like he was in boot camp."

"Yeah, it's a good thing, Clive. I have a good feeling about it. Well, I will get a hold of Anne and get her to take Madison somewhere. I think between the two of us we should be able to reach everybody. I can call Jack, Mike, Nick, Andrew and the rest of the younger crew. You get in touch with Jim, Butch and the rest of the Saint Andrew's retirement home prospects. We will all meet at my house at six. That gives everybody time to have suppah," said Russell.

"Saint Andrew's retirement prospects…. you ain't to far from that you old barnacle" Clive fired back and with that the two old men parted ways.

Russell drove home knowing that Anne would be there cleaning up the house, tending the gardens and taking care of other chores. When he got there she was out in the garden. Her salt and pepper hair was tucked up under a F/V Red at Night hat. She had a t-shirt tucked into her blue jeans that were soiled on the knees from years of gardening. When Russell stepped out of the truck he could hear her humming and singing the song Melissa had sung last night. Russell leaned against his old truck in awe of the woman he had been married to for 35 years. She was timeless. Her age did show, but her spirit was full and powerful. She was wise. She had absorbed the knowledge of her mother and her mother's mother and down the line. She could cook a Thanksgiving supper and never break a sweat or open a cookbook. She had stuck by Russell's side even when he lost his boat to the bank and had to fish out of a twelve-foot skiff. She had also slapped sense into him when he got out of line. She was as tough as an old hard-shell lobster but as gentle as a new fawn.

"What you doing?" Russell asked his wife.

"Planting the vegetables, and also some watermelon," Anne replied.

"Watermelon! Christ Jack will eat them up before you can pick um."

"Speaking of Jack, we need to talk, Russell. What do you think of Melissa and all that is going on?"

"Well," he was stumbling a bit not expecting that question after joking about the watermelon. "To tell you the truth… I swung by Stephanie's grave this morning to ask her to give Jack a little help. I think it worked because when I got down to the dock I saw Jack kissing Melissa."

Anne took a long stern breath as she stood up tall in the garden placing her hands on her hips. "So I assume you approve of this?"

"Yes I do. Jack is happy, Happier than he has been in a long while."

"Yes, he is happy now, but what happens when she gets tired of this town or of him, and heads back to Hollywood. Where does that leave Jack?"

"I don't know, Anne, but Jack is a big boy. He has fallen down, he is getting back up. If he falls again he will get up again. We took his training wheels off long ago, Anne."

Anne relaxed her guard a bit. "I know Russell. I guess I would feel better about it if I knew her better."

Russell got a huge grin on his face. "Funny you should say that. I was going to ask you to spend some girl time with her so I could get Jack's attention at a meeting here tonight. Clive and I are going to meet with all of Tommy's fisherman to see what is on everybody's mind."

"Russell, just what the hell are her and I going to talk about? She is a movie star, she has nothing in common with me. When I said get to know her I meant over time, not all in one night." Anne folded her arms with slight agitation.

"Calm down, yes, she is a movie star, and one you are a fan of last I knew, but she is also a girl. Christ, underneath all that glamour and fame she is a normal woman. I noticed it on the boat, and I think you did too."

Anne let her arms down and placed them back on her hips. "Alright, I guess." Anne still had no idea what she and Melissa would do or talk about.

"Good then, I will text Jack and let him know about the meeting and he can tell Melissa that you two are going to have some "girl time." With that, Russell pulled out his phone and glasses and started texting Jack.

Back at MacIntyre Lobster Tommy sat in his chair looking out at the dock. He watched Clive finish stuffing bait bags. He was plotting in his head how to get even with Clive for making him look foolish this morning. "Nobody pokes their finger in my chest," he said to himself. Wouldn't be the first time he had to take care of somebody for telling him his business. He shrugged it off for the moment. He had other things to take care of. The shipping receipts that Elizabeth had brought to his attention were still sitting on his desk. He had to figure out how to make them look right. If that seventeen year old girl could figure out something wasn't right, surely his accountant would figure it out. Maybe he could just pay his accountant off. That would be less money for him and he was already paying two truck drivers. Maybe with his accountant in the loop they could do more business. He could always take some more money from the lobstering side, but he was already on thin ice with his fishermen and he had to keep the lobstering business as a cover. He stroked his goatee and weighed his options.

Conversation in Jack's truck was interrupted by the dinging sound of Jack's cell phone. Up until the interruption Melissa and Jack had been making small talk. In their heads they were wondering when the next embrace would happen and how far it would go. Jack looked at his phone and gave a long sigh. He looked over to Melissa wondering how to word his next statement.

"Well, we have done it now," Jack said with a slightly concerned look on his face.

"What, what did we do…we just kissed…who cares?" Melissa said with an air of panic.

"My mother, she wants to have some girl time with you, which means she wants to question you. She wants to make sure you're not going to hurt her boy."

"OH, I am going to hurt you." She stopped herself doubting how appropriate that comment was. "I mean…I could get hurt too…I mean you're not the only one with something to risk here."

Jack grinned a bit at the first comment, knowing what she meant "I know, Melissa, like we said this is going to be complicated, and for more reasons than the obvious. I think I know what my mother is worried about, and I didn't know how to talk to you about this."

"What, Jack?" Melissa tightened her grip on the door handle of the truck. Nervous about what Jack's next words were going to be. She had been so caught up in the moment, but also worried for the other shoe to drop and crush the great feeling she had.

"Melissa," Jack paused and took a deep breath. He rubbed his eyes and face with his right hand. "Open up the glove box."

Melissa opened the glove box of the truck. Amongst the paperwork and condiment packets there sat a little felt black box. She reached in and took it out while closing the glove box. She slowly opened the box. There inside was a silver ring with a small diamond on it. Simple and humble but shiny and warm. Melissa looked over to Jack who had a tear rolling down his cheek.

Jack took another long breath and started to speak. His normally strong deep voice was shaky and wavering.

"Her name was Stephanie, Stephanie Anne Turner. I grew up with her. I loved her." Jack paused to regain composure. "She died in a car accident before I could ask her to marry me." Another pause. "She died because I didn't take her home. She had been drinking. She said she was fine, but I got a call that night that she had died in a car accident. That is what is so hard about us. You make me feel so good. I love the way I feel when you're around, then I feel guilty about feeling good." He paused again. "Damn I am so fucked up in the head."

Melissa wiped her own tear away. She wasn't sure what made her sadder. The fact that this man, Jack, who not a moment before, seemed so strong and bullet proof, was now weeping beside her or the story she had just heard. She hunted in her head for what to say next.

"Jack, the last thing I want is for you to be hurt or feel guilty. If you want to put this…us on hold or stop it altogether, I will understand. It won't be easy for me, but it's your call." She paused, taking a long breath while choosing her next words carefully. "I am sure I am not the first to tell you this, but it's not your fault."

"Somedays I would agree with you and the others. Then I think if I had just told her no and driven her home myself. It just doesn't seem fair for me to start feeling happy while she is dead."

"Jack…you both made a decision. You can't punish yourself for the rest of your life. I don't think she would want that. Nobody would. You are a good guy, Jack, and I don't want to cause you pain. I want to help you."

By now both of them were crying.

"Well, it's not every day you get to date a movie star," Jack said to displace some of the stress of the conversation and to hint he wasn't going to let Melissa go. "We just have to work together on this."

Melissa smiled through her tears and laughed a little. She reached over the center console and gave Jack a hug and a kiss on the cheek. She gently closed the box and placed it carefully and respectfully back in the glove box and closed it. She thought to herself, "If that was the other shoe…I am glad it dropped."

Jack gave a long sigh of relief and wiped his face again. The feeling of a big weight was now off his shoulders. He knew that it wasn't over yet. There would be more talks, tears and unloading, but in a way it felt good.

"I think dad wants to tell the guys about the plan to buy Tommy out. He wants to have a meeting with all the fishermen while you and Mom are hanging out."

"I am nervous about this. What are we going to talk about? She and I are so different."

"She will ask you about all the fuss in the tabloids. Just be honest. We Finn's don't judge. She will want to know what your goals are. One of her favorite things to say is, 'You can't go anywhere without a direction.' She will also want to know how long you plan to stay in the Harbah."

"Tabloids and goals…that's funny. Up until the tabloids changed from making me the next Julie Andrews to the next Lindsey Lohan I would have said to act the rest of my life. Now I'm not so sure. Nobody there cares about you, just the money they can make off you. As far as how long I am in "The Harbah" as you call it, I was thinking a month. By that time the tabloid incident would be old news."

"Melissa, what happened that night? All I saw on the news was you beating the shit out of a reporter after he had woken you up in your car. They said you were passed out laying across the back seat with your legs hanging out the open door."

"There was a party after the opening of my last movie. I had been so stressed that week and was drinking more wine than usual. I told my agent I wasn't feeling well and was going to get a ride home. She gave me a pill and said it would make me feel better. Next thing I know, I am waking up in the back of my car with a camera man trying to take a picture up my dress. So I swung at him, but the pictures that everybody caught looked like he was trying to help me and I was going ballistic on him."

"What was the pill your agent gave you? Do you think your own agent set you up? That's what it sounds like."

"I don't know Jack. She has been my agent and publicist since the beginning. Just lately she has been doing things without asking me first. Like that butt shot of me in the "Beach Days" movie. The contract was already signed by the time I realized she had agreed to that. She had been hinting on doing something that would get the tabloids printing my name. She kept saying that bad press is needed. I told her that was not what I wanted. I can't believe she would do something like that. I told her I was going to disappear for a while and wait for all this to blow over. She tried to convince me it was no big deal."

"Damn...I thought Tommy was an asshole."

"That is what I like about you, and your family, and your town. You are all real and honest. I'm tempted to stay the summer, but I am worried that someone might figure out who I am."

"I think if you stayed the whole summer you would have to get a job. Something where people see you, like bar tending or waitressing. No one would ever think that Melissa Andrews would be a bartender in Boothbay Harbor. You would be hidden in plain sight."

"That's good, Jack, but I have never done anything like that in my whole life."

"You're an actress, just act."

"Well, I guess...I will tell my agent that I am going on an extended sabbatical. This could work."

"Mom could find you work easy enough. Talk to her about it tonight."

"Do you think she will help me?"

"Of course she would. Anne Marie Finn loves to help people, from strangers to family."

"What else do you think she will want to talk about?"

"I don't know. Just be yourself. Ask about her."

"OK," Melissa replied nervously.

She leaned back in the seat of the truck and looked out of the window. She saw green trees and grass. It wasn't like where she was from. All the highways there were surrounded by more highways and buildings. Here in Maine the roads were carved in amongst hills and trees. Mother Nature had the right-of-way here. She got out her phone and texted her agent that she was taking the rest of the summer off. She wouldn't be taking any calls, doing any advertisements or giving press releases. She texted her housekeeper that she would be gone for a while and to just keep an eye on things. She thought about texting some friends, but what would she say? She would wait for them to reach out.

"What are you doing?" Jack asked.

Melissa looked at him and smiled "I am in. I am doing it. I am clearing my schedule for 3 months or so."

"We are doing it." Jack reached over the center console and held her hand.

Jack pulled into the marine supply store and parked the truck. They hopped out of the truck and walked into the store. Jack was immediately greeted by the man behind the counter. He was an older man with tan pants and tan shirt. He had on red suspenders that he kept rubbing up and down as he talked. The brim of his ball cap was turned up. He was a comical sight to say the least.

"Jack Finn!" the old man practically shouted. "How you doing, young buck?"

"Doing good, doing real good. How you been, Larry?"

"Christ, I can't complain…I'm vertical." He laughed and slapped his suspenders. "How is your father doing? When I saw him at the fisherman's forum up there in Rockland he was complaining about his back."

"You know Dad. Been fishing by himself for years, I finally talked him into taking a sternman this season. He is taking Michael Williams's boy Josh. Seems to be working out too. That kid's a hard worker and a quick learner."

"Well, ain't that something." The old man paused and looked past Jack to see Melissa standing there. "Ooh, my goodness, Jack, you caught yourself a good one. Ain't she cunnin"

Melissa was a little stunned. "Cunnin?" she thought to herself.

"Calm down, old timer, you look any harder and you'll give yourself a heart attack. This is Madison. A-uh friend of mine"

"Pardon me, young lady, I don't have a filter. My name is Larry, I own the store."

"Nice to meet you, Larry." Melissa was still trying to figure out the "cunnin" statement.

"Jack, you going to run next week at the races?" Larry asked Jack

"Oh yeah, Michael is going to clean my aftercooler sometime next week before the races. I will beach the boat out, change the prop and clean the bottom before Saturday. Are you coming down?"

"Yup, I will be with Marshall Westin. Are you going to have a crew on board?" Larry asked looking back at Melissa.

"I don't know, I haven't formally asked her yet. We will see."

"Jack, I am going to look around." Her eyes were wandering around the store. She felt as if she was in a store in a foreign country. She recognized some of the stuff from Jack's boat but had no clue as to what it was or what it did. She glanced at a rack of the funny overalls. "GuyCotton," she said to herself out loud looking at the brand. She smiled to herself when she looked at the sizes. They ranged from XS to XXXL. "What, no women's sizes?" she joked to herself. She turned to Larry and Jack and asked.

"If I wear a size 2 dress what size of…these do I need?"

Jack was a little shocked and confused. "Um, I think medium. You buying some?"

"Yeah, we are setting traps later, right?" Melissa replied, hoping that she had worded that right. She picked out a pair of medium overalls and wandered over to the boot section. She kicked off one of her sandals and tried on a couple pairs of boots until she found a size that would fit. She continued glancing around the store. No carpet on the floor, no sales associate waiting on you hand and foot. The prices were all posted on little handwritten tags. The store smelled industrial. Concrete floors and steel shelves. "Not in Kansas anymore," she said to herself laughing. It seemed funnier to her having just played Judy Garland in her last movie. She could hear Jack was wrapping up his business with Larry so she headed back to the counter. She put the overalls and boots up on the counter. Without a scanner or even looking at the price tags Larry pushed the numbers on his cash register.

"177.95," Larry shouted as if Melissa were standing thirty feet away.

Melissa pulled out a credit card and paid. They walked out the door and Jack looked at her. She was smiling ear to ear. Beaming with pride that she had bought her own gear. Sure, she had bought a lot of stuff before, but nothing like this. She felt like she was slowly melting into this lifestyle.

"Who was that guy?" Melissa asked.

"That was the one and only Larry Edwards. His dock drifted out of Linikin Bay and Dad helped him find it, then towed it back. Ever since then he tells a harrowing story of how his dock went right out through the bay and how him and Russell Finn saved it."

"Crazy… You guys almost have your own language and vocabulary up here."

They hopped back in Jack's truck and started back to Boothbay Harbor.

"So…your turn." Jack said to her.

"My turn, what do you mean?"

"Well you know all about me, now I want to know about you."

Melissa slightly froze. Then slowly relaxed, "What do you want to know?"

"Well I read your bio on IMBD.com. So I know a little about you. I know about your mom and dad, but I want to hear your side of it."

Melissa was a little annoyed. "Stalking me, Jack?"

"No, no, no. I went on there long before we met, trying to find a picture of you."

Melissa was laughing a little now. "Picture of me…why would you be doing that?"

Uncomfortable being caught in slightly perverted behavior, Jack replied. "In the movie "Summer Days" there are several scenes you were wearing a bikini. I…I…well just because I haven't dated five years doesn't mean I…well…you know. Anyway this is about you."

Melissa was giggling a bit now. "My version isn't much different. I never knew my dad, and my mother couldn't handle me being more famous than her. I have no brothers or sisters. Does it hurt? It used to, now not so much. I have done well without them. My life has been moving so fast I never really found myself needing them."

"But like who do you talk to when life just sucks, like when you found out your mom died? Ok, you didn't have a relationship, but there must have been some remorse."

"I always hoped she would come around and want to be involved, and when she died I knew that was never going to happen. Chris Pratt and I were doing a movie together at the time. He actually was a great friend and helped me through that. He is still a good friend."

"Now how does that work? When I want to hang out with my best friend, we just meet up and have a beer or watch football. It's not like you and Chris can just go have a beer without the press twisting it all out of shape"

"We talk on the phone mostly. Sometimes we will go to each other's house and hang out."

"That's cool. I can't imagine what it would be like to sit and watch football with Chris Pratt."

"Oh, so you're star struck by Chris, but not me?" Melissa fired back while laughing.

"Don't get jealous. I didn't go looking for pictures of Chris in a bikini. It's funny, and maybe it's because I met you in such an awkward, way but you just don't seem…Hollywood to me."

"You are not the first to say that. I think it's because I grew up in a car and hotel rooms. I also know that sometime maybe even in the near future people might be saying, "who is Melissa Andrews?"

"See, that right there breaks the stereotype that everybody thinks. Anyway, when you watch movies are you criticizing the other actors and actresses? Do you watch your own movies? What movies are your favorite?"

"I sometimes critique roles, Jack" she said smiling at him. "If I have other actresses and actors over we take turns acting out the scene to see who can do it better. I will tell you Chris would have made an awesome Jason Bourne. I do watch my own and criticize myself. It is hard to watch a movie I have been in and enjoy it. Except this last one I am very happy with my performance in "Over the Rainbow". I like action films and comedy. There is too much drama in Hollywood to want to sit and watch it. What about you? What are your favorite movies? What kind of music do you like? What is your favorite food?"

"Action and comedy as well, hard rock, rock and roll. Cheeseburgers. What about you? What music do you like? What is your favorite food?"

"Music, I am all over the place. My playlists go from Five Finger Death Punch to Frank Sinatra, from Garth Brooks to Aretha Franklin. Favorite food is a hard one. I have traveled to so many places and tried so many things. When I am home and trying to relax I go for pizza. It's my comfort food."

They talked all the way back to Boothbay Harbor. It had been so long since she had been able to ask someone else about them. All the interviews and meet and greets with fans, you just sit there and answer questions. This was so refreshing to be able to ask someone else what they liked or what they did. Melissa felt so good just talking to someone that would listen. Getting to share all the little details of her life. Things she had taken for granted for so long. She was falling more in love with Jack with every word he spoke. What made her feel better is he wasn't perfect. She could tell he was still pretty guarded and that was fine. He drove too slow and mumbled a little. He was cute though. Handsome, in a gruff kind of way. His dirty Red at Night hat was pulled over his short blonde hair with brown roots. She wondered how the sun bleached his hair with his hat on. His eyes were the same color blue as the ocean in the Caribbean. His warm smile gave a small glimpse of his white teeth. His voice was deep and calming. He looked lean, which was a surprise for his large appetite. Even sitting in his truck he looked tall and sure. His white t-shirt gave plenty of clues about his build. The cuffs of the t-shirt were tight on his biceps.

Jack interrupted her thoughts, "So I forgot to ask you. Do you want to hang out with me for the Boothbay Harbor Lobsterboat Races?"

"Maybe, if I am not with my other lobsterman boyfriend," Melissa said back with wit.

"Well, ask him to come along too."

"Sure, what is it all about?" She laughed while she spoke.

"Other lobstermen, boatbuilders and some others come from all around to race their lobster boats. I race Red at Night. I will probably tie up alongside Dad and my buddy Mike. We drink beer and grill burgers. Then after the last race we head to Rockland for their races the next day. Boothbay's is one week from today."

"Sounds like fun. I've got to get some more clothes, though, so I blend in better. Maybe that is what your mom and I could do. So we stay overnight in Rockland?"

"Yeah…uh I have a big berth, or bed as you call it, down forward in Red at Night."

"So we would be sleeping together…what happened to taking it slow?" Melissa grinned at Jack.

"Well two people can sleep in the same bed without any fooling around. We can sleep in two different sleeping bags." Jack's face was turning red.

"Oh Jack," Melissa sighed. "We are going to have a great summer," and with that she leaned over the console of Jack's truck and gave him a kiss on the cheek. Jack's nerves settled with that, and he smiled back at Melissa. He turned into his driveway and parked the truck. Russell's old Chevy was there next to Anne's Ford sedan

"Here we are, Finn Village. That is my house." Jack pointed to a small house, about the same size as the cottage that she was renting. "That is my mom and dad's house" He pointed to a bigger house with a wraparound porch closer to the water. "And up there on the hill is where my sister lives." Jack pointed out another small house at the top of the driveway.

"Wow…Not really sure what to say."

"I know, a family compound is a little odd. My great-grandfather bought this land, built a small house where my mom and dad's house is. My grandfather bought a piece of land from him and built my sister's house. Shortly after my grandparents started having kids, my great-grandparents died. Mom and dad started out in my sister's house. Her and I actually grew up in that house. After my grandparents died my parents moved into that house and rented out my sister's. My sister bought it from them. I bought a piece of land from them and built my house."

"I'm not surprised that you and your sister had to buy from your parents."

"Yah, that is my parents for you. It works well. We all respect our space. I mow all the lawns and plow the driveways in the winter. Mom and Lucy take care of the gardening."

"What does your dad do?"

Jack chuckled. "Talk."

Anne came out of the house while Russell came up from the dock.

"Well, back from Brunswick. Oh and look, you got yourself some oil skins and boots! What did you think of Larry?

"He is very loud, and he called me…cunnin," Melissa said back, still confused by the word.

"Oh, that's a good thing Melissa, means your cute." Russell explained.

"Ahh. I get it now. He was very nice. The store was much different than I am used to, but very interesting. Everything from clothes to rope to stoves. Some stuff I had no idea what I was looking at. I think if I'm going to be here a while I'll still need to get the lingo down."

"Be here a while…" Anne paused a bit. "How long are you planning to stay here?"

"Until the end of summer. Actually I have a favor to ask. Jack says you're the best person to talk to about finding a job around here."

"I can find you a job easy enough."

"Wait…I got an idea…Jack will you take Josh as your sternman?" Russell interrupted.

"Of course I would, but who is going to go with you? You can't go by yourself and what does this have to do with Melissa?"

"She can be my new sternman…woman…sternwoman. Best way for her to keep a low profile. Josh is getting bored on my boat. I think he would like the pace of your boat better."

"I like the sound of that but I'm going to have to get up early, won't I?" Melissa asked.

"Yes, but you will love the entertainment. Hell, you should pay me"

"Ok then, I'm going to be a sternwoman". Melissa was beaming. The thought of working on a lobster boat thrilled her. It would keep her close to Jack which is right where she wanted to be. "When do I start?"

"Monday morning. You be on the Spruce Point dock at five in the morning. Anne packs the lunches so just tell her if you're allergic to anything. No smoking or drugs on my boat. We crack a beer after the boat is washed and passes my inspection. No asking how many more, or when are we going in. You will keep a knife on you at all times and you will learn to run the boat. I like to have fun at work, but my life is in your hands out there and yours is in mine. That's nothing I take lightly."

Melissa was a little shocked. It was the first time she had ever been talked to so sternly.

"Yes, sir," was the only thing she could think to say.

"I will call Josh and let him know the change," said Russell.

"Melissa, what were your thoughts for us tonight?" Anne asked.

"I was thinking shopping. I need more…normal clothes if I am staying here until the end of summer. I'm going to need some work clothes, too."

"That sounds good, if you don't mind going back to Brunswick. We can go out to eat too"

"Shopping! There goes last week's haul." Russell chuckled.

"Alright, that's enough bullshitting. I have traps to move. Melissa, let's get going." Jack barked out jokingly.

Melissa turned to Jack, "Can I use your bathroom?"

"Of course you can. Go right in the door and through the kitchen. The bathroom is the first door on your right."

Melissa walked into the house and immediately saw a picture of Jack and Stephanie on the wall. They looked happy. Both of them were smiling and sitting on the porch of Russell and Anne's house. She wanted to say something to Stephanie, but didn't know what to say. What was there to say. It was her time now. She took a step away then looked back. "I will take care of him," Every window in the house was open, so it smelled like the ocean even in the house. There were a few dishes in the sink, but nothing overwhelming. It was pretty clean. Not spotless, but neat. When she came out of the bathroom Anne was in Jack's kitchen leaning against the counter.

"So Melissa…I have to tell you I am a little nervous about tonight." Anne said.

"Really, me too."

"Why? You are a movie star. I am just an old woman from Maine."

"Yes, but you are so sure of yourself and so solid…and you're also Jack's mother."

"About that…" Anne took a deep breath. "To be honest with you Melissa, I am still not sure about you and Jack."

Melissa felt a huge lump in her throat; she was hurt and upset and it showed.

Anne could see Melissa was upset. "Wait, wait, wait, dear, hear me out please. It is not that I don't like you, you seem very nice. I just worry about Jack. What is going to happen at the end of summer when you go back? I don't know what you know, but this is a big step for Jack."

"Worry about Jack? He has you and Russell. He has this town that is like a huge support group. What about me? When I get back? Who will take care of me? Mrs. Finn, I am falling for Jack. In less than a day he has made me feel more like a person than I ever have. Yes, we could just be caught up in this moment, but we are willing to risk it. He told me about Stephanie and that there is still a lot of healing to do. Maybe I'm the one to help."

Anne took a second to look at Melissa. Here she was, a woman in love with a man. Deep in her heart, with all of her wisdom and all of her intuition, she knew this was right. Anne smiled at Melissa and opened her arms and gave her a big hug. "We will take care of you. Please, call me Anne."

Melissa took a big breath. Nobody had ever said those words before with such honesty and integrity. It was like she had been drowning and someone threw her a life ring. More of that feeling of sinking into this lifestyle came over her.

All she could think to say was "Thank you."

They walked back outside and saw Russell standing there puffing on his pipe.

"You two ok now or are you going to sing 'Coom-By-Ya'?" Russell asked while puffing his pipe

"Oh, shut up, you ox." Said Anne. "Now Melissa, he may be the captain, but don't be afraid to speak your mind."

Melissa chuckled and said, "O.K."

"Melissa, Jack went down to the boat. We will talk about pay and all that stuff Monday when I pick you up."

Melissa walked down the path to the boats. She could hear Jack's boat start up, followed by the squelch and chatter on the VHF. She heard Jack singing along with the radio. The closer she got she could see the bright red hull shine against the water and the reflection of each wave in the transom. The name "Red at Night" in the gold leaf lettering with grey background seemed to dance with the reflection. Everything had a place on that boat, and everything in its place. His boat was cleaner than the house. On top of the cabin was a radar, a smaller dome and a small antenna, and white handrails going up each side. Two work lights attached to the back of the cabin pointed down at the deck. Between the two lights was a speaker. On the left side of the boat the cabin was fully enclosed with two antennas attached to the side. On the right side of the boat it was completely open. The big disc-looking thing he called a hauler, and the crane-looking thing he called the davit. Tied to the right of the dock was Russell's boat. It had similar lines to Jack's boat but it was smaller. The hull was black and shiny. The name "Old Smoke" on the front in silver lettering. Russell's boat was no different than Jack's. Organized and clean. She walked down the ramp and on to the dock. Jack was loading traps on to the boat. He already had his oil skins on. Melissa couldn't help but watch Jack's arms flex as he lifted the traps and tossed them up on the stack.

"What can I do?" Melissa asked, anxious to help.

"Put your oil skins on and your boots...don't tuck your oil skins into your boots."

Melissa set her boots down and started putting her oil skins on. She stuck one leg in, being careful not to have them backwards. She was wearing shorts so the material felt weird against her skin. She put the other leg in and pulled them up to her waist. She flipped the shoulder straps on and was disappointed to see that the legs appeared too long.

"Come on over here, I'll adjust those straps."

She went over to Jack and he stepped out of the boat and stood in front of her. She felt slightly awkward while he took up slack in the shoulder straps of the overalls. He stopped and looked at her making sure they fit and she wouldn't trip over the legs. He held her by the waist and took a small step towards her and bent down. She tipped her head back with her arms down by her side. Their lips met once again. While they kissed she slid her arms up between them and embraced his face. They slowly pulled apart and Jack picked her up playfully and put her on the boat.

"There. I wanted to get that out of the way before telling you what you're doing next."

"Alright, what am I doing next?" she said, rubbing her hands together and beaming at him.

"I am going to bring a trap to the rail. While I coil the rope up. You take a bait bag and tie it off to the cleat in the trap. I took a pair of Josh's gloves from dad's boat. They should fit you."

Melissa looked at the tray filled with twine knit bags with dead fish in them. It smelled like Jack's hooded sweat shirt, but worse. She slid on the cotton gloves that felt a little big for her. Taking a bag from the tray and holding it up, she walked it over to the open lobster trap. She looked at the trap slightly confused.

"O.K." Jack saw her confusion. "This is the front of the trap, also known as the kitchen or galley. These things here are called the heads. In between them is the bait line. Up top here is the bait cleat. All you got to do is wrap the pull string from the bait bag around the cleat then go over that with the bait line. Then close the trap and make sure you got all these bungee straps over the door." Jack demonstrated everything as he went along. He got the next trap from the stack on the dock and brought it to the boat. He opened the trap and pulled the rope out and neatly coiled it top on of the other rope on the boat. Melissa did everything he said. Jack went about what he had to do but she noticed he kept an eye on her as well. Soon Red at Night was loaded with traps. Jack untied the boat and with a few movements of the steering wheel and controls they were on their way out of Lobster Cove.

"Alright we got a bit of a steam until we get to Damariscove. Let me go over the basics with you. The front or forward end of the boat is called the bow, the back or aft end of the boat is called the stern, the right side of the boat as you face forward is called starboard, and the other side is port. No matter which way you face, starboard side is always there and port is always there," Jack said while pointing things out. "Dad may ask you to go "down forward," that is down in the cabin of the boat. Some call it the saloon. We are standing in what is called the cockpit."

"Red at Night, you on this one" The VHF radio interrupted the lesson. Jack grabbed a microphone and spoke into it.

"Yah, go ahead, Mike."

"Just got off the phone with your father. Where do you want me to drop Josh off on Monday?"

"I got to get bait in the morning, so drop him off at Tommy's. I will pick him up there around five thirty. My plan is to haul four days in a row, then have you take a look at this thing sometime Friday."

"Sounds like a plan, bub. I guess I'll be seeing you latah."

"Yaah, see ya latah."

Melissa chuckled listening to the Maine accent between Jack and Michael. It seemed thicker when they talked to each other.

"Can I take a look…down forward? I want to see the accommodations for next weekend."

"Yaah, sure. Go ahead. By the way the toilet is called the head, too." He was grinning at his own word play.

Melissa opened the door and stepped down into the cabin. There was a large bunk all the way in the bow. There were some small shelves with lobster bands, and other miscellaneous stuff that she couldn't identify on the port side. There was small door all the way to starboard. She opened it and found a small toilet, er—head. She closed that door and took another look at the entire area. It was roomy yet cozy. She couldn't wait to spend the night with Jack. Even if they just laid there and talked. In some ways she hoped that was all that would happen. Sex often complicated things and she didn't want to ruin what they had going, but in the same time she was anxious to give herself to Jack. Would he be ready? Would she be ready? If her and Jack were going to take that step she wanted it to be something they wouldn't regret. She turned around and came back up.

"What do you think? Is it Hollywood star quality?" Jack asked.

"No, and that is fine by me. Jack, may I ask a small favor?"

"Sure."

"No more Hollywood jokes. I know you're just kidding, but I want to forget that life for the next few months. I want to be… normal…average…regular."

"No problem, but let me tell you something that dad told me. Back in high school some of the Patriots players were coming to watch our practice. I started getting so nervous I was getting sick. Dad sat me down and said, "They put their pants on the same way we do… one leg at a time."

"How does that apply to me?"

"You need to remember no matter how famous or rich you are, you still are whatever you want to be. You just keep doing what you're doing. Nothing you have done in the…well, day that I have known you suggests that you are anything but normal. Except your singing. That is…well, damn, I don't have the words for that."

"Thanks, Jack. Funny you see me as normal, you don't see me as a movie star, but here you are a normal average guy and I see you like a movie star."

"Well I guess I chose the wrong profession."

Melissa smiled and kissed him again and said, "No you chose the right one."

They continued the day setting and moving traps. Melissa learned more about the lobstering industry and what was going to be expected of her on Russell's boat. She loved the feeling of the boat underneath her. She liked watching Jack push the traps overboard. The idle chatter of other lobstermen on the radio was entertaining. Sometimes they would call Jack, some even asked about her. Jack just said, "Some PFA that drank too much sea water" but she knew she meant more to Jack than that. She looked forward to the next few months of getting to know him better. She already knew a lot. It still hadn't been a full 24 hours yet and she had fallen for him completely. He wasn't perfect, he had his issues, but he was honest and real. It was going to be a good summer.

Chapter 3

Anne was cutting up vegetables and getting snacks ready for Russell's meeting. She always had food ready for guests. Even if it were someone stopping by unannounced she could put a plate on the table. Looking out the window down towards the water she could see Russell down at the dock fiddling around with traps and tools. "Cleaning" is what he called it. She knew the meeting they were having tonight weighed heavily on his mind. You wouldn't be able to tell unless you knew him. Russell was very much like the ducks he liked to feed and talk to in the cove. Calm and peaceful on the surface, but paddling like crazy underneath. No matter what they went through, Russell always had a steady demeanor. Only when nobody was looking, and he was by himself, would he ever show emotion. When the bank took his boat back when Lucy and Jack were just toddlers, he seemed unphased. Later that night Anne found him taking an oak runner from a trap and swinging it at anything he could find in the dock house. When Russell's father died he held himself together for his mother. That evening Anne went down to the dock to find him sitting on his bottom on the dock much like a child, crying his heart out. The issues with Tommy MacIntyre had been festering for a while. Every time they spoke to Tommy, he knew just what to say and do to get his fishermen off his back. That had come to a head. The fact that there was going to be a meeting showed the frustration on everybody's mind. Russell, Jack, and Michael had been talking about buying out Tommy for a while. They had it all planned out. Michael's wife Abigail would handle the overall business affairs. Anne would run the restaurant. Russell and Jack would run the lobstering side, while Michael would run his mobile marine service as a part of it. Anne had always dreamed about running her own restaurant. She had even started thing about redecorating it. "I am getting ahead of myself," she thought. "We will see," she said out loud to herself.

"We will see what?" Lucy said, sneaking up on her mother.

Anne half startled. "For heaven's sake, don't sneak up on me like that."

"Sorry, mom, what were you saying?"

"Nothing. Just talking to myself. What have you been up to?"

"Nothing much really. I did some grocery shopping…lots of people asking about Jack's new girlfriend."

"What are they asking?" Anne asked, concerned that people had started figuring out who Melissa was.

"Who she is? Where is she from? How long have they been dating?"

"And how did you answer those questions?" Anne asked. She had stopped cutting vegetables and had her full attention on Lucy.

"Mom relax, I said her name was Madison. I told them I had no clue where she was from and Jack had just met her. I told them about the kayak and Jack saving her."

"Good, Lucy." Anne picked up the knife again and continued cutting vegetables. "I have some news for you. Melissa is going to stay in the Harbor until the end of summer. She is going to go lobstering with your father. She and I are going clothes shopping tonight out in Brunswick and then going out to dinner."

"So…this is getting serious…Is this a good idea, Mom?"

"Honestly, Lucy, I don't know, but Jack is 32 years old. He can handle whatever is going to happen. I don't think Melissa intends any harm. I'm not saying that no harm will come of this. All we can do is sit back and watch. If Jack gets hurt, we will help. Until then, we do our damned best to make sure nobody figures out who she is."

"Yes, Mom. It is kinda cool though…I mean did you hear her voice last night?"

"I have had that song stuck in my head all day." Anne giggled. "She is really something special, Lucy. I talked with her a little."

Just then Russell came through the door.

"Finished with the oars devors." Russell asked jokingly.

"Yes, there are veggies, chips, ranch dip made extra thick the way you like it and finger sandwiches," Anne replied.

"What have you been up to today, dad?" Lucy asked her father.

"Getting more gear ready, setting up the boat a little differently. I got a Hollywood actress as a stern…woman now. The Old Smoke has to be at tip top shape. That, and Melissa hasn't been on the water as much as Josh, I made it so she can hold on to something. Also went and bought a toilet seat for a five gallon bucket and a curtain so she has a little privacy."

Anne looked at Russell trying to keep a serious face. "OOOHHHH Miss Movie Star gets all this nice stuff but what about your wife?"

"Or your daughter?" Lucy chimed in.

"You two stop that," said Russell slightly flustered. "You two are Maine born women of a lobstering family. You were practically born with a five-gallon bucket strapped to your stern. This is going to be awkward for the poor girl and I want her to be comfortable."

"Just teasing you, dear," said Anne.

Russell was saved by the sound of Jack's boat backing into his slip at the dock. Jack tied up his boat and shut everything down. After Jack walked up the hill, Russell asked him, "Did you throw her overboard?"

Jack chuckled, "Yup…I used her for bait on the last string. No, I took her over to Tommy's to get her car. She is going to take a shower and then head over here. Mom, she is still a little nervous, I think. Go easy on her."

"Don't you worry, Jack. She will be alright. I won't lie; I still have mixed feelings about all this, but I will go along with it."

"Alright, Mom. Dad, I talked to Mike; he will just drop Josh off at Tommy's in the morning when I go load up. I'm planning on beaching the boat Thursday night to clean the bottom and put the race wheel on. While I'm on the beach out, Michael is going to bump the engine up and clean my aftercooler, not that it has to be up there for that. I should be able to be off the beach out in enough time for you to use it."

"I think I'm all set. Did you go over stuff with Melissa?"

"Yup, just the basics. She will do alright, I think. I gotta go to my house and take a shower. See you in a bit for the meeting."

Jack went over to his house to get into the shower. He intentionally diverted his eyes from every picture of him and Stephanie. It didn't help. As the water poured over the back of his neck the feeling of guilt washed over him as well. This wasn't fair. He was alive and happy while Stephanie was dead and gone. Why didn't she just let him take her home? She wasn't that drunk really. From his memory, she had only had a few beers. Maybe that's why she insisted on driving herself. The real reason Jack wanted to take her home was to pop the question. The police never said anything about her blood alcohol level. The fact she had been drinking had never come up. The guilt started to wash away along with the dirt and grime from the day. His mind went to the meeting tonight. He figured that most of the guys were pretty fed up with Tommy's crap. It was a matter of if they would trust their livelihood in the hands of people that had never run a retail business or restaurant. Would they want to sell lobster to people that go lobstering themselves? There was a little bit of conflict of interest there. It's not like Jack and Russell would use what people were catching to chase them around and set traps near theirs. What would Tommy do when they approached him? That in itself was a mystery. Tommy, for the most part, was very predictable. Up until recently anyways. Now things around the dock had changed. Locked rooms that were never locked before. Bait and fuel had gone up but the price of lobster was down. Even the cost of bands for banding lobsters had gone up. Jack finished his shower and dried off. With his towel around his waist he stepped out of the bathroom. As soon as he closed the door he was startled by Melissa standing there.

"Uuuhhh, what are you doing here?" Jack was a little embarrassed in the awkward moment.

"Jack, you're not shy are you? You saw my butt in a movie, why can't I see yours?" Melissa said stepping forward and reaching for his towel.

"Wait— that was in a movie, millions of people saw your ass. We are not doing well at taking it slow."

"Just playing, Jack. I just wanted to say good luck with your meeting. Will I see you later?" said Melissa as she leaned against the wall pulling her arm back from the towel.

"Don't know. Depends how this meeting goes and how late Mom and you stay out. I ain't doing nothing tomorrow so I think I will stay up late and watch a movie…you want me to wait for you?"

"Sure… please nothing with me in it, and don't get me wrong. I love all your questions about the movie business, but can we just sit and watch?"

"No problem, I have a guilty pleasure of watching 80's movies anyway."

"Aahh, the 80's. Hair spray and IROC Camaro's."

"It's a date then."

Melissa smiled and stepped back toward him. She put one hand against his bare chest and kissed his lips. She started to step back and grabbed his towel and pulled it off of him. She saw his bare butt as he turned and jetted towards his bedroom.

"Damn, you pervert," Jack said, as he closed the bedroom door.

Melissa walked back out of the house and onto the patch of the dooryard that the Finn family used as a common area. A courtyard of sorts. There was such a sense of family and togetherness here. She still felt like a bit of an outsider, but still a welcome guest. Russell was sitting in a lawn chair with a beer in his hand. Anne was putting out veggie platters and chips. There was a man she didn't recognize standing by the table with the food. He had a pretty husky build with a greasy hat, wire rim glasses, shaved head and short beard. His clothes were dirty and greasy from head to toe. He was steadily snacking on the food being placed. Anne slapped his hand and told him to leave it alone until the guests arrived.

"Ain't I a guest, Mum?" The man spoke in a deep voice.

"You stopped being a guest here many moons ago, Mr. Williams, and go wash your hands for Christ's sake," Anne responded.

"Yes, Mum."

Melissa wasn't surprised to see Anne's power over the man. She felt Anne could order King Kong to go wash his hands and it would happen. The man headed towards Melissa. When they finally caught eyes he stopped walking. "Does he know who I am?" She thought to herself. He started to smile when Russell spoke up.

"Mike, that is the Madison you have heard so much about. Madison, that is Michael Williams."

"Nice to meet you", Melissa stuck out her hand to greet him and realized she was still holding Jack's towel.

Michael held his hands up that were covered with oil and grease. "I would love to shake your hand, but I am kind of a mess. Nice to meet you, too. Do I know you from somewhere? You look familiar."

"Nope, I am new in town. Going to be spending the summer here."

"Huh, I swear I have seen you before. I gotta go wash my hands before Anne shoots me. I will talk at ya latah."

"You and Mom headed out shopping?" asked Lucy.

"Yes, I will be here for a while so I need more clothes. Also going to be going sternwoman with your dad so I may need some work clothes," said Melissa

"I heard. That is going to be different. Are you ready for it?"

"I don't know…we will see. I think I did ok helping Jack today. Those traps are heavy though."

"Don't you worry about a thing. We will be doing pairs and singles on Monday. I will go easy til' you learn the ropes. When you first get on board, we will do a safety talk, also a quick "how to" operate the boat and VHF. Then we will discuss pay. I hope you don't mind country western music," said Russell.

"I guess I will learn to like it. Thank you for giving me a job. You don't have to worry about paying me…I…have…"

"Just stop right there. A Finn doesn't take free help. You are here to forget Hollywood so whatever you have doesn't matter. I will pay you a fare rate. What you want to do with it is up to you."

"O.K." said Melissa. There was obviously no arguing with Russell.

"Alright Melissa, are you ready?" Anne spoke up.

"Yes, I'm ready," Melissa answered.

"We will take my car. Russell, you behave yourself and good luck."

Melissa and Anne got into Anne's car. Melissa still had a few butterflies in her stomach. This was all so new and happening so fast. She looked out the window and saw Lucy waving. As nervous as she was she liked the family atmosphere. She hesitated for a moment and then turned to Anne.

"Anne, I know this was meant for us to get to know each other better, but what about Lucy."

Anne paused for a moment. "What about Lucy?" she quizzed.

"She is Jack's sister. I am sure she has just as many questions and probably would like to get to know me, too. If I have learned anything about the Finn's, it's that you all look out for each other."

"So you want her to come along?"

"Yes, if it is o.k. with you."

Anne put her window down and yelled out the window to Lucy and she quickly got in the back seat of the car. Melissa somehow felt better. Even though she was outnumbered she felt it was a little better than one on one. Even though she and Anne had a moment in Jack's kitchen she still felt like Anne didn't quite trust her completely yet.

As they pulled out of the driveway she saw Jack walking out of the house with Michael. She waved and he waved back. She took a deep breath and sighed a little. She would rather be with Jack, but she knew if this was going to work she had to earn Anne's trust.

Anne, hearing the sigh, responded, "Don't worry, he will be there when we get back."

Melissa laughed, "I know. I just. Well…you know."

To break the awkward moment Lucy spoke up. "So where are we going first, girls?"

"All that getting food ready got me hungry. Are you guys hungry?" said Anne.

"I am starving," Melissa spoke first.

"Me, too. Let's take her to that place next to that boatyard where Michael used to work," Lucy answered.

"OOOhhhh yes. The Harraseeket Lunch and Lobster," Anne replied.

"Who is Michael? I mean, I know I just met him and I have heard Jack talk about him, but how do you guys know him?" asked Melissa.

"Michael is Jack's best friend. He is a bit older than Jack. Michael is married and has two kids, Elizabeth and Josh. Great kids, great family. He is a boat mechanic, and his wife, Abigail, manages a hotel."

"Oh yeah, I saw Elizabeth at the dock. Jack wouldn't let me meet her. He said she is one of my biggest fans. Funny, Jack being best friends with someone that much older than him."

"Yes, Jack has always been that way. Jack has always been mature for his age. When he was a kid he would hang around us adults. He listened to Clive, his father and the other fisherman talk about lobstering, boat building and life in gerneral."

"I can see that. He does seem very focused and driven. What does Jack do for fun? Does he have any hobbies?"

"He loves to watch movies, which is a bit ironic meeting you. It was funny to see a thirty two year old single man want to watch the life story of Judy Garland. Most of the time he waits for them to be released on DVD or online but he actually took off to Brunswick to see that," Lucy answered.

The conversation went on. With every word spoken, Melissa felt more and more a part of the Finn family. Lucy and Anne were feeling better about Melissa as well. Melissa was just a woman. No different than they were. Melissa loved hearing stories about Jack and Lucy growing up and the stunts they pulled. All the memories that a normal family has. Melissa didn't have much to contribute to that conversation. Instead she gave the girls inside information on Hollywood. Told them about what actors and actresses were actually nice verses stuck up. She told them what a typical day was like on set. When they arrived at the Harraseeket Lunch and Lobster, Lucy pointed out a small boatyard next door with a small marina.

"That is Strout's Point Wharf Company, where Michael used to work. It is also where we stay for the Long Island, Portland lobsterboat races," Lucy said.

"Tell me about these races. Jack has invited me to go to the Boothbay Harbor races then stay with him on the boat overnight for the Rockland races."

"Ooooohhhh overnight with Jack. Mom, you hear that! You better raft up next to someone else." Lucy teased.

"Lucy Anne Finn, you know better than to tease like that. They are adults. Whatever they do is no business of mine...or yours," Anne barked back.

Melissa was blushing at this point. "Jack and I are taking it slow. This is a very complicated...relationship and neither of us want to mess it up."

They walked up to the counter and ordered their dinner. Melissa pulled out her card to pay, but Anne gently pushed it away.

"You're our guest, you save your money," Anne said.

"Anne, I know you must know how much I am worth. The least I can do is buy you and Lucy dinner," contested Melissa.

Anne shifted on her feet a bit. Melissa in her heart was a great person. She could see that but sometimes that Hollywood arrogance would pop up like an old shag by a dock. It was innocent in Melissa's case. She didn't mean any harm by it. It would just take some Finn

Schooling to break her of that habit. "Don't you let that Hollywood stuff out again. If I were you I would forget all about that and live off what you make with Russell. Don't worry, we won't treat you like a guest forever." Anne paused, a bit hesitant to say the next part and thinking on how to word it, "Melissa, your worth has nothing to do with how much money you have, cars you own, or the size of your house. Around here, around us, your worth is your word, how you treat people, and how you treat yourself."

Melissa smiled back and nodded her head to Anne. The words she just heard carried far too much importance to reply with a simple "yes" or "o.k."

The girls sat down overlooking the lobsterboats. Melissa was about to have her first Maine Lobster roll. She was surprised by the size of the meal. Big chunks of lobster meat with a little mayonnaise mixed in, on a twelve inch sub roll. A basket of French fries the size of a football. Melissa looked at it a little overwhelmed.

"Don't worry, dear, you don't have to finish it," Anne assured her. "Not many places make them like that. Most places it is a 50/50 mix of lobster meat and mayonnaise on a hotdog bun for the same money." Anne wanted to say how she would do hers if they bought MacIntyre's but didn't want that secret out yet.

They sat and had their meals while watching the boats going by. Melissa listened as Anne and Lucy told her more about Maine and their lifestyle. She kept thinking to herself about never going back to Hollywood. Did she feel this way because of how hurt she felt by the media who had just been on her side and quickly turned on her? In a little over 24 hours she had fallen in love, not only with Jack, but his family and their way of life. The conversation around her had stopped. She looked to her right and looked at Anne. The tough Maine woman, with a heart of gold. To her left was Lucy; she didn't know what to think of Lucy yet, but she was nice, and funny.

Anne was trying to think of what to ask Melissa. Her whole life had been on T.V. and the movies. Much like her own kids, she had watched Melissa grow up. Anne had always enjoyed watching the actress. Melissa had true talent even as a little girl. Anne had felt saddened when the news reported that Melissa's mother had died. She remembered Melissa giving a press statement. On stage all by herself. She stood tall and gracefully addressed the press on her and her mother's relationship, or lack thereof, and how she had wished someday they would get past it and bond. Melissa had strength, that was for sure. She also had heart. She may still be a little naïve as to life in the blue collar world but Anne couldn't fault her for that. After a summer with them she would have a different perspective on life, that was for sure. The Finn family was a good place for her. Jack would be a good man for her, and she would be a good woman for Jack. If they went their separate ways at the end of summer both of them would be better people knowing each other.

The air was a little different at the Finn compound. All of the lobstermen that fished for Tommy MacIntyre had shown up. Jack sat next to Michael at the back of the group while Russell stood up and started the meeting.

"Thank you, guys, for showing up on a Saturday evening. You guys all know the issues we have had with Tommy and the lobster price. We also know our bait and other supplies are higher than other places. Suddenly there are paddle locks on doors and new truck drivers. This bullshit started 5 years ago and I don't know about you guys, but I have had enough of it. I know Jack and Clive feel the same way, but we want to know what you guys think."

Hazel Smith spoke up, "I am getting pretty sick of it. I mean I get price drops, that happens, but not in the middle of the day."

"Me, too," said another.

"What are you guys planning to do, start a strike?" a young man, Dale Rines, asked.

"No, a strike is the last thing we want. We care about the business, and a strike doesn't pay the bills. Jack, Michael and I have been thinking we want to buy out Tommy. We have been squirreling away our money and we will get financing for the rest from the bank. Jack and I will run the lobster side and Michael is going to run his mobile business out of there. Anne will run the restaurant and Michael's wife Abby will be the general manager."

"Oh, so you and Jack can see what we are catching. That is convenient," the same young man spoke again.

"Yes, we will, but if you think I am going to start chasing your traps with mine you got it wrong. I have my own places and honey holes. I don't need yours. You guys will have to trust us. What you catch stays with me and Jack," answered Russell.

"And what about Michael's mobile business? Does that mean we will be giving up dock space to a broke down yacht?" Dale kept prodding.

"I will take this one, Russ," Michael stood up and spoke "My business is mostly commercial, but I do take on the occasional recreational boat. I will have the docks far over from the unloading dock. My boat will be there and if there is any broke down boat, my boat will be on the mooring. I will do my best to stay out of your way. What me being there means to you guys is all your maintenance parts will be right here. Reduced rates for you guys and I will be around more to give a hand."

There were more questions and statements made, but the general feeling was they were ready to move on from Tommy. Too many lies, too many issues. Russell, Jack and Michael seemed to have a good plan in hand.

"Before we go too far into this let's have a show of hands. How many of you will have an issue with us buying out Tommy?" Russell spoke out.

The only person that raised his hand was Dale Rines. He looked around and saw he was the only one that had a hand up.

"Great…that's just fucking great, you guys will see when the Finn family starts setting all over you," Dale barked at the group. He stormed off to his truck and tore out of the driveway.

"Well I bet he is calling Tommy right now," said Clive.

"Looks like we got to get our ducks in a row. I will call the bank and set up a meeting with them and have Abby put a business plan together," said Michael.

"I figured this meeting was going to take longer. You guys feel free to hang out, have a couple beers, and eat some grub." announced Russell.

"Can I talk with you a bit?" Michael asked Jack.

"Sure, man, lets walk down to the boat," Jack answered.

"So…Madison. Big step man, big step."

"Yeah, but it is the right time and she is the right girl. I have something to tell you too, but you have to keep a lid on it."

"O.K." Michael answered back hesitantly.

"Madison is not her real name. Her real name is Melissa Andrews…The Melissa Andrews."

"Holy shit, you're banging Melissa Andrews! I knew I had seen her before. Lizzy had her picture up in her room."

"No…not yet I mean. We have only known each other for a day."

"Wow!"

"I know man, from the minute I got her on the boat I have felt like I haven't felt in a long time. She is going to stay here the summer."

Michael took a long deep breath and stopped walking. He looked at Jack all smiles like a teenage boy. "Jack," he paused for a minute. "Slow down a bit, man. I am glad you are taking this step, but you're not taking a step here. This is a giant leap and you are going to fall on your face. You need to stop and think. Three months from now the summer will end. She will take off back to Hollywood and never look back. You will still be here. What then?"

"Look Mike, I don't know what will happen three months from now, but for right now she wants to hide from Hollywood and be a normal person."

"Is that what she told you? From the tabloids it sounds like she should be in rehab. Try explaining that to a seventeen year old girl that has adored and idolized her since she was six."

"Michael, she is not like that. She got set up by her manager."

"O.k. I can see you are head over heels for this chick. Mark my words, she will hurt you in the end, but I am willing to play nicey nice for the summer. I take it she will be going to the races with you then?"

"Yes, she is at least going to Boothbay and Rockland races. Trust me man, by the end of summer you will change your mind."

Michael rolled his eyes and the two walked back up the hill. Clive and Russell were still talking with some of the fishermen. They were all comparing notes on some of the inconsistencies that had been going on at MacIntyre's.

"I had come down about midnight to get my boat off of the beach out a few nights back," said Jim Lowe, one of Tommy's oldest fishermen and good friends with Russell and Clive. "One of the new drivers had just pulled in and Tommy was in a hurry to unload the empty crates. I thought it was funny to be unloading empty crates at night. Why not wait until morning? What was funnier was he was putting the crates in the storage shed and locked them up. The next day when I came in from fishing, Elizabeth had brand new crates. I asked her why we had new crates, and she said Tommy sent her to Larry's first thing that morning to get crates because the truck hadn't come back yet, and they needed more."

"That reminds me." Clive spoke up. "Michael, do you mind asking Lizzy to keep a close eye on things? Maybe even document what she sees. I know she already saw some shipping receipts that didn't make sense to her."

Michael already was a little tense finding out his best friend was dating what he thought was a druggy movie star. "Yup," he responded in a sharp tone. "I will get her to keep an eye out and keep track of what she finds but that is it. I don't want her going into any place Tommy has locked or snooping around his books."

"No, of course not," Russell answered. "We love that kid almost as much as you do."

With that, the men finished their beers. Clive and Michael got into their trucks and drove out the driveway leaving Russell and Jack sitting outside.

"That went well, Dad…except for Dale Rines, but we kind of knew he would be a dink."

"Yeah, and I know the bank will give us the money. I just don't know how big of a price tag Tommy has in mind for that place, or if he will even sell it."

"He could retire for a reasonable offer on the place. I don't see why he wouldn't go for it."

"You never know, Jack. He has something going on. Anyway, how are you and Melissa doing? Well, other than playing sucky face in a lobster shack."

Jack chuckled, "We are doing good…I think. Michael doesn't seem to care for her."

"Did you tell him who she really was?"

"Yes. I can trust him. I think as soon as he gets to know her he will warm up to her. What does Mom think?"

"Well, she is worried about you getting hurt, but she knows you are a big boy. We are all happy to see you so happy. Even Clive picked up on that. How do you feel about it Jack?"

Jack turned squarely to his father and looked him in the eyes. "Dad…I am in love with her. I know that is crazy. First girl I have been with since Steph, and I have only known her for a day. There are more reasons that it is stupid than it is smart, but I don't care."

Russell smiled. He lit his pipe and took the last swallow of beer. "That's o.k., Jack. Do you still feel guilty?"

"Off and on. Sometimes I go hours without thinking about Steph. Then I remember something, or see a picture, or see something that reminds me of her. Then I feel guilty about forgetting her."

"Son…you will never truly forget about her. You will move on. Hell, you have started to already, but she will always be in your memories. You just have to learn to smile at those memories. Jack, it wouldn't hurt to go talk to her about it."

"Talk to her?"

"Yup, go right up to her grave. Put your hand on that stone and dump your ever living heart out."

"I will, Dad. Thanks for the talk. I'll see you tomorrow at breakfast."

"Are you going to invite Melissa to the Finn Family Sunday Breakfasts?"

"I am waiting to see if Mom invites her. That will be the final seal of approval."

Jack walked into his house and started picking up a bit. It wasn't too much longer when his mother's car was pulling in the driveway. As he stepped outside to greet Melissa she was putting several bags of clothes into her rental car.

"Holy shit, did you buy out Walmart?"

Melissa laughed, "It is crazy how much you can buy at that place."

"Jack, we almost lost her in L.L. Bean, she was all over the place," called Lucy.

"Beans? What did you get at Beans?"

"Sleeping bag…for the races," Melissa responded with a smile. She turned to Lucy and Anne, "Thanks, you two. I will see you at breakfast."

"Oh, you got invited to Sunday Breakfast?"

"Yes," Melissa said beaming with absolute pride, "And I am getting my first cooking lesson."

"That was fun Melissa, we've got to do that again," said Anne.

As Jack and Melisa went back into the house. Jack felt so relieved. He valued his mother's opinion and she had obviously approved of Melissa.

"You make yourself comfortable and I will toss a bag of popcorn in the microwave, grab a couple beers and get the movie going. You have had a long day. Put your feet up and relax."

Melissa sat down on the couch and leaned back. She could smell fresh Fabreeze spray in the air, only to be overtaken by the smell of popcorn. Jack's living room looked plain. Not that you would expect any different from a single guy living by himself. White walls, blue curtains, and hardwood floor. The windows looked past his parents' house and down to the cove where the boats were.

"What movie are we watching?" she asked.

"The best 80's movie of all time. "Back to the Future"," Jack answered, while carrying a bowl of popcorn and two beers.

They sat and watched the movie as any normal couple would. Melissa wanted to tell him that Michael J Fox was a real good guy in person, but she really wanted to leave Hollywood behind tonight. Melissa sat cuddled in Jack's arms, watching an old movie, eating microwave popcorn, and sipping a cold beer. When the movie was over she glanced at the bedroom door. She could see the bed. "We could," she thought to herself. Instead she stood up. She wrapped her arms around Jack and they kissed for what felt to be an eternity. When it ended she rested her head against his chest.

"Jack..." Melissa spoke, but didn't know what to say to express what she was feeling.

"Ssssshhhh...I know, Melissa, I feel the same way," Jack responded.

Tommy MacIntyre was a sitting in his office smoking a cigarette with his feet up on his desk when Dale Rines barged in.

"So, Dale...how was the meeting? Are they going on strike?" Tommy asked as he exhaled a puff of smoke that circled his head like a looming cloud.

"No, not that easy. They want to buy you out," Dale said

"Who? Who wants to buy me out?"

"Russell, Jack and Mike. They have it all planned out".

"What did the guys think of this?"

"All of them are behind them. They are tired of the all the crap, Tommy. I told you. You are getting too greedy. You need to stop with the bullshit and concentrate on the lobster side of things"

Tommy exploded. He hopped out of his desk chair, sending it rolling across the office until it found a file cabinet to crash into. The noise distracted Dale but only for a second. In the same instant Tommy had his finger in Dale's chest. "Don't fucking tell me what to do. The last person that did that is dead. I got away with it once. I can do it again. Don't forget...you're into this, too. You're in up to your fucking elbows."

"What are you going to do then, Tommy? I am with you... whatever you want to do," said Dale taking a step back from Tommy.

"It's easy. It's not for sale."

"But what about the others? What if they go on strike, or go to another place to sell their lobsters."

"I will throw another dime on the price and drop the price of a barrel of pogies to $115 a barrel. That'll shut'em up. They can't leave. Other places aren't taking in any new fishermen. We'll be alright. The police don't know what we are doing, we are going to be jumping up a bit too. We will be bringing in a boat at night as well as the trucks. I have decided to get my accountant involved, too. I need help making all this paperwork look right. Hell, Lizzy found some of my shipping receipts that didn't add up. If I am going to keep this up I got to do a better job of keeping a lid on it. Speaking of which, that wasn't too smart of you going out and buying that new truck. People aren't stupid, Dale. You can't be only hauling once or twice a week and going and spending 60K on a new truck." Tommy paused a bit to think. He may be telling Dale a bit too much. Dale had been his best friend since kindergarten, but he was dumber than a box of rocks.

"Alright, Tommy. I will haul more. Hey, you got a fix on you?"

Tommy and Dale shared a couple lines of cocaine off of Tommy's desk. They sat inside that office riding the poison buzz. Outside, the night ended in Boothbay Harbor with the sound of music from the bars, sea gulls calling from the bait shack and people fulfilling their needs…good or bad.

Chapter 4

Anne had just stepped out of the bathroom when she saw Melissa's rental car pulling into the driveway. She watched as Melissa hopped out of the car and at a fast walk came directly to the front porch of their house. The door was already open and Melissa gave a small knock on the side of the door frame.

"Come on in and wash your hands. I found a spare apron you can have; it's hanging on the stove. I am surprised you didn't pop over to see Jack first."

"I am anxious to learn how to cook. I have never cooked before," Melissa said as she put the apron on.

"Never. What do you do when your home?"

"I usually go out..or have Maureen make something for me?"

"Who is Maureen?"

"She is my house maid. She takes care of the cleaning, cooking, and laundry. She also calls people to take care of the house."

"I need a Maureen to keep up with Russell's messes. How does it work? Does she live with you?"

"Yup…well it's a different house on my property. I just give her a buzz and she comes over and makes me dinner, or whatever."

"Melissa.,. do you mind me asking…what do you pay this Maureen?"

"She gets forty five thousand a year."

Anne had to pause for a minute.

"Are you o.k., Anne?" Melissa asked.

"Yes, dear, first I was thinking how nice it would be to have someone come and here and clean up and do all the cooking. Then I thought how nice it would be to get paid to do what I already do here."

"She gets paid, she pays no rent or any utilities, and she has an SUV at her disposal."

"Oh, what kind of SUV?"

"Mercedes."

"Oh dear, are there any openings with other stars?"

Melissa laughed, "I am sure there are, but some are not nice to work with."

"I would straighten them right out."

"I have no doubt about that Anne. You seem like you don't take much crap from anybody."

"Well, I just believe there is a certain amount of respect that should be given to anybody. No amount of money, fame or whatever should change that. Now that is enough jabber jawing for now. I am going to start you off with something easy. You are making pancakes. Last night I wrote down the recipe for you. I will be working on the biscuits and gravy and as soon as Lucy gets here she will start on the eggs. Now don't be afraid to ask me any questions. The only stupid question is the one you don't ask."

"O.k." Melissa answered as she looked over the recipe. Anne had also laid out some measuring cups and spoons. A big mixing bowl was on the counter. The ingredients in bulk were laid out as well.

"Now, Melissa, I didn't lay this all out for you because I lack faith, or think you couldn't do it. This is how I taught Lucy; it's how my mother taught me."

"Thank you," was all that Melissa could think to say. Lucy came into the kitchen and greeted Anne and Melissa and the three went to work preparing breakfast. Melissa followed the recipe closely. She could see Anne looking over every so often. Melissa felt a level of confidence that she had never had, and a feeling of sisterhood with the other women in the room. There were no words. Except Anne humming the song "Over the Rainbow". Melissa thought about joining in, but this was Anne's kitchen, her stage.

"O.k., Anne, I am at the mixing part. It says tip bowl and do figure eights with a whisk."

"Ahh yes. Lucy, show her the Finn way of mixing," Anne ordered.

"Alright, Melissa, you want to tip that mixing bowl a little. Hold it tight. With your other hand use the whisk and do figure eights in the bowl. Start slow and as you get the rhythm, go faster."

"How come I don't put the blueberries in now?" asked Melissa.

"Because if you mix them now, they will get all smashed up. You put them in after, and gently fold them in…don't worry I will show you"

Melissa mixed the batter as instructed. She got a lesson on folding the blueberries into the batter. Soon she was scooping out the batter and putting it on a hot plate.

"Now watch for the bubbles to stop and then flip them. I have a special spatula for pancakes. It is extra big so they don't fall apart on you," said Anne.

Soon the Finn kitchen was filled with breakfast aromas. It was a bouquet of onions and peppers, biscuits and gravy, sausage and bacon, blueberry pancakes and coffee. Just the smells could put one in a food coma. Lucy went around and asked how everybody wanted their eggs. Meanwhile, Melissa didn't dare take her eyes off the pancakes. Anne assured her she was doing a good job. Melissa felt an enormous feeling of pride wash over her. All Anne said was, "Good job, dear," but it meant so much to Melissa. Nobody had ever said that to her. Yes, people had congratulated her and praised her, but it was just something about the way Anne said it. It felt so real. She now knew what she had missed, not having a mother in her life. She could feel her eyes welling up. A wash of emotion had taken over her. Before she could fight it, Anne had come over.

"Melissa, are you o.k.? What is wrong, dear?" Anne asked, while placing her hands on Melissa's shoulders.

Melissa felt a big lump in her throat; she wanted to say she loved Anne but wasn't sure how to say it. She took a deep breath and said, "You're a good Mom. Jack and Lucy are so lucky to have you."

Anne, the strong Maine woman, felt a stiffness in her chest. Here in her kitchen a Melissa Andrews was almost in tears. She had traveled the world and was adored by many. Of all the things Melissa had in her life, she didn't have a mother who cared. No one had ever told her they were proud of her. That was when it had clicked for Anne. Melissa had driven herself to this point not for money or fame. She wanted someone to be proud of her. That was one of the biggest intangible gifts a parent can give a child and Melissa had never received it. She remembered the glow in Lucy's face every time she had ever told her "good job" or the way Jack strutted to the house the first time he docked the boat all by himself. Even remembering her own feelings of accomplishment when her parents had said "We are so proud of you". Melissa needed the Finn's. She needed a family. Yes, she could date Jack, but the Finn family was going to take care of this girl. "You're my daughter, too, now. You just take care of my boy, and I will take care of you"

Lucy had come over and joined the embrace. "You are family now, Melissa. We Finns take care of each other."

They held each other for a few more seconds and then got back to business. They would be sitting outside for this breakfast.

The Finn women came out and grabbed each plate. Lucy put the eggs on the plate according to whose plate it was, followed by Melissa putting on the pancakes. A bowl with biscuits and gravy was taken out as well. Fresh coffee was poured in mugs at each place on the table and big pitchers of orange juice were set out. Finally, when every plate was full and everybody was at the table, they sat down to eat. Melissa next to Jack, Lucy next to her boyfriend Sam, and Russell next to Anne. Jack, Sam and Russell got up for seconds, then Jack for thirds. Melissa was stunned that he ate so much for being so thin. Russell pushed his chair back a bit and sat up as tall as he could.

"I would like to officially welcome our guest and newest member of our family. Melissa, welcome…hell of a job on those pancakes," Russell announced as if he were king of a court.

"Thank you, Russell."

"Now this is the part where we say the highs and lows of last week and what our goals are for this week. No holding back, say what's in your heart. Melissa, you are the guest so you get to go first."

Melissa had to think. There were so many highs and she couldn't think of a low.

"Well, my high was meeting Jack, and all of you. You all have been so kind welcoming me into your family. For my low…I always thought that I wasn't missing anything not having my parents around. Now seeing what a real family is like, I feel sad. Sad for myself a little bit for not knowing what it felt like until now, but also sad for other kids that grow up the same way. My goal for this week is to do a good job on Russell's boat."

Jack spoke next. "My high was meeting Melissa and getting to know her. She is very far from the Hollywood stereotype and I look forward to the rest of summer. My low was Michael not really approving of Melissa, but I think by the end of summer he will see what we all see. My goal for this week is to get the rest of my traps over and learn more about Melissa."

Melissa felt a little disappointed but liked the fact that Jack had faith that Michael would see her for who she was. They went around the table discussing their highs and lows. Meeting Melissa was the high for everybody, except Sam who announced he had been promoted to manager at the grocery store. They sat at the table and talked. Sometimes as a group, and sometimes in pairs. The discussion was interrupted by Anne.

"O.k. boys…your turn to do your part."

Melissa turned to Lucy and asked, "What is their part?"

"This is the best part. All the men have to clear the table, do all of the dishes and clean the kitchen."

"What do we do?"

"We do what they were doing while we were cooking….sit on our asses and talk!"

They shared the laugh. Soon the table was clear, and it was just Anne, Lucy and Melissa sitting outside. Anne sat up and spoke.

"Alright, girls, if you haven't heard by now, your father, Jack and Michael are planning to buy Tommy out. If this plan goes through, I will be in charge of the restaurant. I have some ideas in mind, but I am wondering if you two have any."

"What are your ideas, mom?" asked Lucy.

"I want to bring back the "Rail Of Knowledge." I think that used to be fun for the tourists to watch the guys come in and unload, and they were able to ask questions. Also, I think it would be neat to have some of the fishermen bar tend. Guys like Russell and Jack that like to talk would be fun. I may have to post a warning on the language. I also want to open the restaurant earlier so we could do a breakfast. Maybe have some breakfast sandwiches to go."

"What about a karaoke night? You guys were all singing along with the band Friday night!" Melissa suggested.

"OOOOHHHH Mom, I would so do that!" Lucy responded.

"That does sound like a good idea. If we get a few drinks into Russell he may sing some Johnny Cash!" Anne responded.

The men came out of the house after their chores were done and joined into the conversation of what changes they had in mind.

"I want to take it back to the way is used to be. When the fishermen had a say in what was going on," Jack said.

"I would like to give the guys as much notice as possible about the change in price. If we knew the price was going to drop a quarter at the close of business Monday, Melissa and I would haul through all of my gear Monday and get the better price," said Russell.

"Couldn't that work the other way too? If you knew the price would go up Monday after the close of business, you would wait to haul on Tuesday," said Melissa.

"Smart girl, yes, it could work that way, too," responded Russell.

"It will be some nice for Michael. It's a pain for him right now if he gets a call. Drive down from his shop, get in the skiff, then get out to the boat and get off the mooring," Jack said.

"Where is the Williams clan? How come they didn't come to breakfast?" asked Anne.

"Oh, he had a bunch of excuses. I am sure he will come around," answered Jack.

Melissa felt a little tense after hearing Michael didn't approve of her at breakfast. On one hand, she didn't care as long as Jack and the Finns still liked her but on the other hand this was Jack's best friend. Would she be putting a wedge between these two for the summer. She didn't want that. Anne could see Melissa had wheels spinning in her head. She decided to break the awkward silence.

"Sam, what are you and Lucy going to do with the day?"

"Well, I think Lucy should answer that one," replied Sam.

Lucy hesitated for a bit, then spoke. "Sam and I have been dating now for 3 years and we think it is time that we lived together. We will be moving Sam's stuff over today."

The group gave some small cheers.

"Do you guys need help? I don't think me and Melissa have anything planned yet," offered Jack.

"Thank you. I don't have much to move really. Most of my stuff is already over here. I was going to ask you or Russell if I could borrow your truck," answered Sam.

"Sure, take mine, it doesn't smell of pipe smoke either."

"Hey hey hey, no picking on the old Chevy. The pipe smoke gives it character," Russell chimed in.

"So what are we going to do today, Jack?" asked Melissa

"Well, Sundays are usually my "take it easy day". I guess we could start by going for a walk and we could think of something to do while walking."

"A walk…that sounds good. Do you know how long it has been since I have just walked?"

"I can imagine it's not something you do often. You ready now?"

"Sure, bye everybody. This was awesome…you guys are awesome."

Melissa started to turn and walk away, but then stopped and went back to give Anne a hug. "Thank you, Anne."

All Anne could do was smile back. She knew she had started to mean a lot to Melissa. Melissa was starting to mean a lot to her.

Jack and Melissa walked up the hill and walked along Lobster Cove Road. They were holding hands and talking about the morning. Melissa wanted to know more about Sam and Lucy. Sam, being slightly pudgy at six feet tall, was a perfect match for Lucy. He was generally shy and didn't say much, giving him a gentle giant demeanor that made him instantly likeable. Melissa started daydreaming to herself what it would be like to have Jack move in with her. She pictured him sitting on the couch watching football with Chris Pratt. Better yet, what it would be like to move in with Jack. Hanging out with the Finn family and cuddling with Jack each night on the couch watching T.V. She knew they wanted to take it slow, but how slow? Other than the fact Jack was handsome, and well built, he was kind, loyal and trustworthy. There was no doubting it, she was in love with him. In less than three days he had won her heart and soul without trying. He didn't have to try. Just by Jack being Jack. Then there is the Finn family, honest and sincere. She had won their trust and respect. Except Michael. what was his problem?

"Jack, what is going on with your friend Michael? Why doesn't he like me? He doesn't even know who I am?" asked Melissa.

"He knows. I told him who you..." but before he could finish, Melissa interrupted.

"You what...I thought we were going to keep it a secret. Jack why?"

He hadn't seen this side of Melissa yet. She was angry and it made him nervous. "It's Michael, we can trust him. He ain't going to go around telling people."

"How do you know that? He already doesn't like me. How am I supposed to trust him? He might go tell people so he can get me out of the picture."

Jack was starting to get a little agitated now. "Melissa, this isn't Hollywood. We don't do that shit here. Michael is my best friend. I told him not to tell, I know he won't tell."

"It's not your secret to keep. It is mine. You should have asked me first. Do you know what will happen if the press finds out I'm here? They will be all over your front lawn... flashing cameras and putting a microphone in your mouth. Before you know it, the press will have our story twisted in more ways than I want to think. Jack, I know you trust him, but I don't know him, and I don't like that he is passing judgement on me when he hasn't even met me."

"Give him a chance. He will come around as soon as he meets the real you. All he knows is what he saw in the papers. His daughter adored you, even considered you a role model. He is just reacting to how she feels."

"Why, have I fallen off of some pedestal? You people don't realize the pressure you put on us. I thought I got away from that. I want to be normal. Now I have to win the approval of your best friend and his daughter. Your family loves me, isn't that enough?"

"You people," Jack felt disgusted. "Just what do you mean by that? And pressure...how about the pressure of keeping a roof over your head, or food on the table for your family. That is pressure. I would gladly have the responsibility of being some teenager's idol over worrying about making my boat payment. That is what YOU people don't understand. You Hollywood people and the singers and the sports heroes don't get that. You complain about all the pressure you're under and how tough all the fame is, while people like me have to work our asses off to cover our asses. Melissa, I am sorry. You are right, it was your secret, I get it. You have a lot to learn about the life we live. I have it easier than most, but I work my ass off for it. My dad lost his boat to the bank once. Had to fish out of a twelve-foot skiff to feed Mom, Lucy and me. Do you understand that?"

Melissa was now choked up. She was angry and sad at the same time. "Jack, I didn't mean to sound like that. The "you people" comment…it's…sorry for that. I understand I live the life most people only dream about, but some day all that will fade. Will I be homeless, or go hungry? No, probably not, but some day some new actress will come on to a set and everybody will forget who Melissa Andrews was. I know it is not the same, but the fear and pressure are real."

Jack took a deep breath. She was stepping into his world but he would never be able to step into hers. He would never know that feeling of being forgotten. He took a step towards Melissa. She took a step towards him. They embraced for another long and heartfelt kiss. The kiss was soon interrupted by the squeaky belt on Russell's truck.

"You two sure find the strangest places to play sucky face!" said Russell.

Jack was shaking his head, "What do you want, Dad?"

"Your mom was thinking of doing some gardening today. She sent me to ask if Melissa wants to join her."

Melissa turned to Jack. "Are we O.K.?"

"Yes, we are okay. I'm sorry about telling Michael."

"I am sorry about the "you people" comment."

"And I am sorry I had to hear this crap. Are you getting in the truck or not, Hollywood?" joked Russell.

"Hold your horses old man," Melissa fired back

Russell grinned with his pipe between his teeth. "She is learning, Jack. Be careful."

"See you two back at the house," Jack answered. He was relieved that the fight was over. He was never much for arguing, and she was right. It wasn't up to him to tell her secret or not. Not even his best friend. As he walked home he was thinking how he was going to keep himself busy while Melissa was gardening with his mother. "Maybe I should go see Steph," he thought to himself. He continued on his walk taking in the fresh air and time to think.

Anne and Melissa were headed to the local florist in Russell's truck. Melissa had the window open to help with the smell of the pipe smoke. It wasn't bad, just too much of the vanilla smell. She was reflecting on the fight she and Jack just had. She was disappointed in herself for saying "you people". It was not how she felt. She had more respect for them than that, now more than ever. She was choosing to become one of them. "What if I did?" she thought to herself. "What if I never went back?" Her thoughts were interrupted by Anne.

"Earth to Melissa. Are you there?" Anne jested.

"Yes, just thinking," Melissa answered.

"You must have been thinking some hard. Everything o.k.?"

"I am OK, just thinking what would happen if I never went back to Hollywood."

"Wow.,. what would poor Maureen do?"

"Funny, Anne. I was just telling Jack how much I stress about the day that comes and nobody remembers Melissa Andrews, but now I am so ready to forget about that life."

"Hold your horses, dear. You have had a good couple of days and I have no doubt you will have a good summer, but do you really want to leave Hollywood the way you did?"

"What do you mean?"

"You left to get away from all the stories about overdosing and flipping out on that reporter. Is that the legacy you want to leave there? I think you should set things straight. If you did make a mistake and overdose, come clean. If the media twisted things up, untwist it."

"Anne, Hollywood doesn't work that way. Honesty doesn't hold the values there that it does here."

"That doesn't matter. What matters is what you believe. If you come out and tell the truth, you will know it and you can move on. Your real friends and family will be behind you."

"Thanks, Anne."

The old Chevy pulled into the parking lot. They got out of the truck and walked towards some flowers that were outside. As Melissa was listening to Anne teaching her about flowers, a voice interrupted the session.

"Anne, how are you? I haven't seen you in a while. How have you been?" said a tall, red headed woman with short hair.

"Hello, Abigail. I've been good. How are the kids? What have you been up to?"

"Well, Josh is excited about fishing for Jack. He was happy to go with Russell, but he seems to be very anxious to step up. Elizabeth is doing great. She has applied at a few schools and we are just waiting to hear back. I got done with the business plan last night and I need you to take a look at the restaurant side, and Russell and Jack to look at the lobster side and we will set a date with the bank." Abigail turned to Melissa and smiled. "You must be Madison."

"Oh, I am so sorry I didn't introduce you sooner. Yes, this is Madison, Jack's new girlfriend. Madison this is Michael's wife, Abigail."

Melissa liked the title "Girlfriend". "Hello," she said.

Abigail then turned and looked around to check if someone was listening, "My husband told me who you are; don't worry I won't say a thing."

Melissa was a little annoyed that more people knew who she was.

"Nice to meet you, Abigail."

"I will let you two talk for a bit while I shop around. Abby, bring that plan over tomorrow and I will take a look at it." said Anne.

"Okay, keep an eye out for Lizzy; she is around here somewhere," replied Abigail.

"So…you and Jack, huh," Abigail said, as she turned back to Melissa.

"Yeah, he found me floating around on my kayak, and things sort of clicked." answered Melissa

"I won't beat around the bush. Jack means a lot to us. He is as much as a part of our family as we are of the Finn family. My husband has his doubts about you because of all the stuff in the news, but for me, if Anne Finn approves, you have got my vote."

Melissa took a sigh of relief. "Thank you, Abigail. I am not the person the news is making me out to be. I was set up. I don't do drugs."

"Like I said, if Anne trusts you, you are alright with me."

"What about Michael, though?"

"He will take some convincing. My daughter idolized you and when the news came out about you it broke her heart. If there is one thing my husband doesn't like is seeing his kids hurt. You will earn his trust but it might take time."

"Okay, thank you. I am sorry that your daughter was hurt," Melissa said as she felt flush. In the argument with Jack she had made the comment "fallen off some pedestal". It was real to her now that she had and it was upsetting her. She did care what people thought about her. She had looked up to actresses while growing up. What upset her more was that it was completely out of her control. She hadn't done anything wrong. She was a victim, and now so was Lizzy.

"She will be ok; she is a tough girl. I have to go find her and head home. It was nice to meet you, and, Melissa.,. I am in your corner."

"Thanks again Abigail, nice to meet you."

They went their separate ways and Melissa was looking at the flowers while keeping an eye out for Anne. She liked touching the flowers. She had gardens at her mansion but rarely ever stopped to walk through them. She was basking in the smells of soils and flowers. What was Anne going to teach her today? What skills would she gain? This morning she had learned to make pancakes. Now she was going to learn gardening. "Wouldn't Maureen be shocked if I took care of the gardens?" She thought to herself. Just then she felt as if she was being watched. She looked through the hanging vines and saw a familiar person. It was Elizabeth. She had remembered seeing her at MacIntyre's. Melissa walked around the display to find a tall, blonde teenager looking at her. Melissa could tell she had been recognized. There was no hiding it. She smiled and spoke quietly, "You know who I am, don't you?"

Hearing those words was all Elizabeth needed to confirm what she was thinking. "Yes, you're Melissa Andrews."

"Yes, I am. You're Elizabeth, right? I saw you working at MacIntyre's the other day."

Elizabeth was a little overwhelmed that Melissa Andrews was right in front of her and knew who she was.

"Lizzy," Melisa paused. This had been a pretty emotional day so far and it wasn't even lunch yet. "Can we sit down and talk a bit?"

"Sure."

"I am not the person the media is making me out to be. I don't have any facts yet and I don't want to get into details but I was tricked and that reporter was not trying to help me. Now from what I understand you were a big fan of mine, but I am afraid that those stories may have changed your opinion of me." She paused again while Lizzy nodded in agreement. "Well, I hope I can earn your trust back. Your opinion means a lot to me."

She wanted to say more but couldn't think of the words. This was the most face time she had ever had with a fan. Despite the circumstances, it felt good. "I think your mom is looking for you. I will be around all summer, so we will definitely get a chance to talk more."

"You ready?" asked Anne walking up to them.

Melissa said goodbye to Lizzy and they started walking back to Russell's truck.

"Those Williams kids are good kids, always have been."

"Have you watched them both grow up?"

"Yes, I babysat for Abigail and Michael. Sometimes Jack and Lucy would babysit, too. Jack is great with kids. It will be good for him to have Josh on the boat with him. Jack calls himself a loner but he really likes being with people, and Josh is the kinda kid that asks a hundred questions a minute."

They continued the small talk as they got into Russell's truck. They were forming an odd friendship. Anne always played the role of mother but also treated Melissa with womanly friendship. Melissa started thinking what her life might have been like with Anne as her mother. She imagined Anne would have been at every rehearsal, every screening, every try out. It was easy to see Anne always put her kids before everything, sometimes with tough love, but she always had their best interests at heart. It showed- Jack was a good man, and Lucy was a good woman.

Jack had pulled his truck up to the grave site. He sat there in his truck for a moment. He didn't want to get out of his truck but he didn't want to leave either. He rubbed his face with both hands, unlatched the door and stepped out. As he walked closer to the grave the lump in his throat got bigger. He planted one knee on the ground and placed his hand on the stone, bowing his head and looking for words. He finally got his air and was able to talk.

"Hey, Steph." Jack paused, looking for further words.

"Steph, this is tough. I have asked you to forgive me over and over, but I don't think it's up to you. I have to forgive myself. I look back at that night over and over in my head and I keep remembering you saying you were fine to drive, and you seemed fine. You only had 2 or 3 beers the whole time you were on the boat. I just don't get it. Anyway…I have met someone. She is great. She is not you, but I love her just as much, just a little different. It is crazy we have only known each other a few days. She came to Sunday breakfast. I was going to ask for your approval, but I don't think that is up to you either. I have to get over this. Whether it's my fault or not, it doesn't change how I feel about Melissa." Jack took a long breath, then another. His fingertips started to tingle and feel numb. "Stephanie, I will always love you. You will always be in my heart, but it is time to move on. I know you would want me to move on." And with that Jack dried his eyes, stood up tall, and walked away. After getting into his truck, he gave a glance at the stone and drove away.

When Jack got home and saw Melissa and his mother working in the garden together, he took a moment to watch. They were quite involved with what his mother was teaching her and every so often the two would laugh or giggle. When his mother started singing some Patsy Cline, Melissa joined, and their voices carried into the air as they both started getting more into it. Jack could see his father turn his head from the paper he was reading to look over at the pair singing. When the duet ended, Russell started clapping and Jack hopped out of his truck and joined in.

The day carried on in a slow easy going pace and Melissa had never felt so relaxed and at peace with herself. She thought of all the money actors and actresses spent on psychologists when all they had to do was come up here and hang out with the Finn Family. After dinner they all went out for an ice cream. Then Jack drove Melissa out to Ocean Point, a scenic part of the Boothbay region overlooking the water. Jack pointed out the islands and told her the names. He pointed in the direction of where he found her just a few days ago. They sat there on the tailgate of Jack's truck talking about the past couple of days.

"Jack, your mom introduced me to Abigail as your girlfriend. Is that what we are now, boyfriend and girlfriend?" Almost as if they were back in high school.

"Yeah, I guess we are. We like each other." He almost wanted to say "love each other" but didn't want to jump too fast. He put his arm around her and pulled her closer. Melissa leaned in to gather more of his warmth. Sometimes it wasn't so much what Jack said but what he did that showed his feelings. She wanted to say she loved him too but figured it was too soon.

"Kiss me, Jack."

Jack turned his head and they entered into a long passionate kiss. She could feel his hand on the side of her face and found Jack's rough hands a turn on. He slid his hand from the side of her cheek to the back of her head slightly pulling her to his face. She in turn put her hands against his chest and slid them slowly up to his cheeks. Lips tangled in passion and hearts beating as one. Anxious to go further but both trying to keep the tension at bay. They pulled apart slowly and caught their breath. Melissa looked at Jack with his little half grin. Jack watched Melissa's hair dancing in the wind. They held hands and looked out over the water, breathing the salt air and listening to the waves crashing into the rocks.

"Finally, a kiss without your dad popping up."

Jack laughed. "Speaking of him, we ought to get you back home. You have a big day tomorrow."

When they got home Jack kissed Melissa goodbye before she drove away. He reached into his glove box and pulled out the little felt covered box that held Stephanie's ring. He carried the box into his parents' house.

"Hey, Mom," Jack called as he went to the door.

Anne was in the kitchen making Russell and Melissa's lunch for the next day. "Yes, Jack."

"Do you have a safe place for this?"

Anne stood there a little shocked knowing this was a huge step. "Yes, Jack, I will put it in your hope chest up in the attic."

Jack passed the box to his mother and in return Anne gave Jack a big mother's hug. She thought of a few things to say but decided the unsaid meant more.

Jack stepped back and said, "Good night, Mom."

"Good night, Jack."

Chapter 5

At 4:45 Melissa was standing on the Spruce Point dock. It was chilly so she had sweatpants over shorts and Jack's hoodie over a T-shirt. Her hair was tied up in a ponytail. From the dock she could look into Lobster Cove almost far enough to see the Finn's dock. Soon she saw the red hull of Jack's boat breaking thru the light fog. He was going along at a fast idle, close enough to see but not in detail. "How can he be wearing shorts and a T-shirt when it's this chilly out?" She thought to herself. She heard a honk of Jack's horn followed by a huge wave of his arm. She waved back and blew a kiss. She heard the rpms pick up as Jack laid on the throttle. Then her phone beeped with a message from Jack.

"Have a good day and good luck."

Behind Jack came the black hull of Russell's Old Smoke. She could see Russell behind the wheel with a puff of smoke coming out of his pipe. He pulled his boat alongside the dock and stuck out his arm for Melissa to grab. Russell's arm was as steady as a handrail. He already had Melissa's oil skins, boots and gloves set out on the engine box. Old Smoke pulled away from the dock and into the middle of the bay while Melissa put her gear on. Once out in the middle, clear of buoys, Russell stopped the boat and shut down the engine. She was a little surprised and didn't know what was happening. Russell grabbed a knife in a sheath up on the dash of his boat and walked over to Melissa with the knife.

"You need to find a place for this on you. Somewhere you can get at it quickly. That sheath will hold the knife upside down if you want it that way," said Russell.

Melissa remembered Jack's knife being on one of the straps of his oilskins. She grabbed the knife from Russell and held it up there.

"I think I want it here," she said.

"That's a good spot," he said and helped Melissa mount the knife to her oilskin strap. Then he looked at her a little puzzled and asked, "Have you ever used a knife before?"

"Yes, to open boxes and stuff."

Russell grabbed a short piece of rope and tossed it at Melissa.

"Cut it…quick. Hurry, faster!"

Melissa panicked a bit then pulled the knife out and cut the rope, surprised how fast the knife went through the rope.

"Good, you want to be careful. Those knives are sharp- very sharp. If you look back aft at the stern you will see I have another one attached to the rail back there. The most dangerous thing on this boat is the rope. If you step in a coil it will pull you overboard. The best thing to do is go with it to keep it loose and try to cut yourself out. Even if it means going overboard. You know how to swim, right?"

"Yes," Melissa answered.

"Good. The next thing is what to do if I go over."

Russell grabbed one of the big orange boat bumpers and tossed it off the starboard side of the boat into the water. He turned and looked at Melissa. "Damn…I just fell overboard. What are you going to do?"

Melissa didn't know what to think of this. Russell seemed so serious and she had never had to think like this.

"Call 911!"

"Your phone may not have any signal out here. I am getting tired, my boots are full of water and my wet clothes are pulling me under. Out here you're my 911 and I'm yours. You need to start the boat and get it over to me."

"O.k."

Melissa walked up to the helm, looked at the panel with gauges, a key, and a few buttons. She turned the key, heard some noises, and the gauges all sprung to life. She tried to turn the key one more click but it wouldn't move. She looked at the buttons. One was black and the other red. "Red usually means stop," she thought to herself and pushed the black button. The engine came to life. She looked back at Russell for a sign of accomplishment.

"Ain't I gett'n tired tread'n water. I hope Anne will be o.k. when I am dead and gone," Russell said, as a sign that the lesson was far from over.

Melissa turned the wheel hard to starboard. She looked at the controls on the dash of the boat. One lever had a red knob and the other black. She grabbed the red knob and slowly pushed it forward. The engine sped up but the boat didn't move. In the background she could here Russell reciting his will out loud. "I leave the house to my wife Anne, my boat and traps to my son, Jack." Melissa pulled the red knob back and the engine slowed back to an idle. She slid the lever with the black knob forward and the boat started to turn. The only problem was it was turning too much. She turned the wheel to port as fast as she could.

"That's a good idea, don't let me drown slowly, just run me over and get it done with," Russell continued to heckle.

Soon the orange bumper was alongside the boat. Melissa knew the boat didn't have brakes, so to stop it she put the boat in reverse and applied a little throttle, as she had seen Jack do a few times. The boat came to a stop with the orange bumper right in front of her. She could hear Russell clapping. She felt great, she felt confident, she had accomplished saving Russell.

"Good job, kid! Now if I am conscious, I can get myself back on the boat with a little help from you, but if I am knocked out you're going to want to get a rope around me and then you call for help. Don't go calling 911. Get on this radio and call for another lobsterman," he directed as he put his hand up on the VHF.

"But the only lobstermen I know are you and Jack."

"If you call for Jack other lobstermen will hear. Whoever is closest will come."

"So the radio talks to all of the lobstermen?" asked Melissa.

"All who are on this channel. I have one radio on 10, the other is on 77. My CB is on 20. No matter what mic you grab, someone is listening."

"O.K." She wanted to ask why so many radios but figured she would wait on that one.

"Now, let's get you set up. Your job is to put bait on the bait irons, bait the traps, push the traps over, band the lobsters and keep the boat clean. As far as keeping the boat clean, all you got to do is hose down the boat every once in a while. Just use this hose that feeds the live tank. I will go slow at first then speed up as the day goes on. You got it?"

"I think so," said Melissa. Her newfound confidence was fading a little.

"We are going to haul the west side of the bay starting at Spruce Point. We will go all the way around by Lobster Cove, head of the bay, and up the east side just until we get to the stuff I hauled Friday. Then we will haul around Cabbage Island and finish at Seal Rocks. Don't worry about remembering all these places at once. You will learn them with the more time you spend on the water. I want two fish per trap. After you band the lobsters they go in a bucket, then you count them up after we finish that spot. It is how I keep track of what places are hot or not."

Melissa nodded her head while she stuck the bait iron thru the eye of a pogie. She felt a little queasy doing it, but Russell smiled in approval. He walked up to the helm and put the boat in gear. They cruised a ways up the shore line. Melissa looked out over the water. It was flat calm and a little bit of fog blocked out the sun. The sea smelled good, refreshing, until she would catch the smell of the bait, but she was getting used to it.

"Hey!" Russell yelled to get her attention. When she looked in the direction he pointed, she could see a small ledge coming out of the water. On the ledge was a little seal pup with its mother. She grabbed her cell phone and took a picture.

"That reminds me," Russell said. "The rules of the Old Smoke. Rule number two- All phones will stay on silent and up here on the dash until break time and lunch. Rule number three- Don't ever ask how many we have left or what time we are going to be done. Rule number four- No changing the station on the tune box. Rule number five- If you have a question, ask."

"What about rule number one, Russell?" asked Melissa as she placed her phone on the dash

"That is a combo rule. Rule number one- Have fun, but be safe!"

Rule number one put Melissa's mind at ease. She was still a bit nervous, but she trusted that Russell would take care of her. He would make his verbal jabs for sure, but that was more for comic relief than malice. Russell slowed the boat down and grabbed a long handled stick with a metal hook on the end. She saw he was closing in on a gray and white buoy on a green stick. He reached out with the hook and grabbed the buoy by the rope that was attached to the bottom of the green stick. Up over the snatch block and into the hauler Russell led the rope. He pushed another lever up on the dash separate from the engine controls, and the hauler started pulling the rope up and putting it on the deck of the boat. Melissa waited with anticipation. She couldn't wait to get thru the first trap and get her anxiety behind her. Soon she could see the green wire mesh trap breaking the surface of the water. Russell lifted it slightly and flipped the rope coming off of it over the snatch block. He put the trap down and turned it sideways. Melissa watched him as he opened the door of the trap. She noticed the hauler was bringing in more rope so that meant there was another trap coming soon. She could see how the old bait was hung on the bait line inside the trap and she remembered watching Jack bait his traps. So she untied the top of the bait line from the cleat, pulled the old bait off, stuck the bait line through the hole on the end of the bait iron and slid two fish onto the bait line. After tying off the bait line to the cleat she closed the door and snapped the little bungee straps at the corners of the trap over the door.

"Good job kid. Now slide it down a bit and make room for the next."

While doing her own job, she watched Russell. As he took the lobsters out of the trap some went straight into the cull tray to be banded and some he held a funny shaped piece of metal to the lobster's back.

"What are you doing?"

"The big ones go into the cull tray, the smaller ones I have to measure. This is a measure." He held up the funny shaped piece of metal. "It has a short side and a big side. If a lobster is too big or too short, it is tossed back. Also if it is a female lobster with eggs on it or has a punch on the tail it goes back in. That's how we keep this industry going for the next generation."

After Melisa baited the second trap and closed it up, Russell turned the boat around. She watched him study his electronics briefly and then pushed the first trap over. She rocked the second trap to let the rope go past it. She watched the rope going overboard until it led to her trap. She gave her trap a good push and watched it hit the water with a splash. She turned to the lobsters in the cull tray. They had caught three lobsters that she now had to put bands on their claws. Russell came over and showed her how to hold a lobster without getting bit. There it was. Melissa had hauled her first pair of traps. Soon Russell turned on his "tune box" as he called it. The boat filled with the songs of Patsy Cline, Hank Williams, Loretta Lynn and other singers of that generation. Melissa didn't particularly care for that type of music, but she could tolerate it. They hauled the shore line up to Lobster Cove. After pushing a trap over, Russell gave the command to count what they had.

Melissa counted the lobsters from the five gallon buckets as she put them into the live tank, "154."

"That's not bad, not super good, but not bad. It's break time, girl. Let's see what Old Anne packed for our break."

"That's good, I am starving."

"Aaahhhh banana bread, my favorite. Here you go."

"Thank you" Melissa took a bite. Just as she suspected, it was delicious. "Oh my god, this is so good. I had no idea you could turn bananas into bread. I think Anne could cook dirt and it would be delicious".

"Well, I will be sure to forward the compliment. You spend enough time with her, Melissa, and you will be able to cook like that."

"Me? No, I did o.k. on pancakes, but this is incredible."

Out of the blue Russell said,

"Anyway, I am surprised. Someone so smart as you would go to work for someone without discussing pay."

Melissa was a little shocked at the comment. "I trust you, Russell. That, and I'm not worried about the money."

"Melissa, you are right to trust me, and I told you I don't care about what you have for money. What you have for money in the bank means nothing about what you're worth. I'm sure you wouldn't step on a movie set without having discussed pay. Normally a sternman that has grown up around the business kind of knows what they should ask for. Now you are a green horn and haven't grown into this like Jack did or even Josh. You're not quite up to speed yet, but you will get faster. So I think we will start you off at $125 a day. You keep going the way you're going and show up on time and give me all you got, you will be up to $200 a day, and get a F/V Old Smoke hoodie."

With no thought of comparing her income from acting to the wages that Russell discussed, she gladly accepted the terms. She nodded her head in agreement while finishing the last bite of banana bread. She took a sip of coffee and looked over the water. The fog had started to lift and the sun was starting to pop out. Her thoughts were interrupted by a familiar voice over the radio.

"Old Smoke, come back, Dad."

Russell stood up off the wash rail of the boat. "Go ahead boy".

"How is my girl doing?"

Melissa liked Jack calling her his girl.

"She's doing good. She saved the polly-ball first try and has been keeping up with me."

"Were you reciting your will out loud while she was figuring it out?"

"Ha ha ha, yup didn't even phase her. We are just finishing up break. We're going to haul towards the head of the bay and up the east side a ways, take a lunch break then haul Cabbage and Seal rocks. How is the Josh man doing? Does he miss me yet?"

"Well he isn't as good looking as your sternman…woman, but he had the bait trays and a bag of bands all down on the dock ready to go. I think he misses your charm but likes my choice of music better".

"That's good. I trained him well. How was the dock this morning?" Russell was hinting about Tommy and if Jack had seen him.

Jack figured what his father was getting at. "Just Clive there this morning. Josh says that Tommy asked Lizzy to unlock this morning."

"Alrighty then, you have a large day."

"And you too, sir."

Russell turned to Melissa, "Alright kid, let's get back at it."

He started the engine and they got back into hauling traps. Melissa was completely happy to be where she was and to be doing what she was doing.

On Red at Night, Jack and Josh had finished their break and got back to work. Josh was enjoying the faster pace with Jack. Jack had gone over some of his safety practices. He made sure Josh had a knife on him and showed him where the spare knife was at the stern. They didn't do the "captain overboard" drill because Jack knew Josh had been running boats since he was six. Jack hadn't had a sternman in a while. He didn't like the idea of having a stranger on the boat and most of his closest friends had their own boats. There was also the responsibility of having a sternman. Another person's life is now in your hands, and in this case the other person was a son of a good friend. Josh being a teenager just working for the summer made it a little easier, but when you have a grown man going with you with a wife and kids to support, there is more pressure and stress. He would take Michael once in a while when Michael needed a break from his own business. The two crews worked into the afternoon. Melissa was feeling more and more comfortable and moving faster.

Jack was getting used to having somebody there.

Russell and Melissa had just set back the last pair of traps on the east side of the bay when Clive Farrin came along side.

"Is it your lunch break, Russell?" Clive asked.

"Yeah, tie right up, we'll have a sandwich and a cup of coffee," responded Russell.

They tied the boats together and sat down for lunch. Russell broke out the lunch box and passed Melissa two sandwiches and a ziplock bag of chips. He tried to pass her a cup of coffee which she kindly refused.

"If I drink anymore of that stuff I'll start growing hair where I'm not supposed to."

Clive and Russell got a chuckle out of that.

"Russell, we got to talk later."

"Why later, why not now?"

Clive made a motion to Melissa.

"She's alright. I trust her. Besides she's a PFA anyway, who is she going to tell?"

Melissa made a mental note to ask what a PFA is.

"Rumor is that Tommy is going to jump the price up fifty cents today."

"How in the fuck is that possible? Oops, sorry, Mel…Madison."

"You're alright," Melissa said shrugging it off.

"I don't know how he can do it, but I think he is trying to win back favor with us," said Clive.

"That's a bold move. We are going to be nailin' the lobsters soon. How is he going to keep the price up?"

"I don't know. Maybe he wants to run it to the ground before someone can take over."

"Well, that's interesting. I don't think the guys will fall for it, do you?"

"Some of the younger guys might, but us old fellas are loyal to you."

"I bet Dale Rines went right over and ratted us out. Well, we will see what happens when we go in to sell. I know Abigail and Anne were going over the business plan today, then Abigail is going to schedule a meeting at the bank for all of us."

"I think the bank is the least of your problems. I think Tommy is going to be an asshole."

"He already is an asshole," Russell said chuckling. "I just hope he doesn't do anything crazy, I don't trust him."

The two old friends enjoyed their lunch and conversation. Melissa sat back and listened to the two old men talk while savoring Anne's egg salad sandwiches. At first she was a little worried about what all this food was going to do to her body, but when she considered the hard work she was doing, she figured she might end up in better shape than when she started. She asked what a PFA was.

"Person From Away. Anybody not born in Maine. Doesn't matter how long you have lived here, how many houses you own. Even if you marry a local, you will always be a PFA," Clive answered.

After the lunch and conversation were over the two old friends parted ways and went back to work.

At MacIntyre's Lobster, Tommy was on the phone with his dealer in Boston.

"Hey, Cashmier, how are you doing?" Tommy said into his cell phone, while looking out over the harbor from his window.

"You piece of shit. How many times I told you? No names over phone. You dumb Yankee ass don't even say right." shot a thick Russian accent on the other end of the phone.

"Calm down, buddy, is the boss available?" Tommy said trying to defuse his mistake.

"Yes, what do you want?"

"I want to talk to the boss; I want to move more…lobster."

"Just a minute."

There was some background noise like a door opening and some voices in the background. Then a female voice with a strong Russian accent came on the phone. "Yes, talk to me. How you want to move more lobsters?"

Tommy loved and feared that voice at the same time. The accent was sexy and made him twinge a little, but the woman it belonged to was vicious. She didn't mess around. Five years ago, back when he first got involved with this, she put him in a corner. She made him take care of a loose end, or she said she would take care of him AND the loose end.

"Hi…" he almost called her by name. "I want to expand our partnership. Move more lobsters."

"And how we going to do that?"

"Over the water. I could have a boat go out to you somewhere outside of the harbor. We could move more than on the trucks and it's less paperwork."

"Hhhhmmm, I see. Why this sudden want to expand?"

"More money, I need to keep my fishermen happy to keep the front up."

"I don't care about fishermen. I care about money and you fucking things up. You almost fuck things up from the start. This is not partnership, I am boss. I let you know when I will have boat in the area. You keep the trucks running, you don't call here. You understand?"

"Yes…I…I got you."

"Good day."

The phone went silent in his hand. He had to collect himself a bit. Talking to her terrified him, but if he was going to keep this going, he had to expand. His accountant wanted a cut of the action to keep the books straight. Dale was in on it as well as the drivers. He opened the door to get some fresh air in. When he had finally cooled off and calmed down, he had to make another phone call. He looked through his numbers on his phone.

"Maine Marine Patrol." He said to himself out loud.

Just outside his door Elizabeth Williams was about to step in and give Tommy the bait and fuel slips from the morning when she heard him on the phone.

"Hi, Sargent. This is Tommy MacIntyre."

There was a pause while somebody spoke on the other end.

"Well, I have reason to believe that a couple of my fishermen may be bringing in shorts."

Another pause.

"Yup, Russell and Jack Finn."

Elizabeth shook her head. There was no way Russell and Jack would bring in short lobsters. She had gone sternman with Russell before and knew there was no way he would bring in shorts. Same with Jack, she had never fished with Jack, but she knew him well enough to know he wouldn't do that.

"They are both out today and should be back in a couple hours, maybe three."

Elizabeth stayed outside the door to listen more.

"No problem, just doing my duty, sir. You can tell your warden to check with me when he gets here and I will show him where the selling dock is."

Another pause.

"Yup, yup, yup, I know, just figured he would want to see me. Well, thanks again."

Tommy put his cell phone down. "That should send a message to the Finns not to fuck with Tommy MacIntyre."

Elizabeth knocked on the door and stepped in and passed him the slips. She left the office and, when out of sight, she quickly texted her brother Josh what she heard. After she sent it, she thought a little harder and texted her dad as well and went back about her business like nothing happened.

Jack had just set back his last string of traps at Squirrel Island and was headed to Fisherman's Island when he looked up at his phone on the dash of the boat and saw one missed text. He looked to see a text from Mike that said "Call me ASAP".

"What's up?" asked Jack in a concerned voice.

"Marine Patrol is going to be waiting for you and your father at Tommy's," answered Michael.

"What the hell for?"

"Tommy told them you've been bringing in shorts."

"That rat bastard. Well, I have nothing to be afraid of. I measure them all myself and if there is a doubt I toss them. How do you know all this?"

"Elizabeth overheard it. She texted Josh then remembered the cell phone rule. If you didn't call I was going to call you on the radio."

"Thanks, man, and tell Elizabeth thank you, too."

"No problem, Jack. How is Josh doing?"

"Good, real good. Hard to believe it's the same kid. Normally he is such a motor mouth, but when he is working he hardly makes a peep. Do you want me to bring him home when we are done?"

"No, he told me this morning he wanted to haul his traps and then come home with Elizabeth."

"Alright then, I will talk at you latah."

"Talk at you later, Jack."

As soon as Jack got off the phone he wanted to call his dad and let him know what was going on. The only problem was Russell kept his phone up on the dash and there was no way that he could hear his phone over the engine and music. He didn't want to say anything over the VHF radio either. Tommy would be listening and even asking his father to call him would catch Tommy's attention. Then he remembered the CB radio.

"Old Smoke, you got your ears on?"

Russell stopped what he was doing. If Jack was calling on the CB, something was up.

"Right here, boy." He answered back.

"Call me."

Now Russell knew something was up. He called Jack and got the whole story.

"Well, I ain't worried," boasted Russell. I don't carry shorts, I know you don't, and I have been doing this for fifty something years. I have made a friend or two. I will call an old friend of mine he will keep an eye on this."

"Who's is your friend?" asked Jack

"Don't you worry about it. The less you know the better."

"O.K., Dad. How is Melissa doing?"

"She is doing real good, Jack. Man, can she sing. I think she could give Patsy Cline a run for her money. How is Josh doing?"

"He is silent as a mouse, strong as a bull and quick as a cheetah. Christ, the only thing he has said all day is the count. He doesn't even ask for help changing out the bait trays."

"That's good. I trained him well. Be good to him, Jack; he's a good kid."

"Oh, I will, Dad. I am about done. You heading in soon?"

"Yup. Maybe we can time it and get to Tommy's together. It would make it easier on the Marine Patrol and make a bit of a statement."

"Sure thing. I can even take Melissa home from there, if you like."

"Yup, that works."

"See ya soon then."

"See ya, boy."

Russell hung up the phone and looked at Melissa.

"Melissa, I am going to call an old friend of mine. He is the Commissioner of the Marine Patrol. I may have to tell him who you really are. Are you o.k. with that?"

Melissa thought about it. If he was a friend of Russell's and Russell trusted him, then she trusted him, too. "Yes, I am o.k. with it. I will even give him an autograph if you think it will help."

Russell chuckled, "It wouldn't hurt."

Russell called his old friend. He stood out of ear shot from Melissa. Melissa knew it wasn't because she wasn't trusted but because the less she knew the better. She took that time and rinsed down the boat and filled the bait irons for the next pair. She went through the rubber bands to separate the ones that had gotten tangled. Russell got off the phone grinning ear to ear.

"He wants an autograph." Said Russell.

"No problem."

"Wait…there is more. He wants an autographed picture of you and him and all his patrol wardens."

"Russell…How am I going to do that and keep it a secret?" Melissa was agitated.

"Hold your horses now. He will wait until the end of summer when you're about to go back to Hollywood and he won't show anybody or post it in his office until you are back. Honestly, Melissa, I don't think you will be able to keep it a secret for that long."

Melissa was feeling more relaxed now. "Yeah, I guess you're right. I was almost thinking of never going back. I have enough money and connections to make Melissa Andrews disappear and be born again as Madison Adams."

Russell puffed his pipe and adjusted his hat. Then he spoke sternly, "Is that how you want to leave your old life? Everybody thinking you are some strung out junkie? I don't think so. I may have just met you but I got a good read on people. You have some fight in you. You're full of piss and vinegar. Oh sure you are a nice person and all, but if someone does you wrong you don't go down. Now this little vacation will end before you know it and you will have to face what you left behind. The Melissa I know, the one that earned the love and respect of the entire Finn family in just a few days will march back into Hollywood and prove them fuckers wrong."

Melissa didn't know whether to cry or shout out a battle cry. Russell, with all of his simple wisdom, put things in perspective. She would have to go back at some point. She would prove she was not a junkie and Hollywood would learn just who Melissa Andrews really was.

They hauled through the rest of the gear, Melissa going a little faster now with her elevated sense of self and pride. After the last trap hit the water Melissa gave the final count of lobsters. Russell wrote down the number in a little notebook like he had done all day. With a few scratches from his pencil to the paper he had a big smile on his face. Melissa guessed they had done good. They did a complete cleaning of the boat. Melissa felt that same sense of pride come over her with the appearance of the Old Smoke. Russell turned from the helm a little bit and looked back at Melissa who was now sitting on the transom.

"Normally this would be beer time and you would run the boat in. Given the situation with Marine Patrol being there, we will play it safe. You can take your oil skins off now and hang them up."

Melissa took off her oil skins and hung them up on the port side of the cabin. Out the window she saw a familiar sight, Red at Night was right beside them. She hopped back to the transom and waved. Jack and Josh waved back. Josh was at the helm with Jack behind him. She could see Jack reach for his radio microphone.

"Should we give her a preview of the races?" came Jack's voice on the radio.

"Let's run'em!" responded Russell, clinching his pipe in his teeth.

With that she could see Jack say something to Josh. Red at Night sped up a little and Russell pushed the throttle ahead a little more. They were side by side and close enough to see Josh push the throttle a little more. Russell countered with more throttle. Things were getting louder. The engines, the wind, and the water were all rushing and racing. Russell looked back at her and said, "That's all she has." The boats were dead even. Then she saw Jack tap Josh's shoulder. Red at Night burst ahead. The sound of the exhaust was like a low flying helicopter. Russell eased back on the throttle and followed Jack in. Melissa came up to the helm behind Russell. "What was that all about?" she asked.

"Just a touch of what the races are going to be like on Saturday and Sunday," answered Russell.

"That was fun."

"I will let you get some more time behind the wheel this week and let you run Old Smoke down the track."

Melissa was nervous and excited at the same time. Then she started thinking about the overnight stay with Jack. If he was ready to take the next step she would give herself to him. She started fantasizing about rolling around inside the Red at Night and grinned at the thought.

"Damn, kid, I didn't think racing would make you all dreamy eyed," Russell marveled.

Russell pulled into MacIntyre Lobster behind Jack and both of them tied up their boats and started draining water from their lobster tanks. Standing on the dock ready to unload them was Elizabeth Williams. She was normally smiling and happy, but today she was pale with worry. Russell wanted to tell her that there was nothing to be worried about. Down the ramp came a young woman in a marine patrol uniform followed by an older man around Russell's age. His uniform had more stripes on his sleeve but his salt and pepper hair and overall demeanor said he was in charge.

"Russell Finn, how are you doing, you old salt?" The older gentleman spoke with a southern accent.

"Depends on why you're here Commissioner Styker," answered Russell, acting as if he didn't already know what was going on.

"Weeellllll Russell, we got a tip that you and your boy were selling short lobsters. I thought there was no way that could happen so I wanted to see for myself."

As Tommy was coming down the ramp, Russell asked, "Who gave the tip?" Watching to see his expression change.

"I can't tell you that Russell, you know that."

"Well, I got shit to do today so let's get this bullshit going," Russel said, going further into the act.

"I will have patrolwoman Rand here collect your paperwork. Your lobster license, driver's license and your sternwoman's driver's license. I will have her run yours and all of Jack's and his crew's stuff at the same time. While she is doing that, this little lady will start to unload you. Now what's your name, little lady?" He said as he turned to a petrified Elizabeth.

"Elizabeth Williams."

"Miss Williams while you unload when I say 'that one' you pass me that lobster and I will measure it."

"Yes, sir," Elizabeth answered

Melissa looked up at the commissioner's face and he gave her a wink to let her know everything would be fine. The patrolwoman collected everybody's paperwork and headed up to the patrol truck.

"I think I will head back to my office," said Tommy, wanting to watch from the comfort of his office.

"You stay right here, Tommy. If the Finn's have been bringing in shorts and you have been buying them, that makes you just as guilty," barked the commissioner.

Tommy felt a lump in his throat. Suddenly, this wasn't such a good idea.

Patrolwoman Rand walked up the ramp to the truck and put the paperwork on the passenger seat, then started looking around Tommy's place. Nothing seemed suspect other than a few locked doors. She needed direction from someone that knew the place. She grabbed the paperwork and headed back to the boats.

"Commissioner, all the paperwork is good. I've got to use the restroom. Can Elizabeth come up and show me where it is?"

"Yes, go on up there, Miss Williams." said the commissioner.

Elizabeth jogged up the ramp and met the patrolwoman. She thought it was funny she couldn't find the restrooms; they were clearly marked. Elizabeth had made the signs herself.

"Elizabeth," the patrol woman said in a low voice. "I am not Marine Patrol. I am a DEA agent. What can you tell me about what is going on here? Where should I be looking?"

Elizabeth breathed a sigh of relief. She told the agent about inconsistencies of the shipping receipts and the funny times the trucks had been running. She said she didn't have a key for the locked rooms but told her that Tommy's office was probably unlocked.

"Thank you, here is my card. You see or hear anything, call me." said the agent.

"Yes, ma'am," answered Elizabeth.

As Elizabeth walked back down the ramp she noticed Tommy's face went pale as the commissioner complained about the waste of time it was that all the lobsters looked good. They finished with Russell and had gone to Jack's boat, so she checked in with Russell to see what he had weighed in at. She entered the number into her cell phone so she could put it into the computer later.

"Elizabeth, thank you for the tip," Russell said.

"No problem, Mr. Finn. Why is this all happening? I am a bit scared."

"Don't you worry, Elizabeth. You will be alright. You just ask your dad what is going on and he will tell you what you need to know."

"O.k., Mr. Finn, you have a good day. You, too, Miss Andrew....Adams."

Elizabeth and Melissa shared a smile and Elizabeth went to Jack's boat.

"Well, Melissa, you did a good job today. Do you like lobstering?" Russell asked.

"Yes, it was fun. Being out there on the water. It clears your head." Melissa answered.

"Good, glad you like it. I'll pick you up at the dock same time tomorrow. We will be hauling strings tomorrow. It's a bit more work and a bit more dangerous. It is also going to be hotter than the hinges of hell tomorrow in the afternoon." Russell paused and looked at Melissa. "Good work today kid, you should be proud of yourself." Russell knew just how much that meant to Melissa. She gave him a big hug and a kiss on the cheek. The old man had a big smile with his pipe held in his teeth. She walked over to Jack's boat and watched them finish unloading. Patrolwoman Rand came down the ramp and gave the commissioner a nod.

"Well, I think we have wasted enough time here. Sorry about the waste of time, Jack, good to see you. Elizabeth, you were a big help. I know it was a tough spot for you, but you did just what you were supposed to do. I'm going over to apologize to Russell," said the commissioner to the group.

He gave Melissa another nod and a grin, and then he walked with Rand back to Russell's boat. Tommy took off up the ramp. Elizabeth recorded Jack's catch on her phone and then got back to cleaning up the dock. Melissa jumped down into Jack's boat and stood aside while Josh finished putting things away.

"Good job today, Josh. Are you going to haul your own traps now?" Jack asked.

"Yeah, I got to haul 50 or so in the harbor here."

"Why don't you take that tray of bait we have left over. I don't want it in the boat overnight."

"I'll take it up to the bait shed."

"Josh….I am trying to give you a little bonus for a job well done."

"OH. Thanks, Jack."

Josh lifted the tray of bait up onto the dock and said one more thank you. They quickly agreed on picking Josh up here at Tommy's and what bait to tray up and how much. Jack untied the boat and slid away from the dock while Melissa sat on the engine box. They waved to the commissioner and Russell as they went by Old Smoke. As soon as Red at Night was clear he put it in forward, jogged up the throttle then turned the boat towards Tumbler Island. When the boat was making way and it was safe to take his eyes off the water and hands off the wheel, he bent down and gave Melissa a passionate kiss. Looking out of the corner of his eye where the boat was going and correcting course with one hand, he wanted the kiss to last forever. After it ended, they both took a deep breath.

"I've been waiting for that all day," said Jack.

"Me too." said Melissa.

Red at Night pulled up to the Spruce Point Dock. Jack and Melissa shared a few more kisses as she stepped out of the boat.

"So what do you want to do tonight?" Jack asked.

"Honestly, I'm beat. That is the hardest I have worked in a long time. I think I'm going to take a shower, have some dinner and go to bed."

Jack was disappointed but understood. "Alright, then. It is going to be a busy week and we are going to have plenty of time together this weekend at the races."

"About these races, Jack. We are still going to camp out on your boat right?"

"Yup, I got a spare sleeping bag. If you want it."

"No. I think one set of covers is enough." She turned and walked up the ramp a little bit taking longer steps to show off the shape of her butt. "By the way Jack.,.I sleep naked."

She walked the rest of the way up the ramp feeling Jack's eyes on her body. Jack stood there processing what was just said. Melissa wanted to let him know she was ready, but in a playful way. She knew this would be a huge step for Jack; he was not the kind of guy that took making love lightly. She could tell from the way Russell and Anne raised him, from the passion he once held for Stephanie and from his subtle gentleman like behavior. She wanted to give him plenty of time to think about it and mentally prepare himself.

Chapter 6

Tommy watched the commissioner and patrolwoman Rand drive away and breathed a sigh of relief. "What an idiot!" he said to himself. He wanted to scare Russell and Jack, but all he accomplished was scaring himself and looking like an idiot, not to mention bringing the law onto his dock with all the drug trade he had going on. "How can I hurt them?" he thought to himself. He saw Elizabeth entering their catch into the computer. As soon as she got up and left the office he went into the office and took fifty pounds from Russell and Jack's catch. "That will show them to fuck with me. I will take their money and they won't even know it." He went up to his office to take care of some of the other side of the business. Just as he sat down his cell phone rang. He looked at the caller ID-"Her"- his nickname for the Russian woman.

"Hello," Tommy said trying to be cool.

"What police doing there?" The sexy Russian accent sounded furious.

"Police….no po…." He was cut off before he could finish.

"Don't fuck with me, Mr. MacIntyre, you be found floating in harbor. I have people watching. You are investment, my property. I watch carefully. Now tell me why Marine Patrol snooping around."

"They were here checking out a couple of my fishermen. They heard they were bringing in shorts and wanted to check."

"Why patrol woman speaking your staff?"

"She asked where the bathroom was. Elizabeth showed her."

"She gave her card."

"It was probably to call her if she saw any illegal lobster."

"We don't work "probable's". You check your people. We have boat will be off Damariscove Island midnight tonight. They give you 100 kilos product 10 bait totes. Two will be yours to sell, give me half your profit. Tomorrow night you meet another boat at cove, at your Damrisove Island. Give that boat the other 8 totes."

"We have been doing that on the trucks. I told you I want to push more."

"This is a test run. I come to your place to check it out."

"When are you coming?"

"You know when I am there."

The phone went silent. Tommy stood there staring at the screen then called Dale Rines next to let him know what was going on.

"Hey, Dale."

"What's up, Tommy?"

"You are on, tonight. We need to catch some herring out at Damariscove." Tommy hoped Dale wasn't so stoned that he couldn't remember the code.

"Ooohhh, ya-" Dale barely remembered what Tommy was talking about. "What time?"

"We have to be out there at midnight?"

"O.k. I will come down to the dock about ten thirty and fuel up. We will leave at eleven."

"Sounds good," said Tommy as he hung up.

Tommy was nervous and excited at the same time. He was already pushing more cocaine than the state of Maine had ever seen. He was making hundreds of thousands of dollars every week. He would soon be in the millions. Then he would cash out and head to the Caribbean. "I am not going to let the Finn clan get in my way. I killed Stephanie when she got too close," Tommy said to himself as he stroked his beard. He thought back to that night. Watching Jack say what were to be his last goodbyes. He followed her while she drove back to her house. As soon as she started around the sharp bend at the head of Mill Cove he gave her car a swift hit with his truck. It was all it took to make her lose control. Her car swerved, then flipped doing barrel rolls into the water. Tommy stopped just for a second to watch the car sink. He picked up pieces of her broken taillight then drove away. Earlier that day she had confronted him. She had come down to the dock one night to get her phone off Jack's boat; on her way back up from the dock she saw men unloading cocaine into one of Tommy's closets. She took a picture with her phone and showed it to Tommy. She had decided to give him a chance to come clean before going to the police. That mistake cost her life. "I hated to do it, but that Russian lady would have killed me!" Tommy took a deep breath, but it didn't make the lump in his throat go away.

In the Marine Patrol truck, agent Rand had just listened into Tommy's conversation with the Russian lady and Dale Rines. She took her ear bud out and closed the laptop with frustration.

"What's the matter?" The commissioner asked.

"He keeps calling the drugs 'lobster or product'. I can't get a search warrant with that. I was lucky enough to get the warrant to put a bug on his cell phone," she answered.

"What did he say to Dale Rines?"

"Something about fishing for herring out at Damariscove Island."

"Hhhmmm," Stryker adjusted his hat as he drove. "Feel like going for a boat ride tonight?"

"What are you thinking, sir?"

"Dale Rines's boat isn't set up for catching herring. We can take a patrol boat out and see what they're up to."

"I'll bring the coffee."

"Bring enough for three. I have to get another patrolman to take the boat out."

"10-4, sir."

He smiled with approval. Agent Rand leaned back in her seat for a bit then turned back towards Stryker.

"So how did you know about Tommy and the drug dealing and how do you know the Finn's?"

"Well some things just haven't been adding up. Dale Rines bought a brand new truck and he doesn't fish enough to make that kind of money. I know he is Tommy's buddy, and the local police have been watching them pretty closely, but like the DEA haven't found anything big enough to do anything with. I heard the Finn's have been wanting to buy Tommy's place. So when Tommy called the office claiming that the Finn's were bringing in illegal lobster, I saw it as an opportunity. I called your office and they sent me you. Lucky we had a Marine Patrol uniform for you. Russell Finn and I go way back. He taught me everything I know about lobstering and the town of Boothbay Harbor. He's a good man; his kids are no different."

"In the DEA we knew drugs were moving into Maine, but we didn't know how. Tommy seems to have skipped over Portland and is dealing with someone else. He never mentions her name, but she has a thick Russian accent. I have her number now at least, but these guys ditch their phones so often. I need to catch them in the act, I need to see them carrying cocaine. I need to get into Tommy's closets he has locked up. Elizabeth told me about some shipping receipts that didn't add up, but I couldn't find them. Those would get me a warrant to search a truck or one of those closets."

"Well I'm sure we will see something tonight."

"I hope so."

They drove back to the Marine Patrol headquarters and got ready for the nighttime run to Damariscove. Agent Rand got in touch with her boss back at the DEA to let him in on what was going on and a plan was set.

Back at Tommy's, Elizabeth waited patiently for Tommy to leave. As soon as he did, she went into his office to look for the shipping receipts. She found them and took pictures of them with her cell phone. She also found the business card for Tommy's new accountant and took a picture of that as well and sent them all to agent Rand. Elizabeth didn't know for sure what was going on around her, but she knew whatever it was, it wasn't right. She heard someone come in downstairs. She closed Tommy's office and went down to find a tall, skinny, bald man who looked out of place and slightly disgusted by his surroundings. He was smoking a cigarette and the smoke lingered around his head.

"Excuse me, sir…there is no smoking inside." Elizabeth spoke to the man. He turned sharply towards Elizabeth. His blue eyes were piercing, and it looked as though he was going to yell or threaten her at first. Instead he gave her a creepy smile and tossed the cigarette into one of the lobster tanks.

"Sorry," he said with a Russian accent.

"Can I help you, sir?" Elizabeth said feeling nervous.

"Maybe, police were here earlier, yes."

"Yes…well, the Marine Patrol." Elizabeth thought that it was odd of a customer to ask.

"Marine Patrol…why here?"

Elizabeth knew it was none of his business but felt it was better off to tell him what he wanted. "They were checking for illegal lobster."

"Did they give you…card, perhaps?"

Elizabeth knew that he must already know if he asked for it. "Yes, they gave me a card so I could call in if I saw anything."

"Do you still have card?"

"Nope, I had it in my pocket but it got wet when I was hosing the dock, so I threw it away." Elizabeth was hoping he bought the story. The card that Rand gave her was a DEA card. She knew this guy was bad news and didn't want to tip him off. "I can look up the Marine Patrol number; it's right on the website".

He could see her shorts were wet. The tanks splashed over and hoses were everywhere. He believed her story. "Thank you, no need for number, good day." With that he walked out of the building. Elizabeth watched him as he walked outside and pulled a phone out of his pocket.

"Is good here. The girl knows nothing, she is just teenager. Is what he said. Marine Patrol checking lobster." He spoke into the phone while getting into his car.

"Good, stay there and watch them. I want you on boat when they leave tonight. Watch things and keep Mr. MacIntyre nervous. I want you watch his partner, I don't know him. We do test run tonight and tomorrow. If goes well, more as summer goes."

"Yes, you want go with them tomorrow night?"

"Yes, keep a close eye on Mr. MacIntyre and his business."

"If he does not like my presence…can I-"

"No, don't touch him. Just show him video, him pushing car into ocean. Will keep him in control."

"Yes, is good. Bye."

Casmiere sat for a moment and decided there was nothing to see at Tommy's for now. If he was going to be spending time in Boothbay Harbor he needed a hotel room. He started the car and drove next door to Capt'n Fish's and rented a room with a view of Tommy's to keep an eye on things. Elizabeth, tucking behind the door, took a picture of Casmiere and sent it to agent Rand. As soon as she got back to work, her phone rang.

"Hello," Elizabeth said.

"Yes, Elizabeth. What is this picture you sent me? Who is the man getting into the car?" agent Rand asked.

"I don't know. He had a Russian accent. I think he had been watching me. He knew about the card you gave me and asked why you guys were here."

Agent Rand took a break from loading her bag for the stakeout. She was happy to be getting so much intel but was nervous that a teenage girl was in the middle of it. "Are you o.k.?"

"Yes, a little scared. I didn't let him see your card, and he didn't see me take the picture. He just didn't look like he belonged here, and the fact he knew you had given me that card is creepy. What should I do?"

"Nothing, Elizabeth, you have done enough, more than most your age. At this point we don't have enough to make a move on anybody. Keep sending me as much as you can, but, Elizabeth, be safe. Can you meet me somewhere tomorrow?"

"Yeah, I work through my lunch, but I can meet you."

"Good. Just to be safe I am going to have our tech guys install a panic button on your phone."

"O.k."

"Elizabeth you will be ok. Just act natural while at Tommy's."

"Yes, agent Rand."

"Alright, Elizabeth, thanks again."

Elizabeth put her phone down. She knew her next call should be to her parents but knew they would freak out and pull her out of there. She wanted to see this to the end…no matter how it ended.

As the week went on Rand slowly built her case. She watched every boat trip Tommy and Dale made. She recorded how many bait totes moved, the names of the boats, pictures of the transactions and people involved. She documented every bit of information Elizabeth gave her. She was building a case but still didn't have enough for a warrant. She asked the DEA branch in Boston for help, but they had an enormous case load and couldn't spare the resources. Surprisingly enough, Commissioner Stryker was her biggest help, providing her with a patrolman and a boat any night she needed. He was going to get in touch with an old FBI friend of his who maybe had some information about the Russians. A drug organization that big had to be on their radar. If they could just see what was in those totes, or in those closets at Tommy's, or if they could search one of the trucks. Rand knew the weak link in all this was Dale Rines. Tommy wasn't smart, but he was clever enough not to show off. Dale had a brand new truck and he had been seen at the bars throwing money around. Stryker had learned he hadn't been hauling his traps lately either, so the money had to be coming from somewhere.

The Finn and Williams families submitted the business plan to the bank and were preapproved for two and a half million dollars. The plan was to offer Tommy two million for the place and use the rest to fix it up and make changes. They were confident Tommy would take the offer.

Jack and Melissa built on their relationship with small dates fishing and picnicking on the Red at Night. A double date with the Williams's was to help Melissa earn Michael's trust. All this was building up for the overnight trip on the first Lobsterboat Race weekend. Melissa also spent time with Lucy, Anne and Abigail doing girl stuff. It felt so good to just hang out and be one of the girls for a change. She had gotten some calls from her agent asking how she was doing and when she would be coming back. "Sometime at the end of summer," she always said, not giving a direct answer. The tabloids and other media had changed direction with her story, printing she was taking time off for rehab. Melissa was also building a relationship with Russell. He was a wise old man. Quick witted, he had a heart of gold. He still called her Hollywood, but she didn't mind. She knew at the end of summer she would have to say goodbye to all these people. It made her cry thinking about it, but the pain was well worth it.

Finally, Friday came. Melissa and Russell were out lobstering while Jack had Red at Night beached out. He was taking off the work propeller and putting on his race propeller. Michael was reprogramming the engine for another 125 horsepower, with Josh helping.

"There you go," said Michael. "800 horsepower. Monday I will flash it back down to the 675, but don't go wide open until you swap the wheel back, OK."

"Yes, I know the same thing you tell me every year. Is the water-meth set up?" asked Jack.

"Yes, I used a bilge pump switch to hide it. Push automatic for the first shot and flip to manual for the last shot."

"Nice. Maybe this year I can beat that damned Marshall Weston."

"Hope so. If you don't, I can sell you a bigger Scania!"

"If we weren't on the cusp of buying out Tommy, I would repower this winter."

"Why don't you have your new sugar momma buy it for you?" There was a long pause. Michael knew he had crossed a line.

"You know me better than that, Michael."

Michael knew he had gotten off easy. "Yeah I know. She still coming to Rockland with you?"

"Yup."

Michael could sense Jack was still agitated. "I was just wondering. Elizabeth and Josh are coming in the boat. I think I will just put a tent up in the back of Overtime for those two."

Jack was easing up a bit, "Sounds good. Josh, you running your boat, or is your sister?"

"I'm running it. Elizabeth just likes to sit and watch now. She doesn't even haul with me anymore. I think she is more interested in becoming a cop," said Josh.

"Really…she would make a great cop" Jack said.

"She wants to be undercover. Either FBI or DEA," said Michael.

"Wow…how do you feel about that.,. Dad?" Jack said with a slightly sarcastic tone.

"Well, if I have learned anything about these two kids, it is not to stand in their way, just move aside and help when I can."

"What about you, Josh? What are you going to do after school?" Jack asked.

"I have no clue," Josh said shaking his head and putting his hands up.

Jack and Michael shared a laugh at the blatant honesty of the teenager.

"I can see Dad and Melissa are in. I'm going to go on over and see them. Tide will be up in a couple hours so we will take this thing for a test spin. I think we will go on the back side of Mouse Island. Nobody will see us there."

"Sounds good to me, I gotta go with you when you test run this thing to make sure your exhaust doesn't get too hot," said Michael.

"Sounds like a plan; how do you think it will go Monday when we approach Tommy?" Jack asked while getting in his truck.

"I have no clue. I'm hoping he will take the money and get out of town."

"Me, too, I will call you when she is floating."

Jack shut the door to his truck and drove over to MacIntyre's. Michael and Josh got out of the Red at Night and loaded all the tools into their truck.

Michael paused and looked at Josh. "You really don't know what you want to do after school?"

"No, not a clue. I like lobstering, I like working on boats with you, but that is all I have ever done," Josh answered.

"Well, don't worry, you have more years of school to figure it out. I am behind you no matter what," said Michael.

They got in the truck and drove off.

Melissa could see Jack pulling into the parking lot. Elizabeth was on the dock as usual, ready to unload the boat when they tied up.

"How many crates today, Mr. Finn?" asked Elizabeth.

"Ten crates, a bucket for hard shells and a bucket for culls," answered Russell.

"Any fuel?"

"Nope. Got fuel this morning. Where is the Boss man?"

"Who knows these days. He is never around."

Russell shook his head.

"You ready for your first boat races, Miss Andrews?" asked Elizabeth.

"I guess so. Russell says he is going to let me drive Old Smoke in the races. I'm a little nervous, but it will be fun."

"Nothing to be nervous about. Just put the hammer down when the flag drops and keep her straight," Russell coached.

"I hear that "Over the Rainbow" is a shoe-in for the Oscars this year. Do you think you will get one?" asked Elizabeth.

"To tell you the truth, I haven't followed it that much since being here. I am dreading going back to that life at the end of summer."

"Well, I hope you get one. Do you think I could get your autograph before you go back?"

"Elizabeth, I will do better than that. You and I will get a picture together and I will sign that. I will give you my number and email address and we'll stay in touch."

"Cool!" Elizabeth was grinning from ear to ear as she finished weighing up the lobster and putting the numbers into her phone.

"What did I get, Elizabeth?"

"818 pounds soft shell, 3.25 on hard shell and 2.5 on culls."

"That sounds about right with what we counted. Elizabeth, do you keep that stuff on your phone?"

"Yes, just in case there is a mix-up I can look back at this and see if I entered something wrong. I delete it at the end of summer after the summer books are closed."

"Good system. Another guy used to keep it in a notebook. He left it out once and some of the guys went thumbing through it to see what others were catching."

"You don't have to worry about that. My phone never leaves my pocket and it is password protected."

"I trust you, kiddo. You ready to be a senior when school starts?"

"Yes, I've been applying to schools. I have it narrowed down to three. Northeastern is close, but I like Sam Houston State or UC Irvine."

"What do you want to go to school for?" asked Melissa.

"Major in Criminal Justice."

"Wow! What do you want to do?"

"Either FBI, CIA, or DEA."

Both Melissa and Russell were taken back by this sweet and innocent child who wanted to expose herself to the ugliness of the world.

"Why on earth would you want to do that, Lizzy?" Russell asked, barely keeping his pipe in his mouth.

"I want to make the world a better place," Elizabeth answered innocently.

Russell and Melissa didn't know what to say to such a simple answer. It was naïve and simple, but the way Elizabeth said it, there was no doubt she meant it.

Jack came down the ramp to meet Melissa.

"Here comes Romeo. Elizabeth you better get out of here before these two start playing sucky face."

Elizabeth laughed. "Ok, Mr. Finn. I will see you tomorrow. Bye, Miss Andrews."

"Bye, Elizabeth, nice talking to you," said Melissa.

"Boat all ready?" asked Russell.

"Yup, just gotta wait for it to float and I will take her out for a test run."

"What did you do to it?" asked Melissa.

"Well, Michael hooks up his computer to it and bumps it up to 800 horsepower rating. He also put in a water methanol injection kit to give me another 50 to 60 horsepower."

"How much faster do you think you will go?"

"I do 32 knots now. I am hoping to hit 36, that would put me at about 42 mph."

"And why do you do this?" Melissa asked in a sarcastic tone.

"Bragging rights, free bait, fuel or a lobster trap." answered Russell.

"Yes, all that and at the end of the racing season they total up the points you have earned and there is a trophy and a custom embroidered jacket. It is also good marketing for boat builders and engine sellers. People see me screaming down the track then also see me hauling year-round. It says a lot for Mike and his product support," Jack added.

"Is there any prize money?" Melissa asked.

"A hundred bucks cash. Rockland gives away a truck in the hat drawing" Russell said.

"Hat drawing?" Melissa asked.

"First, second, and third place winners get entered into a hat drawing for more prizes," Jack answered.

"How many people race?" asked Melissa.

"We usually see fifty to sixty boats here. Some places get more, some get less. They will start showing up soon," stated Russell.

"It's really less about the money and trophies for most of us. It's about getting together and having a few beers. We get to meet other lobstermen, talk about the prices and such. A few of the boat builders and engine dealers show up, like Michael. It's what some people call "networking," Added Jack.

"Well, Melissa, today is payday. I will go on up and close out my week. You can wait here, or I can pay you later," Russell said, changing the subject.

"Later is good. Friday night that means beer, burgers, and dancing right!" Melissa said with excitement.

"Yes, it does. How about I give you a ride home in the truck. We'll both get cleaned up. I will pick you back up, take the boat out for a test spin, then head back here."

"I can't believe I went from taking two hours to get ready to go out, to getting ready and going for a boat ride in two hours."

They all shared a good laugh and went their different ways. Jack had just dropped off Melissa when his father called him on his cell phone.

"Miss me already?" asked Jack.

"You're not going to believe what that fucking snake is up to now," Russell screamed into the phone.

"What…who…Dad, slow down."

"Fucking, Tommy! He shorted my sales slips."

"How do you know?"

"I keep track of what I catch, and luckily Elizabeth keeps what she totals on her phone."

"How much did he short you?"

"Fifty pounds every day this week."

"Holy shit…what are you going to do?"

"I went up to his office, but the piece of shit wasn't there. I am on the boat now headed home. Then I'm going to drive to his house and beat my 250 pounds of lobster out of him."

"Christ, don't do that…give me a chance to think."

"You're right, I will go home and simmer down a bit, but that is a lot of money, Jack."

"I know, Dad, we'll get it back. We are making an offer on that place Monday, we don't want to mess that up."

"Good thing you got your mom's temper and brains boy."

"Thanks, Dad. Talk at you on the dock"

Just as he hung up the phone, Michael called him.

"Jack, you ain't going to believe what the fuck is going on."

"I will, Dad just filled me in."

"Nope.,. you don't know the full story. Elizabeth just filled me in. You'll get the rest of the story when you get back to the boat."

"OK."

Jack's mind was reeling. What could possibly be going on? What did Elizabeth know? He got home and took his shower, threw on a pair of his "good" blue jeans and a white t-shirt and he was back out the door. Melissa was waiting outside for him. She was wearing a denim skirt and black tank top. Her hair was pulled back in a ponytail. She looked sexy, but simple. Just what he liked. They drove down to the boat and saw Michael and Elizabeth there. The patrolwoman from Monday was there but in plain clothes. He parked the truck and went down to the wharf. Red at Night was already floating and had been moved to the dock.

"Jack, I moved the boat because this may take a bit," Said Michael

"Ok…what is going on, what is she doing here?"

"Hello, I am DEA agent Carla Rand."

"What the….DEA…, what?" Jack said trying to understand what was going on.

"Jack.,. just listen. Trust me, I was as shocked as you were when Lizzy told me this," said Michael.

"I have been building a case against Tommy MacIntyre. I think he is using the lobster business as a cover for selling and shipping cocaine."

Jack felt numb. It all made sense but he still couldn't believe what was going on. "OK…so what does that have to do with the rest of us?"

"Elizabeth has been sending me information and pictures of some of the stuff going on here. I have also been tracking Tommy and watching him steadily. Elizabeth called me almost immediately after your father left the dock. She told me about the missing pounds of lobster. She also told me that she checked your sales slips as well and Tommy shorted those, too."

"That….Elizabeth, cover your ears….I am going to beat the daylight out of him," said Jack with his face turning red, fists clenched and vessels starting to pop out of his fore arms.

"No, you're not. I need you and your father to act as if you know nothing. The only reason I am telling you this much is so my case doesn't get messed up."

"So what do you want us to do and what was up Monday with you posing as Marine Patrol?" asked Michael.

"First off, we never had this conversation. You tell nobody. Jack, you need to tell your dad so he won't go off on Tommy, but that is it! Second, don't change a thing. Still make your offer Monday, but you know he will turn it down. The Commissioner had his suspicions about Tommy so he saw it as an opportunity to get me down here and start looking around."

"What about my daughter? I want her out of this mess," Michael stated.

"No, Dad.,. I…" Elizabeth tried to argue but her father cut her off.

"Elizabeth, I am already mad that you were doing this and not telling me or your mother," said Michael.

"Mr. Williams, I understand your concern, but Elizabeth is a great source of info and her safety is our main concern. We installed a panic button on her cell phone and we have an agent watching Tommy's 24/7," Agent Rand said, trying to keep Elizabeth's help.

"Dad, I am seventeen. Next year I will be graduating school and going off to college. Then I will be doing this for real," argued Elizabeth.

"That is not for five or six years from now, Elizabeth. We have no idea how bad this could get or how big it is."

"Dad, I can do this. All I am doing is giving agent Rand information and taking pictures of people I see that look out of place. Tommy doesn't even know how I keep track of the guys catch." Elizabeth continued her argument.

"Mr. Williams, I have also told Elizabeth not to go digging around, just report what she sees normally. Like I said, we have an agent watching the place and most of the time it is me."

Michael took a long deep breath. Elizabeth was getting older. She was smart and strong. She looked so sure of herself. Agent Rand seemed to care about her, too.

"O.k." Michael paused, "but you have to tell your mother and she has to agree with this, too. You listen to agent Rand, no digging around. Just report the stuff you see and hear. Agent Rand…Carla, you make damn sure nothing…I mean nothing happens to my daughter."

"Yes, sir," Rand responded.

"OK, thanks Dad." Elizabeth gave her father a big hug. Melissa could see a moment of softness in Michael. He loved his daughter and cared for her.

"Alright then, I need to get back to watching Tommy. Like I told you all, not a word of this to anybody other than your father," Rand said as she pointed to Jack, "and your wife", as she pointed to Michael. "I am so close to breaking this case I don't want to mess it up." She finished and walked away to her car.

"Wow!" Jack said. "I don't even know what to think anymore, but it has me wondering about something."

"What is that Jack?" Asked Melissa

"Steph told me she knew something about Tommy, but she wouldn't tell me. Something about giving him a chance to come clean."

"Well, that is enough drama for now. Elizabeth you go back and finish your work day. When you get home, you and I and your mother are going to have a talk," commanded Michael

"Yes, Dad," Elizabeth answered before walking back to her car.

"You still ready to try her out?" Michael asked Jack.

Jack was still a little zoned out. "…yeah…let's go."

"Josh is already down on Overtime. Hollywood, why don't you ride with him, Jack and I will be in Red at Night."

She was annoyed with being bossed around by Michael and his use of the "Hollywood" nickname but decided to go along without question. "Alright."

She walked down to see Josh standing in a black lobster boat similar to Jack and Russell's but a bit smaller. The engine box was a bit bigger than Jack's, almost too big for the boat. Melissa was a little nervous having a fourteen year old boy driving the boat, and Jack could see the look of concern on Melissa's face.

"Don't worry. He has been running boats since he was six. The good thing is he is finally tall enough to see."

Melissa watched as Josh untied the boat and maneuvered away from the dock. It was no different than watching Jack or Russell do it. Except the boat seemed to jump more when he put it in gear. Once away from the dock, Josh fell in behind Red at Night. Melissa walked up to the port side of the engine box to see out the window. Jack was running Red at Night and Michael was checking his laptop and looking over the engine. Soon they were on the back side of Mouse Island and Jack motioned Josh to come up the port side of Red at Night.

"Ma'am, if you want a good picture, you should stand over here," Josh suggested.

"Ok Josh, thank you." Melissa answered.

Melissa got her phone out and stood on the starboard side of the Overtime behind Josh. She got the Red at Night in focus. Soon she could see Jack give more throttle and Josh soon answered. Then Jack gave some more and Josh matched that. As she continued to take pictures, it seemed that Jack was at full throttle. Melissa looked at Josh. He had a big grin on his face and said, "Hold on." Suddenly Overtime lurched ahead and she had to hold on as Josh swerved in front of Jack but she managed to get a good head-on picture of Red at Night before Overtime pulled far ahead. Soon Josh pulled the throttle back and turned back towards Jack and his father. The two boats came side by side.

"We got thirty-six knots. I am pretty damned happy with that." Stated Jack

"What did you get, Josh?" asked Michael.

"Forty-three," Josh Answered.

"That was awesome!" declared Melissa. She gave Josh a peck on the cheek that turned Josh as red as Jack's boat. She jumped up onto the rail and into Red at Night. Michael got into Overtime.

"You coming down to Tommy's for a beer?" Jack asked Michael.

"After this talk with Abigail and Elizabeth, I may need it. That girl is growing up too fast."

"See you later then. Thanks again for your work."

"No problem, your boat is my floating advertisement."

The two boats parted ways. Jack headed towards Tommy's.

"What a day," Melissa let out with a sigh.

"Yeah, that is crazy about Tommy and the drugs, but it sure explains a lot. Just sucks he isn't going to want to give up his cover. I wonder how long this is going to drag out."

"I know you and your family really had your hearts set on that place. It will happen eventually. When they bust him he will need to sell it to pay for a lawyer."

"True. I guess it is a waiting game now."

"And to think Chris thought I would get bored here."

Melissa and Jack shared a laugh, then shared several kisses before reaching the dock. Melissa looked up at the crowd. Sure enough, Lucy and Sam were there along with Russell and Anne. She could recognize a few more faces this time. During the week she had seen and met some of the other lobstermen and their sternmen. They walked up the ramp and almost instantly Jack pulled Russell aside. Melissa went to Anne who was talking to another older lady. Melissa didn't hesitate to give Anne a hug as part of the greeting and Anne didn't hesitate to return one.

"Hello, Madison. This is Evelyn Turner a…friend of ours." Anne had a little pause in her introduction.

"Hello, Madison, it's nice to meet you. I have heard a lot about you," said Evelyn.

"Good things I hope." Melissa replied.

"Oh yes. I am just happy Jack has finally moved on."

Melissa was shocked. She put two and two together. The name Turner and the "moved on" comment. She was stuck on what to possibly say next. She glanced at Anne who was giving her an assuring smile.

"From what I understand, it was a long time coming. Jack and I are taking it slow and letting wounds heal."

"You're a nice girl; Stephanie would have liked you. I'm going to say 'hi' to Jack. Nice to meet you"

"Nice meeting you as well."

As Evelyn walked away towards Jack and Russell, Melissa paused and turned to Anne "That was Stephanie's Mom wasn't it?"

"Yes."

"Oh my god. I feel…I don't know what I feel."

"You did fine. She is happy Jack is moving on."

"But why say that Stephanie would have liked me. That is…"

"That is her way of saying Stephanie would be happy Jack found you."

Melissa stood there a moment taking in all the emotions that were whizzing around in her heart and mind. She looked up and smiled at Anne. She turned to see Jack hugging Evelyn, with a tear rolling down his cheek. Drying his eyes, he walked over to Anne and Melissa.

"You going to be ok?" Melissa asked Jack.

"Yeah, just a little more closure." Jack smiled back at Melissa.

"Talking about closure, let me close out my week by paying my sternman…sternwomen, sternwoman," said Russell, barging in on the conversation.

"Pay me boss," said Melissa with her hand out.

"Here you go $625. Now I am paying you cash, so don't be surprised to see tax paperwork come at you."

"Great, my accountant will have no idea what to think when I tell her I went to work on a lobster boat," responded Melissa.

"Christ, she might come bugging me for a job."

The group shared a laugh and went on with the festivities. Michael and Abigail showed up and joined the group for beer and burgers.

"So Abigail, Elizabeth was telling me about the colleges she will be applying to. If you want I can write a letter of recommendation,"

Melissa said.

"We don't need any help from you, Hollywood," Michael said flatly.

"Michael Williams!" Abigail blasted out. "Get off your high horse,… and yes, Melissa, a letter from a Hollywood elite would be great."

"Sorry, hun," said Michael in a low voice.

"Don't apologize to me. Melissa is trying to help out our daughter and extend an olive branch to earn your trust. Apologize to her," Abigail insisted.

Michael saw the tension of the group bearing down on him. He looked over at Jack who was staring right back at him with a steely gaze.

Michael shifted his eyes to Melissa. She looked hurt and mad at the same time. He took a deep breath and said, "Sorry, Melissa, and thank you."

"Apology accepted, but sometime here in the near future you and I need to have a talk…just the two of us."

"Weellll, that's enough drama for now. Melissa, we gonna dance or what?" Russell spouted to break the tension.

"I thought you would never ask," Melissa responded gladly.

"Come on, Sam." Lucy grabbed Sam and dragged him to the dance floor.

Michael was still feeling some tension and tried to break it. "You wanna go hit the dance floor, hun?"

"Nope. Not until you toss your gavel and take off your robe your honor. You need to remember you're not perfect either. Jack, how about you take me out on the floor?"

Jack, feeling about as awkward as he could, nodded his head in agreement and took Abigail to the dance floor.

"Look, Mike, I get it. I didn't trust her at first either, but she has earned my trust ten times over by now. She is humble and a bit naïve. She is also very honest. I believe her story about what happened that night. I know it hurt Lizzy but she got over it. You need to get over it. I know you have a lot on your plate right now. It's better to have more support than pushing all your friends and family away."

Michael sat and pondered Anne's words.

After some dancing, drinking and eating, Michael and Abigail said their goodbyes, and the Finns went on their normal boat ride around the harbor. Jack pointed out a bunch of lobster boats "from away" all rafted up at Browns Wharf. He knew most of the boats' names, hulls, engines and the owners. Jack pointed out a boat named Minor Details.

"That is Marshall Weston's boat. That is who I am gunning for. He and I have been racing each other since we were in skiffs."

"Damn, it was fun to watch you guys as kids racing each other. That has got to be my favorite of the races. The kids with skiffs. All the big hopes and dreams." Russell chimed in.

"What do the kids get for prizes?" asked Melissa.

"Tommy usually puts a free meal in for first, second and third. We kind of make sure that happens," stated Russell.

"Too bad you guys couldn't put enough money together for a college scholarship," said Melissa.

Jack laughed a little. "Most of these kids have no intention of going to college. Most of them will leave high school and go right to lobstering, or into a trade of some sort."

"Scholarships don't have to go to a big college, Jack. Why not a trade school or something like that?" Melissa said.

"I guess that would be good. It would be hard to come up with that kind of money," said Jack. That statement had Melissa lost in thought, until her thinking was interrupted.

"So how did you like your first week living here in Boothbay Harbor?" asked Sam

"It was nice. I think next week I will venture out more. Do some shopping here in town. It has been nice to get out on the water. The mornings are the best. The water is calm and all lit up from the sunrise. I like the afternoon's too. Russell lets me run the boat into the dock, and unloading the catch to see how we did. I like talking to Elizabeth every afternoon. Russell even let me pick where we set a few traps, and it was neat to see if I caught any or missed them completely. This is a great life you guys have here."

"Well, I think you fit right in Melissa, I hope if you go back to Hollywood that you can come back here once in a while to visit," said Lucy.

"Thank you, Lucy, but I don't want to think about that place for a while."

"Last Friday you sang us a song. Care to give us another one?" asked Anne changing the subject.

"Any requests?" Melissa answered.

Before anybody could speak, Russell spat out "I Fall To Pieces" by Patsy Cline."

"Russell, she doesn't know any of that old stuff you listen to," Anne replied.

"Yes, she does. She was singing to it the other day on the back of the boat. I could barely hear it over the hauler, engine, and the VHF squawking," argued Russell.

"I got it, Russell," Melissa said with confidence. As Melissa started singing she thought to herself that never in a million years would she have felt so comfortable with people to just openly sing. She did "Over the Rainbow" last week for the Finn's but she had rehearsed that song so much. This was a song she had only heard a couple times on Russell's boat. She looked around and saw nothing but warm smiling faces. "This is family…my family," she thought to herself. When she was done there was a round of applause. Even some people from another boat cheered as they cruised by.

Eventually, Jack went back to Tommy's to drop off his family and Melissa stayed on board.

"What is the plan, Captain?" Melissa asked, while Jack pulled away from the dock.

"Well…I have to take this thing and tie it up over at the other dock where my truck is, but I think we can sit for a bit and have a beer and listen to some music."

"Sounds good. Jack, this week…it has been the best week of my life."

Jack looked at her and smiled.

"Seriously, Jack. I have had a blast out there with your dad. Your mom treats me like her own daughter. Lucy gets me laughing so hard my ribs hurt. Then there is you…I can't even describe the way you make me feel. I never thought it would be possible for someone to make another person feel so good. Jack, most people would say I am nuts or naïve, but I know deep down inside of me in a place that I haven't had open in a long time that… I love you. I do. I love you, Jack Finn," Melissa said with her bottom lip quivering and a single tear rolling down her cheek.

"Melissa…I love you, too." He reached out with both hands to embrace her face, cupping her cheeks with his hands. He pulled her face to his and kissed her. He slid his right hand up to the back of her head pulling her closer. He placed his left hand on the small of her back. Her hands held his shoulders tightly. Lips and tongues danced with an intense passion. Their breaths became one breath, and their hearts pounded on each other's chests. Jack pulled back and said, "I can't wait to tomorrow night."

Melissa smiled back playfully. "You don't have to."

Jack throttled the boat up to get to the dock faster. While Jack tied up the boat, Melissa slipped down forward into the bunk area. After the boat was tied up, Jack shut down the engine and took a quick look around to make sure everything was set. He opened the door to go down forward and closed it behind him. He turned his head and saw Melissa standing there just in front of the bunk completely naked. She took the elastic that held her pony tail out of her hair and shook her hair down. She turned around giving Jack a complete view of her body. Jack could feel himself getting hard already. She stepped forward to him and pulled his white T-shirt off. They kissed again. Jack could feel Melissa's breasts against him. He put his hands on her back then slid them down to her butt. While they kissed, she undid his belt and pants and they dropped on the floor. Melissa pulled away and laid down on the bunk on her back. Jack went to her and they made love until they were exhausted and fell asleep in each other's arms.

Melissa woke up and lay on the bunk watching Jack sleep. Watching his chest slowly rise and fall with every breath. She wanted to wake him up to talk and make love again. Though the sex was great, it was sharing herself with someone that really loved her and cared for her that felt so good. "I am yours forever, Jack Finn," she said to herself with a whisper. She laid back down on her back, staring up through the hatch at the stars.

"And I am yours forever" said Jack as he sat up a bit and rolled over to kiss her. She smiled back at him. He slid her hand down between his legs and held him.

"Ready to go again?" she said then pushed him down on his back. She climbed on top of him and started sliding herself up and down on him. Just then they heard voices and footsteps on the dock.

"We should climb on board cut a hose or two and let her sink," said a raspy high pitched voice.

"No, he might still be around, his truck is still here." said a more familiar voice.

"He is probably with that nice piece of ass that has been following him around. We could steal it and use it for the run tonight."

"No, leave that fuckin' boat alone. We don't want to attract any more attention to ourselves. Them Russians wouldn't like us showing up in a strange boat anyway. We need to get your boat over to my place and get it loaded up. Fuckin' twenty-five crates came in by truck last night, and we need to get them to the pick-up boat by midnight. Casmiere will be over there soon, and I don't want to piss him off. Now quit fucking around and get your boat going."

Melissa and Jack had stopped to listen. Soon they heard an engine start and the sounds of a boat making its way through the water. Jack peaked out the window and saw Dale Rines's boat idling by with Dale and Tommy on board.

"I got to call Michael. He can get in touch with that DEA agent," said Jack.

"Well, it was fun while it lasted," said Melissa while putting her clothes back on.

Jack looked at her and then interrupted her getting dressed to hold her. She smiled back at him and caressed his arm. "Sorry we got interrupted, Melissa."

"Don't worry about it. We have all summer and we are going to make love every chance we get." Melissa responded.

Jack grinned back. He then put his clothes on and called Michael. Michael relayed the message to Elizabeth who then texted Agent Rand.

When Tommy and Dale tied the boat up at Tommy's, Casmiere was waiting there, smoking a cigarette. The smoke lingered around his head like a haunting fog as he watched Dale and Tommy load the crates onto the boat. One crate fell and broke open on the deck of Dale's boat.

"Guns?" Tommy said surprised. "I didn't agree to moving guns."

"Who cares what you move? You're getting paid to move stuff for us no matter what it is. Now pick up and put in another crate," Casmiere said.

"Look. You can't boss me around on my dock. I agreed to move and sell drugs. If you want me to move guns you need to pay me more."

"Mr. MacIntyre, come here. I show you something."

Tommy feared he had crossed a line, but walked up the ramp to Casmiere, who slowly reached into his coat. Tommy nervously watched his hand gripping a black object.

"Sorry, Casmiere, I…." Tommy stopped as soon as he saw it was a cell phone he had reached for. Casmiere had a grin on his face reveling in the fear Tommy showed. He opened up a video and showed it to Tommy. Tommy could see the back of his truck driving down the road. In front of him was Stephanie's car. You could hear the engine in Tommy's truck rev up before hitting the back of Stephanie's car. The car swerved, rolled and went into the water. Tommy got out of his truck and watched the car sink. He stood there for a while making sure she didn't come back up. He then picked up the pieces of taillight and then the video stopped.

"I was supposed to kill you and the girl that night, but because you killed her we decided to let you live. Now if you don't do what we want you to do, this video will be sent to the authorities, or you can continue to work for us and this video will stay right here and you will be a very rich man. We are always watching you. You may not see us, but we are always there," Casmiere said while putting the phone away. Casmiere smiled and motioned for Tommy and Dale to go back to work.

Across the street from Tommy's, Rand was camped out in her car where she had heard and recorded the conversation.

"Holy Shit," she said to herself. "I need to get that phone," she thought as she watched them load the boat and took more pictures. She left to catch Stryker and the crew that would be heading out to watch the transfer. While driving over to the Marine Patrol dock, she started thinking about what she had just heard. She couldn't see the screen on the phone Casmiere was holding but she could clearly hear that Tommy had killed somebody and the act was caught on that phone. "Who did he kill?" she thought to herself. "How and why?" When she got to the Marine Patrol Dock she found the crew ready to go. The FBI agent was an older man and looked like he had spent the past ten years driving a desk. Slightly overweight but still pretty husky. Blue jeans with a blue sport coat. A black FBI hat covering a balding head. He was talking to Stryker when she approached.

"Agent Carla Rand, meet an old friend of mine, FBI agent Dan Ross." Stryker said, standing up greeting agent Rand.

"Hello, Miss Rand. I understand you're the reason we are here tonight." Agent Ross spoke as he stood up to shake her hand.

"Thank you, and nice to have the FBI on board. Our reason for being here just got more complicated," She said while shaking his hand.

"How so, Carla?" asked Stryker.

"They are moving guns as well as the cocaine, and…there has been a murder."

"Murder…who….when?" prodded Stryker.

"I don't know who or when. I just know Tommy did it. The Russian, Casmiere, has the act recorded on his phone. I recorded the whole conversation, but you can't make out the video on the phone. I was too far away."

"Can you send me a copy of that video? Maybe one of our tech guys can enhance the video enough to make out the video on the phone," asked Ross.

"Yes, but please keep me in the loop."

"Carla…I am three weeks from retiring. From my point of view, you are the loop. I am just here as…mutual aid, let's call it," Ross said to reassure her.

Rand was thrilled. She had worked hard on this case. She wanted the credit for making the bust but most of all didn't want to see the case turned into a shit show and the bad guys to get away.

"Well, let's get going then. We need to get behind the island and into position, so they don't catch us on radar," Said Stryker.

Melissa and Jack had gotten dressed and left the boat. They made a quick stop at Melissa's so she could grab a few of her things. Jack was quiet in the truck; he was zoned out, driving with his right hand on the wheel and rubbing his face with his left.

"Jack, you ok?" asked Melissa.

"Yeah, just taking it all in."

Melissa paused a bit, then asked, "Any regrets?"

Jack had been thinking so hard about Tommy, Dale and the drugs he had almost forgotten he had just made love to Melissa. He put his left hand back on the steering wheel and held her hand with his right.

"Yes…we got interrupted," he said while smiling.

"Well…we have all night and all summer and…well, as long as we can keep this going," Melissa said.

"What are you saying? You aren't going back to Hollywood?"

"No. I am going back. I have to. I can't leave it the way I did. I'm not done being an actress yet. What I am saying is, I think we should try to stay together…after I go back."

Jack felt so relieved. He had been wondering what would happen at the end of summer. He had fallen in love with Melissa and dreaded letting her go. "It will be tough..but I know we can make it work," said Jack. Then started to boyishly giggle.

"What is so funny?"

"I am dating Melissa Andrews…I had sex with Melissa Andrews. THE Melissa Andrews."

"I am dating Jack Finn…I had sex with Jack Finn. THE Jack Finn," Melissa mocked back.

They laughed together, then soon pulled up to Jack's house. The lights were out at his mom and dad's house and it looked like Lucy and Sam had turned in for the night. As they walked towards the house Jack froze in his footsteps.

"Everything ok, Jack?" Melissa asked

"I have to take care of a couple things before you come inside," Jack said awkwardly.

Melissa had a feeling that this might happen. She waited patiently as Jack darted inside. In a few moments Jack came back to the doorway and waved Melissa in. As she walked in she noticed the picture of Jack and Stephanie was missing. She paused for a moment, wondering if Jack felt ashamed of bringing another woman into the house.

"Melissa…it's ok. I did it out of respect for both of you," said Jack from across the kitchen. Melissa smiled and her apprehension lifted. She walked to him. They kissed intensely for a moment. Melissa looked up into his eyes and spoke, "Let's get in bed."

Chapter 7

The Marine Patrol boat pulled up to a small dock on the northern end of Damariscove Island. Stryker and the other Marine Patrol officer stayed with the boat while agents Rand and Ross hiked across the island to an old, abandoned coast guard station that overlooked the harbor. The station was nothing more than a single room shack. A couple of windows looked towards the water. Agent Rand got her surveillance equipment out of her backpack. As she was setting up, a huge object appeared at the end of the small harbor. It was a yacht, around 60 feet in lenght. It came slowly into the small harbor. Once inside the harbor it turned so the transom was now visible. Rand turned on her video monitor. Looking at the laptop screen she could see the name of the yacht. "Красный утром" was written in black letters across the stern of the white hull. "Kransyy Utrom," Rand said to herself. Once the yacht was settled it dropped its anchor and killed all its lights. With the video equipment Rand could make out that there were three men tending to a small inflatable center console that was being put into the water. A woman was sitting at a table on the back deck of the boat with her legs up on the table and sipping a glass of something.

As Dale Rine's boat cut through the water, just outside of the little harbor everything was dark; the island just a shadow. He slowed down and navigated into the harbor, keeping an eye out for pot buoys and trying to stay in the channel. His eyes were straining to see what was in front of him when suddenly the small lobster boat was blasted with a shower of radiant light. Casmiere's cell phone rang and he lifted it to his ear. He listened briefly then abruptly said, "Stop the boat." Dale slowed the engine and took it out of gear. Before their eyes could adjust an inflatable tender sped out from around the stern of the yacht that had a spotlight fixed on Dale's boat. The inflatable came alongside and two huge men hopped onboard, grabbed Tommy and Dale's arms, and bent them behind their backs. Then the woman from the yacht climbed onboard leaving a third large man at the wheel of the inflatable. She was slender with dark scarlet hair. She wore a maroon leather jacket that was unzipped and a black shirt and black pants that left nothing to the imagination. When she turned, her stunning but cold glare directed at them. They began to struggle vainly out of both pride and fear.

"What the fuck is going on? Let go of me," said Tommy fighting to get away. The woman pulled a gun from the inside of her leather coat and held it to Tommy's head. Tommy stopped moving.

At that point Agent Rand started to scurry to her feet, trying to think about what to do. Agent Ross put his hand on her shoulder and motioned her to stay down.

"I hear you saw a video this evening, Mr. MacIntyre." Tommy recognized her voice as the one he identified as "HER" on his phone. "Did you like the video? I am sure the Boothbay Harbor Police would like it. I think the young woman's boyfriend... what is his name...Jack, would like it, too. My name is Katiya, we have talked before. Now let's be very clear about something, Mr. MacIntyre, you and this piece of shit work for me. If you want that video to remain a secret and you want to stay alive you will do what I say. Casmiere is my brother. If he gives you an order, consider it is me giving it to you. Do you understand that Mr. MacIntyre?" Katiya said, while still holding the gun to Tommy's head. Pushing it so hard against his forehead he could feel the muzzle against his skull.

"Yes...yes, Katiya," Tommy said shaking, while looking at the gun at his head.

She took the gun from Tommy's head and put it on Dale's. Dale started crying. "Please don't shoot me."

"Shut up, you little bitch. I know about new truck and blowing money at bars. I don't pull trigger because bullet is worth more than you."

She put the gun back in her coat and nodded to her men holding them. They let go of their arms but stayed standing behind them.

"Now, you listen. I have agreement to exchange much cocaine for money and guns. Your cut, Mr. MacIntyre, 18 million dollars to split with your boyfriend here. I will be riding back with you to give this deal full attention. Next few weeks you will receive trucks with my cocaine. When we have at your location, we will bring here and meet with buyer. Nothing can go wrong, do you understand. Now let's get these crates loaded onto my boat. Casmiere, go with my boat back to Boston," she ordered.

"Yes, Katiya. You sure you want to ride back with them?" Casmiere asked.

"I don't think they try anything. If they do, I shoot them," Katiya stated.

Dale, feeling a little brave, spoke out. "If you shoot us who will drive the boat?"

Katiya turned back towards Dale and walked to him. She reached down and grabbed him by his balls and squeezed as hard as she could without changing a facial expression.

"Your life on planet is my control. I- DON'T- NEED- YOU!" she said squeezing even harder between each word for emphasis. Her eyes flashed angrily as she let go of him, then quickly clipped his jaw with her elbow. He dropped to the deck holding himself.

"Enough fucking around, get cargo moved!" Katiya barked out. Tommy started loading crates into the inflatable. Dale fumbled uselessly behind him.

Agent Rand was beside herself trying to wrap her head around everything she had just heard and saw. She knew for sure now, who Tommy killed. She just didn't know when or how it happened.

"Carla, you know why I stopped you, right?" Ross said interrupting her thoughts.

"Yes, I would have blown the case for no good reason. Not much we could have done from here."

"Not only that, we only have two Glock 19's against God knows what."

"That's true, too."

"Carla, you are one hell of an agent. Just remember to stop and look at the big picture."

"Thanks, Dan."

"So, what is your next move?"

"I am going to call my boss in Boston, let him know everything I know and send him copies of everything I have. I am thinking we wait until they do the big move and bust them out here."

"Sounds good. I do have to call into the Bureau and let them know what is going on here. I will let them know it is in good hands and it is your baby. If you need anything, tell me. I can make it happen."

"Thanks."

They watched as the totes made their way from Dale's boat to the big yacht. When the inflatable had made its last run, the yacht shut off its lights and started bringing up its anchor. Dale, Tommy and Katiya headed out of the little harbor, then turned toward Boothbay Harbor. The yacht eased slowly out of the harbor and into the darkness.

As soon as the Kransyy Utrom was out of sight Rand and Ross walked back to the patrol boat to let the Commissioner know what was going on.

"Tommy killed Stephanie?!" Stryker spoke with more emotion than they had ever seen.

"That slimy piece of shit will be lucky if I don't kill him myself," Stryker continued.

"You knew her?" Rand asked.

"Everybody knew her. She was a sweet lovable girl. Always smiling," Stryker said while staring out the window of the boat.

"She volunteered a lot. Very active, just a damn good kid. Everybody thought her and Jack were going to get married. Russell loved her. She was like daughter to him. When she died I watched Russell stay as strong as he could for Jack, but when he thought no one was looking that man would cry." He reminisced further. Stryker gathered himself a bit then turned to Ross and Rand. "We have to nail that son of a bitch."

"We will get them all, Commissioner," said Rand.

They waited for Dale's boat and the yacht to get out of radar range then untied the boat and headed back to Boothbay Harbor. Everyone was quiet on the cruise back. All were processing everything they had just learned. Commissioner Stryker was thinking about the next time he and Russell would talk. How would he be able to talk to him, look him in the eyes and not say what he knew. He thought back to Stephanie's funeral, watching Russell with his hand on Jack's shoulder. He remembered sitting at the bar at Tommy's listening to Russell worry about his son because Jack was blaming himself for Stephanie's death. While the real person responsible was probably snorting a line off his desk. Agent Rand was lost in her thoughts as well. Feeling overwhelmed and under qualified. She thought she was just busting Tommy, a small time dealer, but now she was against the Russian mob. Drugs, guns, cash, and murder all in the fire with a lot of innocent people dangling over it. She planted her face in her hands trying to gather tangible thoughts. She felt a hand on her shoulder. Dan Ross had seen agents do this many times in his long career. "Carla," he said to get her full attention. "You are doing a good job. If your feeling overwhelmed it is because you care, you give a damn. You are going to nail this case. I know you will. If I didn't, I wouldn't be letting you run with it." Rand smiled and said, "Thanks, Dan."

Back at Tommy's Dale had tied up his boat, and the three were walking up the ramp. Katiya turned to them both at the top of the ramp.

"Remember, I am always watching you." She walked away and got into Casmiere's car and drove off.

"This shit is getting out of hand Tommy. We almost died. If Jack Finn finds out you killed Stephanie, he will kill you," Dale said in a panic.

"He isn't going to find out, and you're the only one that almost died, mouthing off. She castrated you, now get your shit together. This is the deal we have been waiting for— eighteen million dollars. That's on top of what we have already made. We can get the fuck out of here and never look back," Tommy said, while trying to light a cigarette with his shaking hands.

"What will you do about this place?" Dale asked.

"Burn it; they will think I went with it. All the evidence, everything gone. Let the Finns start up from ashes."

"What should I do?"

"We can have your boat tied up at the dock. When this place goes, it will go with it…with a little help."

Dale and Tommy got into their trucks and drove off. Over at Captain Fishes Hotel Katiya was settling into the room that Casmiere had been in. The window looked right over at Tommy's. She could watch him very closely right from there. He had sound equipment set up and video recordings. There was a 3 ring binder with pictures Cashmiere had taken of people at Tommy's with names and notes. She sat down on the bed and looked through it. The first set of pictures was of Tommy. Then some of Dale. He had their home addresses with pictures of where they lived. A basic schedule of what they did. The next set of pictures were of Elizabeth. He had written: No threat. Just works for Tommy's real business. Pictures of Agent Rand in her Marine Patrol Uniform and Commissioner Stryker said: Possible threat watch carefully. Then there were pictures of Jack and Russell Finn. On Jack's picture it said: No threat. Boyfriend of girl Tommy killed. He had pictures of all the truck drivers, the real ones and the drug runners.

"Good work, Casmiere," she said to herself out loud. She put the binder down on the table and undressed herself. She got into bed while planning out just how to get rid of Tommy and Dale when the big deal was over.

Jack woke up to his cell phone alarm going off and rolled over expecting to see Melissa, but she was not in his bed. He got up and put on his boxers and pants and walked through the house to find her. He found her sitting in a chair on the front porch. She had found one of his flannel shirts and put it on. She looked so sexy with her bare legs resting on a small table in front of the chair, sitting listening to the sounds around her and sipping a cup of coffee. She looked so relaxed he almost didn't want to disturb her. He leaned out of the doorway putting his foot down on the deck. As his foot pushed down on the deck board, it let out a small creak. Melissa turned and smiled warmly.

"What are you doing?" she asked.

"Enjoying the view." Obviously, he was referring to her.

"Me, too," she said, as she turned her head and looked out over Lobster Cove.

"Whatcha thinkn'?"

"Nothing. For once my mind is at peace. I am just sitting here in this old chair in my underwear and an old flannel shirt. I am watching a squirrel. I hear birds. I smell the ocean."

Jack didn't know what to say. Melissa looked so happy and peaceful.

"What ta' hell are you two doing hanging out outside half naked?" Russell broke the tranquil moment.

Jack was about to get mad at his father for interrupting Melissa's moment of peace, but he saw her smile and respond, "Why are you staring at me half naked you old pervert?"

"Ha, Jack, you hear that. She's learning. She don't take any shit!"

"What are you doing out here, Dad?" Jack asked

"Well, if you don't remember, I only live a hundred feet away. I was walking by to get the paper and heard voices. That's when I stumbled on to this.....business." Russell said, while motioning towards them with his arms. "Now you two put some clothes on and we can all head down to Ebb Tide for some fish hash and pancakes. My treat." Russell answered, as he continued on his way to get the newspaper out of the mailbox. Melissa thought it was cute that he wouldn't look at her directly. She stood up and walked back into the house, giving Jack a kiss as she walked back in. Jack stood in the doorway watching Melissa walk thru the house in bare feet. The flannel shirt seemed to dance around her body, airy like a sheet hanging on a clothes line. She had the sleeves rolled up just a bit and the tail of the shirt would float up enough to see her black underwear once in a while. When she turned to face him he saw it was just buttoned high enough to cover her beasts, but still show some cleavage. "Jack, Do you mind if I keep this shirt?" She asked.

"No, I don't," Jack responded with a childish smirk on his face.

"Stop grinning, you pervert. I would think you had enough by now."

Jack walked to Melissa and wrapped his arms around her and gave her a kiss. "Melissa, I could almost blow off the fish hash and the races, just to spend the weekend in my bed with you."

"That would be boring," Melissa replied.

Jack was completely shocked. He thought Melissa enjoyed him, at least that is what it seemed like. He looked at her. She started to grin and said "I mean...just in your bed? What about the living room, or the kitchen, or in the shower?" They kissed, then laughed, and then kissed some more. Eventually they got dressed. Jack packed a small gym bag for the weekend. Melissa grabbed her bag and they met Russell and Anne in the driveway, got in the car and headed into town.

Ebb Tide was a small diner in downtown Boothbay Harbor. It served homestyle New England dishes. They opened at 5 o'clock in the morning to cater to the lobstermen crowd and closed at five in the afternoon so older people could come for an early dinner. The breakfast menu was simple: however many eggs cooked however you liked with whatever you want in them. Plain, Maine blueberry, or chocolate chip pancakes stacked as high as you wanted and bacon, breakfast sausage, hash browns and toast available on the side. They rotated several dishes for specials, biscuits and gravy, cinnamon rolls the size of a dinner plate, breakfast steak and french toast an inch thick just to name a few. This morning was Russell's favorite, a big bowl of fish hash, made from smoked Atlantic Codfish, fried with finely diced potatoes and onions and served with a slice of grilled toast.

As the Finn's and Melissa walked in, a waitress waved at them from across the diner and made her way to their table. She was tall and looked to be in her 50's. Her navy blue uniform was clean and pressed. Her long blond hair tied up in a bun. Melissa thought it was odd that she didn't have any note book or pen.

"Hey guys, how is it going? Haven't seen you guys in a bit."

"We are doing good; it's been busy. The shedders came a little early this year." Russell answered.

"That's what I have been hearing. I also have heard all about you, Madison. You are as pretty as all the rumors."

Melissa blushed. "Thank you, didn't know I was so famous." Melissa said while she considered the irony of what she just said.

"It's a small town, dear, with lots of mouths and ears. A few people said you are a dead ringer for that Melissa Andrews, but she is a little chunkier and a brunette. Anyway, I hope she gets an Oscar for that movie. I think she was a better Judy Garland than Judy Garland."

The Finns and Melissa had to fight back their laughter.

"How have you been, Andrea?" Anne asked to change the subject.

"Oh, I am good. Working here and taking care of Henry keeps me busy."

"How is Henry?" Russell asked.

Andrea paused, you could tell something just struck a note. "He is doing alright. He is comfortable and happy."

"If you need any help around the house, lawn mowed, wood stacked, or trash taken to the dump, let me know," Jack said as he wrote his cell phone number on a napkin and started to pass it to her. Melissa intercepted it and stole the pen out of Jack's hand. She wrote down her alias and her real number.

"I can help, too…if you don't mind."

Andrea bit her lip holding back emotion. "Thank you." She paused a bit. "What can I get you folks."

While they gave her their order Melissa was amazed that she didn't write any of it down. After they were done she repeated the order back in the same order she got it without missing a single detail. Andrea walked away and gave the order to the kitchen.

"Melissa, I am some damn proud of you, kiddo. You are catching on to this small town living thing," Russell said, while Anne nodded in approval. Melissa smiled proudly. She didn't know the story with Henry, and she didn't have to. She saw enough with expressions and gestures to know something was wrong. Soon their breakfast was on the table and they ate and talked. Melissa furthered her education on the locals and some of the town history. She was listening carefully when an ad in the local paper that was sitting on the table caught her eye.

Tindal & Callahan Reality: For Sale 2 bedroom 1.5 bath 1000 sq.ft. On a wooded .5 acre lot. Located at 11 Old Stone Wall Rd in Boothbay Harbor. Private secluded location. Cozy fireplace.

She reached over and grabbed the paper. It had a small black and white picture of the house. She stopped and thought for a bit. She showed it to Jack and said, "Am I nuts or does this seem like a good idea?"

Jack looked at the ad and rubbed his chin and said, "Are you thinking of living here and not going back to Hollywood?"

Russell and Anne were now paying attention to the conversation.

"No, I am going to go back, but I am going to want to come back here as much as possible. I don't want to rush me and you, so having my own place makes sense."

"Yeah, it does make sense, but there are bigger and nicer places than that around here."

"I have a mansion, Jack. When I come back to Boothbay Harbor I want to forget that lifestyle. I want small and hidden. This place is perfect!"

Jack looked at the ad a little closer. "Hey, this place is close to where you're staying now."

Russell and Anne took a look at the ad. "We know the real estate agents. We could get in touch with them for you. We could tell them we are looking to use it for a summer rental," said Anne.

"Would you? That would be awesome!"

"I will give them a call Monday."

They were finishing up their breakfast when Tommy MacIntyre strolled in. He found an empty seat and practically fell into it. You could tell by the look on some of the faces of the people sitting close to him he stunk to high heaven. He was still wearing the clothes they saw him in on Friday and looked like he hadn't slept all week. He was constantly sniffing and wiping his nose. He peered over at the Finns almost like he was looking past them. He gave a halfhearted wave in their direction. The Finns all responded with a nod or wave.

"We should get going," Russell stated.

"I can't stand to look at him. Filthy…just filthy." Anne said, shaking her head. They got up from the table. Russell left a $50 dollar bill to cover the bill that was a little over thirty dollars. They were just about at the door when Tommy spoke up.

"Jack," Tommy said loud enough to bring the whole diner to silence. "Just about two weeks until the anniversary." Tommy paused for a bit. "Five years, ain't it?"

Jack had a lump in his throat. Every bit of good feeling he just had drained from his body.

"Well, it looks like you've moved on." Tommy drove the last nail in the coffin. Jack's tightened his right hand, veins started showing down his arm. Suddenly he felt a soft warm hand hold his tense fist. "She wouldn't want this." Jack turned to see Melissa holding his fist. Suddenly the lump in his throat was gone. He took a deep breath and relaxed. Jack turned back toward Tommy and spoke. "I have moved on, Tommy, thank you, but she will never be forgotten." With that the Finns walked out of Ebb Tide.

"I am proud of you, Jack. He dealt a low blow and you handled it well." Russell said proudly.

"Like you said, I got Mom's temper and brains." Jack replied.

"Damn, Jack, you owned that moment." Melissa cheered.

"It would have been a lot worse if you weren't there, thank you."

"So, what's the plan, Jack? I got to head back to the house to get my boat loaded with all the coolers and the grill. Then bring her around into the harbor." stated Russell.

"Why don't I go with you guys and help load the boat?" Melissa suggested.

"That's not a bad idea. I can walk to my boat from here. Michael and I can get a spot next to the track toward the finish line," said Jack.

"Sounds good, Cap. We'll see you soon," Russell said.

Melissa gave Jack a quick kiss goodbye and got into the car with Russell and Anne. Jack started at a fast pace towards his boat. While he walked over the footbridge that stretched across the inner harbor, he looked out over the Harbor. He could see Clive Farrin was out setting up the race coarse. Boats were starting to leave Brown Brothers Wharf. He could see the dock where his boat and Michael's boat were tied up. Michael and his family had just pulled into the parking lot with their minivan. Josh and Elizabeth hopped out. It was a scene he had seen many times. He swore every time those kids jumped out of that van they grew. Elizabeth was just six years old, and Josh was three when Michael had moved back into Boothbay Harbor. Michael had grown up here and joined the Navy right out of High School. After getting out he found work at Strouts Point Wharf Company in Freeport, Maine. Soon he met Abigail, got married and along came Elizabeth and Josh. Michael had always wanted to work for himself. So, with the support of Strouts, Michael built his mobile marine mechanic business, being one of the first to offer assistance while on the water. Soon they moved back to Boothbay Harbor, and Jack was one of Michael's first customers. Despite a big age difference, they became tight friends, with Jack even babysitting once in a while. Now Jack looked at kids, not all grown up but pretty close. Jack hoped Michael would lighten up on Melissa. Michael was dead wrong about Melissa. What would it take to get him to see it?

"Hey, there he is. Hi, Jack." Abigail greeted him with a hug.

"Hi, Abby, how are you guys this morning?" Jack asked.

"Well, the kids and I are good. Mr. Grumpy Pants down there is all wound up."

"Why is he all wound up?"

"After he got your text last night he put two and two together."

"What do you mean?"

"Jack.,.10:30 at night and you are down on your boat…with Melissa."

"Oh, for Christ's sake. What is his problem with her."

"He is super sensitive right now. With Elizabeth going into her senior year. All the colleges she picked are out of state. She is too busy to hang out with him. Now this deal with Tommy."

"What should I do?"

"Give him space. She seems like a really nice girl, and I am so happy for you. He will figure it out soon enough."

"Thanks, Abigail. Let me grab one of these coolers for you."

Jack grabbed a cooler and carried it down the ramp. He could see Michael shuffling stuff around on board the Overtime.

Jack tried to start the conversation outright. "Morning, going to be one hell of a day out today. Where do you want this cooler."

"On the boat," Michael replied in short.

Jack fought back the urge to pick the fight that Michael was looking for. "Where? Up under the transom or just behind the engine box?"

"I will just take it from you, for Christ sake." Michael snatched the cooler from his hands.

"Michael!" Jack yelled.

"What?" Michael responded, staring shocked at his friend.

"I love her. With all my heart. For once in five years I feel good again. I trust her. I would trust her with my life. She is a good person. My whole family thinks so. Your wife and daughter think so. I love you, man. You are my best friend. You and your wife held me up and kept me going when all I wanted to do was lay in bed and cry. You have trusted me with your kids. Your son's life is in my hands everyday he steps aboard. Trust me on this. Don't make me choose between you and her."

Michael looked at his friend. He didn't dare ask who Jack would pick. If he was about to take this stand for her, she must be worth it. He set the cooler down and extended his hand. They gripped each other's hand in a firm hand shake while smiling at each other.

"You guys will have to come over for dinner one night."

"Sure thing, man." Jack responded.

After getting the boats loaded, started and untied, they headed away from the dock. They let Josh lead the way in his skiff, with one hand on the wheel and the other on the davit. He looked like he was a champion race car driver headed for the race track. He held his head high with his hat turned backward. He spotted the Old Smoke and headed in that direction. Michael watched his son from behind the wheel of Overtime and Jack brought up the rear with Red at Night. When all the boats were tied together and anchored securely Elizabeth and Abigail set up chairs and Melissa climbed onboard Red at Night. Michael headed over to see her.

"Melissa----"

"She turned to him wondering what was coming.

"I...I'm sorry. I've been an ass."

Melissa smiled and responded, "From what I understand, you were being protective of your daughter and your best friend. I can respect that."

"Thank you, just do me one favor. Take good care of him. He is a damn good man."

"I will, and you're not a bad man yourself."

Michael blushed, then gave Melissa a big bear hug. Everyone noticed, no one commented, they just smiled.

Soon a familiar voice boomed over the VHF. "Welcome everybody to the 35th Annual Boothbay Harbor Lobsterboat races. I need all of the Boothbay Boats gas classes to head down to the starting area. I also have a young sternwoman in the crowd that has volunteered to do the National Anthem. Madison Adams, you have our undivided attention," Clive Farrin announced.

All were shocked except Melissa and Russell. Melissa made her way to Russell's boat and grabbed the VHF microphone. The harbor filled with the sound of Melissa's voice. When she finished there was a round of applause that could be heard up on shore.

"Glad I bought that new radio," said Russell.

"You two are sneaky. I had no idea." Jack said shaking his head.

Michael started laughing.

"What's so funny, Michael?" asked Abigail.

"This whole harbor just heard Melissa Andrews sing the National Anthem live and they have no clue," he chuckled.

"So what happens now?" Melissa asked.

Russell explained, "All the local boats that have gasoline engines race. They split them up in two classes — small block and big block. Then the two Boothbay boat diesel classes will race. You and I are in the first class because we are under 500 horsepower. Then Jack and Michael are in the second class, which is 500 horsepower and over. After those races, the real races start. They start off with the outboard classes, then gas powered classes, then the diesel classes. All the classes are broken up by length of boat and horsepower. You and I will head up after the first gas class. You still up for running the boat?"

"Yes, who is going to be racing us?"

"Clive and Jim. Maybe Dale Rines if he is up and about."

"How will we do?"

"We will smoke Jim. Dale has the same hull with the same horsepower so that will be a good race. Clive will toast us," Russell grumbled.

The conversation was interrupted by the sound of the gas powered lobster boats coming down the track. Most of them were more noise than speed, owned by guys that were just getting started in the business, part timers or older lobstermen that were just too stubborn to retire. Russell untied the boat and Melissa jumped on board. The Old Smoke made its way down to the starting line with Melissa at the helm. After getting to the starting area, Russell chimed in with instructions and pointers.

"Listen. That blue boat over there is the start boat. They will raise a big pirate flag here in a bit. When they do, you want to be right beside them. Keep one hand on the throttle and the other on the wheel. You got to bounce your eyes back and forth a bit from looking ahead to watching the flag. When that flag drops you creep that throttle up nice and steady. You won't hurt anything if you push it too fast. She just takes off better under a steady hand. Check the gauges once in a while. If the temp gauge goes over 210, back down slow and easy. She'll want to roll a bit when Clive goes by. Just make small corrections. You'll do fine."

"You're going to be right here, right?" Melissa asked.

"Hell no, she goes better with the weight aft. I am going to sit on the stern and have me a pipe," Russell said as he packed a load of tobacco into his pipe.

Melissa was nervous now. This was the craziest thing she had done in a long time. She felt like she was going to puke at any moment. She was about to wave to Russell to have him take the wheel, but the flag went up. She throttled up to match speed with the start boat. She glanced ahead briefly to make sure she was headed straight, then she looked back to her right to check the start boat again. Just as she did, the flag dropped. Melissa whipped her head back around and focused down the track. All nervousness gone in that instant. She pushed the throttle ahead until it stopped and kept it pinned there. As predicted, Clive's boat, Sea Swallow started going by. Old Smoke rolled some, but Melissa kept her straight and true. Then suddenly, a giant puff of black smoke belched from the Sea Swallow and slowed to a stop. Melissa kept the throttle pinned as she went by. She passed the finish boat and slowed down easily. She turned back to Russell who had his old ball cap on backwards and his pipe firmly in his teeth with a big grin.

"Holy shit, Russell, that was awesome!" She was beaming.

"Good job, kiddo. First place! Now swing by the finish float and get your prize. Then we gotta check on Clive."

Melissa had become a natural at running the boat. She eased into the finish float and collected the prize. She passed the envelope back to Russell, then headed toward Sea Swallow.

"Pull up on his port side. I will put some bumpers out. Make sure my davit is behind his cabin." Russell ordered. She eased up alongside and backed down bringing Old Smoke to a stop. They tied the boats together.

"Where do you want to go, Clive?" Russell asked.

"Take me back to the finish float. I am fucking done with this Caterpillar piece of shit. I'm getting Michael to order me a Cummins first thing Monday morning."

Russell motioned to have Melissa start going.

"I have never towed a boat before," Said Melissa.

"Well you are today. Just put him on the back side of the finish float so he can still announce and be out of the way," Russell ordered.

Melissa put the boat in gear and started pulling the Sea Swallow along. When they started getting close to the dock, Clive started calling out how many feet were between the dock and his boat. When Clive called out "1 foot" she figured that was close enough and backed down hard to get both boats to stop and drift towards the dock. After Clive was tied up, she and Russell untied and headed back towards their group. When they got back, it was just Josh and Abigail sitting in Josh's skiff.

"Where did everybody go?" Melissa asked while tying up to Josh's skiff.

"Jack and Michael are both in this race. Elizabeth went with Jack and Anne went with Michael." Abigail answered.

"Don't worry, kiddo. Jack will take you for a race before the day is out. He has two, maybe three, races left," said Russell.

"Miss Andrews, you can race with me!" Josh suggested.

"That sounds like a wonderful idea Josh."

"We are in the second outboard class so we can watch Dad and Jack go at it."

Just as Josh said that, Clive could be heard announcing the race. Melissa looked towards the starting line. There were five boats in the race. Overtime was closest to the start boat. To his port was Heather Thompson in Gold Digger, then there was Jack in Red at Night. To his port was a lobsterboat she had seen at Tommy's called Lucky Catch. The last boat was another boat she had seen around but didn't know. Soon the flag went up and all the boats lurched forward. All the boats were lined up even when the flag dropped. Overtime jumped into the lead with Red at Night close behind. Right on Jack's stern was Gold Digger. The three of them came down the track for a one, two, three finish.

"First place, Overtime with a speed of 45.5 MPH. Second place, Red at Night with a speed of 32.9 MPH. Third place, Gold Digger with a speed of 31.5."

"Wait a minute. Jack and Michael were going much faster than that yesterday afternoon. What gives?" Melissa asked.

"Both Dad and Jack have competition here today. They don't want to show off what they can do just yet." Josh answered.

"These guys…you would think they were racing for a million dollars. What a blast," Melissa exclaimed.

"Alright, Miss Andrews, you ready?" asked Josh.

"Sure am, Josh, let's go," Melissa responded and they headed to race.

Melissa had a blast watching Josh from the stern of his skiff. He was racing against some of his friends from school, so the teenage boys were all a little shocked to see a beautiful grown woman riding with Josh. Melissa grinned as she figured out Josh was just showing off to his friends. Josh placed second and collected his prize, a free pizza at a local pizza joint. He was quite happy with that. In all the commotion, Melissa realized she had never checked what she had won. It didn't really matter, she was having one of the best days of her life. When they got back to the raft of boats, she climbed back aboard Red at Night. The group talked and watched the races while Anne fired up the grill. Before long there were burgers and hotdogs all around. Out of the Williams's cooler came a big bowl of pasta salad. Jack told Melissa quietly that it was the best pasta salad on the planet, even better than his mother's. Soon it was time for Jack to race again. This time he pulled the engine box off and moved it to the stern. He told Melissa to sit low and not on top of the transom. They made their way down to the starting line. Off to his starboard, Jack could see Marshall Weston in Minor Details trying to get the spot closest to the race boat. Jack gave a wave to Marshall and Marshall returned the wave. Minor Details slid between the Red at Night and the start boat. Jack waved for Melissa to come up to the helm.

"This is a tight race with lots of boats," Jack yelled over the sound of the engine. "I need to keep my eyes forward. Slap my shoulder when the flag drops, ok?"

"Ok," answered Melissa.

Jack grabbed one of the ropes that were tied to the rail of the boat. "Hold on to this. When I hit the throttle, it pulls like all hell."

The flag on the start boat went up. Jack hit the throttle and matched speed. Melissa had her eyes locked in on the flag. She kept watching while listening to the throttle changes. When it dropped, Melissa slapped Jack's shoulder and he pinned the throttle. Red at Night jumped out in front. Jack came off the throttle a bit to keep Minor Details just behind amidships. Then suddenly, Minor Details gained ground. Jack answered with more throttle, but it wasn't enough. Melissa watched Minor Details slide by slowly and take first place. She looked at Jack expecting to see him disappointed, but he had a big grin on his face.

"What's so funny? He beat you."

"I still had some throttle left and I never hit the water meth injection," Jack said, grinning from ear to ear.

"I got second place. That puts me in the Diesel Free For All. I won't hold anything back on that one."

They idled back to their raft of boats. Michael was heading up for his race, with Elizabeth and Josh riding along, but when Overtime was headed down the track it was Josh at the helm. A boat named Piss Pot was trying to make a move past him, but Josh kept giving just enough throttle to stay ahead.

Soon it was time for the Diesel Free For All. All boats that had placed in the top three in their race could run in their respective Free For All gas or diesel. Melissa decided to sit and watch Jack race for a change. Jack had Elizabeth on board while Josh ran Overtime again. The flag dropped and they came screaming down the track. Overtime leading the pack with Piss Pot tailing close by. Battling for third was Minor Details and Red at Night. It almost seemed that Minor Details was going to win when Red at Night made a sudden lurch forward. It was so close they had to wait for Clive to announce the results.

"First Place goes to Overtime with a speed of 51 MPH. Second Place goes to Piss Pot with a speed of 50.5 MPH. And third goes to Minor Details with a speed of 38 MPH."

"Damn, That was close. Jack must have waited too long before hitting the water meth," said Russell

Jack came back to the raft of boats and tied up. He was shaking his head as he shut down the boat.

"What happened Jack?" Melissa asked.

"He snuck up on me. I hit the first water meth but hesitated. Before I hit the second time, he was already going by."

"You will get another chance in Rockland, don't you worry," said Russell.

"It will be tight. He has done something. I used to get him right out of the hole." Jack said.

They all turned their attention to the last race of the day, the Fastest Lobsterboat Afloat. At the starting area, Josh had Overtime closest to the start boat, then next to him was a red, gas powered boat named Thunder Bolt. Marshall Weston was next to him in Minor Details, with four more boats off to his port.

"Overtime and Thunder Bolt will be one hell of a race!" Jack said as he stepped up on the rail.

The flag went up and all the boats lined up and were heading down the track, then the flag dropped. Thunder Bolt sprung out ahead of Overtime by a boat length. The gap slowly closed. Overtime started breaking away; it seemed like half the boat was out of water. You could see Josh at the helm with his hat turned backwards and a big grin on his face. At the finish Overtime had it by half a boat length. Everybody cheered. After visiting the finish float for the prize, they came back over to the raft of boats.

"Good job, Josh!" Abigail cheered.

"Josh didn't mess around. He nailed the throttle and hit the first water meth right off the start. He dumped the second one about half track." Michael was almost shouting with excitement.

The Races were over, and it was time to go in and collect whatever hat drawing prizes they had coming. Jack and Russell talked to Marshall Weston and a few other lobstermen from the other towns. Clive pulled Michael aside to have him order a new engine. Melissa, Abigail, Anne and Elizabeth had some girl time talking about the guys. Josh was talking to his friends about running his dad's boat down the track. After all the awards were collected and everybody had their fill of food and drinks, they headed back out to the boats and steamed for Owl's Head just outside of Rockland Harbor. Melissa sat in a chair perched on the engine box with her feet up on the dash of the boat. Relaxing with a beer in her hand, she started thinking about the house in the paper. She liked the idea of a place to stay when she came back. She might even buy a small car to keep here so she wouldn't have to worry about renting a car. When would be the next visit? She didn't know what she was going to be getting into when she got back to Hollywood. There would definitely be press conferences.

"Over The Rainbow" had become a major hit in the box offices so there would be interviews about that. The Oscars would be in February. She definitely wanted to be back before then.

"Jack, what is it like here in the winter?" Melissa asked.

"Cold, very cold and snowy."

"What do you do for fun?"

"Well, that is a tough question. Pre-Melissa, Jack would just work on boats, lobster when I can and sit around the house."

"What about post Melissa, Jack?"

Jack grinned. "Work on boats, lobster when I can and have sex around the house."

"Pervert," Melissa said, slapping his shoulder.

"I don't know. Whenever you come back, we will have to think of something. The harbor gets very quiet during the winter. In the fall I watch Josh play football and Elizabeth play soccer. In the winter I go watch their swim meets."

"You love those kids, don't you?"

"Yes, it's hard not to, they're good kids."

"Do you want kids someday, Jack?"

Jack was caught completely off guard. He hadn't thought about having kids since Stephanie. He knew he loved kids. He always considered it a privilege to be a part of Elizabeth's and Josh's lives.

"Yes, I do. Someday," He answered.

"Me, too." Melissa answered, faster than she could think. With her childhood non-existent, she always felt she could possibly gain some of it back with her own children. They smiled at each other both knowing they were getting a little ahead of themselves.

"Are you still thinking about buying that house?" Jack asked.

"Yes, I am just trying to figure out how I can do it on the down low. I don't want to use my agent or lawyer for it. I want as much separation between that life and here as possible. I also think I want to get a car while I am here. Nothing special, I don't want to have to rent a car every time I come back."

"If you want to stay under cover while you're here and be able to get around, you should get a truck with four wheel drive. Roads can be terrible in the winter especially where that house is. That would be a site for the paparazzi. Melissa Andrews driving in an old pick-up truck."

"It wouldn't be the first time a celebrity has done that. Colin Farrel drives an old Ford Bronco."

"Why? With all his money, I would be driving a Mercedes G class AMG."

"It's hard to stay low profile when you do that. Jack, I know we have talked about this, and I don't mean to sound like the cliché "poor famous celebrity", but it is tough. Think about this. You get up and head down to the dock on a day you're not lobstering, right?"

"Yeah."

"Ok, you get out of your truck and someone you don't know suddenly wants a selfie and an autograph."

"I got the time, why not."

"Fair enough, you get down to the dock and start having your coffee and within fifteen minutes there is a ton of people showing up at the dock all wanting selfies and autographs and asking personal questions."

"How does that happen? They don't know I'm there."

"Yes, they do because the first person posted that selfie on Facebook and gave away your location. Now you have to leave to get clear of all the people."

"Ok, it sucks but I get in my truck and leave."

"Not that simple. While you are trying to leave, the mob gets bigger because everybody is posting their selfies with you. Your truck is surrounded by strangers that think just because they are your biggest fan they are entitled to your time. As you try to slowly back away you accidentally back into one of them. Now you're all over YouTube, Facebook, and whatever else. There's a lawsuit against you. Suddenly you're the bad guy and all you wanted to do is have a cup of coffee with friends."

Jack stared at Melissa thinking for a bit. This was a side of the Hollywood life he never saw. He understood now why she wanted to keep that life so far away from what she had here.

"So is that your dream car if you won the lottery, a Mercedes G class AMG?" Melissa asked to lighten the mood.

"Yeah, I actually went on line and did the build and price thing. It came out to a little over $229,000. I could sell the boat and get one, but I can't haul traps in an SUV."

"No optional trap hauler?" Melissa asked jokingly.

"Or radar, but it did have GPS," he said chuckling.

Melissa took a long deep breath of the salt air and studied the rocky coast as they were going by. She could see on the GPS names of the islands and towns they were going by. Names like Pemaquid and Musgongus reflected the rich Native American history. While other names like Allen Island and Port Clyde were clues to early English settlers. The Coast looked jagged and hard. Mostly rock and ledges, but some small openings of beaches and soft terrain. The Maine coast to Melissa was much like the people that lived on it. Hard and tough on the outside looking in, but once you get inside you feel the warmth of the local hospitality. She looked at Jack staring out over the bow, leaning against the davit with a beer in his right hand and the wheel in his left. What would it be like to be married to him? How would Jack react to the Hollywood lifestyle? He would probably argue with Maureen about doing his own dishes and cleaning up the kitchen. Jack would look so handsome in a tuxedo escorting her on the red carpet. Would he be shy at first, then slowly adapt to the environment? What would the media say? She laughed to herself, who cares what they would say? How would Boothbay Harbor treat her if they knew who she was? All these questions and the only way to answer them is to jump in and find out.

"Jack, have you ever traveled?" Melissa asked.

"Not out of the country. Went to Disney in Florida when I was a kid. Went to Colonial Williamsburg for a high school trip. Why?"

"Just picturing you in Hollywood visiting me. Maybe going to the Oscars with me."

"Holy shit, really…that would be nuts. Could I?"

Melissa was almost shocked. Jack looked like a kid all excited for Christmas. She figured that there would be some hesitation, but there he was ready to go now.

"Sure, um, the Oscars are in February at the end of the month. Do you want to come to Hollywood then?"

"Sure, get away from Maine in the winter. Go somewhere new. Meet some more celebrities."

"Ok then…it's a date." Then Melissa had a thought. "Do you think your mom and Dad would come?"

"I don't know. The first thing dad will say is "that's a lot of money" and start listing off all the expenses."

"That is easy. I will fly them. They can stay at my house. Don't worry, it's big enough so we will all have privacy."

"Well, you may be opening up another can of worms with that. Dad may see that as a hand out, and you already know how he is with that."

"Well, I will ask them. It would mean a lot to me if they were there."

Jack nodded in agreement; he knew that his folks meant a lot to Melissa. If they tried to argue about it he would give them a little nudge.

The boats set anchor in Owls Head Harbor and soon the air was filled with the smell of sizzling steaks and chicken. Food was shared from boat to boat and from family to family. Melissa decided to wait to ask Russell and Anne to come to the Oscars. After food and plenty of drinks, the stories and jokes came out along with some music. The night of partying and enjoying friendship ended with a slow dance to Russell's favorite song. Eventually all the boats pulled away to find their own anchoring spots. The night fell quiet as everyone turned in for the night.

Chapter 8

Monday morning Agent Rand sat at her kitchen table with a cup of coffee and bagel in the other. She opened her laptop, logged in and saw an unread email from the FBI agent Ross. She clicked on it at once and soon the message was open with an attachment. The message read, "Here you go Carla. Almost like we took the video ourselves." She couldn't wait to see the video. She clicked on the attachment. Soon she was watching a late model Dodge pickup with a wooden flatbed following a small blue car. The video was so clear she could see the plate numbers on both vehicles. She took a moment to catch a screenshot, then continued the video. The small blue car started around a sharp bend; just as it did, the truck sped ahead slamming the car, spinning it sideways. The car slid off the road and rolled violently into the water. The truck stopped and a figure stepped out which could be clearly recognized as Tommy MacIntyre. He watched the car sink into the water, picked up all the pieces of a broken taillight and tossed them into a toolbox in the back of the truck. As Tommy turned his truck around you could hear a male voice with a Russian accent saying, "He took care of her, you want me take care of him?" There was a pause then "OK, let him live." As Tommy's truck went by you could see the front bumper was bent and had some blue paint on it. Rand didn't know whether to cry or jump for joy. Sad that a young woman was killed, but overjoyed that she had solid evidence linking Tommy to it. She took more screen shots of the blue car and Tommy's truck. She already knew who the car belonged to, but she needed confirmation. Stryker would be able to ID it along with DMV records. She forwarded the email and attachment to Stryker with a message. "You are going to want to sit down. Call me when you can." She leaned back in her chair recovering from the video. Just as she got up to get dressed her phone rang. It was Stryker already.

"Good morning, Commissioner. How are you?"

"Bouncing between grief and all outrage."

"I figured. I need you to confirm that that is Stephanie's car, and I am also going to run the numbers through the DMV. I haven't seen Tommy driving that truck around. Did he sell it?"

"I haven't seen that truck in years…. probably five years. How about you get suited up in that Marine Patrol uniform I gave you. I will come pick you up and we can go visit his house."

"Sounds like a plan, but he will want to know why we are there. What will we tell him?"

"I don't know yet, but I will think of something."

"See you soon. I'll make some extra coffee."

"Carla…after that video…I don't need coffee."

Rand got showered up and into the Marine Patrol uniform. Soon Stryker was at her door. She got into his truck, closed the door and looked at his face and could tell he was upset.

"Are you going to be able to do this?" she asked.

"Yah, just opened up an old wound. The local police never looked too hard into Steph's accident. They all just assumed she had been drinking and probably didn't want to smear her memory by digging into that. She must have seen something or knew something. Sounded like if Tommy didn't do it that Russian guy would have. The worst part is I am going to have to hold on to this for a while. I will be running into Jack and Russell and can't say a word. Jack has beat himself to death thinking he let her drive drunk.

Seems like he has forgiven himself and moved on, but this is going to reopen that wound…Carla, do me one favor. I want to be the one that puts the cuffs on that piece of shit."

"No problem."

Before long they were at Tommy's house. Stryker pulled into the driveway next to Tommy's truck. It wasn't the Dodge in the video. He looked out into Tommy's yard that was littered with bait trays, barrels, and old lobster tanks. Out in the far back corner of the lot was a brown tarp covering something in the shape of an old pickup. He pointed it out to Rand, who nodded. They took a breath, got out of the truck and went to Tommy's door and knocked. After repeated knocks, Tommy came staggering to the door. He looked like a zombie and when he spoke, he was barely coherent.

"What you doing here?" Tommy mumbled, hardly opening his mouth and not making eye contact.

"Good morning, Tommy. I suppose you heard the gunshots earlier, right?" Stryker spoke in a loud voice to annoy Tommy. Meanwhile Agent Rand was giving him an odd look.

"Gunshots?"

"Yeah, Gunshots…you would have to be high not to have heard them."

Tommy paused and had a look of deep thought.

"Yeah…gunshots. I heard them."

"Well, Tommy seems like your neighbor may be doing some summertime poaching. We would like your permission to take a look into your back yard to see if we can find any shell casings, maybe a wounded deer. I'm sure you won't have a problem with me looking around since you have nothing to hide, and you wasted my time at the dock the other day."

Tommy, still trying to get his brain in gear, mumbled, "Sure, you can go look."

"Thank you, Tommy. I appreciate it."

Tommy closed the door and went back inside. Stryker motioned to Rand to go straight to whatever was under the brown tarp. She walked briskly to the tarp and lifted a few rocks to peel the tarp back. Sure enough, it was a late model Dodge pickup with a wooden flat bed. She took pictures of the damaged bumper and the blue paint transfer. She was taking a picture of the license plate when Stryker got there. He pulled back more tarp and opened a toolbox on the back of the truck. He looked in and saw broken pieces of tail light.

"Carla…take a picture of this. Do you have an evidence bag?"

"Sure do. Gunshots, Commissioner?"

"There is an old friend of mine that lives out here. I called him on my personal cell and asked him to call me back on my work phone that was recorded."

"Stepping into some gray areas, don't you think?"

"I don't care. Tommy needs to go to jail for this. Along with those Russian dirtbags. Now let's get out of here before shithead figures anything out."

They went back to the truck and left. On the way back to Carla's they called Dan Ross who had been doing some homework of his own. He told them that the Russian voice in the video matched the voice of one of the men from Friday night. It was Cashmere Sokolov and the female was Katiya Sokolov. They were the kids of a Russian mob boss in Boston who had passed away a few years ago. They owned a seafood business as a front for a drug and firearm ring. The Boston PD and FBI had been trying to pin them down but never could find anything to stick. The FBI was onboard to render full assistance with Rand in charge. He had also gotten in touch with the director of the DEA and commended Agent Rand on her case. The DEA was now…finally behind her. They would have a meeting soon to come up with a tactical plan for the takedown.

At the town dock Michael and Jack were working on the Red at Night. Michael was detuning the engine while Jack put his working prop back on.

"Jack…what do you think is going to happen at the meeting?" Michael asked.

"Damned if I know. I know we will not be walking away with the place. Just sucks to be so close, but so far away," Jack answered.

"It pisses me off for so many reasons I lose count. The drugs, screwing you and your father over, I was really hoping to push my business to the next level. You know, Elizabeth has no interest in it, but Josh is one hell of a mechanic and even though he has no idea what he wants to do, it would be nice to give him the option."

"I know what you mean. Mom had her heart on running that restaurant. Dad needs to slow down a bit. Running the dock would have been perfect for him. You never know what could happen. It could work out."

"How? When Tommy gets busted the place will go up for auction. We can't compete with the money in this town."

"Ain't you some negative."

"I just have my mind on a lot. All this talk of colleges and helping that DEA woman made me realize that Elizabeth isn't my little girl anymore. She's all grown up, it went by so fast. She doesn't need me anymore." Michael started choking up on the last few words.

Jack had finished tightening the prop nuts, put the cotter pin in then climbed up the ladder and into the boat. "Michael, if I have learned anything from Melissa it's that we always need our parents. She never had any and now she so attached to mine I have to remember she isn't my sister. Hell, I'm thirty and still need my parents. Just try to remember what it was like when you were her age."

"Damn it, Jack, you're thirty but you act like you're fifty…You are some damn wise, you know that?"

Jack just shook his head and smiled at his old friend.

"Speaking of Melissa, you guys seem to be going pretty good. You guys looked good together this last weekend. You were right, she don't act any bit of that Hollywood bullshit either."

"Yeah, she is something special. She is going to fly me and my folks out to Hollywood in February so we can go to the Oscars. Can you imagine that, Dad and Mom in Hollywood?"

"Hollywood will never be the same."

"Well, I guess I should head back to the house and get cleaned up before we meet at Tommy's."

"I got to meet that DEA woman. She wants me to wear a wire just in case Tommy says something incriminating."

"That's a good idea. Tommy suffers from diarrhea of the mouth and constipation of the brain."

They shared a laugh and headed in separate directions. Jack would come back later tonight when the tide was up to take the boat off the beach-out. He looked out over the harbor as he was driving by the church. He could see his father's boat coming in by Tumbler Island. He guessed Melissa was at the wheel while his father was sitting on the transom puffing away at his pipe. He knew his dad would be anxious about the meeting with Tommy. It was hard knowing that there was no way Tommy was going to give up the dock and they couldn't mention anything about what they knew about the drug dealing. He shook his head at the whole situation and continued his drive home.

Down at MacIntyre Lobster, Elizabeth was stacking crates on the dock to get ready for the afternoon rush of boats coming in to sell. She could see Old Smoke making its way through the harbor. Melissa was at the wheel and brought the boat up to the dock. Russell and Melissa tied the boat up and Melissa shut the engine off.

"How many crates today, Mr. Finn?" Elizabeth asked.

"Six crates and we don't have any hard shells today. How you doing, Elizabeth?"

"Good, Mr. Finn. I have been busy today. This place was a mess after the weekend. How are you doing, Miss Andrews?"

"Just call me Melissa. Miss Andrews sounds like a kindergarten teacher. I'm good… I had a blast this weekend at the races. Did you have fun?"

"Yeah, I like the camping and watching Dad and Josh race."

Russell broke up the small talk. "All right, you two. Let's finish up here. Elizabeth, you are still keeping track on your phone?"

"Sure am, Mr. Finn. Are you getting bait today, any bands, or fuel?"

"Yes, I'm going to have Melissa tray up a barrel of herring while I top off fuel."

"Ok, just give me what you got for numbers before you leave."

Melissa grabbed the bait trays and headed up the ramp. The bait shed was its usual stinky self. Barrels upon barrels of dead fish. She had learned to just get to work and ignore the smell. She dumped out a barrel of herring and started shoveling it into the trays. She felt someone's eyes on her and glanced back and saw Dale Rines staring at her. She kept shoveling but shifted her position to keep an eye on Dale.

"You're Jack Finn's new woman, ain't ya?" Dale said with a slimy tone.

"I am his girlfriend yes." She responded.

"First time I've seen shoveling bait look so sexy."

Melissa felt dirty, dirtier than the dead fish she was shoveling. "What do you want?" she asked, realizing that both Elizabeth and Russell were down on the dock.

"What do I want…. well, I think you know what I want. Not much stopping me from getting it. That old man and teenager won't hear you if I close the shed door."

"Russell will come up here if I am not back with this bait."

"Maybe so," Dale started walking towards her. "Or maybe he is too busy telling fish stories."

Dale was now within an arm's reach. Then she realized she was holding a bait shovel. She quickly slammed it down on Dale's foot. Dale fell to the ground holding his foot, yelling in pain. Soon Russell and Elizabeth came running up the ramp to see the commotion.

"What the hell happened?" Russell asked surveying the scene.

"I was shoveling bait and accidentally hit Dale's foot. I am sorry, Dale. I hope I didn't hurt you."

Dale got up off the floor. His clothes were soaked in bait juice from laying on the floor. He limped around and said, "I'm fine". He was confused on why Melissa didn't tell Russell what really happened.

"Well, finish up, Melissa, we got to get going," Russell said and walked out of the bait shed.

"Next time it won't be your foot," Melissa said to Dale as he gimped out of the shed.

Elizabeth stood there in the shed for a bit while waiting for Russell and Dale to leave.

"Did Dale make a pass at you?" Elizabeth asked after Russell and Dale were out of ear shot.

"If that's what you want to call it. Has he tried that on you?"

"No, but dad caught him staring at me once and threw him overboard."

"I am not surprised."

"You have a good day, Ms.....sorry, Melissa."

"You too, Lizzy."

Melissa finished traying up the bait and loaded it on the boat. Soon they were cruising back around Spruce Point. While running the boat she started thinking about Elizabeth and what her own life was at that age. Melissa had already been in 10 movies by the time she was seventeen. She had been tutored while on set and between movies, not setting foot in a school since she was eight. She had no friends her age. She lived a dream but never got asked to prom or went to a slumber party. She really had no childhood.

Her thoughts were interrupted by Russell coming up from the stern to talk. "Sorry I'm so grumpy today. Just thinking about that meeting is pissing me off. I was really hoping to get that place for Jack and Anne.....and maybe, me too." Russell spoke with his pipe clenched in his teeth.

"I'm sorry, Russell. Maybe when they bust Tommy the place will go up for sale, and you can buy it then," Melissa answered trying to keep him positive.

"No, he'll get busted, and the place will go up for auction. Some out-of-stater millionaire will buy it and turn it into a hotel."

Melissa paused and thought for a bit. "What will you and Jack do?"

"We will fish for someone else, which is a good thing at this rate, but I have a lot of years there. I just wanted to get that place for Anne. She has wanted a restaurant her whole life, but she always put the kids and me before her. It would also leave Jack in a good spot, along with Michael and Abigail. Anyway, ain't gonna happen now. No sense letting a wish bone grow where a back bone should be. I'll see you in the morning, kiddo."

Melissa pulled the boat up to the dock. She gave Russell a big hug and a kiss on the cheek. She stepped off the boat and looked back at Russell. "Russell…don't forget good things happen to good people."

"Really.,. you got proof?"

"Yeah, I met you guys." She gave Russell a big smile and walked up the ramp. Russell laughed and some weight was lifted off his mind. As she walked up the ramp, she sent Jack a quick text wishing him good luck and to call her when he got out of the meeting.

A couple hours later at MacIntyre Lobster the Finns and Williams were sitting down at a table in the back with Tommy who looked sober for a change. After everybody was sitting down a tall red headed woman came walking to the table and sat next to Tommy. You could tell her presence made Tommy uncomfortable. There was a pause while everybody waited for someone to talk. Russell broke the silence.

"Good afternoon, Tommy," he paused and looked at the redhead, not knowing if he should address her too. "We called this meeting to make you an offer. We would like to buy this place from you."

Tommy shifted in his seat a bit and glanced at the redheaded woman sitting beside him then asked, "What's your offer?" He really wanted to say "No fucking way," but had been advised against it.

Abigail Williams spoke next. She was going to be the president of the company, so she felt this was her part. "We can offer two million."

"Not enough," Tommy answered quickly. When the woman turned and looked at him. Tommy froze like a deer in the headlights of an oncoming car.

"He means to say maybe come back when you make better offer," the woman interjected with a Russian accent. Michael knew right away this was the Russian woman Elizabeth had told him was around lately.

"How much better and who are you?" Russell responded agitated.

"Mm, maybe five million. I am Tommy's -financial adviser."

"Five million?! Are you f....." Russell stopped when he felt Anne's hand hold his.

"Ok. We will see you when we are prepared to make a counter-offer."

As the Finns and Williams were walking out, the Russian woman smiled and said, "drive safely."

As soon as they were out of earshot Russell piped up, "Well, I am glad that's over. Who tah' hell is that foreign woman Tommy had beside him?"

"She's been kicking around the dock lately. Elizabeth told me about her, said some Russian dude asked her a bunch of questions a while ago, too," Michael said.

"This is getting crazy. Russian drug dealers in Boothbay Harbor. We need to talk to Agent Rand and get this taken care of before someone gets hurt," Jack said, shaking his head in disbelief.

"Not only that, don't forget Tommy is skimming our catch," Russell added.

Michael said, "Well, there is nothing more we can do today. I am going home and having some beer, hotdogs and Abigail's pasta salad, and forgetting all about this meeting. Elizabeth will take this recording to Agent Rand, not that there is anything much on it."

"I don't even know what I am doing for dinner yet. I gotta call Melissa and see what she wants to do."

"Why don't you guys come over and have dinner with us. We have plenty of hotdogs. I always make a big batch of pasta salad. Just grab some chips and whatever you want to drink. Tell Melissa I have wine I can share," Abigail suggested.

"Ok, sounds like a plan. I will give her a call and we will head over," Jack replied.

Jack called Melissa and filled her in on the dinner plans and she happily accepted the invitation. When Jack pulled into the driveway, Melissa came out, hopped into the truck and gave him a long kiss. It took his breath away. He was in awe of how beautiful she was, it didn't matter if she was in a fancy gown on T.V. or in cut offs and a T-shirt. She was simply gorgeous. He smiled at her while recovering his wits then put the truck in gear and headed for the Williams place. Along the way they picked up chips and beer, and he also caught her up on what happened at the meeting.

The Williams place was a modest, white, two story house with dark blue shutters and trim that sat in the middle of a big green wide open lawn. At the end of the driveway to the side and behind the house was a garage almost as big as the house. The door was open, and Josh was inside tinkering with a dirt bike. Off the back of the house was a deck where Elizabeth was setting out napkins and silverware on a picnic table. When the truck came to a stop, Jack and Melissa stepped out. Jack went into the shop to see what Michael and Josh were up to, and Melissa took the chips and beer up to the house.

"Hi, Elizabeth, nice to see you so soon. Can I help?"

"Nope, I got this. Thanks though."

"Where's your mom? I want to talk to her about something."

"Her and Dad are inside. Go right in if you like."

Melissa stepped in and heard Michael and Abigail talking.

"Why can't she go to school closer to home. Why does she need to take off to Texas? What if she needs something? What if she gets sick?"

"Michael, you know her. She wants to be on her own. She is independent. She doesn't even let us buy her school clothes anymore. She registered her car by herself last week. She is always going to be your little girl, but she is growing up… she is grown up. I know this hurts you. It hurts me too, but if she starts to see how much it bothers you, she will change her mind. Texas is one of the best, if not the best," Abigail explained.

By now Melissa could see their reflection in a picture on the wall. Abigail was hugging Michael while Michael was weeping. Melissa had to hold back her emotions as well. Hearing that conversation and seeing the bearded, old, gruff Michael crying had shocked her a bit. She had just turned to open the fridge when Abigail and Michael came out of the living room. Michael kept his head down so the visor of his hat covered his eyes.

"Hey, Melissa," Michael mumbled as he went by.

"Hi, Michael," Melissa replied.

"Hi, Melissa. Glad you came," said Abigail.

"Yeah, me, too. I had so much fun talking to you at the races. Jack told me about the meeting with Tommy. I'm sorry he didn't take your offer."

"We all knew he wasn't going to take it, but it still sucked to hear him say no. Then that Russian lady."

Abigail and Melissa carried their conversation out onto the porch where Elizabeth had finished setting up the table and was now putting hotdogs on the grill. Michael had made his way out to the shop where Jack was talking to Josh as he finished putting his dirt bike back together.

"You about ready to fire that thing up, Josh?" Michael asked as he came into the shop.

"Yup, gotta put my helmet on then kick it over."

"Just make sure you test the brakes before you go too far…or fast."

"Yes, dad."

"You ok, your eyes look red…and puffy?" Jack asked Michael.

"Never mind my eyes and get out of Josh's way."

Jack knew all he needed with that answer. Whenever something was bugging Michael he got short and temperamental. With a couple kicks the dirt bike fired up. Josh revved it up a couple times then eased off the clutch and left the shop. He tested the brakes,..briefly, then cracked the throttle and shot down a path next to the drive way. He kept on the throttle and banged through the gears.

"That's your old CR250, ain't it?" Jack asked.

"Yup, he dug it out, took it completely apart and rebuilt it piece by piece," Michael answered.

"Damn…sounds like he did a good job."

"Yup…wouldn't let me help. Wanted to do it all on his own."

"Michael…that's a good thing."

"I know, Jack, but this is getting real. It's Elizabeth's senior year, she wants to go to Texas for college. She is always working or with her friends. Josh is getting the same way. They don't need me anymore." Michael started getting choked up again.

"Michael, we have talked about this; if there is one thing I have learned, we always need our parents. I still ask Mom and Dad for advice. I bet if your old man was still here, you'd be calling him. You got it easy. Your daughter is going to Texas for college. You…you went into the Navy and not only that you were all over the world fixing stuff Navy Seals broke. Now it may seem that they don't need you, but the only reason they are as independent as they are, as smart as they are, and as good as they are is because of you and Abigail, mostly Abigail," Jack ended with a grin.

"I guess you're right. Just a really tough transition."

"Christ.,. It won't be long before you're walking Elizabeth down the aisle," Jack jabbed again.

"Don't even go there, you prick."

The banter was interrupted by Josh coming back into the driveway. He pulled up into the shop and shut it off.

"How did it go, Josh?" Michael asked.

"Holy shit, dad, this thing is fast."

Michael and Jack laughed a bit "Good to hear, but don't let your mother catch you talking like that."

"Yes, Dad….Dad?"

"Yeah, Josh."

"Thanks for the bike."

"You're welcome, bud."

"Dinner is ready," Elizabeth called from the porch.

They sat down and began to eat. Melissa looked around the table and listened in on the conversations. Jack was telling Abigail some of the stories about Josh out on the boat. Michael and Josh were talking about the bike. Elizabeth was sitting next to her, kind of taking in the conversations as well. It looked as though she was in deep thought.

"What are you thinking about, Elizabeth?" Melissa asked.

"It's just crazy to think that a Hollywood movie star is sitting at this table and everybody is talking about lobstering and dirt bikes."

Melissa laughed a bit and said, "I guess they don't think of me as a star anymore. Do you still think of me as a star?"

"Well, yes, but you're a lot cooler now than I thought you were before."

"Why is that?"

"Even though I had seen you do interviews and in gag reels you seemed cool and laid back, but there is still a camera there so you could have just been faking it. Now that I've met you, you're not fake at all. You are caring and nice to talk to."

"Thanks. Some interviews I did have to fake nice, but most of them were the real me. The gag reels are the real me. I like to laugh."

"What is your average day like?" Elizabeth asked. By this time the group had started focusing on their conversation.

"Well, that's a tricky question. If I am filming a movie my life basically evolves around that. I usually stay in a hotel close to location. I try to get there a week or so before the movie starts so I can take in the area and get into character a little bit, but some movies we film all over the place like "Over the Rainbow". I went to Grand Rapids, Minnesota to see where Judy grew up. I went to the library there and looked at old newspapers from her childhood and during her career. Some of them I photocopied and posted around my hotel room to help me get into character. During filming I don't go out much, I stay away from people to help me stay in character. I stopped using my cell phone as much, watched black and white tv, anything I could to parallel Judy's life. Watched hours and hours of her in movies, interviews, and on tv. For every hour spent on set there was two hours of homework."

"Yeah, but what are you doing when you're not filming? Chilling by the pool, driving fancy cars, going to exotic places like Boothbay Harbor," asked Michael with a slightly snarky tone.

"Yes, sometimes I do that, but also, I have interviews, promotions, benefits and other stuff. It's not like we get a lot of down time. I was offered the role in "Over the Rainbow" before we ended filming "Beach Days". When we were filming in New York I got to do a cameo for "Blue Bloods". So, I was technically filming in two spots."

"Wow, so like what time do you wake up?" Elizabeth asked.

"Between 7:00 and 9:00, unless the director wants a specific shot. Like in "Beach Days" my character Madison was a surfer that surfed before work. Sunrise in Hawaii when we were filming was around 5:30 so the director wanted me there at 4:00 to have time to do make-up, wardrobe and prep. Of course, she lifeguarded after work so we would shoot until around 8:30 at night. After filming we would read through our lines for the next day and talk about what was going to happen. I wouldn't get back to the hotel until 10:30 or 11:00. Madison didn't drink, so I didn't drink during that film. She was also vegan, so no meat or dairy. It actually set me up perfectly for playing Judy Garland."

"So how do you find time for a personal life. I mean you have had a few boyfriends?" Abigail asked.

"Like you just said, I have had a few boyfriends. It's tough, you see each other for a month then you're off in two different directions. You turn on the news and there he is kissing some model." Melissa paused a bit. "Listen there are times when it sucks and sometimes it's a lot of hard work. Then there is the pressure of someday being forgotten. The media will turn on you in a heartbeat, you have seen it. On the other hand, I own a mansion, a Mercedes, a limo, and always fly first class. I have traveled all over the world. I don't want to sound like the "poor little rich girl" but I don't want people to think it is easy either. No different than you guys. You guys worry about your mortgages, boat payments, the price of lobster, fuel and bait, but you also have a blast on the weekends. Most of all you have each other. Of all the places I have traveled and all the people I have met, I have never seen a group of friends and family tighter than you guys."

Jack raised his beer and said, "I can drink to that. Here is to the Finn, Williams and Andrews family of friends."

Melissa gave Jack a warm smile. They all raised their glass to the toast.

"O.k. That's enough about me. Lizzy, what's your day like?"

Even though Melissa was less like a Hollywood star and more like an old friend now, Elizabeth was beaming that she was curious about her life. "Well, as you know, I work down to Tommy's. I get there at 8:00 and I clean up from the morning rush. I help customers buy lobster, clams and other stuff. I have a working lunch. I get crates ready for the afternoon. Then the afternoon rush starts at around 2:30. It's kind of crazy because you still have customers buying stuff and you have boats coming in to sell, but I like the excitement. It's my favorite part of the day. After the rush I pick up and close out."

"What do you do for fun? Do you have a boyfriend?"

Elizabeth started to blush. "Well, there is a boy I like…. but it's hard to talk to a boy when you smell like bait. For fun my friends and I will go to the movies or to the beach on my days off."

"What is your school like? Do you play any sports?"

"It's a small school. My class is only 36 people. I play soccer in the fall, swim team in the winter, and tennis in the spring. I lifeguard at the pool in the evenings and have violin lessons twice a week."

"Wow!...Busy girl. What about you, Josh?"

Josh started blushing as well. He had a small crush on Melissa. "Well, this time of year I go sternman with Jack and help dad out fixing boats. When school starts, I play football in the fall, swim team with Elizabeth in the winter and baseball in the spring… and I play the drums."

"Oh my gosh, you two. You guys are so busy."

"That was Michael's and my plan from the start. Keep them busy and less chance of them getting into trouble. It has worked pretty well. Learning music helps them in school. Having a lot going on teaches them time management. The sports keep them active and healthy and have social aspects to them, too." Abigail chimed in.

"I will have to remember that. Sports and music. Keep them busy."

"Are you planning on having kids soon?" Michael asked chuckling.

Melissa wanted to say yes. She wanted to say she was going to marry Jack. She wanted to say they were going to have two kids, a boy and a girl, like Josh and Elizabeth. She loved Jack. There was no other man she ever wanted to be in her life or build a family with. She knew she couldn't say that, even though she was so certain it was going to happen.

"Someday," she answered, giving Michael a slight wink.

Michael saw the wink and at first didn't know how to take it, but after thinking a bit, he answered the wink with his own warm smile. "That's good.,. you'll make a great mother."

The group finished their meal and conversations. Then after a round of goodbyes, hugs and handshakes, Jack and Melissa got back into his truck and headed out.

After Jack and Melissa left, the Williams family picked up from the dinner. After picking up, Elizabeth went up to her room to read and get some quiet before going to bed for the night. While reading, there was a knock on the door.

"Hey, Kiddo, can I come in?" Michael asked.

"Yeah, sure, Dad."

Michael walked into the room and looked at the pictures on the wall. There was a picture of Melissa on the set from Beach Days. Also, some posters of boys and other stuff you would see in a teenage girls room. He grabbed the chair from her desk and sat down. He rested his elbows on the tops of his knees. Elizabeth could tell this was going to be a serious talk.

"Elizabeth, remember that movie you watched as a kid? The one where the little girl finds a baby dolphin. She brings it back to health then returns it to the wild? Remember how hurt that little girl was when she found out she had to let it go?" Michael stopped to regain composure.

"Yeah, Dad, I remember we cried together, and Mom and Josh giggled at us."

"Yeah, kiddo. Well, I am starting to feel like that little girl and you're my baby dolphin, except you're not a baby anymore. You are a woman. A little more than a year from now you are going to be headed to college and it's gonna fly by. Before you know it, you'll be in your car headed to wherever."

"Dad, I can stay close by and…"

"No, Texas is the best and I know you want to go there. So come hell or high water you are going…if you really want to."

"Oh, Daddy, I do, thank you."

"Now, hold on now, this comes with some strings attached. Like I said, this year is going to fly by, so you need to spend some time with your brother and your mother. Got it."

"What about you, Daddy?"

"I suppose you can hang out with me a bit," he said with a cheeky grin.

Elizabeth gave her father a big hug. Michael squeezed his little girl. No matter how old she got, she would always be his little girl.

On the front porch of her rental cabin, Jack sat sipping a beer with Melisa in his lap, her legs dangling over the arm rest. They looked out over Linekin Bay, watching the waves and taking in the night air.

"What are you doing tomorrow since Dad's not hauling?"

"Sleeping in! Then your mother and I are going to look at that house," she answered happily.

"So, you are seriously going to buy it?"

"Yes. I really like it here. I want a place of my own when I come and visit. I know I could stay with you, but I don't want to force this. We are moving fast, but I think we're doing good."

"I don't think it's a bad idea. Are you still thinking of getting a truck?"

"Yes, I am going to try to get a house and truck before I leave. You're lobstering tomorrow, right?"

"Yes, it's gonna be a long one, too. Clive is going to borrow my boat on Wednesday. Then on Thursday Josh is going with Michael to pick up the new engine for Clive."

"That's right, he is using your dad's boat tomorrow. How does that work? Does he pay you for rental?"

"No, we take care of each other. Knowing Clive, he will top off the boats with fuel, no matter how much he used, and leave a bottle of rum somewhere."

Melissa sat there taking in what she had heard. It was almost like going back in time. These people, even though they all had smart phones, internet and were well aware of the world around them, didn't stop sticking to the core values that every human should hold dear. They were by no means perfect. They all had their flaws, but they would take the shirt off their back and give it to a stranger.

"You got quiet all of a sudden. What are you thinking?"

"I am thinking we need to get to bed. You have a long day tomorrow."

Chapter 9

When the sun came up shining through Melissa's window, she was already awake, laying there thinking more about Jack, the Finn's, and Boothbay Harbor. She got out of bed and took a shower. After her shower she went out to the kitchen and found a note under her cell phone. "I love you, Jack." Simple and to the point as always, she thought to herself and smiled. She glanced at her phone and saw a flood of missed texts, calls and emails from Hollywood. She shook her head. She wasn't dealing with that today. Today was about setting more roots in Boothbay Harbor. As she sipped her coffee and stared over Linekin Bay there was only one thing that weighed on her mind - the upcoming 4th of July weekend. She heard Anne pull into the driveway and come up onto the deck. Melissa met her at the door and opened it.

"Good morning, Anne, how are you this morning?" Melissa asked.

"Oh, I am good, kind of excited really. Never been house shopping before. Russell already had a house when we got married," said Anne.

"That's right. You lived in Lucy's house, then moved to the house you're in now."

"Yup…. moved right across the lawn. Now I have been wondering about this buying a house, how do you buy a house and keep your cover?"

"Easy, my new accountant has a shell company made for me. Nothing illegal, just used to make big purchases without bringing attention. So, if I like this house, I call my accountant and he has the shell company buy it."

"Wow, does that happen a lot?"

"Yes, it's the best way to keep press and crazy fans away. Anne, I need to ask you about something."

Anne took measure of the serious look on Melissa's face and posture. "What's on your mind?"

"I want to get Jack out of Boothbay Harbor for the 4th of July weekend."

Anne took a deep breath. It was a good idea. The past five years Jack just went through the paces on the fourth, but he never looked to enjoy himself. Almost like he would rather not be out on the boat and watching fireworks. "That would be great. Getting him to agree to it. That is the challenge. What do you have in mind?"

"Camping. Not on the boat, somewhere way away from here."

"Yes, away from the boat, away from us, anything that will remind him of Stephanie."

"Where could we go? Does he even like camping?"

"Yes, we used to go……That's it, Cadillac Mountain! We used to go there once a summer when Jack and Lucy were little. Oh, I've got an idea! When he comes in from hauling, I will plant the idea in his head to take you camping. Get you away from the coast and see some more of Maine."

"Hopefully, it will work."

"If it doesn't, hit him in the head with a frying pan, then drag him out to the mountain."

They shared a laugh before getting into the car to check out the house. As Jack said, it wasn't far from where she was staying. The driveway was steep and curvy, and Anne made a comment about having Jack plow it in the winter. As they crested the hill, the house came into view. It was small, but cute, with white clapboard siding and blue shutters. A small SUV was parked in the driveway and the real estate agent was walking around on the deck. As usual in Boothbay Harbor, the real estate agent and Anne knew each other, which prompted a ten-minute conversation catching up with each other. It was a custom that Melissa was getting used to. The agent opened the door and allowed Melissa to walk in first. The smell of cedar and pine put a smile on her face. It was a large open room on the first floor with the kitchen and living room separated by a breakfast bar. In the center was a stone fireplace. To her left was a set of stairs leading up to a loft that was a bedroom. It was small and cozy. She already knew she wanted it; the rest of the tour was a formality. The real estate agent talked and talked, selling a house that was already sold. Anne would speak up once and a while with decorating ideas. Melissa didn't want to change a thing. At the end of the tour the real estate agent kept going on, pushing the sell. Melissa politely interrupted her. "I will take it."

The agent stumbled a bit. "Oh, ok I will schedule an inspection for you."

"No….no inspection. Here is the number for my accountant, he will take care of everything." Melissa passed the agent a card.

"Ok….um, very well then. Thank you, nice meeting you. Nice seeing you again, Anne."

They got in the car and left. The real estate agent was calling the seller as they left. Melissa was happy to be getting a place of her own in Boothbay Harbor. She had fallen in love with the town as much as she had fallen in love with Jack and the Finn's. After dropping Melissa off, Anne went home to tend to her gardens and get some household chores done. A few hours after lunch she heard the distinct sound of Jack's boat coming up into the cove. She went and sat down on the porch and waited for Jack to come up the hill.

"Hey, Mom, how did it go with Melissa and the house today?" asked Jack.

"She loved it. She said she will take it; she didn't even want an inspection."

"Really…. I wish she would slow down a bit. There are plenty of houses to choose from."

"Well, Jack, she really likes that house. When Melissa likes or loves something she doesn't hold back. You know that better than anyone."

"I know. It just seems she has been going straight out for the past few weeks working for dad and now buying a house. Just wish she would slow down and relax."

Anne shifted her stance. She was now picturing Jack as a fish, and she was the fisherman. He just took a nibble on her hook. "Well, that's where you come in, Jack. It's your job to take her somewhere so she can relax. Away from Boothbay Harbor, away from us even. Just the two of you. You guys can relax and spend some time with each other."

"You are right, Mom. I should take her out in the boat for a weekend."

Anne jiggled her metaphorical rod a bit. "All she sees are boats, Jack. Take her away from the coast a bit. Show her some of Maine."

Jack pondered the idea, staring at the ground, rubbing his chin a bit.

Anne decided to set the hook. "Take her up to Cadillac Mountain, Jack. Let her see some forests and wildlife other than damned old lobsters and dead fish."

"That's a good idea, Mom. Maybe next weekend we can head on up there."

"Don't wait, take her this weekend. They have a great fireworks display up there. Take the whole weekend. Head up there Friday and I don't want to see you until Sunday evening."

Jack hesitated a bit. The 4th of July had been kind of sacred to him since Stephanie died. He was thinking of an excuse to tell his mother.

"Jack…. there is no reason to be here on the 4th of July," Anne said, fully aware of what Jack was thinking.

Jack nodded in agreement. After cleaning up, he headed to Melissa's and was surprised to find how anxious this Hollywood movie star was to spend the weekend camping. They spent the rest of the week planning out the weekend and stocking up on camping gear. Michael had found an old blue 1986 Chevy K5 Blazer. He told Jack about it, thinking it was the perfect vehicle for Melissa and just like the house, she loved it. It was old and had minor flaws, and nobody would suspect a Hollywood elite would be driving it. Before long it was Friday, and they had Melissa's K5 Blazer loaded and hit the road for Cadillac Mountain.

Tommy MacIntyre sat in his office chair looking out the window at the boat traffic in the Harbor. Some people were going around the harbor making a tour before the fireworks. Others were just sitting at anchor or on a mooring waiting for the show to start. Tommy was nervous, wondering how the night would go. He just wanted his money and to get out of town. He had all the cash he had made up to this point in a duffel bag hidden in the bait shed. His plan was to grab it as soon as they got back in from this last deal and got paid. He'd get in his truck, go to Portland and get on a plane. Hopefullym, Dale would come, too. He just wanted to get as far away from Boothbay Harbor and the Russians as he could. Having both Katiya and Casmiere around this week was crazy. Both of them watching him and Dale closely. Late night boat trips and trucks coming and going all night. He hadn't had a good night's sleep all week. He was just about to daydream about what warm tropical place he was going to run off to when Katiya came into his office.

"Are you and Dale ready?" she said, leaning on his desk.

"Yes, Dale fueled up the boat this afternoon and is on his way. All the crates are ready to be loaded. As soon as the sun sets a little more, we will start loading him up."

"Good...you will be a very rich man, Mr. MacIntyre. What will you do with all your new fortune?" she asked, grinning, knowing she had no intent of paying him or letting him live.

"I'm getting way out of here. Nobody will ever find me."

"Good. I want no strings attached after deal."

Just then Casmiere came through the door with Dale in a headlock, his feet mostly dragging behind. Dale's face looked like he had been in a boxing match and lost. The left side of his face was red and puffy with one eye swollen completely shut. He was bleeding heavily from his nose and a split upper lip.

"What is going on here?" Katiya yelled.

Casmiere tossed Dale onto the floor. "Piece of shit was at bar drinking and talking about buying islands in the Caribbean. He is too drunk to run boat."

"I can run it," Tommy spat out. "I can run the boat. We can still do this."

Katiya smiled at Tommy. "You can drive boat?"

"Of course, I know his boat inside and out."

Katiya took a gun from the inside of her coat and shot Dale in the head. He fell limp on the floor lifeless.

"Noooooo!" cried Tommy. He went to Dale's side but there was nothing he could do.

"Get up. Your friend is dead. Don't end up like him, you do what I say," said Katiya.

Tommy got up from the floor slowly. His only friend lay bleeding from his head. One good eye open staring into nowhere. Tommy felt like fighting for a brief second but just as quickly he realized his chest felt tight and hurt. He was also short of breath with numb lips and fingertips. He was lucky to keep his feet underneath him as he meekly followed Katiya and Casmiere out of the office. He gave Dale one last look as he closed and locked the door. The sun was setting as they walked to the docks.

Tommy went down and got Dale's boat started and brought it over to the loading area. Even now out in the boat away from them he felt their power. They knew he wouldn't make a run for it. What could he do? Where could he go? Standing there in his friends boat he couldn't help but feel guilty. It was all starting to catch up with him. He had gotten Dale involved. He killed Stephanie. He was sure he wasn't going to make it out of this alive. Before he reached the loading area, he texted Jack real quickly. "Jack I killed Stephanie. I ran her off the road." He sent the message then tossed his phone overboard. He didn't want to take the chance of Cashmere or Katiya seeing what he texted. He pulled the boat up to the loading dock and tied up. "Get loading," Katiya said. Within a couple hours all the crates were loaded up. By this time the fireworks had just started. They slowly cruised way out around the crowd of boats so as not to draw attention. Little did they know all the law enforcement on and off the water were watching them like a hawk. As soon as they passed Tumbler Island, Tommy bumped the throttle to cruising speed and headed for Damariscove.

Out on Damariscove Island, Rand and Ross were hiding in the old Coast Guard station where they had hidden before. A helicopter was hidden on Fishermen's Island nearby, as were a number of tactical officers. The Coast Guard and Marine Patrol were also standing by out of site. Soon the big yacht came into the little harbor, dropped anchor and waited. Several people on board were moving around and at the top of the big yacht some crew were getting a small crane ready. Rand took pictures of everybody out on deck with her night vision camera. Commissioner Stryker sent her a text to tell her that the running lights of Dale's boat should be coming into view. She pointed her camera to the opening of the small harbor. Sure enough Dale's boat came into view. She focused in on the boat and could see Tommy behind the wheel. Cashmere and Katiya were sitting on some crates. She leaned over to Ross.

"I can't see Dale. Do you think he is down in the cabin?" she asked.

Agent Ross pulled out his thermal binoculars and looked. "No, only three on board." Agent Ross responded.

"I'm not holding this up for him, we'll wait until the crates start moving then make the jump."

Agent Ross nodded in agreement.

Tommy brought the boat beside the big yacht and Katiya climbed on board while Casmiere kept an eye on Tommy. Agent Rand turned to her laptop that had the audio and video surveillance. She could see Katiya greeting an older man.

"Hello, Mr. Balfour. How are you this evening? How was cruise from Sherbrooke?" Katiya asked.

"It was a nice cruise. Maybe you would like to join me on the way back…after we do business." he answered with a French like accent.

"No, tonight is just business. Are you ready to transfer money?"

"Are you ready to show me what I am buying?"

Katiya leaned out of the window and spoke to Casmiere in Russian. He opened two crates. One containing guns, the other cocaine. Balfour motioned to one of his men and the man jumped onboard the lobster boat and inspected the contents of both crates. He then gave a thumbs up. Balfour smiled from ear to ear, then opened up a laptop and punched some keys. He turned it to Katiya.

"Put in your banks routing and account number."

Katiya began to type in the numbers while Balfour gave the order to start loading crates.

When Rand saw the crates starting to move from the lobster boat to the yacht she made the call to have the Boothbay Harbor Police Department move in on Tommy's place. She also gave the order for the Coast Guard to block the entrance to the harbor. As soon as she saw the harbor was sealed off she gave the signal to turn on the lights and advance on the two boats. The dark little harbor lit up like it was daytime. A couple of Balfour's men went for their guns but were shot down quickly. Rand's voice boomed over a loud speaker for everyone to put down their weapons. Guns hit the deck and everybody put their hands up. All agencies involved converged on the two boats. Stryker and Ross boarded Dale's boat. Stryker stepped up to Tommy and looked at him with such disgust he could almost taste it. He reached his arm back for his hand cuffs then paused and caught eyes with Rand who was on the yacht arresting Balfour. A big grin slowly stretched across his face. He then clenched his fist as tight as he could and swung his giant fist around with all the force he could muster, putting every muscle into it from his wrist to his hips down to his feet. When his fist hit Tommy's lower cheek he could feel and hear Tommy's jaw bone break. Tommy's eyes rolled back into his head and he fell to a heap onto the deck of the boat, where he lay lifeless for a few minutes. Stryker put handcuffs on him and propped him up against the side of the boat.

"Commissioner just got a call from BHPD. They found Dale Rines dead in Tommy's office. Gunshot to the head," Agent Rand yelled down to the boat.

A muffled contorted voice came from Tommy's bruised face. "She did it. She shot Dale. Katiya that Russian bitch killed my friend."

"Tommy you might as well have shot him yourself getting him mixed up in this, and Stephanie...." Stryker's voice cracked. "What did she do to deserve to die?"

Tommy spit out a tooth and blood onto the deck, then took a couple breaths between sobs.

"She caught me. That night before getting on Jack's boat she had come up to go to the bathroom. She caught me and Casmiere over there making a deal. She waited until he was gone and approached me. She told me to turn myself in or she would go to the cops first thing in the morning. I called Katiya and told her about it. I was going to leave town, but they said for me to kill her or they would kill the both of us. So I waited until she got back. I followed her...."

"I know what happened. I saw the video and found her broken taillight in the toolbox of your truck. You took her away from her parents, Jack and the town that loved her. Tommy, you can count on me being at the trial. I will pull every string and call in every favor to make sure you rot in prison. I'm going to send you pictures while you're in jail too. Pictures of the town and the people in it having fun out and about. Pictures of Jack and his new girlfriend. Pictures of whatever happens to your place. Then every Fourth of July I will send you a picture of Stephanie's grave." Stryker stopped, nearly out of breath, his body under tension like a guitar string about to snap. He wanted to beat Tommy. He wanted to slam him around that boat like a dog shaking a chew toy. He couldn't though. It wouldn't be worth it. Instead, he took a long, deep breath. He looked up at Agent Rand and spoke. "Let's take them in."

They brought the yacht and Tommy's boat into Boothbay Harbor and tied them up at the Coast Guard station. Rand walked out onto the pier to clear her head and turned to see Ross getting off his phone and walking up.

"How you doing, kid?" He asked sked.

"I don't know what to feel. On one hand I am glad we nailed them but on the other I feel guilty we hadn't done It sooner. Two people lost their lives while I've been assigned to this area. If I had only caught things sooner."

"Carla, you can't go down that road, it has no ending and it is a dark, dark path. You nailed them. You, with some help from Stryker and me, but you got the wheels turning." He paused to get his words together. "Bad people do bad things. All good people can do is try to stop them; we can't blame ourselves for what they do."

Chapter 10

Russell Finn sat in his truck on the side of the road looking at the police tape around MacIntyre Lobster. During the fireworks last night the police had stormed the place with the blue lights on and sirens screaming. Most people didn't even notice it until the fireworks were over and came back to the dock. They were told to go somewhere else; they would release vehicles after being searched and cleared. Rumor had it that an ambulance had arrived at some point but nobody knew why. Russell had tried to call Jack but there was no cell signal where Jack and Melissa were camping. Russell had sold his first lobster at this very dock. There was a lot of history there, some bad, and some good. As he looked out the windshield he looked up into his rear view mirror and saw Clive pulling over behind him. Russell hopped out and walked back to Clive's truck.

"Where are we going to have coffee?" Russell asked, trying to be funny.

"Coffee…. You're worried about coffee? How about where in the fuck are we going to sell our lobsters on Monday. Where are we going to get fuel or bait?" Clive fired back.

"I know, Clive, just trying to lighten things up. Jesus, don't forget I am a lobsterman, too. I know what is at stake here. I've already been thinking about that."

"You got a plan?"

"Well... I was thinking of calling all the retailers and have a meeting somewhere Monday morning. We can hash out where everybody is going to go. I think where you and I are the oldest, it kind of falls on us to get the ball rolling. What do you think?"

"I think it's a good idea. That will give'em time to talk to their guys and figure out how many they want to take on."

"Yup. I will check with Hughie over to Robinson's first. Maybe he will let us have the meeting there."

"Yup."

There was a long pause while both the old lobstermen looked over at Tommy's.

"This needed to happen, but don't it suck?" Russell said taking a puff on his pipe.

"Yeah.,. just a shame it had to go this way. Would have been nice if you guys could have got it. Now who knows what will happen to the place."

"Yup…Well, I'm gonna head back to the house and make some phone calls. Talk at you later."

"Let me know what ya find out. I will get the word out."

Russell walked back to his truck and watched Clive drive away. He had just started his truck when Rand and Stryker pulled into Tommy's. Stryker waved him over, so Russell started his truck, drove across the street, and pulled up next to them.

"Morning, Commissioner, morning, Agent Rand," Russell greeted them. He noticed both of them looked tired, like something was weighing on them.

"Good morning, Russell. You got a second to talk to us?" Stryker asked.

"Sure, I imagine there's a lot to talk about."

"There is, Russell. First off, we had to go through Tommy's records to figure out just how much drugs and money came through here. While looking into that, we looked into Elizabeth's records of how much Tommy was shaving off of your catch, along with padding out your bait and fuel. At the end of all this we can help you with the paperwork with the Office of Victims of Crimes so you can be compensated for all of it."

"That's good news. Jack is up north camping with Melissa and I can't get a hold of him right now, but I will be sure to tell him."

"There is some bad news. After this place is cleared and the investigation is over, Tommy will probably have to sell it to pay for legal fees, but until then it is closed so you and the other guys will need to find another place to sell your lobster."

"I figured that. I think Agent Rand here warned us that may happen."

"Russell, just listen for a minute. This is hard to get through. Dale Rines is dead. I can't say how or who, but he is dead."

Russell took a long puff from his pipe. He never liked Dale. Dale was a problem child all his life, but it still hurt that he was dead. Russell did catch the little hint that Stryker had put out. The "or who" was a hint that he had been murdered. That bothered Russell.

"Russell, this next part is hard to tell you. It is going to open up old wounds and at some point you are going to get mad…. rip roaring mad." Stryker paused to compose himself a bit. "Russell…. Stephanie wasn't drunk driving the night she died…she was pushed off the road… she was murdered."

Russell took the pipe out of his mouth. He flashed back to the morning when Jack had come over crying that Stephanie had died and it was his fault. He remembered his own pain. The double sided pain of losing Stephanie and watching his son blame himself.

"Who?" was all Russell could mumble out.

"I can't tell you right now. I will as soon as I can, but we have the person that did it and they will pay for it".

"Can I tell Jack?"

"Yes, but keep it in the family, Russell. The Feds don't want any details of anything released yet.

"Got it…thank you…and thank you, too, Agent Rand."

"Thank you, Russell, for all your cooperation. I will need to question you about everything you know about this sometime soon. Jack and Melissa as well," said Agent Rand.

"Yup… I figured that. Just let me know when and where. I will be there."

"We can do it at your house if you like; you tell me what time works for you."

"I will let you know as soon as I talk to Jack."

"That's fine, Russell. Have a good day."

Rand turned and walked towards the crime scene that used to be MacIntyre Lobster. Stryker nodded his head, gave a wave then followed Rand. Russell headed back to his house.

Melissa opened her eyes to find Jack still asleep lying there next to her. Normally he would have been up making breakfast, or coffee, or looking at the weather. She decided to get up, get dressed and spend the morning outside. She stepped out onto the grass with her bare feet. The morning dew tickled the soles of her feet. She took a deep breath in, arched her back, stood on her tiptoes and stretched her arms to the sky. Then she decided to get a jump on breakfast. Anne had given her the recipe for blueberry pancakes, and she was going to try to make them before Jack got up. She was a little nervous at first because she had only made them once and that was under Anne's supervision. She read through the instructions first. At the end there was a little note for Melissa:

"Melissa, cooking is mostly confidence. The confidence is passed on from generation to generation. You have made them once. All I did was the measurements and that is the easy part. Don't forget to heat the syrup. Good luck, Anne."

Melissa smiled a confident smile and started mixing ingredients. She could almost hear Anne telling her to be gentle with the blueberries. She started a fire and watched it closely. Anne had included in her recipe tips on cooking on an open fire. Melissa put some butter on the pan and it immediately sizzled away. Melissa paused for a moment, hesitant on pouring in the pancake batter. The way the butter acted just seemed different, then she went ahead and poured in some batter. The batter and pan reacted violently. She knew it wasn't right. She hadn't waited long enough for the fire to cool down a bit. "I should have started the fire, first then mixed the batter," she thought to herself. Her face got warm as the feeling of failure started creeping in. "I should just let Jack do it," she told herself. She looked at the burnt pancake, then looked at the recipe. She could see that there was writing on the back of the recipe. She turned it over to find two words "try again". At first she was a little upset. Did Anne expect her to mess up? After taking a moment she smiled. Yes, Anne knew she would mess up. Probably because Jack messed up his first and Lucy messed up her first. She bet even Anne messed up her first pancake. Those two words started to mean more than just pancakes. "Try again" seemed to be the Finn family code. When Russell lost his boat, he tried again. Jack was "trying again" with Melissa. Any time Melissa messed up on the boat Russell would just say, "Try again, Hollywood". She looked around and found some rocks to elevate the cooking grate, cleaned the burnt pancake out of the pan and started over. Soon there were a stack of pancakes sitting on a plate near the fire to keep warm. Melissa took a picture with her phone and tried to send it, but forgot there was no service. She went on to make coffee and warm the butter. Melissa heard Jack moving around in the tent.

"Hurry up and get out here, breakfast is ready," Melissa shouted.

"What are we having? Milk and cereal," Jack responded teasing.

Jack came out of the tent to find the fire going and a stack of blueberry pancakes next to it. Coffee was ready and Melissa was sitting there beaming with pride.

"Wow…umm…wow. I don't know what to say," Jack stumbled to say.

"How about, "Thank you for breakfast."

"Yes. Yes, thank you."

Jack made himself a plate of pancakes and a cup of coffee. He stared at Melissa, who had the look of an Olympic gold medalist basking in her achievement and enjoying every bite. It was funny to think that someone who had overcome being abandoned by both her parents to become an Oscar nominated movie star could find so much accomplishment in making pancakes. "I am going to marry her," he thought to himself. "Not now, when the time is right, but I want to spend the rest of my life with her. It won't be easy, but she is worth it."

He took a bite of his pancakes and they were delicious. After breakfast they got ready to go for a hike up Mt. Cadillac.

When Tommy MacIntyre cracked his eyes open, he was looking at the inside of the holding cell in the Boothbay Harbor Police Station. He hadn't slept much because every time he closed his eyes he saw Dale lying dead on the floor, eyes wide open staring into nowhere. He looked around his cell and he was alone. Katiya and Casmiere were not there. He sat up and put his face in his hands. A heavy, deep feeling of regret started to settle over him. A lump formed in his throat and his eyes started to well up. It had been five years since he killed Stephanie. Since then he had convinced himself it was her fault for meddling in his business. Now he felt the guilt. It was her kindness that got her killed. If she hadn't given Tommy a chance to turn himself in, she would be alive. If she had just gone to the police, he would have just been arrested for some drug charges. Now he would be going on trial for murder, drug trafficking, trafficking illegal fire arms and whatever else they could dream up. Everyone would know he killed Stephanie, the three time Miss Shrimp Pageant winner, Homecoming Queen, Boothbay Harbor's favorite. Tears started rolling down his cheeks. He wanted to kill himself. The door to the cell opened up slowly. Boothbay Harbor Police Chief Upham walked in.

"Tommy, an agent from the DEA is here to see you," said Chief Upham.

"Ok, Nick," he said as he stood up.

"Its Chief Upham to you."

"Alright, Chief."

Tommy had known Nick Upham since childhood and had always called him Nick. That time was over. Chief Upham put hand cuffs on him, they felt cold as ice, and led him down the corridor to his office.

"Sorry we don't have a formal interrogation room, Ms. Rand," Upham said to Rand. Tommy looked at agent Rand and suddenly recognized her as the warden with Commissioner Stryker that day he had called in on Jack and Russell.

"Hello, Mr. MacIntyre. I am sure you are a little confused about who I am. I am Agent Carla Rand with the DEA. I was undercover as the warden the other times we have met. I am in charge of the investigation against you, Katiya and Casmiere Ornikoff and Robert Balfour. Your charges are murder in the first degree, trafficking narcotics with the intent to sell, selling of narcotics, trafficking of illegal firearms and theft."

"Theft?" Tommy interrupted.

"Yes, you were changing the numbers of Jack and Russell Finn's catch, bait and fuel to steal from them. How much is still undetermined until we look through Elizabeth Williams's log of what they actually caught and used for bait and fuel."

Tommy dropped his head. He had forgotten about all of that.

"Mr. MacIntyre, at this point you can ask for a court-appointed attorney, hire your own attorney, or proceed with providing me with a statement of what has happened, starting with your first encounter with the Ornikoff crime family. You will need to include the murder of Stephanie Turner. Do you understand!"

Tommy paused for a moment. He had seen plenty of crime T.V. and movies. Something was missing here. "Wait, don't I get a deal?"

Carla Rand leaned back in her seat. This moment is where all that waiting and watching comes into play, all the collecting of evidence and recording conversations. She knew her case was air tight. She decided to lose her professionalism for a moment.

"Mr. MacIntyre, do you remember the OJ Simpson trial? How everybody knew OJ did it, but his lawyer managed to somehow get him out of it. If you had him for a lawyer you would still be screwed. We have you on video, we have video of that video, we have your confession last night…"

"And my text to Jack," Tommy interrupted.

"What…" Carla was a bit shocked that Tommy would give a hint of more evidence against him, but also needed to know who else knew about what had happened.

"I texted Jack last night that I killed Stephanie. After they killed Dale I figured I wouldn't be far behind. I figured I owed it to him."

Rand took a deep breath. She would have to find Russell again. He had mentioned this morning he couldn't get in touch with him. She would have to find out why.

"Well, like I said, it's up to you. You can get a lawyer or you can give me your statement now. It's up to you."

Tommy was tired. The kind of tired that didn't involve sleep. He just wanted this to be over. "Can you record me rather than me writing it all out?"

"Yes, Mr. MacIntyre. I will get it set up."

Tommy gave the full story, from the beginning five years ago until last night. It took eight hours, with a couple of breaks and a pot of coffee. After finishing he signed some paperwork and Agent Rand took him outside for a cigarette.

"What's going to happen to my dock, house and other stuff?" Tommy asked.

"After we finish our investigation you can sell it all or have a family member take care of it for you."

"I want to give the dock to the Finns and sell my house and give the money to the Turner's."

"I can help make that happen."

"I know I will be spending the rest of my life in prison. It's the least I can do. Will Dale get a funeral?"

"That depends on his family. If no one comes forward he will be cremated and stored in a vault in Augusta."

"What is going to happen to me?"

"You will be moved up to county jail until trial then moved to the state prison."

Tommy took a long drag of his cigarette then dropped to his knees and cried. He cried harder than he ever remembered. Cried so hard he had a hard time breathing. There was no island with sandy beaches in his future. His best friend was dead and he would be spending the rest of his life in prison.

Jack and Melissa made their way up Mt. Cadillac. The mid-morning air was cool and fresh. Melissa was taking in the movement around her. Squirrels and chipmunks scurried about, birds flying and chirping around the tops of the tall trees that surrounded them. She wasn't a complete stranger to the outside world, but now acknowledged it more. Out on Russell's boat he would always stop to watch an osprey or bald eagle and point out seals to her. When hauling further offshore, or "outside" as he called it, he pointed out whales and porpoise. She wondered how much she may have missed on some of the locations she had filmed at. Always focused on work and not what was going on around her. "Maybe if I had paid closer attention, I would have been more aware of my agent's agenda," she thought to herself. Then she remembered the Finn family code of not dwelling in the past. Jack walked behind her, letting her set the pace. He, too, was taking in the wildlife and nature around him. This was a different environment for him. He was used to salt air and the sound of seagulls. He focused on the sounds of their footsteps. Most of the time they were in step with each other. Every so often a root, or rock that had to be stepped over or around would take them out of synchronization, but shortly after a few steps their rhythms would find each other. To Jack it was symbolic to all relationships in life. Most of the time two people who are on the same page, would once in a while get off track but with a little work and time, find each other again.

"I'm glad you talked me into this. I spend so much time on the water. It is nice to get away from it for a bit."

"Well, I wanted you all to myself this weekend. I love your family but they are always popping up. I have never been camping before. It was the perfect little get away. We can just be us…with just us."

"Nice play on words there. Have you talked to anybody back in Hollywood about us yet?"

"Not yet. I told my accountant about the house and I fired my agent. Other than that, I left Hollywood in Hollywood, but I have had some thoughts."

"Really? Like what?"

"I want you to go back with me in September."

Jack stopped walking. "What for?"

"I am going to put all my cards on the table. What happened the night I was drugged. Why I fled to Boothbay Harbor. Meeting you. Working for your dad…everything." She had stopped walking and was facing Jack.

"Why? I thought you wanted to keep Boothbay Harbor away from that life?"

"I do, but I can't hide from it either. It's a part of me. I want to be able to come to Boothbay Harbor and not look over my shoulder or worry about someone recognizing me. Yes, there will be times when people will hound me, but after the novelty of it wears off, I will be able to live a normal life."

"Ok, so how does that involve me? Why would I need to be there in September?"

Melissa's tone was changed a pitch into sounding a bit annoyed. "Because you're my boyfriend and a Finn. If I have learned anything, it's a Finn stands up for a friend and backs them up."

Jack paused for a second. She was right. It was his duty to stand behind her. "So what is the plan?"

"Have you ever watched The Jim Sterling Show?"

"Yeah, a few times. He is like Graham Norton and Ellen DeGeneres in one. You get the funny side of the celebrities he has on the show, along with some of the serious back story."

"Well, I am glad you like him because we will go on the show, introduce you, talk about lobstering with your father and talk about that night at the party."

"Uuummmm...me on The Jim Sterling Show. I think this mountain air is getting to you."

"He had asked me about going on his show a while ago. It will be perfect. He is light hearted, funny and genuine."

The look on Melissa's face was so confident. She had really thought this through. This was her world. She knew it and he trusted her. "Ok. Looks like I will be going on The Jim Sterling show."

Melissa wrapped her arms around him. "Thank you Jack."

"This is crazy, just a few weeks ago I was lonely and depressed, now I will be going on The Jim Sterling show with the Melissa Andrews."

"Well just a few weeks ago I didn't think I could trust anybody. Now I have not just found you, but a whole family."

"This has been the craziest summer I can remember. Meeting you, Tommy dealing drugs, agents lurking about."

"Yes, about the agents lurking. Agent Rand came to see me the other day."

"What about?"

"Just to give me a heads up that they would be moving in on Tommy soon and my name might be dragged into it. She was worried about the headlines. I mean it doesn't look good. One minute I am suspected of ODing, the next I am in a town with drug activity. I already told you how the media work. If there are dots the media will connect them no matter how far apart they are. That is another reason to go on T.V. with my…our story. We can tell our side."

"Man…what a shit show Tommy created."

"She said I would need to be there for you to…. then she said, 'she had said to much'."

"Me? Whatever. I am so tired of that whole deal. I just want it to be over. I was really hoping we could get that place, now I just want to move on."

They continued their hike up the mountain side. Jack started thinking about what Melissa had said about Rand's statement. "What did she mean, be there for me?" Jack pondered it for a while then started daydreaming about going to Hollywood. He had always been drawn to movies. He loved watching the actors and actresses mold themselves to their parts. Melissa was no exception. When she played a part she really got into her role. He had admired her for that long before they had ever met. Then some of her offscreen activities had impressed him as well. Visiting children's hospitals and veterans' hospitals. She had always seemed real in any of the interviews he had seen. Stephanie was a fan of hers, too. Jack paused a bit. He hadn't thought of her in….well, a few days. Last night he and Melissa danced to the radio by the camp fire then made love in the tent all night. He started to feel guilty again. He had stopped walking and was staring at the ground. How could he just take off on the anniversary of her death. He heard a voice calling him.

"Jack…. are you ok? Jack…JACK!"

He had come out of his trance and Melissa was standing there next to him.

"What am I doing?" Jack said out loud.

Melissa felt something was up. She had seen that vacant expression before.

"Hey Jack…you are ok… You haven't done anything wrong," She said softly.

"Damn it…I remember everything! Her mother calling me. Going to see her car….to see her. Why didn't she let me drive her home? Why didn't I just take her keys?"

Melissa took a deep breath to help cope with the awkward situation. She felt like an imposter, but also like a referee between Jack's blame for himself and that part of him that knew it wasn't his fault.

"Jack…I want you to look at me. Bring your eyes right up to mine." Melissa paused as Jack slowly made eye contact.

"Listen. If there is one thing I have learned about Steph it is she was forgiving. You told me that. Your mom and dad told me that. Now stop and think. You asked to drive her home. She said no. It's not your fault. Even if it was, do you really think she would want you beating yourself up like this? I love you, Jack Finn, and she loved you. Neither of us wants to see you hurt."

To Jack it seemed like Melissa and Stephanie had a talk between themselves, like a changing of the guard. He picked his head up, took a deep breath and dried his eyes. He gave Melissa a big hug then looked into her eyes. They were a little watery, but she was smiling at him. She was right.

Russell Finn slowly rocked in his old rocking chair while he puffed on his pipe and sipped his scotch. Sitting out on the deck, looking out over the cove, he was in deep thought. He thought about all that had happened in the past five years and what he might have missed to prevent some of it. Also, he was thinking about how he was going to tell Jack about Stephanie. And, wondering what it was going to be like fishing from another place. He could hear humming and singing in the garden. It gave him peace to hear her. No matter what unfolded in the future, Anne would be by his side. He thought the same about Melissa for Jack. He could tell she really loved him. Not just the fresh puppy dog love that people get, then a couple months down the road it's all fizzled out. What they had was as real as the air, the ocean and the earth. His thoughts were interrupted by the sound of a truck door closing. He recognized the voice greeting him and the footsteps coming up on to the porch.

"Hey old man, how are you?" Michael said as he sat down in the chair beside him.

"Old Man?….You ain't too far behind me, old boy. You better order yourself a walker and a case of prune juice," Russell bantered back.

"I'm feeling it today. All this commotion got me stressed out."

"Well, I can tell you I have seen bait scares, price strikes, changes in regulations and license restrictions. I started fishing for Tommy's grandfather, then his father, then Tommy. I might have been nervous a few times, and maybe pissed off more, but this…This has me sick to my stomach."

"I know how you feel, Russell. To think my daughter was right in the thick of it. On the right side of it, but right in the middle of it. I am proud of her, but wow. At least nobody got hurt."

"Hold your breath on that. I can't tell you what I know. That agent lady told me some of the story. I can't tell you any details. This bullshit claimed two lives."

Michael wanted to press him for more, but if Russell was told to keep his mouth shut, it was shut. Michael stood there pondering the possibilities of who might have died. His thoughts were interrupted by Russell speaking.

"Your daughter was key in this whole thing. Her record keeping saved me and Jack a bunch of money. She is a good kid, Michael. Both of them are."

"Thanks, Russell. Any word from the love birds?"

"Nope, I think that was the idea. To get away from here. Melissa had that thought out. What are Abigail and the kids doing today?"

"I think Abigail and Elizabeth are job hunting for her since Tommy's is closed. Josh is either out riding his dirt bike or rebuilding that old 6BT Cummins I had kicking around the shop."

"What are you up to?"

"Driving around trying to wrap my head around everything. Just a lot of changes lately with Jack and Melissa, Elizabeth talking to colleges and this mess at Tommy's."

"Well, the good thing is most of what you're worried about is a good thing…really. Your best friend has met a great woman and is moving on. Your daughter is about to finish high school and go to college, and Michael, I would bet my boat that she will be a thriving success. This crap with Tommy…well it's done for the most part. Given, we all got to pick up the pieces, but at least the drugs are out of here."

"Yup. I guess you are right. I think I am going to round up the family and go for a boat ride. What are you going to do with the rest of your day?"

"Anne is out in the garden picking flowers to put on Stephanie's grave. We have always done it today."

"Yeah, we did it yesterday morning…never gets any easier."

"No, it doesn't."

"Alright old man, I am going to hit the road. When you hear from lover boy tell him to give me a call."

"I will, Michael. Have a good one."

Chapter 11

Carla Rand had just pulled into the Twin Bridges Detention Center and there waiting by his truck by the service gate was Dan Ross. He was standing, looking at his cell phone, drinking a Dunkin' Donuts coffee. Dan had made her a job offer. He and his superiors really wanted her on the FBI. She hadn't had time to think about his offer yet, but she almost wanted to turn it down. She liked Dan more than a friend or colleague. His big goofy smile was complimented by a deep voice. Not handsome or ugly, his husky build, cheap glasses and balding head all housed a heart of gold. If she took the offer, she would be working for him and that would stop any chance for a relationship. He said he would be retiring soon, but how soon? She had kept these feelings at bay for a while, but now that the case was moving away from investigation and would be going to trial, it seemed that she could act on them. Maybe in a subtle way, just some coffee. Then again, the two had drank enough coffee with each other during the investigation it would hardly seem like a step forward. Dinner…going out to dinner might be nice. She stepped out of the car with the intent to start the conversation off about going out to dinner.

"You ready for this, kid?" Dan asked her. She hated it when he called her that.

"Yes. Dan…I was thinking, what if we went…" He cut her off before she could finish.

"Do you have a plan for the interrogations? Want me to take one and you the other?"

Carla was shocked. Dan was all business.

"No, I think we should go in as a team. Question Casmiere first. One of the charges against him is accessory after the fact. It's a good bargaining charge to drop for more information."

"We can try that. We have a ton of solid evidence against the both of them, but I don't want to show our cards yet. We are still searching the hotel room, Tommy's place, their phones and their place in Boston."

"Are you ok, Dan? You seem edgy."

"That Balfour guy scares me. He wasn't on our radar. We have no info on him. That… and he showed no emotion when being arrested. Like he didn't care. He never even asked about the guys we took down."

"I am surprised that surprises you, Dan. You expect these guys to care?"

"I guess you're right. I'm just tired of this shit. I've had enough and I'm retiring after this trial. I am going to move to some island in the Caribbean and never think about this job ever again."

"Any of it, Dan… Not even me?"

Dan's answer was drowned out by the sound of the laundry truck leaving the detention center. "Funny," Carla thought to herself "a laundry truck leaving on a Saturday." Before she could ask Dan to repeat what he had said an alarm from the detention center rang out. They ran towards the gate but the automatic lock-down gates started to shut. They looked at each other and said in unison "laundry truck" then bolted back to their vehicles. "My truck," Dan yelled as they sprinted towards his truck with hopes of catching the laundry truck. Just as they opened the doors, a huge explosion knocked them to the ground. Ears ringing, they looked towards the driveway going into the facility. There, the laundry truck, or what was left of it was sitting, turned so it was blocking the driveway, engulfed in flames.

There was a faint sound of another car that couldn't be seen fleeing the area. After the gates opened and they were cleared to go into the facility, they found a number of guards had been shot with tasers. Katiya and Casmiere were in separate cells, both shot in the head. Balfour was gone.

Carla Rand dropped to her knees. Dan Ross squatted down beside her. In an effort to lighten the mood Dan Ross with his deep goofy voice said. "Well….I am either retiring really soon, or not for a while." Carla Rand wiped the tears from her face while she chuckled a bit. The case would be out of her hands now. She would be able to see Tommy get what he deserved, but this part of the case, the big part, was now bigger than she ever knew about and could handle.

The FBI crime scene investigators were on scene now and taking statements from all people at Twin Bridges Detention center. They reviewed security footage which just showed people in masks. They appeared to be well trained and knew what they were doing. They used tasers and stun guns on all the guards but shot Katiya and Casmiere in the forehead with handguns. Single shot each, quick with no words. Katiya and Casmiere both looked startled and tried to get up and away, but they had no chance. The door opened, and bang, both times. Then they picked up their shell casings and left the cell. Balfour was nowhere to be found. His prints were not in the system; he was a ghost. The only evidence left behind were the bullets inside Katiya and Casmiere's heads. The agents in charge of the investigation questioned Carla and Dan. All they saw was the van that had exploded and burned. There would be no evidence there either. Dan and Carla sat outside having a cup of coffee waiting to be cleared to leave.

"So, what are you going to do with the rest of your weekend?" Dan asked.

"Well, I have to run back to Boothbay Harbor and tell Russell that Tommy killed Stephanie. I guess Tommy texted Jack that he did it. He was worried that Casmiere and Katiya were going to kill him, too, and suddenly felt remorse or something".

"I'm sure seeing Dale shot in front of him shook him up quite a bit. Tommy was in over his head from day one."

"Apparently Katiya and Casmiere were, too."

"This Balfour has got to be a bad dude. I don't get not killing the guards but killing Katiya and Casmiere. I'm thankful, but most mob activity is shoot everybody…twice."

"What I don't get is what was the plan after the exchange. I mean they were definitely going to kill Tommy, I am pretty sure of that, but what about Dale's boat? Were they planning on bringing it in themselves? Is there another boat out there somewhere? So many questions and the people that could tell us are dead."

"Well, there is still a lot of investigating to do. Tommy's is still being searched, the yacht, the hotel room and now this mess. As soon as we are cleared, they will keep us in the loop on what they find. They may even bring us in on the investigation. Have you thought about the offer?"

"Well, no and yes…Dan, I like you. I like working with you, but I also like not working with you…. I mean, like when we have put the case files down and just talk. Few people understand our lifestyle and our jobs. It makes having a relationship hard, but we understand it. I haven't said anything because we were working this case. When you came to me with that offer, I was happy, but also scared. If I come to the FBI, I would be working for you, and you know that wouldn't work trying to build a relationship. I know you're considering retiring soon, but now we have this mess. As much as I like you and want to move forward on that, I also want to see this through to the end."

"Carla, I liked you from the moment we met. I made the mistake of bragging you up to my superiors, which turned into that job offer. There is nothing I want more than to watch you succeed in the Bureau. So let's do this. You take that offer and you come work for me. More than likely, they will keep us on this case and let us finish what we started. We can work this case together and maintain our friendship…nothing more. Then when we close this case, I will retire, and we can hump like rabbits." Carla burst out laughing. They both did. They sat there on the curb leaned against each other shoulder to shoulder until they finished their coffee. Dan Ross got into his truck and drove off. Carla got back into her car to head to Boothbay Harbor.

Standing on top of Cadillac Mountain, Melissa and Jack gazed over the trees and landscape. The ocean was not far and now they could smell the sea breeze. All the trees waved gently in the small breaths of air. They turned to look over the water twinkling with sunlight. The boats looked like little sea fleas scurrying about. Looking out over the land, they could see almost every shade of green ever conceived. They held each other, lost in the vast world around them. There could have been a thousand people on that mountain top, but to them they were the only ones there. A small quick kiss followed by "I love you's" capped the moment.

"You ready for lunch?" Melissa asked

"Yeah, that hike burned my tank dry."

They set out a blanket and dug out their lunch. They sat on sun warmed rocks and enjoyed the scenery while they ate.

"So, if you were not an actress, what would you want to do? Like a normal job. Would you have gone to college or a trade school, military or straight to work after high school?"

"That's a good question. When we were filming "Summer Days" I got to play the part of a surf instructor. I spent a lot of time with the kids that were in the cast. I had to give them some pointers on acting and it was fun to pass on that knowledge. So, I think I would be a teacher. Working with kids, molding minds, influencing them to be something."

"I could definitely see you being a teacher. You would be good at it."

"What about you, Jack, if you could be a famous celebrity, what would you be? Singer, actor, comedian, or professional athlete?"

"Well, I do love football, but I think singer. I love to sing. It helps me think. It helps me deal with life."

"We should go out to a karaoke bar some night!"

"Hold on there. I like to sing by myself. No one around to hear how terrible I am. That would be funny though. You going up on stage and singing karaoke. People would be getting a free Melissa Andrews concert and never know it."

"I've heard you sing in your truck and out on the boat. You're not that bad. If you guys had got Tommy's, your mom was going to do a karaoke night."

"Well, I guess it's a good thing we didn't get it then. Now we don't have to listen to a bunch of drunk roughnecks singing!"

"Oh Jack…" She thought about bringing up Tommy's but didn't want to dampen the mood. She liked just sitting and talking to Jack. He was easy to talk to. He was honest and sincere. She wanted to buy Tommy's herself and just give it to the Finns but that wouldn't work. They didn't take handouts. They sat there for a while in a friendly and calm silence, enjoying the simple presence of each other. Their peace was interrupted by a little girl who had walked over and was now standing and staring at Melissa. She looked to be only four or five years old. Sporting a cute smiling face, she held her hands in front of her, fiddling with her fingers as if shyness had derailed her courage. Melissa waved to her, and she waved back. Her blonde pig tails dance in the wind. Her smile doubled with the brief interaction. Soon her mother darted over.

"Sorry…she insisted that you were that actress, Melissa Andrews. I tried to tell her that there was no way that Melissa Andrews would be on a mountain in Maine."

Melissa hesitated a bit then spoke. "I am Melissa Andrews. Would you like an autograph?"

"Oh my gosh! I… we're your biggest fans.…I didn't bring anything to sign.…I didn't think I would be meeting a celebrity on Cadillac Mountain."

"That's ok, I have a sharpie in my back pack. I can sign my hat… if you don't mind."

"No, of course not."

"Can you do me one favor?" Melissa asked while getting out her sharpie marker.

"Sure, what can I do for you?"

"Please wait until Monday before you post any of this."

"Oh, yes, of course. Nobody is going to believe it any way."

Melissa paused in thought for a moment. "Yes, they will, especially when you post a picture of us together."

"Oh my gosh, would you?"

"Sure, my boyfriend Jack will take it if you give him your phone."

Melissa signed her hat and gave it to the mother. The mother passed Jack her phone and snapped a few pictures. The mother took a moment to look at the now autographed hat.

"F/V Red at Night? What is that?"

"That is my boyfriend's lobster boat. He's a lobsterman in another town." Melissa didn't want to say what town. She just wanted to give her a little information.

"Melissa Andrews is dating a lobsterman. Wow!" The young mother, still a little star struck, was at a loss for words. "Well, thank you so much. Sadie, say thank you."

The shy little girl managed a big smile while partly hiding her face in her mother's side. Melissa smiled and waved back.

"Wow, very cool, Melissa. That little girl will remember that for the rest of her life," Jack stated.

"I hope so. I like doing stuff like that. It's like your dad said. 'With great power comes great responsibility.' I have a responsibility to my fans. They are the reason I am where I am. I think I am going to be doing a lot more reaching out to my fans and being more interactive with them. Go to more hospitals and stuff like that. Try to be more tangible." Melissa said.

"Is that why you gave her that hat and made a point of letting her know you're dating a lobsterman?"

"No!..Yes….I did take advantage of the situation a bit. Monday she will post that picture and talk about meeting me. People will learn that I didn't go running to a rehab center. They will learn I went on a vacation and have a new boyfriend. Some media rags will run with the story and spin it in some negative manipulation. I am fine with that. I will come out later with two powerful things on my side."

"And what are those?"

"The truth….and you."

After they finished their picnic lunch, they headed back down the mountain. It had been a good day.

It was five o'clock in the evening when Rand pulled into the Finn family compound. She walked up onto the back porch to see Russell sitting in his rocking chair, smoking his pipe and sipping a tumbler of scotch. No cell phone in his hand, just the local newspaper. If she didn't know better, she would have sworn she had just walked back in time. The radio in the kitchen was playing some old golden country music, with Anne singing along while she was getting dinner ready. She felt like she was looking at the flat calm ocean just before a storm hit and she was the storm. She knew the fact Tommy was willing to give them the business wouldn't soften the blow. She was planning the conversation in her head when Russell spoke up and interrupted her thoughts.

"This must be something else if you're standing there for that long thinking on what to say," Russell said.

"Hi Russell…." She paused trying to think a little more.

"Good evening, Agent Rand. Come on up and take a seat. Would you like a cup of coffee, a scotch, or something".

"No, thank you. I have had too much coffee over these past few weeks and I am here officially so I can't drink."

"Suit yourself…but please take a seat. You standing there makes me think I am about to get arrested."

Rand smiled at the small bit of humor trying to make the situation a bit lighter and took a seat next to Russell. "Russell, some information has come out and I need to share it with you. It's about how Stephanie died."

"Mind if I get Anne out here to hear this?"

"No, of course not."

Russell went inside the house and soon both of them came out. Russell sat back in his chair while Anne stood next to him with her hand on his shoulder.

"The night of the Fourth of July Stephanie left Tommy's place, headed to her house, but she was being followed by two men in separate vehicles. The first vehicle was close behind her while the second was a ways back. The first vehicle slammed into the back of her car forcing her off the road. The person in the second car recorded it on their cell phone." She paused to let that settle a bit and could see the emotion in Russell's and Anne's faces. "The driver of the vehicle that pushed Stephanie's car off the road and killed her was Tommy MacIntyre."

Before she could take a breath to finish what she was about to say, Russell had hopped out of his chair knocking over his drink.

"That miserable piece of shit took our Stephanie away. Why?.... I don't care... I am going to rip his heart from his chest and shove it down his throat. How could he do that?.... How?.... Why?...."

Russell was fading to tears now. Anne was choked up as well but held her husband tight.

"He was given an ultimatum. Either he killed her or he and she would both be killed. Stephanie had overheard Tommy talking to one of the dealers. She gave Tommy a chance to go to the police himself and come clean. Tommy told this to his dealers. That's why they gave him that ultimatum."

"Stephanie...If she hadn't been such a nice person.... always giving people a second chance," Anne muttered.

"He's confessed. He gave me a statement. He didn't need to though; we have him on video and pieces of Stephanie's broken taillight found in an old truck of his. Another thing, he texted Jack last night that he killed her. I know Jack is out of cell phone range but what happens when he isn't. I am sure this will hit him hard. Is he going to be ok?" Rand asked.

"I don't know when he will get that message. I would think he would call me or Anne first. Melissa is with him. She will take care of him." Russell answered.

"Well, I would hate to say there is a silver lining in all this, but I do have some good news. Tommy intends to give you the business."

Anne and Russell looked at each other.

"Just give it to us?" Anne asked in astonishment.

"Yes, he would end up losing it anyway. I think he knows nobody would fish for him again after all this gets out. He feels he owes it to you. He is also giving Stephanie's mother his house and property."

"Does he think all that makes up for what he did?" Russell barked.

"No, I think the guilt is overcoming him. I don't feel sorry for him, but I think in the big picture he went in over his head. He had no idea what he was getting into and once he realized the mess he was in, it was too late. Now I have a very long week ahead of me. I will be interrogating you two, Jack and Melissa, the Williams family and all the fishermen. Russell, I may need you to keep an eye on the stuff down at the dock. The pumps are still running and bait freezer is still cold, but I may have you and Elizabeth come in and check things out during the week until we wrap up."

"What about a trial?" Anne asked.

"Unless I turn up more suspects during the interrogation, which I don't think I will, there will be no trial. We will have an arraignment in which Tommy will plead guilty. Then it will go to sentencing. He is being charged with first degree murder and a stack of federal and state drug charges, so he will be spending the rest of his life in prison. That's not even including the little things like cooking his books and stealing from you and Jack, which you can press personal charges for."

"What if he pleads not guilty?" Russell asked.

"Well, he can try but I have so much evidence against him my case is solid. He has already confessed, to me today. Not to mention the text he sent Jack. I also have video of him in the act. I am not even offering him a plea bargain."

"Well about these interrogations?" asked Russell.

"Just a formality. I have to warn you though, I have to play bad cop with you guys. I can't show any favoritism. You are more than welcome to have a lawyer present."

"We have nothing to hide. I don't think we will be pressing any personal charges either. We just want the dock," Russell stated.

"Ok then, I will leave you two alone. Try to have a good weekend, with what is left of it."

"We will. Agent Rand…. Thank you…. for everything," said Russell.

"No problem. Just doing my job." Rand felt a blast of pride wash over her when she said that. It was her job and she had done it well.

Russell settled back in his chair and looked at his wife. There were no words to say. With Jack constantly blaming himself for Stephanie's death they never had complete closure. With Melissa in the picture now it felt like closure was close and Jack had seemed to have forgiven himself and moved on. This was the final piece they didn't know they needed. At the same time there was the weight of anger. Some at Tommy for what he had done, but some at themselves for not pushing for more when she died. Everybody assumed she was drunk driving but didn't push any harder for an investigation because they didn't want to tarnish her reputation and her memory. Everybody made excuses for her like "it's a bad corner", "if they had just put a guard rail in" or "must have been a deer". Nobody looked at the accident any harder than they wanted to. Everybody was worried about proving she was drunk driving. All this thought overshadowed the news of getting the dock.

As agent Rand drove out of the driveway to head back to her hotel room for the night, she thought about the discussion she just had. She didn't bring up what had happened to Katiya and Casmiere for the simple reason they didn't need to know. Even though she was certain that none of the Finns, Williams or other lobstermen were involved, it was best to keep them in the dark about that. The FBI wasn't going to release any information about the jail break until Wednesday, so if someone brought it up before then, they would have to be involved. She started wondering who Mr. Balfour was. Maybe he was just a sheep in wolf's clothing. If so, why not execute him like the other two? Tomorrow she would check out the yacht they had brought in from the arrest. Hopefully, it had some answers on it. She really didn't need to check it out for her case. Her case against Tommy was already strong, and he had confessed. Katiya and Casmiere were dead, and she had solid evidence against them anyway. Also, now that they were dead, Tommy would have no reason to hold anything back. Monday she would start her interrogations with Elizabeth. She had a lot of information on what was going on. She would also get Michael, Jack and Russell out of the way. She couldn't wait until the investigation was over so she could sit down and have a drink with these people. It had been hard to be so stoic with good people.

Melissa and Jack came down from the mountain and had dinner, a simple meal of hotdogs and pasta salad. Jack paused to take in the moment; there had already been several times where he had stopped and saw Melissa for who she was. Yes, she was a Hollywood actress, there was no denying that, and her practical down-to-earth side was clear as well. She was also strong, confident and smart. At first, he had some apprehension about going public with their relationship. He was worried that all the attention would somehow mess up what they had made. Her leadership and backbone with starting to let the general public know about them put his mind at ease. Yes, it would have its trials and tough spots. He knew it and was sure Melissa knew it. She probably knew it better than him. "Any issues or drama, any tears or anguish that happen are worth calling her mine," Jack thought to himself. They sat and enjoyed a cold beer together amid idle conversation about Boothbay Harbor, Hollywood, and their future, as the fire slowly went out, and the sun painted the sky shades of red before it dipped below the mountain.

Chapter 12

With fresh coffee in hand and the sun just starting to peek over the horizon, Rand walked across the Coast Guard Station parking lot. She stepped aboard the Kransyy Utrom with the plan to start at the top of the yacht. She went up to the bridge and started looking around. One thing she noticed first was that the forward fuel gauge was showing empty. What was the plan? They certainly wouldn't be getting fuel at midnight. Were they going to wait until morning, then get fuel somewhere local? That didn't seem very smart. She figured that they would have wanted to get out of there. Also, the name on the boat was in Russian, but Mr. Balfour was French Canadian, or at least that was what she thought from his accent. More questions kept circulating in her head. She noticed four men in suits headed to the yacht. Behind them was Dan Ross shuffling to keep up. Soon they were up on the bridge with her.

"Agent Rand, what are you doing here? You have no reason to be on this boat," spoke one of the suits.

"I am investigating a drug case against Tommy MacIntyre," she answered.

"From what I understand, he has already confessed. Your case is done. No need to poke around anymore."

Rand looked at Ross for some type of back-up. When their eyes met, he shook his head. Like it was out of his hands. She wanted to argue, she wanted to find out who Balfour was.

"Agent Rand," Ross spoke up. "These men are from the FSB, that's Russian intelligence. We are done here."

She walked through the men and went with Ross off the vessel.

"I'm hoping you are going to tell me what in hell is going on here?" she snapped at Ross.

"Listen, Carla…this is some next level shit. These FSB guys arrived in Portland this morning. They are not messing around. We are done here," Dan Ross explained.

"That's it, some Russian big shots come over and you're done? What about Balfour? What about Katiya and Casmiere?"

"What about them? They are dead! And Balfour…Balfour. I think he is one of these FSB guys," Ross said, hoping to convince her.

"Really?"

"Come on, Carla, you're smart…put it together. Balfour was so smug and wouldn't speak a word other than a few pleasantries."

"Ross, what about his accent? He was French Canadian."

"With enough practice anybody can pull off an accent. How come the only people killed in the jailbreak were Katiya and Casmiere? All the guards were just stunned. Carla, I know you want to chase this case to the end. This is it. This is the end. Tommy is going to jail for the rest of his life. Casmiere and Katiya got what they deserved. We are done."

"It doesn't feel done. There are so many unanswered questions. Casmiere and Katiya should have gone to trial and Balfour, whatever he is, needs to be held accountable."

"Well, if you want to roll Casmiere and Katiya's cold dead bodies into court and sit them up for a trial, be my guest. If you want to go toe to toe with the FSB, go for it. I am retiring the minute Tommy MacIntyre steps into prison and his case is closed. My advice to you is let it go. You nailed Tommy, and if those other two were still alive, they would have been nailed too."

Carla Rand took a deep breath. Dan was right. It was over, or pretty much over. She wanted to see Casmiere and Katiya behind bars, but it wasn't going to happen. Whatever Balfour had to do with it was over her head. She stared out over Boothbay Harbor trying to figure out what to-do next.

"If you're trying to figure out what to do next, let me help you. Say, 'Dan, you are right, and I owe you a cup of coffee and a breakfast sandwich.' Then after we do that, we go our separate ways. You enjoy a day off, relax, have some fun. Monday you and I start questioning all the parties involved with the Tommy MacIntyre case. We tie up any loose ends with that. When that case is closed, and Tommy is behind bars, you ask me out on a date."

"No…" She snapped at him then added with a smile, "You ask me out."

They shared a laugh and went to a local coffee shop. Carla didn't want to let this case go, but she had to, for now.

Jack opened his eyes slowly as the morning sun was coming up over the horizon and lighting up the inside of the tent. Melissa lay peacefully still sleeping. They had taken two sleeping bags and zipped them together. Jack wanted to get up and look outside, but his arm was under Melissa, and he couldn't slide it out without waking her. He rolled onto his back and looked up at the roof of the tent. He listened to the peace and quiet. He started thinking about how he didn't want this weekend to end. Today they would head back to Boothbay Harbor. As much as this weekend away had helped, he still felt like he should go to Stephanie's grave to pay respect. He felt kind of awkward to be thinking of her while laying naked next to Melissa. The thoughts of Stephanie had been fewer and far between until this weekend. He wondered if he should make one more visit. One last goodbye, before starting his life with Melissa. They hadn't talked about marriage, but the writing was on the wall. It was just a matter of time. It was too soon now, but he couldn't picture his life without her either. "Damn, my head is all over the place" he thought to himself. Melissa rolled over and faced him. She opened her eyes and looked into his. They lay there staring at each other.

"What are you thinking?"

Jack wasn't about to tell her where his train of thought had been going. "I'm thinking that if you don't get off my arm soon my fingers will go numb."

Melissa grabbed her pillow and hit Jack with it. Soon, play wrestling turned into love making. After they got up and dressed, they stepped out of the tent.

"I don't want to go, but I'm ready for a shower and my bed," said Melissa.

"Same here. How about we pack up now and take the scenic route home? We'll find some diner for breakfast and lunch. As soon as we get cell signal back, I can ask mom and dad if they want to go out to eat," Jack replied.

"Going out to eat three times in one day…I think some of my Hollywood habits are rubbing off on you."

"No, no, no, out to eat twice. When I ask my parents if they want to go out to eat they will just invite us to their place for dinner."

"You're terrible, Jack, using your parents for a free meal."

"Hay hay hay. I mow the grass and plow the driveway. Free my butt."

They packed away the camping gear and loaded it into the Blazer. They shared one more quick kiss on the camp site, then got in the truck and began their way home. It wasn't long after they hit the main road that both their cell phones started beeping with missed texts and phone calls. Jack was busy driving, so Melissa checked hers first. The first one she opened was from Russell; it read:

I hope you get this before Jack looks at his. The DEA lady did her big bust on Friday night. Tommy MacIntyre was arrested. Dale Rines is dead and we found out how Stephanie died. Tommy killed her. Tommy sent a text to Jack Friday night confessing to it. Be ready this will shake him up.

Melissa felt nauseous. She looked over at Jack who was singing along with the radio.

"Jack," she called, just over the radio. Jack turned and looked at her. "Pull over. Stop the truck."

"Are you alright? You look like you've seen a ghost."

"Just stop the truck and check your phone."

Jack pulled to the side of the road and picked up his phone.

"Check your text messages. There will be one from Tommy."

Jack was confused why Tommy would text him, and how Melissa knew. He saw one message from Tommy and opened it. Melissa watched him as he stared at the screen on his phone. The veins in his arms, hands and head became more visible. His eyes welled up. She wanted to say something but couldn't. It was like watching a train wreck in slow motion and not being able to scream for people to get out of the way.

"AAAAAAAAAAAAAAAAAAAAAAAAAAA!" Jack screamed at the top of his lungs. So loud it startled Melissa and hurt her ears.

"AAAAAAAAAAAAAAAAAAAAAAAAAAAAA!" He let out another yell. "Wwwwwwwhhhhhhhyyyyyyy?"

"That son of a bitch. He killed her. He took my Stephanie away."

At this point Melissa was completely lost as to what to do. She wanted to reach for him and hold him, but wasn't sure and started to cry herself. It felt like all the progress she had made with Jack had just faded away.

"Jack…" Melissa tried to draw his attention.

Jack turned and looked at her. His face was red, tears rolled down his face and his hands clenched the wheel. She had never seen him like this. The wound had been opened; the scab of time ripped off in one text.

"He took her from me. He took my Stephanie," Jack sobbed.

It hurt Melissa to hear him say that. In a sense it made her feel like she didn't matter. All the time they had spent together, all the love they made, was a distant memory for him right now. His thoughts were on the pain of losing his first true love. Melissa's heart was breaking, and she couldn't say it. She knew it would be selfish to say anything about herself. Right now, she had to care about one person.

"Jack…I'm sorry."

Jack took a deep breath and eased up on the steering wheel. Then another big breath as his body's tension slowly eased. He rested his head on the steering wheel. Melissa reached over and placed her hand on his back. It was hot to the touch. She rubbed his back slowly as she stared out of the windshield. Suddenly Jack's big arms wrapped around her and squeezed. He started crying. Big sobs and hard breathing. She held him tight while fighting back her own tears. It hurt so much to see him in so much pain. They sat there on the side of the road holding each other. Jack slowly eased up and looked at Melissa, his new girlfriend, helping him mourn the loss of a past love.

"Melissa…this is going to seem weird, but I want you to go with me to Stephanie's grave. I want you there as I take this next step. I think she would want you there."

"Whatever this life has in store for us, I will be by your side. I love you."

Jack took one last deep breath, put the truck back in gear and headed back to Boothbay Harbor.

Anne Finn was already up getting ready for the Finn family breakfast. Even though Jack and Melissa wouldn't be joining them, the Williams family would be over, along with Lucy and Sam. Clive was also coming over. She wanted to have a good breakfast and a good Sunday before next weeks drama got started. Her head had been spinning in so many directions lately that she just wanted to sit and eat with good people. Russell was also up milling about the house. He had been stirring about a lot lately. Whenever he had a lot on his mind he would pace and stir. Anne had decided to let him be for now, she pretty much knew what was on his mind. Lucy came into the house, then the Williams pulled into the driveway. Abigail and Elizabeth joined Anne and Lucy in the kitchen. The women got to work making sausage and gravy, eggs, and pancakes, while the men sat outside and talked. Russell sat in his rocker with a piece of rope showing Josh every knot he knew, and Josh would replicate it. Sam and Michael watched while discussing the grocery store and Michael's business. Clive arrived and joined in the knot tying lessons with Josh and Russell, which had turned into more of a life lesson tutorial.

"That is a lucky kid. All that knowledge and wisdom, and he is just soaking it up. I wish I had mentors like that growing up," Sam observed.

"Yup. I never had it either. It's good to have someone else to look up to. As a dad I can preach my head off and not get through, but when an older person like Russell or Clive repeats what I have said in a different way, it seems to take," said Michael.

"How does he like going with Jack?"

"He loves it. He thinks the world of Jack. How are you and Lucy doing?"

"Good. Living together is a bit of a change."

"Ha Ha, I bet. I thought Abigail was going to throw me out the first week. I kept leaving beer bottles and soda cans out. She took them and piled them in my truck…that took care of that."

"Yes, we had a dish war…well more like she stopped doing dishes and I didn't start doing them. It got to the point that the sink was piled up so high you couldn't use the faucet. I asked her when she was going to do them. She quickly replied she wasn't. So, I did them. Same thing happened with the laundry."

"Ha Ha Ha. Sounds familiar. Now the kids help out with the chores. Makes things easier."

"I bet."

The conversation was interrupted by Anne announcing that breakfast was ready. They all came to the picnic table on the porch. They sat and ate and enjoyed each other's company. All the conversation stayed away from the recent events. Everybody was just tired of all of it, and knowing that the upcoming week was going to be more of the same, they instead talked about upcoming boat races, Jack and Melissa and other plans for the summer. They discussed their highs and lows for the week, still avoiding anything to do with Tommy MacIntyre and that mess. Everybody had it on their minds but just didn't want to talk about it. After breakfast the men did the dishes while Anne, Lucy, Abigail and Elizabeth sat outside and enjoyed a cup of coffee.

"What are you guys doing with the rest of the day, Abigail?" Anne Asked.

"I think yard work is the plan. Michael has been out straight lately, so we need to get caught up with that. It will be a good distraction," Abigail answered.

"Yes, distraction is just what we need today," replied Anne.

"How is dad?" asked Lucy.

"He is ok, just tired of this mess."

They sat and made idle conversation until the men came out of the kitchen. Russell walked over to Anne and placed his hands on her shoulders. He looked down at her and asked, "You ready?" She gave him a nod.

"Thank you all for coming over for breakfast. Before you leave I have some news Agent Rand told us last night. I don't know what is the best order to tell you this." Russell paused a bit. "Dale Rines is dead. I don't know the details, but he is dead. Tommy MacIntyre is under arrest. One of the charges is murder. Not Dale's, but Stephanie's." He stopped to gather himself. Everybody in the group had a change of expression. "Tommy rammed her car off the road."

Everybody sat in shock. Nobody could speak for several minutes. Clive finally spoke up sharply, "Why?"

"She had seen Tommy with one of the dealers and told Tommy to go to the police or she would. Tommy told the dealers. They gave him a choice, kill her or they would kill them both."

"Does Jack know?" Michael asked.

"We don't know. He and Melissa are out of range. Tommy sent him a text Friday night when he figured his life was over," Anne answered.

"There is some good news in all this." Russell chimed in to lighten the mood. "Tommy is giving us the dock. We will be signing papers tomorrow. Agent Rand says she will be done with it by the end of the week."

"That hardly makes up for taking Stephanie away from us," Clive jeered.

"Of course, it doesn't, he is also giving Stephanie's mother his house and property. That doesn't change anything either. I still want to rip off his head and …" Russell paused to compose himself. "What we have to take from this is, justice will be served."

"What about Casmiere and Katiya?" asked Elizabeth.

"Agent Rand didn't mention them, but you know better than all of us about the case she was building. I am sure they will rot in prison, too," Russell Answered.

Anne addressed the group. "This has been a difficult time for all of us, and the interrogations this week are not going to be easy either, but we are nearing the end. None of us had anything to do with the drug dealers and none of us are murderers, so we just need to get through this week, and we can move on. I'm sure Melissa is taking good care of Jack; we all will be here for him as well."

They all shared hugs and handshakes as they departed. Soon it was just Russell and Anne standing in their front yard watching Lucy and Sam walk up the hill to her house.

"Russell, do you want to make a bet?" Anne asked.

Russell could already read his wife's mind but decided to play along. "What are we betting on?"

"Who gets married first. Jack or Lucy?"

"My money is on Jack. Him and Melissa have been playing sucky face all over Boothbay Harbor. Every time I run into them two, they are stuck together like two old barn owls."

"Really? I think Lucy and Sam."

"From what I overheard, Lucy is getting him trained on dishes and laundry"

"See, it's just a matter of time."

"So, what are we wagering?"

"If Melissa and Jack get married first, I will paint the bottom of your boat the next haul out. If Lucy and Sam get married first, you help me weed and plant the gardens…all of them."

"You're on, Mrs. Finn."

The two started laughing and nudging each other. They held hands as they walked into the house.

The three-hour drive from Cadillac Mountain to Boothbay Harbor was quiet. Jack hardly spoke a word. He went over that night in his head almost every mile he drove. Stephanie was found with her seatbelt still on and a big gash on her forehead. More than likely she smacked her head, so when she hit the water, she was unconscious. Jack thought about if it had never happened. What if Tommy never killed her? He and Stephanie would have been married by now. Probably a couple of kids. Instead, he had wasted the past five years blaming himself for something he had no control over. He shook his head in aggravation.

While shaking his head he caught a glimpse of Melissa. Her head was resting on the side of the truck while staring out the window. She was hurt. This had been a battle for her as well, competing with a ghost. She caught him looking at her and gave him an assuring smile. Melissa was strong, and she had been patient. He loved her. There was no choosing one over the other. Melissa was here, now, and she would be here five, ten, a hundred years down the road. It wouldn't be easy, it wouldn't be perfect, but then what is? They would make it work.

Soon the truck was pulling into the graveyard and Jack pulled up to Stephanie's stone. Her grave was decorated in fresh flowers and well taken care of. Jack slowly got out and walked over. Melissa got out as well, but didn't know where to stand, or what to say. Jack stood staring at the stone. He seemed to be lost for words. Melissa took a step forward and kneeled down. She wiped her hand across Stephanie's name.

"Hello, Stephanie. From what I hear, you were quite a woman. Jack loved you very much, still does and always will. It's not fair that you had to lose him so early. I am sorry you didn't get the chance to make a life with him. I am Melissa Andrews and I love Jack. I swear to you to I will take care of him. I have a strong feeling that you approve of this. Thank you." Melissa stood up and took a step back. Jack crouched down now. "Steph. I have spent some time here apologizing for your death. I thought for a long time that it was my fault. I'm sorry Tommy took you away from me. I hope now that everyone knows what really happened, you and I can sleep easier. Stephanie, I will always remember and love you."

Melissa and Jack turned, got into the truck and headed for Jack's house. At Jack's house the family gathered around to discuss all the good points and bad points of everything going on. Russell and Jack intended to go lobstering the next day and would be selling to Hugh Tompson, who owned Robinson's Wharf. After talking everything over about the upcoming week, they all shared a toast to Stephanie as one last parting motion.

Chapter 13

Melissa was standing on the dock as usual when Russell and the Old Smoke swung in to pick her up. Russell watched her jump onboard and he headed out away from the dock. Melissa went about her normal routine. First, she put on her oil skins and gloves, then set up her bait trays and cull tray the way she liked them. Melissa had gotten pretty tough since going out with Russell. She used to have to ask him for help moving the trays around, but now she could do it on her own. There were no more questions either. Melissa had learned how Russell liked to fish. She knew if the fish were tender, to double them up on the bait needle. If bagging bait, which she hated, she knew the size Russell was looking for. Russell had really enjoyed having her onboard. He liked teaching almost as much as he liked lobstering. It was great to watch her going from a bumbling green horn to a confident stern woman. Much like he had watched Jack. They started breaking traps over the rail and going through the motions of the day. Soon it was break time and Russell broke out the lunch box for their morning snack.

"Here you go, kid. Anne made some blueberry chocolate chip muffins for us," said Russell as he passed one over.

"Thanks. I successfully made blueberry pancakes for me and Jack while we were camping."

"Good for you. We sure missed you on Sunday breakfast. How was camping?"

"It was great. Jack did have a moment of guilt being away with me for the 4th of July, but we got through it. We met a little girl who is a big fan, so I took a picture with them."

"Wow. That's going to blow your cover a bit, isn't it?"

"Yeah, but it's time. I can't hide anymore. It's time to face this head on."

"Good, kid. Proud of you."

Melissa let that soak in. She could never get tired of hearing Russell say he was proud of her. "Thank you. Jack is going back with me in September. We're going to go on the Jim Sterling show and I'm going to tell everything. From what happened the night of the party, to meeting Jack and you."

"Christ, nobody will come to Boothbay Harbor if you tell them about me!"

"Oh, they will. You will start getting a bunch of offers from actors and actresses wanting your advice and the Old Smoke workout plan."

"I imagine they will want to put me on one of those infomercials like that Sham Wow guy."

They shared a good laugh and got back to work. Russell checked his phone and saw a message from Rand. She wanted to interrogate him and Melissa when they got in. After checking with Melissa he sent a message back saying he would come to Tommy's by boat after selling the lobsters at Robinson's. Rand agreed to that. Russell and Melissa finished the rest of the day. Selling at a new place was a bit of a hassle. They had gotten used to Elizabeth's system, and these guys didn't go onboard and help load up the crates like Elizabeth did. After selling, they steamed over to Tommy's and tied up. Ross was there to greet them.

"Hi, I am Agent Ross with the FBI. I have been assisting Agent Rand in this investigation. She wanted me to come down and talk to you a bit before I send one of you up there. This is going to be an interrogation. The gloves come off; she and I are going to come at you like pit bulls with rabies. We have to. We have no friends here. Even as closely as Elizabeth worked with us, and as much as she did for us, she still left the office in tears. Now that is your warning. Russell, you go up to Tommy's office and Agent Rand will be there waiting for you. Ms. Andrews, you will come with me."

Russell went up to Tommy's office where he could see Rand sitting there at Tommy's desk. She already looked mean and cold. He opened the door and walked in.

"Take a seat, Mr. Finn." Her voice had a tone so serious it sent a chill to Russell's bones.

Before he could greet her, she fired her first question. "How long have you known Tommy MacIntyre?"

"All his life. I remember when his dad brought him down to the dock when he was just days old."

"So, you knew Tommy all his life, but didn't know he was dealing drugs?"

"Well, no, I suspected something was up, but didn't know what was going on."

"What made you suspect something was going on?"

Rand continued to fire questions at Russell. She tried to rile him up but he remained steady. Agent Ross was questioning Melissa at the same time.

"Ms. Andrews…or is it Ms. Adams, I am confused."

"It's Ms. Andrews. Melissa Andrews. Madison Adams was just a name Jack cooked up so I could lay low."

"Yes, big Hollywood superstar. You were recently found almost overdosing, then used your purse to beat the reporter that saved you. Gave him a black eye, I believe."

"No, I was drugged by my agent. The reporter was working with her trying to remove my underwear to get an up-skirt photo of me."

"Do you have any proof of this?"

"No and I don't need it. What does this have to do with Tommy MacIntyre anyway?"

"Well, you're a smart woman, Ms. Ad…Andrews. You can put these puzzle pieces together. Big Hollywood star comes into town after an overdose and suddenly drugs start popping up in town."

"No, the pieces don't fit. Because you guys know there was drug activity here long before I got here."

Ross rocked back in his chair. Melissa Andrews was a strong woman who wasn't going to be shaken by accusations.

Rand had just finished with Russell and pulled more paperwork out of her briefcase.

"More questions? Come on, you know I didn't have anything to do with this."

"Read it and sign it…. if you want to."

Russell looked down at the paperwork. It was the deed to Tommy's. He had already signed it over to Russell. He looked up at Rand, who had a smile on her face. He signed the paperwork, shaking his head the whole time.

"As soon as I finish the rest of the interrogations, which should be by Wednesday, this place can be opened for business."

Russell smiled so big he almost lost his pipe out of his mouth. "Thank you". Rand nodded back. Russell went out of the office and down the stairs and found Melissa was waiting in the boat for him. Jack had pulled in behind them. Russell kept a straight face as we walked down the ramp.

"So how was it? Was she as savage to you as that Ross was to Melissa?" Jack asked.

"She was rough. For a minute she almost had me convinced I did have something to do with all this."

"Well, I might as well get this over with. Come on, Josh, I am sure they want to question you too."

"Hey, Jack…want a little good news before you go in there?"

"Sure."

"We got it, this place is ours. Tommy signed the deed over to us. We can open as soon as Wednesday."

"That is awesome!"

"I figure I will call Michael and have them come on over after dinner so we can plan this all out."

"Sounds good."

Jack and Josh went up the ramp, while Melissa and Russell untied the boat and headed for home.

"I will drop you off at the dock, then send you a text when we are having our meeting, ok?" Russell said to Melissa.

"You want me there?"

"Now, come on now. You know damn well you're a part of this family. We do this together."

Melissa smiled and sat on the stern while Russell ran the boat to the dock. After he dropped her off, she checked her phone for the first time all day. There were several missed calls and text messages, and over a thousand alerts on her Facebook account. The lady that had taken her picture with her daughter had tagged her in the photo and it had gone viral. As she looked through the Facebook feeds, several articles popped up. "Actress Melissa Andrews dating local fisherman.", "Melissa Andrews seeks rehab on Maine mountain top." Melissa was ready for this and as she looked through all the feeds nobody knew where she actually was, just somewhere in Maine. The only hint was the hat on the little girl's head that had the boat name on it. There had to be several boats in Maine with that name. She checked her missed texts and Chris Pratt had sent her a message asking her to get in touch ASAP. She decided she would call him after the meeting with the Finns. She breezed through her voicemails quickly. Other than Chris there was nobody she cared to talk to. She felt she probably should have let Chris know what was going on. They were pretty close friends. She got herself showered and made herself dinner. While eating, she saw a new text had popped up on her phone from Jack. It said "Meeting at 6:00. Have you checked the news? Love you, see you soon." She checked the news app on her phone, and sure enough, there was the woman and the little girl being interviewed. As much as the reporters tried to pry into the story and ask questions that could be damaging, the lady stuck to what happened. They had met Melissa Andrews on Cadillac Mountain with her new boyfriend, Jack, who owned a boat named Red at Night. As much as the reporters tried to dig and ask about rehab or drugs, the lady stuck to the facts. The next news article was about a big drug bust in Boothbay Harbor. Only a few details were released. No names or exact locations, just that it was the biggest drug bust in Maine. Ten times bigger than any previous bust. As she ate her dinner, she hoped the sequence of the events to come would not collide. She guessed by mid-day tomorrow the town would be buzzing with the news of her and Jack. Madison Adams was no more. Her real identity would be out. Also, the details of the drug bust would start getting out. She hoped that people would not make the leap that Ross had insinuated. That would be a disaster. To change her thoughts to something more positive, she started thinking about the meeting at the Finns. She really wasn't surprised they had invited her. She really liked the idea of having a karaoke night. As her mind started filling up with ideas, her phone rang. It was Chris Pratt.

"Hi, Chris, how are you?"

"How am I? … How are you, Miss Run off to Maine Without Telling Anybody?"

"Chris, I am sorry I didn't say anything to you and haven't called. I have had a lot on my mind."

"I guess so. New boyfriend! When and how did that happen? Do you think that is a good idea right now?"

"Well, how it happened is kind of comical and we have only been together a few weeks. He is a really great guy. Honest, sincere, and he cares about me. I don't really care if it is the right thing to do right now. The media can say what they want. I love Jack and he loves me."

There was a momentary pause on the phone as Chris processed what he had just heard. "So, what have you been doing up there, other than falling in love and climbing mountains?"

"I have been going lobstering with Jack's father…" Chris interrupted her.

"Lobstering! You have been going lobstering. Like real hard labor."

"Yes, and I know how to drive a boat now. I have been to lobsterboat races. Chris, I have even been learning to cook from Jack's mother."

"Wow, Melissa. It seems you have found some good people over there."

"Yes…. Yes, I have…. Wait, how about you come on out here. Jack is a fan of yours; he would love it."

"Sure, I don't have anything going on. When can I come?"

"How about this week?"

"Alright, I'll start looking at flights and see how soon I can get there."

"That's great, Chris, thank you."

After some more small talk Melissa got off the phone. It was time to go to the meeting, and she didn't want to be late. She pulled into the driveway and walked into the house. Anne had chairs sitting out on the porch with a table of snacks at the center. Michael, being his usual self, was taking snacks one after the other.

"Abigail…don't you feed him?" asked Anne.

"I do. We just had dinner, but you know Michael, if there is food out, he eats it."

Melissa laughed then looked around for Jack.

"Don't worry, Melissa, Loverboy will be here in a minute," piped up Russell.

Melissa gave Russell a playful roll of the eyes and took a seat. Soon Jack hopped up on the porch and sat down next to Melissa. Russell stood up and started the meeting.

"Thank you all for coming. Most of you know by now that Tommy MacIntyre has given me the dock. As much as I would like to shut it down and redo everything, we just don't have the time. We can move in as soon as Wednesday. I want to open the lobster retail that day. The restaurant we want to open on Friday. That means we have to get busy and get that place cleaned up. Michael, you can move in as planned and start setting up shop. You can move your boat to the outside dock. Friday will be the grand opening of the restaurant. The only problem is we need a name. Any suggestions?"

The group started spit balling names around but nothing that all of them liked.

"The Harbor" Elizabeth shouted out.

"I like it," said Jack.

"Me, too," Anne agreed.

"Going once…. Going twice…. The Harbor it is." Russell finalized the name.

"How about a karaoke night for the first night?" Melissa suggested.

"Sounds good to me," said Anne

"I think it's a great idea… Melissa are you going to sing?" Said Lucy

"Probably not. My cover is pretty much blown. I have to lay low for a while," Melissa said with a shifty grin that only Russell saw.

The group discussed more details on how things would be run. Russell would run the lobster retail business and Anne would run the restaurant. Michael would move his business to the dock but pay rent to "The Harbor". Abigail would oversee all the businesses. Sam and Lucy were going to give their current jobs two weeks' notice, then come work full time. Elizabeth would work the dock like she used to for Tommy and had some ideas on how to modernize the record keeping. Josh would work the dock too, when not out with Jack. Russell and Jack said they would work the bar on Friday and Saturday nights as a bit of entertainment for the tourists. Melissa would do as much as she could, while trying to keep a low profile.

"You want to walk down to the boats with me?" Jack asked Melissa.

"Sure," Melissa answered.

"So, what do you think of the news tonight?"

"What part? Facebook blowing up about me, or the whole Tommy thing?"

"Facebook… how long do think we got before everybody figures it out?"

"Not long. I didn't think about the hat with your boat name on it. Locals will figure it out real quick."

"That's all right. That was the plan right?"

"Yes, but I just wanted to drop a subtle hint. The locals that see that picture will recognize your boat name, then the whole world will know where I am and who you are. I just didn't think about that stupid hat."

"Let's see what happens. Are you spending the night here tonight, or do you want me to come over to your place?"

"I think I just want to chill at home by myself tonight; it's been a rough day with that interview and all. I want a glass of wine, YouTube some funny videos, and go to bed. Tomorrow is an outside day, so it will be trawl strings all day."

Jack smiled at hearing her talk like a real sternman. She had really taken hold of that job. "Listen to you, 'outside day' and 'trawl strings' you are really loving it out there aren't you?"

"I do. That's why I am kind of upset that I jumped the gun. I may have ruined a good thing. Out there with your dad, I'm relaxed. Yes, it does get a little stressful when we aren't catching anything, or the wind and tide is against us. At the end of the day your dad says, "good job, kid" and that is better than the pay. I don't want to lose that."

"Hey. One thing is for sure, my father's pride in you will not change. He could have every news network, every bit of paparazzi circling you guys and he would grab his gaff and beat them back, then thank you for the opportunity to do it. Like I said, let's see what happens."

"Alight, Jack. I'll see you tomorrow. Love you."

"Love you, too."

They kissed each other goodnight. Melissa went home thinking about how the rest of the week would play out.

The next day went as usual. Russell picked Melissa up at the dock while Jack steamed on by. Melissa's favorite thing about Russell's "outside day" was the scenery. The first stop was Bantam Rock, which was about eight miles out. Russell's boat cruising at 18 knots it made for a nice half hour trip. Sometimes she would see right whales or a few porpoises. There were only five five-trap trawl strings out there, but Russell said it let him know when the lobsters were moving out. From there they worked their way inside, hauling around Pumpkin Island, Pumpkin Ledges, Pinkham Shoal and Damariscove Island. They would stop and have a break in Damariscove Harbor before hauling around Outer Heron Island, the White Islands, The Hypocrites, and Fishermen's Island. After lunch they hauled around Wylie's Rock, Card's Rock, and Squirrel Island. They were steaming in from Squirrel when they saw Jack's boat just off of Burnt Island. There were five or six pleasure boats circling him and it looked like they were trying to get close and take pictures.

"Red at Night, you alright over there, Jack?" Russell called Jack over the radio.

"I'm good. I got a bunch of boaters over here looking for…. somebody. Josh and I just cranked up the radio and ignored them. You guys done for the day?"

"Yup. Headed on in."

"Listen…I am just about done, too, but I don't want to trail them into Robinson's while you guys are there. I will take them on a wild goose chase. You give me a call when you're done, and I will head in."

"The secret is out." Hugh Thompson interrupted the conversation. "I got a stack of people here asking where Melissa is."

Melissa started to look discouraged; this was what she was worried about.

"Hold on… operation Rescue Hollywood is now in effect. I'm out here in Overtime. I can grab her from Russell and take her to her dock." Michael called over the radio.

Russell looked back at Melissa "You ok with that?"

"Yes, I am so sorry."

"Nothing to be sorry about. We look out for our own here… you know that. We can hide you from anybody. Except the IRS, those fuckers can find anybody."

Melissa chuckled and the plan went into action. Michael took Melissa into the Spruce Point Dock while Jack and Russell went into Robinson's to sell their lobsters. When the reporters and fans asked about Melissa, they played dumb, saying they didn't even know who she was. The reporters questioned the boat name being the same as the one on the hat, but Jack just replied there had to be more than one Red at Night. Hugh Thompson was happy with all the fuss because his restaurant was full. After selling their lobster and loading up bait for the next day, they headed home. Melissa was at the dock waiting for them, happy to hear that they had played it off.

"I want to haul tomorrow, Melissa. Just a short day, then we will take the rest of the week off to get The Harbor up and ready to go as soon as agent Rand releases it. You can work with me doing that or help Anne with the restaurant. Either way it will help you keep a low profile," Russell said.

Melissa wanted to say she had a friend coming in the next couple days but didn't want to give up the surprise. "Ok, we'll see who needs the most help and I will jump in there. I am sure the press will be lurking around for a while. It would be good to lay low. I do have to check in with the real estate agent about that house and do some other stuff," Melissa informed him.

Russell said his goodbyes and walked up the hill to the house. Melissa gave Jack a hug and a kiss and hung off his shoulders. She stared up at his face that had a small half grin.

"What are you doing tonight?" asked Melissa.

"I'm going to ask my hot, Hollywood actress girlfriend if she wants to sit outside and eat tacos."

"Well then. What is holding you up?"

"Well, it would be kind of hard to ask Jennifer Lawrence to dinner with you right here."

Melissa slapped his chest. "You jerk... Jennifer Lawrence... really!"

"Just kidding, you're my only hot Hollywood actress girlfriend."

"That is good, because I brought my work clothes for tomorrow with me. So, I can spend the night."

Jack held her tight and gave her another long kiss. They enjoyed a night of tacos and sitting out on the porch overlooking the cove.

The next morning Melissa met Russell on the boat at the end of the dock. Russell was a little surprised to see her there rather than having to pick her up at the usual spot. Jack came down shortly after and both boats untied and made their way out of Lobster Cove. Russell stuck to the plan of having a short day. He received the call from Rand that Tommy's place was now officially cleared. Tommy had given his house and property to Stephanie's mother. After the short day of hauling, Russel, Melissa, and Elizabeth started getting the place ready to do business again. Melissa broke away to talk to Chris, who would be arriving tomorrow. By late afternoon the entire Finn and Williams family were there getting the restaurant ready. Elizabeth and Melissa made pages for different social media. Abigail worked on making a website. Anne was working on a menu while telling Jack and Josh where to move chairs and tables. Michael and Russell went through all the plumbing and other mechanical stuff to make sure it was ready. Anne cooked up some lobsters, corn, and onions for dinner for the crew. They sat and ate while passing around ideas.

"One thing I am stuck on is the menu. It looks just like every other menu on the coast of Maine. I want to be different," Anne stated.

"You're doing the breakfast sandwiches to go… that's different." Michael replied.

"I know, but I need to do something else. Those breakfast sandwiches are mostly for you guys and other lobstermen. The summer people aren't up that early."

The minute she said summer people something clicked in Melissa's head. One of the great things about being in Maine, and being a part of the Finn Family, was Anne's cooking. Not so much how she cooked… that was always good… but what she cooked. Homemade mac and cheese, homemade Sloppy Joes, not just the Manwich out of the can. Jack told her about so many dishes that his mother made that were just as good.

"Anne, I've got it," Melissa spoke up. "Out of Anne's Kitchen… you make one of your meals out of that cookbook in your head. The type of dish that takes people back in time to sitting at the table as a kid and having their mom put a plate in front of them. Then you're not just selling a dish…you're selling a feeling," Melissa finished.

"That is a good idea," Lucy added.

"Meat loaf with green beans and tator tots," Russell blurted out.

"Your boiled dinners…" Abigail added.

"Yes. Do a different one every week. Maine is more than just lobster and clams," said Melissa.

"I like it. I will do it," Anne said.

"Could you do your baked stuffed lobster?" Michael asked.

"I could but that would have to be limited to maybe a hundred plates," Anne answered.

"I think you should do that on opening night. That will bring them in," Russell said.

"Ok then, but I'll need some help. That's a lot of work. Tomorrow night I will need Abigail, Elizabeth, Lucy, and Melissa to help."

"That reminds me… how are we on staff? Cooks, someone on the window, someone calling out orders that are done and someone to clean tables?" Abigail asked.

"Most of the staff are coming back." Said Anne.

"I also got my friends Amy Williams and Justin Lewis. They want to work here," said Elizabeth.

"Jack, Michael and I can bartend. We will put on some fresh oil skins and pour on the Maine accent a little more," said Russell.

"Russell… if you pour on any more accent, nobody will understand you," Melissa jested.

"What about karaoke? I think we should do karaoke on the first night," Lucy Stated.

"I don't know, Lucy. We have a lot to do and not much time to do it," Anne said.

"Mom, we already have a stage. We can get the sound system easy enough," Jack added.

"But who is going to host it? We need an MC to help organize and introduce people," Anne asked.

"I got a guy…. I do. I know the perfect MC," Melissa said mysteriously.

"Who…?" Jack asked.

"Trust me…you will see."

"Ok then… we are doing karaoke, but, Lucy, you are in charge of getting the sound equipment," said Anne ending the debate.

After the dinner meeting they went back to work cleaning and moving stuff around. They worked until ten o'clock, then called it a night. The next morning they were back at it again making signs, menus and other things. Elizabeth was showing Russell, Jack, and Josh how the point of sale worked at the retail part and showed them her system for keeping track of the lobsters, bait, fuel and other purchases. Russell let all of Tommy's lobstermen know that he was open and ready to make them new accounts. He would even pay off their balance at whatever retailers they had gone to. Every surface of every room was cleaned until it shined like new. Jack and Russell got three new sets of oil skins and wrote names on them in Sharpie. They worked all morning right into lunch. Anne cooked some hotdogs and hamburgers for lunch and Melissa asked for an extra burger and fries. She said it was for the MC she had found. All day she had been checking her phone, which was strange for Melissa. While everyone was sitting and eating lunch out on one of the picnic tables, a voice called out.

"Hello… anybody here?"

"Chris, you made it!" Melissa called out.

"Chris?" Said Jack confused.

"Hey everybody, I want you to meet my best friend, Chris Pratt. Chris… this is my new family."

They got up from their seats and greeted him. After the introductions were over, they all sat back down to finish lunch and talk to the new guest. He heard the stories how Jack and Melissa met, about learning to be a sternman and lobsterboat racing. After lunch, Chris joined the work force with little hesitation.

"Where are you going to stay, Chris?" Russell asked.

"I saw some nice bed and breakfast places. I think I will stay at one of them."

"That's not a good idea. Lots of people around and you stick out like a sore thumb. How about you stay at my place. I got a spare room and you can get a ride here with me tomorrow," said Jack.

"Okay, I wanted to talk to you a bit anyway."

Anne and the girls got all the lobsters prepped so all she would have to do was bake them in the oven. All the food was now stocked and ready to go, and trays all cleaned and ready. They all sat down for dinner again. Russell stood up to make a toast. He took his pipe out of his mouth and looked out over the table of family and friends. He had been thinking of this toast all day, but now…there were no words. All he could do is hold up his beer. Everybody else held up theirs.

"To The Harbor," he said out loud, getting a bit choked up.

"The Harbor." Everybody sounded off with beer bottles and glasses clinking.

After dinner Melissa, Jack and Chris went back to Jack's house to get Chris settled in. They sat out on the porch talking and having a beer. Melissa decided to call it a night, knowing Chris wanted to talk to Jack and that tomorrow was going to be a long day. She also had to go see Abigail for one last trick up her sleeve. After Melissa left, Jack and Chris sat there in silence for a bit. Jack started chuckling.

"What's so funny?"

"I just kissed my girlfriend Melissa Andrews and told her goodnight. Now I am sitting on my porch having a beer with Chris Pratt. Normally this would be considered odd or absolutely crazy. But now I really am not…well, I don't even know."

"I am glad you said something. I need to talk to you a bit, Jack. She loves you. She is completely in love with you and your family. I have known her for a long time and been with her at the best and worst of times. Never have I seen her this happy."

"I love her, too, Chris. This hasn't been easy for me, but she has changed me. I have been able to put a lot behind me because of her."

Chris took a sip from his beer and looked out over the cove. "Jack... Melissa means a lot to me. Like Lucy means a lot to you. Melissa is the sister I never had. Don't hurt her. Things are going to get tough after you two are made public, really tough. Tabloids will twist every little thing you do, they will learn about Stephanie and exploit that, they will twist this whole drug deal thing. Are you ready for that? Are you tough enough for that?"

At first Jack started to get mad. Who was Chris, who made a living acting, to question how tough Jack was, who made a living out on the water. Then he thought a second. This was a different kind of tough he was talking about. He took a deep breath.

"Chris... there is nothing I wouldn't do for Melissa. Someday when the time is right, I will ask her to marry me. We will spend the rest of our lives together. There is nothing... nothing that anybody will every do to change that."

Chris shook his head in agreement. There was no disputing it.

"Ok... let me ask you a question," Jack continued.

"Go ahead."

"You have been by Melissa's side almost her entire life. How come you and her never tried to be anything more than friends?"

"Wow... you don't hold back. Melissa and I are really good friends. We have talked about the what if's, but having a solid friendship means more to both of us. If we started dating and something messed that up, it would ruin our friendship. The media can say all they want. We know what we are."

Jack nodded his head. Chris continued,

"When the news came out about her being high on drugs that night of the release party, I knew it was all bullshit. I had seen her drink and party, but she never crossed that line. She is a good person, Jack. Good woman. God knows she has helped me at my worst."

Jack and Chris sat out and had a few more beers before going to bed.

Chapter 14

Everybody met up at The Harbor at six o'clock as planned and, as usual they went straight to work. Russell, Elizabeth, and Josh worked the dock. The first bait delivery showed up and they unloaded the truck. Russell was impressed by how well Elizabeth could run the forklift. They also loaded up a few trucks with lobster headed for local restaurants. Russell was getting the hang of this end of the business. He could tell Tommy hadn't been doing much and Elizabeth was what kept the place going. Chris was having fun working with Anne, Lucy, Sam and Melissa. All the tables had been set, the karaoke system was in place and everything was spotless. They took Jack's boat out for lunch to get some time away from the restaurant. After lunch Anne sent the crew home. She wanted everybody rested and ready to go for opening night. Elizabeth and Russell stayed to run the dock and everybody else left to get some rest. It seemed like forever waiting on four o'clock to roll around. Everybody was so anxious to get the restaurant open. Anne sat in her chair out on the porch, rocking the minutes away, when Russell came up on the porch.

"Justin take over for you down on the dock?" Anne asked.

"Yup, he is a good kid…and a brute at that. Elizabeth is going to leave him and that other new kid down there."

"That other new kid…. Russell, you've got to learn their names."

"I know, I know. Especially since Elizabeth will be leaving when school starts. This is quite the change. I have only ever been the boss of one person. Now I got a handful. How are you doing?"

"Nervous, anxious, happy and scared. I hope we do well."

"Anne… there is nothing you don't do well. I think we will do great. I am actually liking the retail side of the house. Depending on how things go, I might take the boat out for the winter and just do that."

"Thank you, Russell."

Chris went over to see Melissa at her place. He hadn't had time to really talk to his friend. A lot had happened and he was anxious to catch up. When he pulled up to her cabin she was sitting outside on the steps singing to a song that was playing on her phone.

"Hey, sounds good. What is that for?"

Melissa wanted to keep it a secret. She had a few things planned for tonight. "Oh, nothing. Russell listens to some old music and I have come to like it a bit. What are you doing here?"

"Haven't had much time to talk to you. How are you doing?"

"I was here about a week before meeting Jack and his family. I spent most of that time sitting in this cabin worrying about my career, going over that night and just depressed. I decided I needed to go out, get some air, and just be by myself, but out…you know. I got in one of the rental kayaks, looked across the bay and said, I am paddling over there. I got all the way across Linekin Bay when a boat wake rolled me over. The water was so cold I just couldn't get back in my kayak. I was in the water, my fingertips were going numb and I was losing my grip on the kayak. All the while I was worried about how I was going to be remembered. Then came this big red boat with this man telling me what to do. Within a few short days I found a family and a man to love me…the real me. It hasn't been easy, Chris; Jack had his issues. Then this whole drug dealing thing with the old owner of the dock. But no matter what, the Finn family stuck together, and I was, and am, a part of it. Russell is the father I should have had. Anne loves me like a daughter. Watching how Lucy at first was very protective of Jack, but now I think she would do the same for me. I have gained so much so fast. It's a little overwhelming, but I wouldn't trade it for all the Oscars or Grammys in the world."

"So does that mean you're not going back?"

"No, Jack and I are going back to Hollywood in September. I am getting in touch with Jim Sterling and we will tell our story, along with the story behind my overdose."

"Normally anybody in our business would ask if Jack were ready for that, but after talking to him, that man would do anything for you. He loves you…I mean, really loves you. A type of love that Hollywood can't even understand. I can tell how these people feel about you. They talk to you like they have known you forever. I mean they talk to me, but it's not the same. I mean, I'm sure if I stuck around and earned their trust, but you are already there. What you have here is beautiful."

"It is. Thanks Chris, Are you ready to MC tonight?"

"Yeah, it's gonna to be fun."

"Do you mind if I disclose that you are the MC on the Facebook page?"

"Sure, I am sure it will help. Are you going to…come out?"

"Just wait until tonight. I am working on something."

"Nice."

After Chris left, Melissa sent a text to Abigail to update the restaurant's Facebook page. "Opening night Karaoke MCed by Chris Pratt, with special guest Melissa Andrews."

Abigail replied, "Are you sure?"

"Yes, but wait until 4 o'clock or so to do it so the crew won't get a chance to see it."

"OK… this is going to be awesome."

Soon it was 4 o'clock and the crew had shown up to The Harbor ready for opening night. Grills were fired up, steamers were heating up and staff was dressed and ready. Russell and Jack were behind the bar. Elizabeth was at the order window and Abigail ready to greet people as they came in. Anne was in the kitchen at the ready.

Chris was on the stage dressed as a regular local, a Red at Night ball cap, blue jeans with holes in the knees and a "The Harbor" t-shirt. Michael, Josh and Sam were ready to take care of any issues that might pop up. When 5 o'clock rolled around there was a long line of people that extended out into the parking lot. Shortly after opening, the place was filling up and orders were being served. Chris told a few jokes and signed a few autographs until the seats were mostly full then, started the introduction to karaoke.

"Welcome all to The Harbor." He paused for the applause. "Tonight, and every Friday from now until the end of summer, starts Karaoke Fridays. A chance for people to come up and make a fool of themselves in front of all their friends and loved ones. But our first official singer of Karaoke Friday will be no fool. She has a voice like no other and has been compared to the likes of Julie Andrews and Judy Garland- none other than Melissa Andrews."

Jack and Russell looked up in shock as the crowd cheered. She walked out on the stage with her new look of jean shorts and tank top. Looking just as plain and normal as anybody else there.

"Hello, The Harbor. Yes it is me, the one and only Melissa Andrews. I have been here for a short while now as Madison Adams. I would like to dedicate the first song of the night to my boyfriend, Jack Finn. For those who don't know, he is the younger of the two bartenders tonight. He saved me after I had flipped my kayak. Since then, Jack has showed me what real love is about. So here is to you, Jack."

Bonnie Raitt's "Let's Give Them Something To Talk About" started playing and Melissa sang. As usual, her voice was stunning. She hopped down from the stage while singing and sat on the bar singing to Jack. Cell phones were out, catching video of it. Some people were streaming live to different social media outlets. There was no covering this up. She had outed herself and Jack completely. At the end of the song, she gave Jack a passionate kiss and the restaurant cheered. The Harbor was packed, and many people got up to sing. Michael and Jack did their best Good Ole Boys by Waylon Jennings. Melissa and Lucy talked Anne into getting up and singing Patsy Cline. Jack and Russell were having a blast behind the bar, even though it was busy. The kitchen had a few hiccups, but nothing major. They sold out of the Baked Stuffed Lobster. The night was going great and even Carla Rand stopped by to have a drink.

As the night started to wind down, Chris brought Melissa back on stage. She addressed the audience.

"Wow, what a night. Thank you all for coming. This will be the last song of the night, but before I sing, I have some great news. I need Elizabeth Williams front and center."

Elizabeth made her way up to the stage.

"This girl played a major part in the recent drug bust that happened here. She put herself at risk. She kept an eye open and reported everything to the DEA." Melissa gave agent Rand a subtle wink. "She intends to go to college in Texas next year. I know this is a little early, but we figured it may take some pressure off her parents. A new scholarship has been made to help local kids go to college or trade school. We named the scholarship after a man that has taught me a lot, has been my boss, and has been like a father to me. So, Elizabeth, you are the first official recipient of the Russell Finn Scholarship."

Everybody cheered. Russell choked back tears of joy. Melissa jumped off the stage and gave him a hug.

"Can I get Anne Finn out here please?"

Lucy grabbed Anne and took her to Russell and Melissa. Melissa turned and faced them.

"You two are the best people I know. Thank you for making me feel like a part of your family. This song is for you."

And she sang Don Williams "I Believe in You." Russell and Anne danced while the crowd watched. The opening had been a success. Melissa continued to sing a couple of songs during the opening weekend and Chris MCed as well. They took time during the day on Saturday and Sunday to talk to fans and answer questions from reporters, but Melissa didn't give any details of her supposed overdose, just that she had been tricked and she had no drug issues. Any questions about Jack were done in the same manner, no details, just the fact he was her boyfriend. When Jack was questioned, he also stuck to the same story. Melissa stated that she would be going on Jim Sterling's show in September and all details would be revealed then. During the following week there were still some reporters swarming around and taking pictures of Melissa working on Old Smoke. By using Elizabeth as a double, Melissa was able to close on her house and move in. The reporters were shocked when they realized they had been following a 17 year old in a wig and sunglasses. By the end of the week the hype had died down and Melissa was able to be herself, with no more hiding or aliases. She would sign autographs for fans and even take pictures with them. Chris had gone back to Hollywood but promised to come back. He had enjoyed his stay and even went sternman with Jack. Jack and Melissa's relationship grew, the more summer went on. More boat races, more camping, more time to really get to know each other. Melissa had started to learn how to garden with Anne's help. She was planting flowers and other things around her house. She had also learned to cook more. She, Anne and Lucy would often do girls' night out. Elizabeth and Abigail would often tag along for those. July turned into August and soon it was getting to the end of August. Melissa had planned on going back to Hollywood in the beginning of September, after Labor Day. In some ways she was anxious to get back. She wanted to get on Jim Sterling's show and set the world straight as to what happened, and about her and Jack. At the same time she had gotten so close to Anne, Russell and the rest of the Finn and Williams family, she didn't want to leave. Jack had started getting himself ready. This would be his first time ever going to the west coast. He hauled through all his traps. Josh was going back to school, so he didn't have to worry about leaving a sternman without work. He gave Josh a big end of the season bonus and agreed to take him next season if he wanted. The Harbor had slowed down a bit, as all restaurants on the coast of Maine do. There were still a few weekenders that would come up to see the foliage, so Anne planned on closing for the season after Columbus Day.

The night before Melissa and Jack were to fly out they got together for a going away party at Russell and Anne's. As everyone sat down to eat Russell stood up to address the group.

"Wow… what a summer. Hollywood actresses, drug dealers, and The Harbor. Melissa, you came into this family wet, cold, and floundering about. You have come a long way. I am proud of you and no matter what happens between you and Jack, you are always welcome here." Russell held out on the sentiment. He was already getting a lump in his throat. He held up his beer. "To Melissa," everyone toasted and repeated. Melissa tipped her head to Russell and said thank you. There was a long pause as Melissa looked around. "Well, come on, girl, you're not getting off the hook that easy. You got to give a speech," Russell ordered.

"Ok…" Melissa paused slightly, scrambling on where to start. "I came to Maine to get away. My plan was to stay hidden and tucked away for time to think. I didn't want to meet anybody. Didn't want to be social. Just wanted the world to leave me alone. Then in a few hours I was at a dock drinking beer and eating hotdogs. Being grilled by Lucy, questioned by Russell and courted by Jack…though I don't think he knew it. In a few days I was part of your family. Facing your challenges, cooking breakfasts and working with you. You have changed me. I am stronger and ready to deal with life again. I can do that because I have you…all of you. I know if I need you, you will be there. Thank you all for being my family."

There was applause then the sound of silverware on plates. Small conversations went around the table, like Melissa asking Josh and Elizabeth about high school. Michael and Jack, talking about repowering Red at Night over the winter and other small conversations. When dinner was done Anne brought out apple pie, blueberry pie, and a chocolate cream pie. After everybody was full, Anne got up again to get a bag and placed it on the table in front of Melissa.

"What's this?" Melissa asked.

"Just a few things Russell and I got for you. Just to remember us by."

Melissa reached in the bag. The first thing she pulled out was a F/V Old Smoke hat, then a F/V Old Smoke hoodie. On the upper right hand side of the front of the hoodie was "First mate Melissa". She felt something in the pocket of the hoodie. Inside the pocket was a bracelet. On the bracelet was engraved a lobsterboat and a message "With great power comes great responsibility". She smiled and remembered Russell saying that, quoting the Spider-Man movie.

"Thank you so much…" Melissa started to say, but Anne interrupted her.

"That's not all." Anne reached behind a cabinet and pulled out a big package all wrapped up. It was thin, but tall and wide. "As you know, these days there are cameras everywhere. So, I asked everybody at this table to take pictures of you and send them to me. Then we all picked the pictures we liked the most. Well, go ahead and open it."

Melissa opened the package. It was a collage of pictures from throughout the summer. From the first night out on the boat, to one of the last days out with Russell. There were pictures of her with Josh and Elizabeth, Lucy and Abigail, and her and Anne in the kitchen. Some of just her up on stage and some of her just out on the water. There were some good pictures of her and Jack: dancing, or just sitting, and one good one of them looking at each other. The one that she loved the most was one Anne took the day she came out lobstering with her and Russell. Melissa was in the middle of baiting a trap and you can see Russell watching her in the background with the look of pride and admiration. She was speechless. She could feel her eyes watering. Jack slid his arm around her, and she leaned into him and turned the collage around for everyone to see.

"Thank you, all," she said, hardly able to get the words out. There were more last minute goodbyes before everybody left. Jack went with Melissa to her house. She wanted to stay there for her last night in town.

The next morning, after making breakfast, she made sure the house was clean before the limousine showed up. Melissa had chartered a private jet with door-to-door limo service. Jack looked out the window as he grabbed his bags. He was little shocked that Melissa had seemed to have already sprung back to her Hollywood lifestyle. Melissa saw the expression on Jack's face.

"I know… I know it's a bit much. When I chartered the flight, they insisted on the door to door limo service. We are taking a private jet. Airports can be a hassle, especially with everything going on," said Melissa.

"I get it… it's just a bit of a shock. I was kinda hoping to ease into the lifestyle, not have it show up in a big black limousine," he said, and turned to Melissa smiling to show he wasn't upset. He opened the door and let Melissa out. He started carrying the luggage out to the limo when the driver started taking the bags from him. Jack let him take his bags, understanding it was his job, but insisted on helping. They got in the limo and were off to a private airport where the jet would be waiting. When they arrived at the airport, the driver and staff loaded the plane. Jack just took it all in. The stewardess came out and said they would be taking off shortly and they would have to buckle-up for take-off. The pilot stepped out and greeted them and the stewardess. Jack took in all the pomp and fanciness of the set up.

"Do you always fly private jets?" Jack asked Melissa.

"Most of the time, just because it is easier to get travel times to fit in my schedule. I will start flying more commercial soon, just to help stay in touch with my fans. This time I figured it may be too much and gives me the opportunity to spoil you a little. You took good care of me in Boothbay Harbor. And you wouldn't let me pay for anything. Now you're in my world. Let me spoil you a bit…a lot," replied Melissa.

The jet made its way onto the runway and was soon in the air. It would be a ten hour flight back to Hollywood. Jack looked out the window and slowly watched Maine get smaller. He thought about what was to come, wondering what Melissa's house would look like. In all their conversations it never came up. Would she let him drive the Mercedes? Did she have a pool? What about this house maid? Would they go out to eat? How soon would they be going on to the Jim Sterling show? He turned his head from the window to see Melissa talking to the flight attendant. She closed the door that separated the stewardess' side of the plane from theirs and locked it and started walking towards him while taking off her clothes.

"What are you doing?" Jack asked, even though it was pretty clear what she was doing and what she wanted.

"I have always fantasized about having sex while flying. Time to fulfill that fantasy."

By the time she got to Jack she was in her underwear. She started taking off his clothes and kissing him passionately.

Between love making, napping, and eating, the ten hour flight went by quickly. Soon they touched down in a small private airport just outside of Hollywood. A limousine was waiting for them.

"Where are we going first?"

"My house. We will get you settled in. Then I will give you a tour of my house and the grounds, then maybe go out for a quick drive and show you around a bit. We will just eat in tonight and go to bed early to sleep off the jet lag. Tomorrow we are going to be busy. I am taking you clothes shopping."

"Melissa, I brought clothes. You don't need to go blowing money on me."

"Jack, I told you… this is my time to spoil you. To be honest, it may overwhelm you a bit, but let me do it. Besides… no offense, but the clothes you brought are not going to cut it where we will be going later this week, and they certainly won't cut it on the Jim Sterling show."

Jack took a deep breath and released it slowly. From childhood he had been taught to work hard, don't take handouts and live inside your means. Also he grew up watching his father being the bread winner. He had been taught it was the man's job to provide. Back in Boothbay, Jack paid for almost everything when he and Melissa went out. This was going against everything he had ever been taught. "Ok, but you're not pulling the whole "Pretty Woman" thing on me."

"Not my plan at all, Jack. I will be there with you. I don't want to give you a new look, just make your look a little fancier. Jack, I know this is going to be a struggle for you. It goes against a lot of the Finn core values. I love those values, but this is my time to take care of you. Don't worry about money and what I spend on you. I got it. Trust me."

His anxiety settled down and he was willing to put aside his ego for a bit. Jack smiled, and leaned over and kissed her.

The limo pulled up to a driveway blocked by a gate. The gate was a beautiful black iron gate with bluish stone pillars on each side. The pillars connected to an eight foot stone wall that disappeared into trees and bushes. Melissa put the window down and typed in a passcode to the gate. To her surprise it didn't work.

"Maureen must have changed the code." Melissa said, as she got out her phone. "Hello, Maureen, it's me, Melissa. We are at the front gate. Can you tell me the new code?"

While this was going on, Jack looked around and checked out the scenery. He couldn't see a single house, just a lot of gates, walls and fences. Soon Melissa's gate opened, and the limo drove ahead. Jack put down his window to get a clear view. The driveway was all inlaid stone. The bushes were all trimmed and well kept, lots of tall trees blocked the view from on lookers. The stone wall seemed to go around the entire property. The driveway made a large sweep to the left and went into some tall trees. As soon as they cleared the corridor of trees the driveway met with the front of the mansion. It was all white with black trim and had large white pillars that went from the ground to a roof that over-hung the entrance. A woman wearing a modern version of a maid outfit stood on the steps ready to greet them. The limo came to a stop and the lady walked up to Jack's door.

"Master Finn, nice to meet you. How was your flight?" the lady said while opening the door. Jack was now grinning ear to ear. He had sunk a little further into accepting this lifestyle. He felt almost giddy at this point.

"Hello, you must be Maureen. You can call me Jack."

"No, sir, you are Master Finn or Mister Finn. To use your first name would be a mark against my trade." Maureen was kind but stern.

Jack was a little taken aback, but could understand she took her job very seriously and had a lot of pride in it. Maureen walked around the car and greeted Melissa. You could see they almost wanted to hug but didn't. There was definitely a bond there but also a respect towards the trade. Melissa asked the driver to take the luggage inside. Jack had to fight to try not to help. He stood looking at everything around him. He had seen this place before when Melissa had invited some media group to come in and take a tour. It was much like the old "Lifestyles of the Rich and Famous Show" except the star gave the tour. It was while watching that on YouTube that Jack started to really be a Melissa fan. Other than being a very talented actress, she seemed nice while giving the tour. Now after spending the entire summer with her, his beliefs were verified. Melissa took him by the hand and asked, "Are you ready to go in?"

Jack nodded yes and they walked forward. Maureen had darted ahead and started opening the huge mahogany door. Jack guessed it had to be at least ten feet tall. They entered into a huge foyer with all white walls with a few pictures and some plants in fancy pots on pillars. A huge mahogany staircase stood in the middle. Jack spun around, slowly taking it all in.

"Holy shit, I could fit the Red at Night in here," Jack murmured. Melissa chuckled and then asked the driver to leave the luggage on the floor. Jack watched her tip him and he started to walk out. Jack waved and said good bye. The driver tipped his hat and said "good day" and walked out. Maureen grabbed a couple of bags of luggage and started to take them. Jack grabbed a couple bags as well; Maureen turned and gave him a stern look. Jack slowly put the bags down while grinning at Maureen.

"Ready for the grand tour, Jack?" Melissa asked.

"Yeah, let's check out your shack here."

Melissa took his hand and led him to a set of white glass panel doors. Through the glass he could see a dark hardwood floor. All the cabinetry and walls were white with dark hard wood trim and polished silver fixtures. As she opened the doors and they walked in, he could see a huge stainless range top that was next to a big white sink that was part of an island in the middle of the kitchen. The counter top was all black marble and hung over in front with 4 barstool type seats tucked under the overhang. Against the wall was a flat screen TV. Directly to his left was a giant stainless refrigerator.

"Wow, my mother would love this kitchen."

"I bet she would; it's a matter if Maureen would let her cook in it."

"Ha-Ha, those two would be a trip to watch, Dad would be even funnier."

Maureen walked into the kitchen.

"Ms. Andrews, I have unpacked yours and Mr. Finn's luggage. What would you like for dinner?"

Melissa turned to Jack. "What do you feel like, Jack?"

Jack thought for a second. He was sure Maureen would want to show off her cooking skills.

"How about pizza? We can sit and watch a movie," he said, winking and smiling at Maureen, continuing the game he had going with her.

Maureen rolled her eyes. "What do you want on your pizza, Mr. Finn. Pepperoni?"

"You pick, Maureen. I will eat anything."

Maureen nodded and walked away. Melissa continued giving Jack the tour of the house. She showed him the pool, work out room, her private theater room for watching movies, and all six of the guest bedrooms. In the garage Jack was blown away by Melissa's blacked out Mercedes AMG GT R coupe. Also in the garage were a Land Rover and Maureen's Mercedes SUV.

"The keys are in this box. The gate out front will open automatically when you pull up in one of my cars. Don't touch Maureen's car."

"Wait, you mean I can drive your Mercedes?"

"Of course. Be careful though. The media know that car very well. You may find yourself being in a paparazzi gauntlet."

"Ok, so I have seen every room but yours. When do we see that?"

"Not until tonight." She paused for a bit and took a deep breath. "Jack, I have to tell you something. You are obviously not my first boyfriend, but no other man in my life has ever spent the night with me in my bed. Every other boyfriend had some angle or was just using a relationship with me to boost their own career. I always knew that, but I wanted some type of companionship. You are the only man I have ever fallen in love with."

He knew he loved her and he knew she loved him. He didn't care about the men before him. He really didn't care about mansion, the cars, or how much she was worth. He did care that he meant enough to her that she wanted their first night together in her house to be special. He pulled her close and kissed her passionately. When they finished, she leaned against him, wrapping her arms around him. He held her close and they stood there just holding each other. Eventually they walked back to the kitchen where Maureen was preparing pizza. Jack saw her grilling what looked like sautéed steak and something else, but she covered up the pan. He looked up and saw her give him a devious grin. They passed through the kitchen and sat by the pool.

"We are having lunch with Jim Sterling at his house tomorrow. Just so he can meet you and get the whole story. After that we will go out and see some of the sights, the Hollywood stars, maybe take you on a set, and greet some fans. We will grab dinner at Madeo, then back here for a break, take a shower, then back out to go clubbing," said Melissa.

"Clubbing?"

"Yes…have some drinks, dance a little and have some fun."

"Ok…" Jack hesitated a bit. This was a major change. He had not been one to go out "clubbing" ever in his life. Now going out with complete strangers had him feeling a bit anxious. He could tell it meant a lot to Melissa. She was trying to make this a memorable vacation for him. Just seeing her house was memorable enough.

They talked more about what was planned, until Maureen came to tell them dinner was ready and waiting in the theater.

"I have Notting Hill queued up and ready to go… I thought that was fitting given the circumstances." Maureen jested.

Maureen guided them to the theatre. Jack could smell the pizza on the way; it didn't smell like a normal pepperoni pizza. As they walked into the theater, Jack could see his pizza.

"That ain't Pepperoni!"

"No, it is sautéed filet mignon and Pacific scallops with chopped scallions. A little surf and turf if you will"

"Wow, Maureen. It looks good. I was trying to make it easy for you."

"Mr. Finn you are a lobsterman, right?"

"Yes."

"Hard work, right? Challenging?"

"Yes and yes; it, can be challenging."

"You take a lot of pride in what you do. You are proud of what you are and where you come from."

"Yes, of course."

"Well, I am very proud to be Ms. Andrew's housekeeper. I take my job very seriously and Ms. Andrews pays me well to do it. I understand this is not something you are used to. But to try to help me, or make things easy for me, would be like me saying you have an ugly boat. Now Ms. Andrews told me you are a beer drinker. Would you like one with your pizza and movie?"

Jack finally understood where Maureen was coming from. He asked for a beer and sat down to enjoy his pizza. Melissa sat down next to him. Maureen came back with a selection of local beers for him to choose from, but kept them in the bottle rather than pouring into a glass to fit Jack's style a bit. As Jack watched the movie, he laughed a bit about how some of it mirrored him and Melissa, but how most of what they had was their own. He thought back to the first moments he had picked her up out of the water. The first time she smiled at him after getting warmed up. When they were done eating, they snuggled in close to each other. Maureen came and took the dishes. At the end of the movie Maureen came back and spoke to Melissa.

"Early start tomorrow, Ms. Andrews?"

"Yes, I want to be up by seven. I don't need you to set out any clothes, but if breakfast could be ready by eight that would be great."

"And what would you like for breakfast?"

"That pizza was filling, so probably just a bagel and tea. How about you, Jack?"

"Scrambled eggs and sausage please, Maureen... and coffee!"

"Cream and sugar?"

"No, black please."

"Ah yes, I should have guessed. Very good. I will be in my quarters for the rest of the evening. See you in the morning."

Maureen left Jack and Melissa in the theatre.

"I am going up to bed. I want you to give me fifteen minutes, then come on up," Melissa said to Jack.

"Ok," he said, knowing she was planning something very romantic and erotic.

Melissa walked away and headed upstairs. Jack sat impatiently looking at the time, waiting for the fifteen minutes to go by. It felt like an eternity. His mind was buzzing with all the ideas of what she had planned. The minutes clicked by slowly and when the fifteenth minute had gone by he walked towards her room. He went up the stairs and came to her door. He slowly cracked it open to find her standing leaning against the foot of the bed. She was wearing a white lace slip that fit loosely, but with the low light glowing through, it showed her curves. Jack slowly walked to her and wrapped his arms around her with his hands resting just barely above her buttocks. They stared into each other's eyes, not saying a word. In that mutual stare all that needed to be said was already known. Jack slid his hands slowly up around her hips and over her breasts. He held her face in his hands like a fragile flower. He pulled her face towards his lips and they kissed passionately. The world went away as the two made love in Melissa's bed in her house.

Chapter 15

Jack opened his eyes to see the white ceiling of Melissa's bedroom. He glanced over to her and she was still curled up sleeping. He slid out of the bed quietly and got dressed enough to be decent to walk around the house. Melissa's room had a balcony just outside of large double doors. He stepped outside and took in the morning air. It was much different than his home. No salt air, no sound of seagulls or lobster boats in the distance, no sunrise coming up over the water. He liked this place because it was new and different but knew if he stayed here too long he would hate it. It was just not his way of living. At first he had thought Melissa had gotten over this type of lifestyle, but now it seemed she ran right back to it. Even last night was a different side of Melissa: the fancy lace slip, the lighting, and the huge bed. He would rather have seen her in one of his shirts on the bunk of his boat. He took a deep breath and released it slowly, and thought about her plans for the day. He really didn't want to do the whole new wardrobe thing. He was nervous about meeting Jim and going out clubbing. None the less he loved Melissa and was willing to do anything to make her happy.

He walked back inside and thought about getting back in bed but being so used to being up and about this early in the morning, he figured he would head downstairs and get himself a cup of coffee. Maureen was already there getting breakfast started.

"What can I get for you, Mr. Finn?" Maureen asked.

"A cup of coffee please. I can get it myself if you're busy Maureen."

"Nonsense. You like blueberry coffee with french vanilla creamer, correct?"

"Uh… yeah, how did you know?"

"Ms. Andrews told me about what you liked. She also warned me you would be up early."

Jack nodded his head. He should have figured that Melissa would make sure he would have everything he would want. Even the microbrew beer last night. Wanting to make small talk, and also curious about what Maureen thought about this whole thing, Jack decided to start a conversation with Maureen.

"So, what do you think of me and Melissa, Maureen?"

Maureen stopped what she was doing and looked at him kind of flustered.

"It is none of my business, Mr. Finn. Ms. Andrews is my employer and you are her guest. I am not allowed to give my opinion on her personal matters, nor do I care to voice them. Now if you would like to make small talk, I suggest we talk about the weather or recent news."

Jack felt so foolish. Of course, Maureen would not talk about such things. Maureen was a professional, very strict and stoic. Maureen finished making his coffee and passed it to him. He started to walk out of the kitchen when Maureen spoke up.

"I will say that she is the happiest I have ever seen her," said Maureen with a smile of approval.

Jack took a sip of his coffee, smiled back at Maureen and walked out towards the pool. He sat down on one of the chairs and stared into the pool.

"Not quite Lobster Cove, is it?" Melissa said as she sat beside him. "Funny, I have only been back here a day… not even, and I already miss that place. I can imagine how you feel. You have lived there your whole life."

"I'm alright. It's pretty cool to be here with you." Jack tried to make it sound like he was fine.

"Jack, I saw the way you looked outside on the balcony this morning. Since you have been here you have been slightly on guard."

Jack looked at Melissa. She was so caring and perceptive. "Melissa, this is just a lot for me to process. This life is very different. You are different."

"Jack, I am no different. I am still the girl you fished out of the water. This is just a part of me you have never seen. I need you to be a little patient and let your guard down. Nobody is going to think less of you for living it up a bit."

Jack leaned in and kissed her. He felt a little better after that talk. It was as she said, another side of her he had never seen. She was still the woman he fell in love with. Maureen brought their breakfast to the table by the pool. After eating, they got dressed and headed out for shopping. While heading for the first store, Jack's eyes explored the interior of the Mercedes: all black leather with carbon fiber trim. Melissa handled it well, flipping through the gears with the paddle shifters on the steering column. She grinned at Jack while at a stop light at the bottom of an on ramp. When the light turned green Melissa took off fast and raced the car up the on-ramp and onto the highway. Jack looked at the speedometer; they were doing 80 by the time they hit the highway. After getting onto the highway Melissa backed off the gas pedal.

"So what do you think?" she asked.

"Damn, this thing is fast."

"Yes, and it handles like a dream. You say the word and you can drive it."

Jack looked around at the busy highway. There was so much traffic, and there were four lanes of it. The most he was used to was two, and that was only when he was headed to Freeport or Portland.

"I think I will respectfully decline. There are way too many cars out here. Not to mention I have no clue where I am going."

"Suit yourself."

In downtown Beverly Hills Melissa escorted Jack from store to store buying different outfits in each one. He was in awe that at each store someone was there at her beck and call, pulling clothes off the rack and showing them to Melissa. If it passed the visual check, Jack would try on the outfit for final inspection. He was kind of getting into it as well; some of his anxiety and apprehension had faded. A couple of the people helping had even suggested that Jack be a model. Melissa didn't like the idea, she liked Jack just how he was, humble and honest, not corrupted by fame. They walked out of the last store with Jack in a new outfit of black designer jeans with a white vertically ribbed V-neck t-shirt. She had also picked out some high-end sunglasses with chrome wire frames and ice blue lenses. He looked like a movie star.

"How do you feel, Jack?" Melissa asked.

"I have to say. I feel pretty damn good. Thank you," Jack answered.

"You're welcome. Let's run these clothes home then we will head to Jim's."

"Crazy. You say head to Jim's like we are headed over to Michael's house."

"Well, we kind of are. It's no different. You met Chris, this is just like that."

After dropping Jack's new clothes off, they drove to Jim Sterling's house. Just like the first time he saw Melissa's house, he was in awe of the big house and luxurious surrounding landscape. Melissa pulled up and Jim walked out of his house. He was dressed very casually, not much different than the way he dressed on his show. He greeted Melissa with a big hug.

"Hello, so nice to see you, and thanks for coming."

"Thank you for inviting us over. This is my boyfriend, Jack."

"Hello, Jack, how are you liking Hollywood?"

Jack still had not figured out how to answer that question yet. "I am getting used to it," he responded. He already liked Jim. He had watched the "Jim Sterling Show" many times and he liked the way Jim handled the celebrities on his show. He kept things light for the most part, but every so often he would pull some emotion from a guest. Jim himself was a funny character. He seemed to be always smiling and jovial, even when caught off guard by the press.

"Well, why don't you guys come inside and have some lunch. We can talk about the show while we eat."

Jack was a little uncomfortable at first. Jim was asking some personal questions about Stephanie and he really wanted to let that rest. Melissa's past was pretty much known. There had already been stories about her and her triumph to stardom, so Jim asked about the night of the alleged drug overdose and what actually happened. Melissa told him her side of that night. When Jim asked about Boothbay Harbor, Melissa lit up and told him all about Russell and Anne. To hear her talk about them, they were superheroes. She had a great pride about Jack's parents. She shared the many pictures of the family, the boats, and pictures taken of her working on the boat. Jim came back to Jack asking about how it felt to be dating a movie star and how it has changed his life, if any. They left out Tommy and all the drug dealing. Jim asked if they wanted a copy of the questions he was going to ask and they both declined. At the end of the lunch Jim saw them out and gave them a hug. They drove out of the driveway and headed to Melissa's house for a snack and a nap before their night on the town. Jack kept bouncing between a state of panic, wanting to go home, and a curious anxiety about what was to come. Jack had never been to a fancy restaurant with dress codes and such, and he certainly had never been to a dance club before. He had never been much of a party animal and was never much for getting drunk. From what he had seen in Boothbay, Melissa wasn't either. Sure she got pretty tipsy a couple times but was always able to function. Who would they be partying with? Would Chris be there? What would he talk about?

Jack woke up to Melissa kissing him on the cheek. He rolled on to his back and looked up at her blue eyes. She was smiling at him, as she did sometimes when she was lost in happy thoughts. He couldn't help but think how funny it was that he was sleeping with one of America's hottest women. Laying there naked with no care in the world. How many men wished they could be where he was.

"What are you thinking?"

"Just how many guys would love to be where I am right now. I am Melissa Andrew's boyfriend."

"Yeah, and if you were famous, think of how many women would love to be where I am. There are plenty of gorgeous women in this world prettier than me. The only difference is the world doesn't know about them."

"Yes, but on top of your looks, you can act, sing, and dance. You are also just as beautiful on the inside."

Melissa's eyes got a little watery. She kissed his cheek. "I love you, Jack Finn."

"I love you, Melissa Andrews."

They kissed each other passionately. Jack tried getting intimate again but Melissa stopped him.

"I have a limo coming to pick us up. We have to get dressed."

"Damn the bad luck."

She asked him to get ready in a separate room, so he picked out an outfit with some help from Maureen and went down the stairs and waited for Melissa. He heard the door open and close. Then came the sounds of her heels gently clicking on the hardwood floor. Then she came into view. She was wearing a black skirt that stopped at the top of her knees and a black tank top that let a subtle amount of cleavage to peek out. Her hair was down just how he liked it. She looked sexy, but tasteful. He couldn't help but start thinking about getting her out of it. Jack was sharp as well, in a black leather Bogetta Veneta jacket over a white button up shirt and black jeans with chrome zippers. Maureen had taken the liberty to gel his hair a bit.

"You look great Jack, It's you…. in a different way," Melissa said.

"You are looking pretty hot yourself. I already can't wait to get you back here and in bed," Jack said, while sliding his hand behind her and squeezing her butt.

Melissa smiled back seductively. "All good things come to those wait."

They went outside and got into the limo. When they arrived at the restaurant it was just like what Jack had seen on TV. There was a man in a three-piece suit greeting people as they went in. He knew Melissa by name. "Hello, Miss Andrews, nice to see you again." Melissa smiled at the man and said thank you. Jack, a little uneasy, just tipped his head. Just inside the door was another man who confirmed the reservation made by the people before them. A waiter came and took them to their seat. The man didn't look up to ask, "Name please?"

"Andrews, party of two."

The man looked through his sheets then said, "I have no reservation for an Andrews."

Melissa cleared her throat to hint for the man to look up. He did, and looked stunned.

"Oh my…. my mistake, Miss Andrews. I assume you would like to be in the private section, yes?"

"Yes, please."

They walked to the back of the restaurant. Some of the people looked up from their meal and pointed at Melissa. Melissa could see that it was starting to bother Jack. "Don't worry about it, Jack, it happens," Melissa assured him. They stepped up a small level into a smaller section that was still open to the restaurant but more secluded. As the waiter seated them, Jack saw Tom Selleck having dinner with Greg Jbara. There were a few more celebrities sitting and eating. Some just went about their meals, some waved at Melissa. Jack gave them a respectable nod of the head to play it cool. He helped Melissa sit, and sat down himself.

"What do you think?" Melissa asked.

"This is crazy. I mean the people in this room…."

"No different than sitting and eating at The Harbor…. just a little fancier."

"Yes, but Lucy would lose herself if Robert Downey Jr. was at The Harbor."

Just as he finished saying that, Jack Nicholson sat down at the table behind him. He gave Melissa a small wave and a smile. He turned in his seat towards Jack.

"So, you must be the new boyfriend. I like your name," said Jack Nicholson.

"Aaahhh yes. Uuuummm thank you."

"I hear you're from Maine. I am thinking about buying a house in Freeport. It's on this place called Wolfe's Neck. Do you know a good contractor to do some work for me?"

Jack had regained his train of thought a bit. "Yes, Knickerbocker Group, great business, good people."

"Thank you, I also have a sailboat. From what I understand in the media, your best friend is a marine mechanic, right?"

"Yes, he is in Boothbay Harbor, Williams Marine, his name is Michael."

"Thanks, I'll look into all that. Take care of Melissa; if you don't, I will."

Jack turned back to Melissa, grinning ear to ear.

"Wow, you didn't look that happy when you pulled me out of the water."

"Well I didn't know who you were at first, then when I did, I figured you were already pretty embarrassed."

During their meal several other celebrities came over to greet them. Different actors and actresses, directors and singers. Before long Jack was at ease making conversation with them. Most would say hello to Melissa, then turn to Jack with questions about Maine and lobstering. Robert Downey Jr. even asked to go sternman with him sometime. After dinner they went back in the limo for a short ride to a club.

The people waiting in line all asked Melissa for autographs and selfies as they walked up. Melissa went down the line and tried to get to all who were asking. The doorman let them in, and Melissa went straight to the VIP section. There was another doorman that let them in. Jack could see more people that he recognized from T.V. Some came up to Melissa to say hello and make small talk. She always introduced Jack as her new boyfriend. Jack was getting used to all the fame. He even felt like a bit of a celebrity himself. Jack was having conversations with actors and actresses, football players and other sports figures. With every new face came another drink in his hand. He had actually lost track of where Melissa was. He looked around and couldn't see her. He felt a little tipsy. He noticed he was starting to slur his speech a little, so he put his drink down and started to look around trying to find Melissa.

"Jack… Jack… are you ok?" Jack looked up and saw Melissa.

"I think I am drunk…. actually, I know I am drunk."

"Ok, just take it easy, I will get the limo to come around."

Jack heard what she said but it was already too late. He tried to take a step but fell flat on his face and everything went dark. When he opened his eyes again, he was in the limo. Then the next time he opened his eyes he was in Melissa's bed back at her mansion. His stomach felt upset, so he got up and went for the bathroom. It felt like he was back on the Red at Night during a storm, staggering all over the place. He was worried he might not make it to the toilet in time. Then he felt Melissa's hands guiding him to the bathroom. As soon as he saw the toilet he dropped to his knees and let it all go. After a couple of vomit sessions he stood up and went to the sink to clean up.

"What happened?" Jack asked.

"Well, I don't know how much you had to drink because you went off on your own completely ignoring me. When I finally found you, you were staggering around completely incoherent. Then you passed out… flat on your face… in front of everybody."

The minute she said "everybody" his stomach turned and not because of the alcohol. He pictured what the scene must have looked like. How could he let this happen? He never got drunk. He embarrassed himself, and mostly Melissa.

"Melissa, I am sorry. I don't know….how….what….?"

"Jack….I am not mad…well maybe a little…but why didn't you stay with me?"

"I don't know… all those people started coming up and asking questions. I felt like a ….."

"Like a star…like a celebrity."

"Yeah."

"Well you kind of are now. It can be fun, but it comes with a price, your privacy. It's a tough price. All the news media are going to be talking about my alcoholic boyfriend."

"But I am not…I hardly ever drink…. that much."

"Jack, it's all about perception, not reality."

Jack put his face in his hands, wondering what had he done. "I am so sorry, so so sorry," he moaned into his hands.

"Luckily, we got you out without being spotted. So you are fine, but you have to be careful Jack."

Jack was relieved that they had taken him out unseen. He wasn't even mad that Melissa had made him feel so terrible. Now if he could just get over this headache, and his stomach would settle down, he would be better. He remembered the last time he had gotten that drunk. It was in high school, at a party. He was just dating Stephanie and they had been invited to a friend's house. It was his first time drinking and being at a party. Just like last night, he lost all control and drank way too much. He walked away from the party and passed out next to the road. A neighbor saw him and called for an ambulance. When he came to, he was surrounded by his parents, Lucy, and Stephanie. He never forgot the look of worry and disappointment in their eyes. From that point on he figured he would never get drunk again. He would have a few beers, but when it started to turn the corner, or if he started getting more than a buzz, he would stop. Last night he had gotten caught up in the moment of having all those famous people coming up and introducing themselves and asking about him. He was THE Melissa Andrew's boyfriend. He had said it to himself a few times since they started dating, but now he saw the full meaning of it. Melissa told him that there wasn't much planned for today so he could take his time getting ready. They would be going on The Jim Sterling show tomorrow and she wanted him to be ready.

After spending the day together at Melissa's house, Jack felt better. They swam in her pool and Chris came over for lunch. For dinner they sat outside in the garden. When Jack woke up the next day he was instantly nervous about the show. He would be sitting on a stage in front of a live audience. Even though he knew what he would be asked, he still feared saying the wrong thing. After breakfast they got dressed and headed out. Melissa kept assuring him there was nothing to worry about. Once at the studio, they sat down to have their makeup done. She sat back all relaxed, but Jack was on the edge of his seat. After make-up, they were guided to a place just behind the stage. Jack could hear Jim talking about Melissa and her accomplishments. He felt Melissa's hand slide into his. He looked towards her and she was smiling at him.

"Thank you, Jack. This means a lot to me."

He figured he had a few seconds to spare so he leaned in and kissed her. Just then the wall they were standing behind moved open and they found themselves kissing in front of a live audience. The crowd cheered and Jim made a comment about needing a room. They walked out on stage holding hands. Jack looked out towards the audience, where everyone was clapping. The lights felt hot on his face, and he could feel himself starting to sweat. They sat down on a white couch opposite of Jim. Jim started the conversation.

"Hello, Melissa and Jack. So glad you could come. I was thinking to start out with introducing Jack here to the audience."

"Glad we could be here. This is my boyfriend Jack, Jack Finn," said Melissa.

"Jack, how are you? How are you liking Hollywood."

There was a moment when he wanted to run right off the stage. The lights were bright and hot, there were hundreds of eyes on him. The make-up felt funny on his face. He glanced over at Melissa who was looking at him with full confidence. "I am good Jim. So far Hollywood has been a lot to take in. Just the other night we went out to eat and I had a short conversation with Jack Nicholson."

"Now Jack, from what I understand you are a…. Lobsterman, right, you catch lobsters for a living."

"Yes, I have my own boat. I have been lobstering on my own since I was twelve. I started out with a 12 foot skiff and 10 traps. Now I have a 38 foot boat and 600 traps."

"Wow, since you were twelve."

"Yes, and I started going sternman with my dad when I was six."

"Oh my gosh, so you literally grew up on the water."

"Yes. I went to school and all, but every summer I was on the water."

"From what I understand, your dad had a new sternman....or stern person this summer."

"Yes, Melissa went with him."

"I actually have a picture of her at work on your father's boat. Do you want to see it?" Jim gestured to the audience.

The audience all clapped and said yes. Melissa's picture appeared on the big screen. She was in the middle of spinning a trap to put on the stern. Wearing oil skin overalls over a bikini top, she looked striking. And the F/V Old Smoke hat on her head with a ponytail coming out of the back completed the lobsterman image.

"Wow, ladies and gentlemen. Melissa Andrews hard at work. Melissa, you look so happy in that picture."

"Jim, going lobstering was the best thing for me at the time. Jack's dad, Russell, is a just a great person. He speaks plainly and honestly. He really put a lot of things in perspective for me."

"Now getting on to that, you went to Maine to get away from the bad publicity you were getting, right?"

"Yes, what really happened that night was, my agent drugged me. She had a deal with the photographer to get some pictures of me. She thought a good scandal would help me in some way. I woke up just as the reporter was lifting my dress up and reaching for my underwear. I just went crazy on him. I hit him with anything I could find. Somehow that got twisted by the media that I was high and passed out and he was just trying to help me."

"So, are you going to sue your agent?"

"No.... I don't care anymore. One thing Russell taught me is, as long as you know the truth, you tell the truth and you stay true to yourself, everything will work out. That is why I am here… to tell you and everybody else what really happened that night and introduce the world to Jack."

After that, Jim cut to commercial. When they came back they went on to discuss how she and Jack met and her future plans to interact more with her fans. Jack talked about the adjustment to this newfound celebrity life. At the end of the show Jack was relaxed. Jim showed a picture of the collage Anne had made, with Melissa pointing out everyone on it.

"So not to sound cliché, but with Jack you found a family. I mean everybody already knows you never met your dad, and your mom left you when you were young. So now you have a family that loves and supports you." Jim stated, while getting emotional at the end.

"Yes. Russell was the first person ever to say 'I am proud of you' It shook me when he said it. Even when Anne just says, 'Good Job' when I help her in the kitchen, it's a great feeling."

"That's awesome, and you have learned to cook, too?"

"Yes…well a little, I can also drive a boat, I'm learning how to garden, a lot of things I had taken for granted I have learned to do."

"So what is in the future for you guys? What are your plans?"

"Well, Jack is here for the rest of this week. I will be showing him around a bit more, maybe take him on a movie set. After he goes back I have to get back to work on promoting "Over the Rainbow" and thinking about future projects."

"What about you, Jack, do you lobster fish all winter?"

"Yes, I bring half my traps in and the other half stays out. I will go lobstering once or twice a week. We just became owners of a lobster retail business and restaurant, so that should keep me busy."

"So you two will be doing the long distance thing for a while. When will you guys see each other again?"

"I plan on going back to Boothbay Harbor for Thanksgiving and Christmas. Then I plan on flying Jack and his family here for the Oscars."

"Well, I am so happy for you Melissa. You have a great guy and a good family."

"Thank you, Jim, I am very happy now."

After the show, Melissa and Jim went out into the audience, signed some autographs and took selfies. Jack found himself being asked for his signature and a selfie as well.

The rest of the stay seemed to breeze by for Jack. Melissa showed him around Hollywood and took him to a movie set. The director allowed Jack to be an extra in a scene. He found himself being less and less nervous around celebrities. Some were too stuck up to really talk to him, but most were quite friendly. They did the club scene again and Jack managed to control himself. He found himself conflicted; on one hand anxious to get home, but on the other he didn't want to leave Melissa. To some extent he didn't want to leave Hollywood. He was somebody here. He was Melissa Andrews boyfriend. He never thought he would like being the center of attention, but he seemed to enjoy it. He liked people coming up and introducing themselves to him. He met so many actors, actresses, directors, sports figures and producers, he felt like one of them. On their last day together, they hung out at Melissa's. Jack could tell she was not ready for him to go home.

"Well, Thanksgiving is right around the corner, then Christmas. You know what my dad would say. Absence makes the heart grow fonder."

"I'm already pretty fond of you, Jack. You fit into my life very well. I think I fit into yours pretty good, too."

"Do you ever have to pinch yourself just to make sure this is really happening? I mean, we only met four months ago."

"I do, Jack, but love has no time limit, no minimums or maximums. It's just love. We love each other. That's all I need to know."

They embraced again. The next morning the limo came to pick up Jack. He would be flying back in a private jet. He kissed Melissa one last time then said goodbye to her and Hollywood.

Chapter 16

The first couple of weeks were tough for Jack. Lots of people asked about Hollywood and being on "The Jim Sterling Show". He was still glad he did it but even that little bit of stardom was overwhelming now. He had gotten used to seeing Melissa every day and night. They kept in touch, texting by day and calling by night. The Harbor kept him busy bar tending and helping his dad run things. Elizabeth was back at school now but had left Russell in good shape as far as systems for accounting. The restaurant was thriving. The breakfast sandwiches were a hit with lobstermen and other early birds as well. When it was Sunday breakfast they would call Melissa and say hello. Melissa had made it a habit to make blueberry pancakes on her own on Sundays. Melissa was pretty busy herself, with all the promotional work for the new movie. She had started going to hospitals and schools dressed as Dorothy from "Wizard of Oz". She took time to read to the smaller kids while getting involved in the teen support groups. With everything she had going on, she still missed Jack, the Finns and Boothbay Harbor. Both she and Jack counted down the days until she would come back for Thanksgiving. Now that the summer crowd was gone from Boothbay Harbor, the town was less buzzing with all the gossip. Everybody knew about Melissa, everybody knew about Tommy and the Russians, and everybody knew what really happened to

Stephanie. Stryker would often swing into "The Harbor" for a cup of coffee, on the house, of course, and to talk to Russell.

"So what do you think Tommy is doing right now, Russell?" Stryker asked his old friend.

"I hope he replays that night he killed Stephanie in his head over and over. I hope her face haunts him…wakes him up every night."

"Yup me, too. How is Jack doing after all that? That poor kid blamed himself for that for so long."

"Jack is doing good. He has moved on. He and Melissa stay in touch. Once in a while some reporter will pop up and try to get some dirt on Melissa, but he doesn't say a word to them. Completely ignores them. How about you? Now that all the dust has settled."

"Well, still not all the way settled. Agent Rand still stays in touch. She is still trying to find out who killed those two Russian birds. Of course, the case is closed, but she keeps looking into it on her own time."

"That crazy kid is going to get herself hurt. I'm just glad it's all over for us."

"I wouldn't say that…. from the looks of things, you've just started. New fishery, new restaurant. I see Michael is getting a permit to put a shop in."

"Yup, and to add on to that, I am thinking of getting out of lobstering altogether."

"What? You not lobstering, why?"

"Too friggin' busy. This place takes up too much time. That, and it just doesn't seem fair to fish alongside the same guys that are selling me lobster."

"You going to sell your boat?"

"Yup… and probably have Jack help me finish off a 23 Crowley. I have always liked them. Maybe fish just a few traps in the bay during the summer."

"Wow…. I thought you would die on Old Smoke while setting a string out."

"Nope…. now I will probably die in the bait shed shoveling red fish."

The two old men shared a laugh. Stryker said goodbye and left the table.

Russell went back to the office. Anybody that was going out was out by now. He kept track of who was out and for how long. This time of year most of the guys moved their gear further offshore and some did multiple day trips. His newfound position made him worry a bit about the guys fishing for him. He wanted everybody to be safe and to come home. He knew the guys fishing for him and knew their fathers, mothers, wives, husbands and kids. This time of year the weather can turn sour quickly. He always had the weather written on a white board. He knew it was a waste of time, with all these guys having smartphones with weather apps. He just wanted the guys to know he cared. To keep himself busy, he would walk around and find projects that needed to be done. He would make a list of things that needed fixing or improvement, then start getting it done.

Anne had decided to keep the restaurant open all year. She closed the outside seating, but the inside was still open. She kept up making breakfast sandwiches for the early birds. She had also started hosting some cooking nights for high schoolers to come and learn how to cook. After teaching Melissa, she found that it was a good way to pass on her knowledge and be involved with the community.

Jack was out hauling traps. He was pulling a short day by himself. It was two days before Thanksgiving and Melissa would be arriving at Portland airport tonight. He wanted to get the heat turned back up at her house and take her Blazer to pick her up. He knew there would be people at the airport bugging her for autographs. The media would be too, with microphones stuck in her face, probably his, as well. Her latest movie was making headlines and was a complete box office hit. He had gotten used to the fanfare for the most part. He was anxious to see her again. To hold her, kiss her, make love to her. He found it hard to believe he spent five years alone, when now he could hardly do two months without her. They had talked on the phone and FaceTimed a bit, discussing what they would do during her stay. Melissa was pretty anxious to be with her Jack for the holidays but also be with her new family. She had spent past holidays by herself, or with a few friends, but this year she would be with the Finns with all their love and warmth.

Jack had hauled the last pair of traps and had washed the boat. He was steaming into the harbor when he heard his father call on the radio.

"Red at Night, how you doing, boy?" blasted over the VHF.

"I'm all done, dad, and heading in," Jack answered.

"Ok, boy, I will see you when you get in."

"He is getting too bored there in that office by himself," Jack thought to himself.

Soon Jack was pulled into The Harbor and tied up the boat. His father came down the ramp, pipe smoking away and coffee in hand. While unloading, they made idle chat about the catch and the weather. Jack decided not to get any bait because it would be a few days before he would go lobstering again. After selling, he steamed back to Lobster Cove, tied up the boat, and walked up the hill to take a shower. The anxiety was building. Melissa had been texting him, letting him know when she was on the plane and where the layovers were. After getting dressed, Jack got in his truck and headed to Melissa's house. He turned the heat up and got a fire ready in the fire place, pulled her Blazer out of the garage and headed for the airport. It was 2 o'clock and he would be at the airport by 3:15. Her flight would be landing at 3:20.

Melissa was seated comfortably in first class. While watching the inflight movie, she noticed that the gentleman sitting across the aisle was looking at her, but when she would glance over, he would look away. He looked young, fresh out of high school. He was in uniform, Navy dress blues. She had heard he got bumped to first class by the captain. She decided to break the ice.

"Thank you for your service," she said, as she stuck her hand out to shake his. She watched his clean shaven face blush as he stumbled for words.

"Thank you… I mean you're welcome, ma'am," the young sailor said.

"You can call me Melissa. What is your name?"

The young sailor looked dumbfounded as the Hollywood elite asked his name. "Ah… I am Justin, Justin Brown."

"Hello, Justin. Going home for the holidays?"

"Yes. I am on leave for a week for Thanksgiving. When I get back, my ship leaves for the Med."

"Oh, so you will be missing Christmas with your family?"

"Yes… That is the way it goes sometimes."

"Well, give me your address on the ship. I would like to send you a care package for Christmas."

"Sure" Justin started writing down the ship's address on a piece of paper that Melissa handed him. "Are you going back to Boothbay Harbor ma'am…with your lobsterman boyfriend?"

"Yes, can't wait to spend our first holidays together." Melissa stopped herself there, not wanting to carry on about it, since this young man would be missing Christmas with his family.

"Jack is a good guy, love his boat. I saw you two at the races. I am buddies with Josh Williams."

"Oh my gosh, what a small world. So you are headed to Boothbay Harbor, too?"

"Yes. My mom is picking me up at the airport. She is a big fan of yours. She tried to get your autograph when you were singing karaoke at The Harbor, but she didn't get a chance."

"Well, I can't have that now. I will give her an autograph and take a picture with her at the airport."

"She will love that. Thank you."

Justin and Melissa made idle chat the rest of the flight until the plane landed safely in Portland. She grabbed her bag and made her way off the plane, keeping an eye on Justin to keep track of him. They walked out of the gate together and she could see Jack standing there with his big grin. Justin had found his mother and was picking her up off the ground with a big hug. As soon as Melissa got to Jack he did the same thing to her. They kissed a long kiss before her feet were back on the ground.

"Damn, I missed you," Jack said to Melissa.

"I missed you, too. I met someone that knows us on the plane."

"Imagine that…. someone that says he knows us."

Melissa gave him a smirk back, then pointed over to Justin and his mother. "His name is Justin Brown, that is his mother. He says he is buddies with Josh."

"Yup, I know of him. He went into the Navy after graduating last year."

"I guess his mother is a big fan of mine. I promised him I would take a picture with her."

Melissa and Jack went over to Justin and his mother and introduced themselves, though they really didn't need to. After taking a few pictures, Melissa asked them if they would like to eat with them. Jack was a little annoyed. He had been waiting for months to see Melissa… now he had to share her. Jack decided to go along with it. After stepping out of the airport a cold northeast breeze blew through.

"Holy crap it's cold," shrieked Melissa.

"Welcome to late fall in Maine. Your truck is parked right over here. It hasn't been off long and it should be pretty warm still."

Melissa was happy to be back in Maine in her old truck. It was like shedding an old skin and getting a new one. She had been pretty busy promoting the movie and with interviews since her appearance on "The Jim Sterling Show". She was also trying to keep her promise to be more engaged with her fans. She was also happy to be back with Jack. The old saying 'absence makes the heart grow fonder' was true, so true. She had missed him so much. His visit to Hollywood had been awkward and not without its challenges, but she felt he handled it well. Now she was back in his territory, in his world. Their world really. Jack had stayed in touch with her, but so had Russell, Anne and Lucy. Even Elizabeth sent pictures of homecoming and Halloween. The family had made sure to keep the bond strong. Her thoughts were interrupted by Jack.

"So tomorrow I have to take up some traps inside and bring them in. I figured you could go with me," said Jack.

"Oh, I am sorry, Jack, I forgot to mention I have a meeting with the high school tomorrow about the College fund. After that, I promised Elizabeth that I would make a guest appearance at her youth group." Melissa responded.

Jack was more annoyed now. "Ok, when do I get to see my girlfriend, can I get penciled in sometime this vacation?"

"Jack, what do you mean? I am right here."

"Yes, and we are on our way to dinner with your fans. Tomorrow you are busy. When do I get some time with my girlfriend?"

"Jack… I am here with you now and I am going to be here until New Year's. Sorry, but you have to share me. Justin Brown is serving his country. The least I can do is treat him and his mother, who is a fan, to dinner. Elizabeth is like a niece to us and you know what that college fund means to me. Part of dating me, Jack, is sharing me with the general public. They are my fans, they deserve my time."

Jack settled back in his seat. What Melissa just said made sense to him, but he was still agitated. There was an uneasy tension in the Blazer. Both were silent. "This is nothing like what I had in mind," Jack thought to himself. They pulled into the Taste of Maine and Melissa shut the truck off. She took a second to think about what to say.

"I am sorry," said Jack. "I just had things kind of planned out. Didn't think about what you wanted to do, or even check to see if you had plans."

"It's okay, we will have plenty of time together, but you have to realize I didn't just come here to see you. I want to spend time with your mom and dad. I want to hang out with Lucy and Abigail. I want to have some girl time with Elizabeth. I love you, Jack, but I also love your family and friends."

As tough as that was to hear, Jack was happy to hear it. She was right, he had been selfish and he had started to realize it during the silent ride from the airport. Now after hearing Melissa's side of it, he realized she was more than his girlfriend. In that moment, as awkward and almost uncomfortable as it was, Jack decided he would ask Melissa to marry him. Not right then, not too soon, but in the near future. She cared about him, there was no doubt, but she loved his family, and that was all he needed to know.

After a great dinner with Justin Brown and his mother, they got back on the road to Boothbay Harbor. Jack told Melissa about all the different events coming up. The Harbor was going to host its first ever Friendsgiving with all the fishermen and their families. Also, between Thanksgiving and Christmas there were a bunch of events in town that had become traditions for the Finn family, including the lighted boat parade, where the lobstermen and other boat owners would decorate their boats in Christmas lights and parade around the harbor. The Finns always attended the tree lighting ceremony. Russell had, for the past ten years, been given the task of delivering Santa Claus and Mrs. Claus by boat to the tree lighting ceremony. Melissa was listening to Jack's every word. He almost sounded like a kid the way he described Santa, and all the festivities.

"Jack… do you still believe in Santa Claus?" Melissa asked sarcastically.

"Sure do. Stop believing and stop receiving," Jack said.

"So…. you still get presents from Santa?"

"Well… sort of. Mom, dad and Lucy all pitch in together and buy stocking stuffers. One of them stuffs my stocking and drops it off at the house. They will probably do one for you this year."

Melissa's face felt hot, she had no idea what to do. She hadn't had to buy gifts or get gifts in so long. She had never really had a Christmas. Buying gifts wasn't an issue, she obviously could afford it, but what to get was a challenge? She knew not to go overboard. She had daydreamed of buying Anne a new car and Russell a new truck but knew they probably wouldn't except such gifts. That's not the kind of people they were. Jack had been thinking about putting a new engine in his boat, but how farnd he feel if she did that? She had time to figure this out. She wanted to do the right thing and wanted to show the Finns how much she cared.

Soon she pulled into her driveway. She took a moment to look at her little house. Jack had been keeping up with the yard work and kept the house looking good. Anne had obviously been by and put up a few seasonal decorations. Jack looked at her and watched a warm smile appear on her face, she was home. Hollywood was where she lived, but Boothbay Harbor was her home. Jack grabbed her bags and followed her into the house. As soon as she walked into the house she started to mention to jack how good it smelled, but he had dropped her luggage and picked her up into the air. Hands holding her up by her butt, she wrapped her legs and arms around him. Bouncing off of chairs and walls and shoving the bedroom door open, Jack tossed her down onto the bed. They tore each other's clothes off in a fit of passion, catching up on days of missed love making. Melissa woke up shortly after midnight. Jack had rolled onto his back and was still sound asleep. She started thinking about their future together. They were both 30 years old. "What if we were married, Jack?" she asked quietly out loud. She thought about how to balance her acting career around being a wife. She would move to Maine and sell her mansion. Most of the time they were shooting on some location anyway. In the past five years she had only stayed there nine months. She would sell her cars… she didn't need them here. She loved her old Blazer anyway. Or maybe, go back to school and become a teacher. Yes…a music and drama teacher. That would be something, a Hollywood actress becoming a small town high school drama teacher. That would be like Tom Brady retiring and coaching varsity football. Kids…. I want kids. Not right now, but soon. Even though my mom was terrible, I know I can be a good mom and break that chain. Jack, no doubt, will be an awesome dad. She rested her head on his shoulder and smiled. Slowly she fell back to sleep, dreaming of their future together.

Jack woke up to the alarm on his phone. He looked down to see Melissa still sleeping, with her head on his shoulder and an odd smile on her face. He grinned and slowly slid himself out from under her. He kissed her gently on the cheek and said, "Love you, have a good day." He put on his clothes and headed out the door to his truck. As he drove to his house, he thought about what he and Melissa had. It had only been six months or so since they met, but he loved her so much. His family loved her. He had dated Stephanie for years before buying a ring, and even then he had his doubts if they were ready. This was different… sort of. Of course he had doubts, it was a crazy match and they had only known each other for a short time. He went into his house and put on his work clothes with plenty of layers. It was going to be cold and windy today. While walking down to his boat he got a text from Michael.

"You up?" it read.

"Yup. Headed down to the boat right now. Going to take up traps inside." Jack texted back.

"Hollywood with you?"

"Nope. She has plans. I forgot she has a life here now, not just me."

"The world doesn't revolve around you. Do you want help?"

Jack did notice that the wind had picked up a bit. It would be nice to have a spare hand even though it was mostly pairs and singles.

"Some help wouldn't be bad. Is Josh playing hooky?"

"No, you idiot. I am bored in this shop today and want to get out for a bit."

"Sounds good. I will pick you up at the dock."

Michael responded with a thumbs up emoji.

Michael was waiting at the dock sipping coffee when Jack pulled in.

"Fill the tank with fuel, I'm going up to get bands," Jack barked out.

"Yes, your highness, want me to fluff your pillows and turn down your bed, too?"

Jack shot back a cheesy grin. Michael knew Jack was all business while at the dock. It would take a few traps over the rail to get him to lighten up. Michael filled the tank with fuel. No bait was needed because he was taking up traps. He looked on as Jack talked to Russell. Michael smiled a bit at the sight of father and son talking as adults. That would be him and Josh someday. Jack read the fuel at the top of the ramp and called it to his father, then shuffled down the ramp and hopped into the boat. He and Michael untied the boat and headed out. Jack told Michael the plan for the day, where they would be taking traps up, how they would be stacked and what size they were. As traps started coming over the rail and were stacked, rope was being neatly coiled up and buoys cleaned and stowed.

"So what is on your mind?" Michael asked.

"What do you mean?"

"Josh said you usually turn on the radio or start talking 4 or 5 pairs into the day. We have 28 traps onboard and you haven't said a word or turned on the tunes."

"If you want the radio on just ask."

"Jack… something's on your mind."

Jack stopped the hauler and turned towards Michael.

"When did you know it was time to ask Abigail to marry you?"

Michael had to stop and think. This caught him a bit off guard. "Uuuummmm why? Wait…I know why. You are thinking about asking Hollywood to marry you."

"Just thinking it over."

Michael had now wrapped his head around what was going on. He thought about this summer. He thought about Melissa. He thought about his best friend being happier than he had seen in years. "Well, let me ask you something. Why not marry Melissa?"

"Well, we have only been dating six months, and some of that was long distance."

"So what…did you believe in her when other people didn't? Did you stand up to me…your best friend, to defend her? Did she stand by you while you hesitated on letting go of a memory?"

"Yeah."

"Well… Do you love her? Because she loves you and that is all that matters, but on top of what you two feel for each other, she loves your family. She loves my kids. She loves me and Abigail, and Jack, we all love her. Let me tell you something. I was flat broke living paycheck to paycheck when Abigail and I were dating. I had my doubts. Tommy Erskine told me something that I haven't forgotten to this day. 'You will never have enough money, you will never be sure enough. If you love her and she loves you, it will work out.' Abigail and I haven't been the model marriage. We have had our rough patches, but we worked through it all. No different than your mom and dad."

Jack took a second to process what he had heard. He gave Michael a nod and turned on the stereo and continued hauling traps.

"Nice…." Michael called out grinning evilly.

"What?" Jack asked

"If you marry Hollywood you will finally have enough money to have me repower this damn thing. The 16 liter V8 motor will look so good in here."

"What do you mean? I might go with a Volvo…. or maybe even a Cat."

"I would disown you, and never let you in my house again."

The two shared a big laugh and continued taking up traps.

Melissa had been up and taken a shower. She was focusing on her meeting with the principal of the high school. This college fund meant a lot to her. Russell's comment, "with great power comes great responsibility," reminded her she had to do something with all her wealth and fame. Giving the students of Boothbay Harbor a chance to do more after high school was a way to do that, but she really wanted to help those that worked on the water. During the summer she watched as Josh would come in from working with Jack, then go haul his own traps. Elizabeth was always the first down to the dock in the mornings and the last to leave. Even on her days off she called into Russell to see if he needed any help. That was just the Williams kids. She also saw Josh's friends working hard hauling their own traps, or shuffling bait and lobster at the dock. The whole culture here was based on work ethic. This was something the rest of the country needed to see. She listened in on the conversations these kids had. They wanted to go to school, some to college, and some to trade schools. Boothbay Harbor was no ghetto by any means, but most families of the working waterfront didn't have the means to send a kid to college, and most rejected the idea of student loans. She had a set of guidelines in her head. Not only did the student have to work on the waterfront, but the family had to be making less than 60K a year. Along with that, the student had to have at least one extracurricular activity each year of high school, in either a sport, club or volunteer program. As far as grades were concerned Melissa decided to keep the bar low. The student needed to maintain passing grades. After talking with Clive Farrin, who used to be a shop teacher, she felt that some of the kids that were good at working with their hands, may not necessarily be able to keep up an honor roll grade average. Along with the new scholarship, she also wanted to donate money to the school. She wanted to make sure her money went to drama, shop and home economics. Also, she wanted to test the waters to see what was the possibility of working at the school in the future.

Soon she was at the school waiting outside of the principal's office. As an adult, she found it quite funny to be sitting in the school office waiting to see the principal. The staff were very nice and welcoming. She could tell they wanted to ask for an autograph or just talk, but that Maine work ethic seemed to overcome that. The staff went straight back to work after greeting her and getting her seated. She reached into her purse and pulled two photos out of a stack. It was just a simple picture of her that Jack had taken one night on the boat. She looked at their name tags and signed them individually, then got up and passed them to the staff members. Both smiled with delight and thanked her. The principal opened her office door and greeted Melissa.

"Come on in," Mrs. Niles said. "Would you like some coffee?"

"Yes, please," Melissa responded, and was happy to see Mrs. Niles getting the coffee herself.

"Sugar…creamer?"

"Black, please,"

"Really….?"

"Well Mrs. Niles, I did go sternwoman on a lobster boat all summer. Russell, my captain, insisted on me drinking black coffee."

"Ahhh, that sounds like the Russell I know."

"You know Russell Finn?"

"Ms. Andrews…. While you were gone, did you forget how small this town is? Russell and I graduated from this very school together."

"I guess I had forgotten. That is very neat. I would assume you would have no problem with me naming this scholarship after him then?"

"No problem at all. I actually like the outline of your scholarship. I do wish the grade average would be at least a B average, but I get why you don't push that bar too high. I would bet that Mr. Farrin has something to do with that."

"Yes, in discussion with Clive…. Mr. Farrin, he told me how he remembered students getting A+'s in his class, but failing writing, math or science. Your science teacher, Mrs. Hersom, said the same students that would excel in the physics portion of science may struggle with the biology portion. There are countless studies into the way students learn, children and adults. Some can sit and listen to a lecture and absorb every grain of information. Yet some will completely miss it. I want to give that student a chance, and I believe they deserve it. Most of those students have to study harder than the rest to make passing grades. That shows me they have a work ethic and determination."

"I couldn't agree more. On the part of working waterfront, but that doesn't seem fair to students that work in construction, electrical or other trades not related to the working waterfront."

"I understand that, Mrs. Niles. My hope is that when this scholarship starts making more headlines and turning some heads, it may wake up some other people of wealth to help."

"I hope you are right. It is odd that so much money can be thrown at a new building or a new park, but not at education."

"I am glad you said that. As you know, I am very close to the Williams kids, Josh and Elizabeth. They have told me that the shop class seems outdated, there is no home economics class and the drama club is struggling."

"Yes, they would be right. I think our mutual friend, Mr. Farrin, installed the equipment that is still there today. It would be great to offer a home economics class again, but that room is out of date and now used as storage, As you know, putting on plays costs money, we don't get much from ticket sales."

"Well, I can help with the financial part of things, but I think in some cases one hand can help the other. Your shop class can build the sets for the drama club. Shop students can also help install new fixtures and appliances in the home economics class room. Once the home economics class is up on its feet they can make costumes for the drama club and baked goods to sell. If I donate money to this, I do have one request."

"Your name somewhere on the school?"

"No, I would like the home economics class to involve some life lessons, so to speak. Lessons on navigating healthcare insurance, maintaining a good credit score and things of that nature. Same thing in the shop class: how to change a bulb in your car or in your house, how to change the oil in your car and how to change a tire. Not every student has a Finn or Williams family backing them up. They need to be taught these skills to be self-sufficient when they leave your building for the last time. Whether going across the country to college or staying here and going to work right after high school."

"Well, Ms. Andrews... I am very impressed by someone who lives the lifestyle you do, you are amazingly practical."

"I have one more request. Upon completion of a degree, I want to teach music and drama. If another teacher is not in your budget, I will happily work for free until a position opens up."

Mrs. Niles was now awestruck by the thought of THE Melissa Andrews as a teacher in her school. She at once started weighing the good and bad of that situation."

"Ms. Andrews... don't you think that would be a bit of a distraction? Having a Hollywood actress as a teacher?"

"I won't always be a Hollywood actress. I have also found that after people get to know the real me, the glitz and glamor wear away."

"Well, Ms. Andrews.... I have to say from what I have heard about you in the recent months, and now after talking to you, the glitz and glamour will never fade, but your honor and goodness will shine through. I will bring this up to the superintendent. From there it goes to the school committee."

"Okay, here is the thing...I do need this to remain quiet for now. I have brought a non-disclosure agreement I will need you and the superintendent to sign. I think as far as the committee goes, for now you can leave my name out of it and just say an anonymous donor."

"I understand completely. I am sure Mrs. King, the superintendent, will be happy to sign it as well. I believe from here you are making an appearance at the teen women's club?"

"Yes, Elizabeth asked me to make an appearance and answer some questions."

"I will give you a bit of a warning…. that group isn't about putting on makeup and shopping at the mall. They discuss real issues. They talk openly about politics, birth control, and other rather serious topics."

"Thank you, Abigail gave me the scoop. Today should be pretty tame. I will be doing a Q&A about myself and the movie business."

"Just be prepared. Some of those girls know no boundaries."

"Thank you for the warning, Mrs. Niles. I will be in Maine until after the new year. After that I go back to Hollywood to get ready for the Oscars. After that….I have no clue."

"Well good luck at the Oscars and have a great holiday season, Ms. Andrews."

"You too, Mrs. Niles."

She walked out of the office and into the hallway. Just as she stepped out, the bell went off and students came pouring out of the classrooms. The hallway she was in was not near the major traffic area. She watched the students go to their lockers, exchange books, talk briefly amongst each other, then go on their way. She took a deep breath to soak in the scene she had missed in her own childhood. She was "homeschooled" by a tutor and did her schooling on different movie sets and locations. She never got to play school sports or have a locker. Her thoughts were interrupted by Elizabeth greeting her.

"Hi, Melissa!" Elizabeth said happily.

"Hey, Elizabeth, how are you?" Melissa replied. She enjoyed having Elizabeth so happy to see her. It was genuine.

"I am good. Are you ready?"

"Well, yes and no… little nervous."

"What? Nervous - you are an actress. You have been in movies and on stage in front of thousands of people. How could you be nervous now?"

"Because this is for you, I don't want to embarrass you in front of your friends."

"Melissa, the fact you are here, doing this, is just awesome. My friends think it's so cool that I am friends with Melissa Andrews."

Melissa smiled; it didn't settle her nerves though. This was new territory for her and Mrs. Niles' statement hadn't helped much. Elizabeth opened the classroom door and Melissa stepped in to see two dozen or so teenage girls looking back at her. There was some whispering and some gasping. In the back of the class there was a female teacher with a polo shirt, shorts and a whistle around her neck. She had to try not to laugh at the stereotype. Elizabeth gave a brief introduction then stepped aside and went to a vacant seat.

"Hello, ladies, you already know me, and probably know my story. Now I could repeat what you already know, but that would just be wasting your time. I would like to go straight into a question and answer session, and see what that brings up for discussion."

There was a long pause and nobody was saying anything. Melissa felt so nervous and confused. Why were they not asking anything? Maybe she should have discussed herself to get the room warmed up. Just as she was going to prompt them a girl sitting behind Elizabeth raised her hand.

"How do you handle all the press and social media going after you all the time?"

Melissa thought to herself, "Wow, jumping right into it I guess."

"What is your name?"

"Laura,"

"Laura, how I handle that has changed a lot since my first visit to Maine. I used to let the headlines bother me. I was worried about what everyone thought of me. I was afraid that I would fall from my stardom in a moment's notice and be forgotten. Now I don't. I learned that it was what I thought of myself, and what the people closest to me think, that matters. Before, I didn't have a real family; now I have solid family and friends that care about me and love me no matter what." Melissa gave Elizabeth a little wink at the end. "And please introduce yourself when you ask a question. I want to know you guys as well."

Another girl stood up and asked a question, "Hello my name is Amanda, what is your favorite food?"

"Hello Amanda, I like hotdogs, Red Snappy hotdogs at "The Harbor". What is yours?"

"Pizza."

Melissa nodded her head in approval.

A girl up front spoke up next. "Hello, my name is Karen. In the movie Beach Daze, you spent most of the time in a bikini and at one point showed your bottom. Do you feel that was necessary? Do you feel objectified by doing that? How do you feel that affects younger women watching you?"

Melissa took a breath and focused on Karen. "Good questions. We do live in an age where women have to think about how they present themselves. When you see me off screen I dress pretty conservatively. Yes, my dresses can be fancy, but I don't show a lot of skin. That is my choice, as it is the choice of my peers to do what they want to. As far as "Beach Daze", my character Madison was a surf instructor in Hawaii. I went to Hawaii and looked into that culture long before shooting began. What I wore during the movie was a reflection of that. I was playing a part and doing my job. It was more of a uniform to me than a bikini. As far as my "butt shot", that was a contract flaw. I never wanted to do nudity, but my agent let that slide. I was already locked into the contract and filming had started. If I had backed out I would have been open to lawsuits. That is why in that scene you don't see my face because I wasn't very happy about it. I didn't feel objectified by that— more upset that my agent let that happen. As far as how you and other young women watching me goes, I have become more aware of what I do, and am working to be a positive role model. Now, would I tell you to never wear a bikini? No, do what you are comfortable with, but I would say do it for yourself and not for anybody else."

Another girl spoke up. "Hi Melissa, I'm Jamie, while we are on this subject. How do you control your weight?"

"The same way anybody else does. I diet and work out. For playing Judy Garland in "Over the Rainbow" I had to lose a lot of weight. I actually had to be unhealthily skinny. Judy only weighed 80 lbs when she did "Presenting Lily Mars".

Jamie continued her question. "Do you feel you would be as successful if you were fat or not as pretty?"

"Wow! No holding back with you guys. That's okay. You deserve the truth. As you know, there are very successful overweight actors and actresses. As far as not as pretty…. What is pretty to you? Everybody's perception of beauty is different. My boyfriend thinks I look my best in a T-shirt and jeans, with no make-up. A lot of people don't recognize me without my make up. So, yes, I think I would be just as successful if I were overweight. I would use that to my advantage. As far as being ugly….to me there is no such thing."

"What do you like to do while you're here in Maine?" Elizabeth asked to try to lighten up the mood.

"Well, this summer, as most of you know, I went sternwoman with Russell Finn on the Old Smoke. That was the most fun I have ever had. So I like to be out on the water— either working with Russell, cruising the coast while going to the races, or just sitting and drifting while listening to music."

The class continued to ask questions. Some were easy, asking about favorites, or about other actors, while others were about appearance, plastic surgery, and feminist issues.

"May I ask a question, Ms. Andrews? I am Ms. Cornagain the PE and health class instructor."

"Of course, and call me Melissa."

"These girls will be going off into the world when they graduate; some bound for college, a few going to serve their country, and some right into the work force. What advice can you give them?"

"For those about to serve our country, thank you. To all of you, know yourself and be confident in that knowledge. Don't get hung up on what others think of you. When wrong, own it. When right, stand up." Melissa paused for a bit to let that sink in. "Okay, I think that is all we have time for. Today was to let you know more about me and to build a relationship with you ladies. I will be back before graduation and we will be doing some mock job interviews and more discussion on how to be successful."

The class said thank you and she allowed the students to do selfies with her, along with group pictures.

It was now about 12 o'clock and Melissa headed to The Harbor to meet Jack.

Chapter 17

When, Melissa arrived at The Harbor, she walked in to find Anne there cleaning up the kitchen. She was humming to herself, as she worked diligently to get her kitchen in order. Even in this slow season, Anne kept herself busy with the upkeep and making the breakfast meals to go. They had talked several times while she was gone. Mostly to say hello, but sometimes to talk about life. Jack was smart and wise, but also her boyfriend. When she wanted advice on life she often called Anne or Russell. Without any knowledge of the movie business, their basic life advice always applied and made the most sense. They just kept it simple. When she had asked Anne what she thought of her moving to Maine permanently, Anne told her simply, "Doesn't matter what I think, or what Jack thinks, or what anybody else thinks…What matters is what you think. What will make you happy? That is what matters. You will always be Melissa Andrews. Whether you're here… there, or on the moon."

Melissa giggled out loud a bit when she thought of the moon part. Anne turned and looked to see her standing there. Anne dropped what she was doing to give Melissa a hug and say hello.

"Hello, nice to see you. How long have you been standing there?"

"Just a bit to watch you work. Nice to see you, too, Anne. I missed you." Melissa replied

"Well, I missed you too. I take it you have been to the school already. How did that go?"

"My meeting with Mrs. Niles went well. She is very nice. She is going to put my proposals in front of the superintendent and the school board. The meeting with the senior girls went well, too. Their questions were all over the place though, from my favorite food to real feminist issues."

"Well, that sounds like teenage girls to me. You must be hungry. I am about to make something for Jack and Russell. Want me to make you something?"

"Yes. 2-3 Red Snappy hotdogs please…. with everything. Is Jack in yet?"

"I just heard him on the radio saying he was just inside of Spruce Point."

"Oh, he should be close then."

With that she headed out of the kitchen and out to the docks. She waved to Abigail who was walking by. Even though she had just spent the night with Jack, it was something about meeting him at the dock that had a girlish feel to it. Like greeting a soldier coming home from tour. The red boat was full of traps and coming into the dock. Russell made his way down the ramp slowly, while puffing on his pipe. Melissa was shocked at how cold it was. She thought she had enough layers on, but the cold November air coming off of the water was getting through. Jack and Russell, on the other hand were just wearing their typical hoodies. It didn't matter how many times Jack looked at Melissa. He always had a big grin on his face and his eyes lit up. After tying the boat up he hopped out. He wanted to give her a hug but didn't want to get her nice clothes messy. He leaned in gently and gave her a kiss.

"Sucky face on the docks again!" Russell jeered, "Brian…. I think we need to put up a sign that says no sucky face on the premiesssssssss," to the dock boy who was following him down the ramp.

"Hi, Russell." Melissa beamed.

"Hey, Hollywood. How ta' hell are you?" Russell answered.

"Glad to be home."

Jack loved hearing Melissa call Boothbay Harbor home. It made his heart feel warm.

"Jack, your mom is making us lunch up in the kitchen."

"Ok…Let me shut this thing down and I'll be right up."

"Oh sure… everyone forgets the sternman," Michael bellowed, stepping out of the boat.

"Hey, Michael. I just saw Elizabeth and some of her class."

"How did it go?"

"Good. Good kids, good questions. Challenging, but good."

"I know most of those girls, watched them grow up. How did it go with you and Mrs. Niles?"

"Good. She will be talking to the school board and the superintendent about my ideas."

They walked up the ramp and into the eating area, where Anne already had their plates ready and waiting. Melissa told them about the promoting of the movie and getting ready for the Oscars. They all got her caught up on stuff happening around town. Melissa missed this so much. Just to sit and talk with people was so nice. After lunch Melissa looked at the walls of the restaurant. Anne had been busy hanging pictures up on the wall. There were some of the town back in the 50's and 60's and some childhood pictures of Jack and Lucy. Elizabeth and Josh were in some as well. She came to a picture of a young couple standing in front of an old car. At a closer look she could see it was Russell and Anne.

"That was me and Anne, Fourth of July 1983," Russell said, looking over her shoulder.

"But that car looks older than that."

"Yeah, that was a 1957 Chevy Bel Air. My dad had it and gave it to me. When things got rough I sold it to help keep the lights on and pay for firewood."

"Oh my god, Russell! I didn't know. Do you know where the car went?"

"No clue. I taped a note under the seat explaining how my dad gave me the car and why I was selling it."

Melissa turned back towards the picture as Russell walked away. She pulled out her phone and snapped a photo of the picture. She had a mission, and only a short time to accomplish it.

Anne had asked Melissa, Abigail and Lucy to help with the shopping for the "Friendsgiving" tomorrow afternoon. It was mostly a potluck event, but Anne had some things she wanted to make. They all piled into Abigail's minivan and headed to the grocery store. While in the van Lucy mentioned that she thought Sam may be "popping the question soon." The women all giggled with cheer. Anne mentioned that Sam had better ask for Russell's permission. Melissa started to daydream about Jack proposing to her. "Who would he ask permission from?" She thought to herself. It was way too early for those thoughts. They haven't been dating for a year yet. Sam and Lucy had been living together. Her train of thought was broken when they arrived at the store. After shopping they went back to The Harbor to get things prepped. Once again, Melissa was feeling very good about where she was and what she was doing. She had been getting some cooking lessons from Maureen. Anne seemed to be impressed by Melissa's new confidence in the kitchen.

"You are getting to be pretty good, Melissa. You did a good job cutting up that celery," Anne complimented.

"Thank you. I have been practicing with Maureen, watching some cooking shows. I can make spaghetti now."

"Wow. I am glad you are taking an interest in cooking. It can be a very rewarding hobby. Have you tried any baking?"

"Well, I did do some of the out-of-the-box brownies where you only have to add egg and milk. They came out pretty good. I may ask you for a recipe for brownies or cake to try before I go back. Anne, how come I never saw that picture of you and Russell in front of that old car before?"

"Russell had that tucked away somewhere. He took it down when he had to sell it. He was so upset when he sold it, but we were broke and we had Lucy, and Jack was on the way. He wrote down the guy's name and number he sold it to on the back of the picture, figured he would buy it back someday. Anyway, no sense living in the past. We are on to better things now. I do miss cruising in that car though. Russell and I felt like movie stars behind the wheel of that thing." She glanced at Melissa. "Probably you think that is silly."

"No, Anne, I don't, but you guys are better than movie stars."

Anne hugged Melissa. They finished up prepping for tomorrow. Before leaving for the night, Melissa glanced at the back of the picture and wrote down the name and number.

Later that day, Jack was cleaning up the Red at Night when Russell came down the hill and onto the dock.

"How many you take up today?" Russell asked, while letting a puff out from his pipe.

"Took everything up from the harbor. I think after the weekend the tides might be right to take up everything in the bay in one or two days," Jack answered.

There was a bit of a pause while Jack formulated a question in his head.

"Dad…. I am thinking about asking Melissa to marry me."

Russell grinned from ear to ear.

"Well…. what you thinkin?"

"We haven't been dating that long, but I love her and I know she loves me."

Russell started dancing on the dock singing the Beatles "All You Need is Love."

"Come on, dad…. I am serious. Should I ask her to marry me?"

"Of all the questions you have asked me, and will ask me in our lifetime, that is one of a few I can't answer for you. Nobody can. You need to sit on that front porch with a nice cold beer and think it through, but don't just use that brain of yours. Use your heart, listen to it."

Russell let a big puff from his pipe and started singing again "Listen to your heart......"

"Dad.... don't give up your day job."

"Well, that is why I came down here in the first place. What do you think of me giving up lobstering and running the dock full time?"

Jack grinned ear to ear "Of all the questions you have asked me, and will ask me in our lifetime, that is one of a few where I can't answer for you. Nobody can. You need to sit on that front porch with a scotch and think it through."

Russell smiled and shook his head at his son.

"Seriously, dad, if you are ready to get out, then do it. I know you love that dock and you care about the guys that fish for you."

"I was thinking getting a small outboard deal. Maybe you and I finish off a 23 Crowley and fish a hundred or so up here in the bay. Just to stay on the water. That, and your mother would still want to have a boat for cruising in."

"So Old Smoke will be up for sale. Man, that would be a perfect boat for Josh...if he wants to stick with it."

They walked up the hill together, chatting the whole way. Anne could see them coming up the hill. She smiled, as the memories of them walking up that hill together over the years played in her head. She remembered Russell with both Jack and Lucy up on his shoulders as he walked up the hill. She always thought it was funny how Russell with a smaller build and stature, was always able to carry both kids up that hill. She heard Russell come into the house.

"We already for tomorrow, Anne?" asked Russell as he sat down in his chair and opened the newspaper.

"Yes, Melissa stayed a little after lunch and helped me get things prepped. She has been learning to cook while she was back in Hollywood."

"That is good. Cooking is a good skill to have....if you are married to a lobsterman."

Anne hopped up and swatted the newspaper out of his hands.

"What do you mean, married to a lobsterman? Is Jack....... did Jack...?"

"No, no, no, not yet, but he is thinking about it. He was asking me about it. If he should."

"What did you tell him?"

"I told him he had to answer that for himself. Are you worried about losing the bet?"

"I don't have to worry about losing the bet. You are going to be selling Old Smoke."

"Who told you that?"

"Nobody.....Russell Finn, I can read you like you read the "Register". You haven't been hauling as much. You haven't been out on the water since I don't know when."

"Well, I guess you are right. I was thinking about getting an outboard boat for us to cruise around in and maybe I would have 100 or so up here in the bay. What do you think?"

"I think you have already made up your mind and you are fishing around waiting for someone to agree with you. Well, I agree with you. We are in a good spot moneywise. You have plenty to keep you busy at the dock."

Russell nodded his head in agreement. He realized they had completely derailed from the conversation of Jack and Melissa.

"I think he will pop the question after Christmas."

"Me, too."

It was two in the afternoon when everybody started showing up at The Harbor. Melissa and Jack arrived and were greeted by a swarm of kids wanting to see Melissa. She took her time and signed autographs and anything else they gave her to sign. They made their way down to the group of people already there. Melissa joined Anne and Abigail at a table, while Jack joined Michael in a group talking about past race seasons. A young couple came walking in with their baby. The husband was one of Russell's new dock guys. They had just had the baby a month ago. The infant was passed around from one woman to the other. Melissa wanted to hold it so bad, but was not sure, since she didn't know the mother. She had never held a baby before. Abigail was holding it when she could see Melissa looking on.

"Would you like to hold her, Melissa?"

"Yes…. if it is ok with the mother?"

"Oh, I would be honored to have Melissa Andrews hold my baby."

Abigail slowly passed the child to Melissa. The small girl started to fuss, but Melissa rocked her and sang to her. Jack looked over to see Melissa with the baby.

"You're all done now, cap. Once a woman holds a baby you got a year…. maybe two before they want one," said Michael.

"I guess I better hurry up and buy a ring then, shouldn't I."

"Are you serious? Just yesterday you were on the fence. What happened? You fall off?"

Jack pulled Michael away from the group a bit. "Look, I dragged my feet before and lost the chance. I am not doing that again. If I have learned anything from this crazy summer we had, it was that you can't take life for granted."

"Alright then…. looks like we will be going ring shopping." Michael gave Jack a pat on the shoulder and returned to the group. Just then, Anne announced everything was ready and it was time to line up to eat.

The group filled up plates and sat down for the meal. Russell had one of his more religious fishermen say grace, then they dug in. The room went quiet with nothing more than the sounds of silverware on plates. Every so often someone would ask who made what and if they could have the recipe. A few got up for seconds, and some even for thirds. After everyone had their fill of dinner, Anne and a few others started getting the desserts ready, while Russell addressed the fishermen. He thanked them all for coming and bringing their families. He also thanked them for fishing for them. He had Elizabeth pass out the Christmas bonus checks to them all. After dessert was finished and the music was turned on, the kids and some of the adults hit the dance floor. Soon the crowd was chanting "sing" to Melissa. So, she took the stage and sang a few songs and even got Anne to go up to sing Patsy Cline's "Crazy". After the festivities, everybody helped clean up. The teenage boys showed off how many chairs they could carry. Everybody said their goodbyes and thank you's.

Later on in the evening, Melissa and Jack were watching TV together on the couch.

"So what were you and Michael talking about?" Melissa asked.

Jack had to think. He hated to lie but didn't want to tell her he was going to go buy an engagement ring. "Oh, we were talking about putting a new engine in the boat." It wasn't a lie. They had talked about it.

"How did you like holding the baby?"

"It was good, she was so cute. At first, I was worried about dropping it or accidentally hurting it somehow. Then I relaxed a bit and started singing to her."

Snuggled up beside each other they sat and watched TV.

The Finns and Williams gathered at Russell and Anne's house the next afternoon for Thanksgiving. The conversation here was more personal than at the Friendsgiving. They went around the table discussing current events and what was going on in their lives. After the meal and dessert, Melissa took a moment to absorb the past of couple days. She watched Russell teaching Josh different knots, and she listened Michael and Jack talking boats as usual. Abigail, Elizabeth and Anne were talking about Elizabeth's upcoming graduation and move to college. She felt so at home and relaxed.

For the next couple of weeks Melissa fell into the daily rhythm of the Finn's life. She was either on Jack's boat, helping Anne in the restaurant or working on the docks with Russell. She also kept in touch with Mrs. Niles at the school, and even attended a PTA meeting as a guest where she was able to talk about some of her plans for the school. She watched the town slowly morph into its Christmas season and soon it was time for the annual Christmas celebration. One cold Saturday morning they all gathered down at The Harbor. The majority of Russell's fisherman had brought their boats into the dock to hang Christmas lights and other decorations on them. Michael had his boat in near where Josh and Elizabeth decorating Josh's boat. Anne had homemade apple cider donuts along with cocoa and coffee. Jack had found an 18 foot tall Christmas tree, and stood it up in his boat. He and Melissa covered it with lights. Russell had a giant Santa in his boat, Michael had made a big sign saying Merry Christmas Boothbay Harbor. Everybody helped everyone and in a couple of hours the boats were all decorated. They had a quick lunch then headed to the school where there was a craft fair and some more events for the kids. Melissa had volunteered to read "Twas the Night Before Christmas" to the younger kids and to sing at the tree lighting ceremony coming up. When the afternoon festivities had wound down, and the sun was starting to set, they gathered at the Christmas tree on the library lawn. A crowd of Boothbay Harbor people had gathered to meet Santa. The kids all ran down to the town dock to greet Santa coming in by boat. He, Mrs. Claus, and the entourage of kids, walked up to the tree. Then Santa gave a wave of his hand and bellowed out a big "Ho ho ho, Merry Christmas!" The tree lit up and all the kids were awed by the majestic light. Santa paused to allow the magic of the moment soak in; he then gave Melissa a nod. She stepped up on the stage, grabbed the microphone and soon the words to "White Christmas" came warmly out of her mouth and over the air. Everybody was silent, listening intently. Next she had all the kids join her on stage and they sang "Rudolph the Red Nosed Reindeer". She sang a few more songs and hopped down off the stage. By then the sun had set and it was time to get in the boats for the lighted boat parade.

The boats untied from the dock and made their way out into the harbor. The coast guard had one of their boats decorated, and as usual, led the parade. They passed by St. Andrews hospital so the patients there could see the thirty or more boats all decorated. They rounded the harbor, receiving cheers from people on the docks. They passed the dock where the judges were and finished the tour around the harbor. Once all the boats had gone through they met up at McSeagulls, a local bar, for drinks, music and to find out who had won. The judges had announced that Nick Page, a lobsterman from Robinson's Wharf had taken first place. Jim Lowe, who fished for Russell, had taken second, and Josh took third. As usual, all the prize money was donated back for next year's celebration. Melissa and Jack spent a lot of time on the dance floor, constantly in each other's arms. After the results were announced, the band fired up again and Jack and Melissa were back on the floor holding each other close during a slow song.

"Jack…. I think I am a little drunk," Melissa bubbled.

"I think you are more than a little…. but that's ok, I am, too."

They laughed at each, as they danced, wavering across the dance floor.

"Jack, I am mustering up any sober I have in me to say I love you. This day has been awesome. I really just feel so good being in your life…..This life."

Jack lowered his head until his forehead touched hers. Their noses touched lightly.

"Melissa Andrews. I love having you in my life. It's our life." Jack thought about proposing right there, but he had been drinking, so had she. He wanted it to be special.

They kissed right there on the dance floor.

Chapter 18

A few more weeks went by and Boothbay Harbor looked more like a Christmas village. A few inches of snow had fallen to give the town the final touch. Melissa and Jack spent more and more time together. Jack had taken her out plowing snow, then out sledding, and bought her a pair of snowshoes to go hiking on local trails. They also shared their time with friends and family, hosting a movie night. They watched their favorite movie, "Back to the Future", at Melissa's house, and she made taco's. She also went along with the ladies for a girls night out of Christmas shopping. She was swarmed by people at the Maine Mall, asking for her autograph or a selfie with her, but she took it in stride and made sure to interact with her fans. The big mystery was that she had rented Michael's big work bay in his new building and had Michael make sure no one could see what was in the shop. Michael pretended to have no clue what was going on.

Melissa was in a place where she had stopped being so awestruck at the love and fellowship the Finns and Williams had showed her. Now she just embraced it, appreciated it, and showed her own love back. If she wasn't helping Anne in the kitchen, she was helping Abigail with the bookkeeping. Abigail had helped her get enrolled in some college courses to get a teaching degree. Her bond with Russell grew stronger as well, often joining him for breakfast in the mornings when Jack had gone out lobstering.

Christmas morning came, and Jack and Melissa started out with the stockings they had stuffed for each other with small trinkets, snacks, chocolates, and other candy. Jack had gotten her the signature Maine stocking stuffer, a car window scraper. After the stockings were emptied, it was time to move on to the bigger gifts. Jack, knowing this was Melissa's first Maine winter, had gotten her some insulated socks, winter boots and winter gloves. But under the tree there was a small jewelry box. Melissa paused before reaching for it. She unwrapped it slowly and opened the lid. In the box was a necklace with a small charm. It contained a nautical chart showing the location of where he had pulled her from the water.

"Oh, Jack." Melissa paused… holding the necklace to her chest. "This is…. Perfect." She reached out and hugged and kissed him.

Jack smiled proudly.

"Open yours, Jack."

Jack started opening boxes. One was a new hoodie with his boat name to replace the one he had given to her. The next was a new hat. But the best one was a vest worn by Michael J Fox while filming "Back To The Future". It was in a display case with a signature of authenticity. Jack was awestruck. He couldn't even think of what to say.

"Look at the back, Jack," Melissa said.

Jack turned it around and on the back was a note from Michael J Fox. It read:

Jack, I hope you have a Merry Christmas. Melissa kicked over every rock in Hollywood to find this vest. She is a great girl. Good luck to you both.

Sincerely MJF.

"Thank you so much, Melissa…. I love this. This is crazy."

After getting dressed and having coffee, they made their way down to Anne and Russell's. Jack was a little annoyed that Melissa was texting someone, but figured it was probably to just say Merry Christmas to her friends. When they arrived, Lucy and Sam were already there. They all exchanged gifts and opened presents. Anne had taken pictures of all of her recipes, then used those pictures to make a cookbook for Melissa and Lucy. Russell had hats and hoodies made for everyone with The Harbor logo and their names. After all the gifts had been opened, there was an awkward silence. There hadn't been a gift from Melissa to Anne or Russell. Then there came a rumble from outside. The rumble got louder, then it revved a bit. Russell peeked up as if he almost recognized the sound. He looked at Melissa, who was grinning ear to ear.

"You didn't….," said Russell.

"Go look…," responded Melissa.

Russell, as if he were a teenager, jumped out of his chair kicking wrapping paper into the air. As he breezed through the kitchen, he didn't slow down to look out the window. As he went out onto the porch the rumbling had stopped. He went around the corner of the house and saw the shiny chrome front bumper against the midnight black of an old 57 Chevy Bel Air. It looked just as it did in the picture. He stopped in his tracks, standing in the snow with his slippers. Anne was close behind, chattering away about the way he had kicked the wrapping paper all over the living room. The chattering stopped the minute her eyes caught what he was already looking at. She rested her hands on his shoulders

"Oh, Russell….," said Anne in amazement.

"Look inside," prompted Melissa.

They walked to the car and Michael stepped out leaving the door open. Sitting in the middle of the red leather bench front seat was a black leather jacket, white T-shirt and blue jeans. Also a black pokeadot dress. The exact outfits they were wearing in the picture taken some 30 plus years ago.

"I had to do some homework and track down the car. It was in pretty good shape; it needed a new engine and some other little things that Michael helped me with, but it's your car. The outfits obviously are not the ones, but they will fit."

Russell and Anne looked on in complete shock. Neither of them could think of any words to say.

"Keys are in it, Russell…. Fire it up," Michael said, holding in his emotions.

Russell stepped in while Jack opened the passenger side door for his mother. As Russell sat down in the seat, in the dash where he used to keep a picture of Anne in high school, was a picture of all the Finns and Williams, including Melissa. He placed his hand on the key switch and turned it on. The rumble that had caught his attention just minutes earlier came back. He revved it up a bit and a grin stretched across his face. He looked over at his wife, his lifelong companion who was sitting next to him fighting back the tears of joy, as was he. He looked out the windshield at his family. Melissa was standing there with a single tear rolling down her cheek. He shut the car off, and got out, and went to Melissa and gave her a big hug. He picked her up right off the ground.

"Thank you…. Thank you so much," said Russell, holding himself together.

"I am glad you like it," was all Melissa could think to say.

"I love it! How did you ever find it?"

"It took some digging, and some work. It ended up in Florida. I had to fly Michael down to take a look at it."

"Michael! You knew about this?"

"Yes…. that's why my shop has been all locked up. Melissa had a private jet take me down there and look at it. I told her what it needed. She had that thing on the back of a flatbed before I was even back on the plane. She had my buddy in Freeport, Dodge Restorations, handle bringing it back to life. Austin put a newer fuel injected engine in to make it more reliable. When he was done we moved it at nighttime into my shop," Michael answered.

"Who else knew about this?" Anne asked.

Abigail confessed she knew but didn't say anything to anybody. To everybody else it was as big a surprise to them as it was to Russell and Anne. Russell started the engine again and backed it into the garage. He didn't dare take it for a ride on the Maine winter roads.

He vowed as soon as spring hit he and Anne would take a cruise down Route 1.

As the week passed and New Year's Eve approached, Jack grew a little more nervous. There was going to be a big New Year's Eve party at The Harbor. He was planning to ask Melissa to marry him that night, but he wanted them both to be sober. He would have to ask her before the party. He would ask when he picked her up. He had played it in his head over and over. She would be coming down the stairs from the loft into the living room. She would probably be dressed up a little, but nothing too fancy. He would wait until she got to the bottom step and then drop to one knee. After that, he didn't know what he was going to say. Obviously, at some point, he would say, "Will you marry me?", but he felt there should be some lead up to it. It should be something about all they had been through. He couldn't think of what to say though. As he was sitting in his truck looking inside and thinking all this, she had already come down the stairs. He decided in that moment to just go do it, let whatever words pour out. These moments can't be planned out or strategically mapped. He had to just jump in with both feet.

He got out of his truck and walked to the door. He opened it up and there she was. She was wearing a simple, yet gorgeous, black dress. Her hair was left down, the way he liked it. The small simple earrings and the necklace he had gotten her for Christmas reflected the evening light. His face suddenly felt hot and flushed. She walked up to him to give him a kiss but instead of bending down to kiss her, he slowly went down to one knee. He took a deep breath to get oxygen back to his brain. The lump in his throat that was almost causing pain slowly went away.

"Melissa, I saved you…. I saved you from the water, but in many ways, you saved me. Now I could go on and talk about every event, every emotion that has brought me….us to this moment, but there is no need for that. You know I love you. I know you love me. I can't even think about what our lives would be like without each other. I want to be with you forever. Melissa Andrews…. will you marry me?"

Melissa now felt hot in the face. She now felt a lump in her throat. This was not what she had expected to happen tonight. Yes, she had thought about life with Jack, and yes, she had thought about marrying him at some point, but she didn't expect he would ask so soon.

"Jack…. I am not ready…" She paused to think how to say what she was feeling, but the pause was too long. Jack had gotten up… and left, with a tear rolling down his face.

Jack was nearly home. His phone was ringing constantly. First Melissa, then his father, then Melissa again. He had driven around Boothbay Harbor so much that he was now driving over some of the same roads again. "How could she say no…." he thought to himself. They had been through so much together. He was hurt, confused and angry, all at the same time. He knew he should have waited, but Michael and his father said it was time. No, no, they didn't, he said to himself. They said this was his decision. "Not ready…. How can she not be ready?…. We were on the Jim Sterling show for Christ's sake." It had been a while since his phone rang so he thought it was probably safe to go home now. He didn't want to go to the party now. He just wanted to go home and go to bed. He pulled into the driveway and sure enough, her Blazer was there and the kitchen lights were on. Jack paused a second. It wasn't too late to put it in reverse and leave again. What good would that do? She would still be here when he got back. He pulled the rest of the way into the driveway and got out of the truck. He walked into the kitchen and Melissa was standing there looking at him. Her makeup had run from crying. He almost felt bad, but the pain of being rejected overcame it. He didn't know what to say. He wanted to tell her to leave, but also wanted to ask all the questions that were running through his head.

"You didn't answer your phone…." said Melissa with a shaky voice.

"Didn't want to talk," Jack snapped back.

"Jack, you caught me by surprise, and you didn't let me finish."

"What…. what else were you going to say? What is there to say? I thought you felt the same way about me that I feel for you. I guess I was wrong."

"No…. you are not wrong. I love you, Jack, I do, but marriage. I am not ready for that."

"Why? We love each other."

"Jack, we have a great thing. I don't want to rush into this and mess it all up."

"It won't get all messed up. Don't you get it? We can handle anything."

"Jack, just give me time. You have caught me in the middle of big changes in my life, you know that." She paused to catch her breath. Jack looked like he was about to speak, but she decided to start and make him listen further. "Jack you are right, I do love you. I love you with all that I am, with all my heart and soul. I love your family and friends. I love your town and this whole new lifestyle that you have brought me into. I do want to spend the rest of my life with you. But before we go jumping into marriage I need to finish these changes that are happening. I hope you can accept that."

Melissa walked towards him and gave him a kiss on the cheek and walked out the door. He stood there numb, as he heard the door close and her car leave.

For the next couple days Jack and Melissa didn't talk much. He was still hurt. Everybody knew something was wrong but didn't know what had happened. Jack distanced himself from everybody and Melissa continued to work with the principal and school board. She called and texted Jack with only short answers in reply. She had been so hurt by Jack pulling back the way he had. The one person she could count on was now pushing her away. She had Russell take her to the airport on her last day.

"You ready, Hollywood?" asked Russell as they pulled up to the airport.

"Really wish Jack would have brought me. Though I don't mind your company."

"I don't know what is going on between you two. None of my business really. I will say that my son is hurt and, when he is hurt, he gets stubborn. Stubborn as hell. Now his head is stuck so far up his ass he might lose one of the best things that ever happened to him."

"Don't worry about that, Russell. I love your boy and if I have to physically remove his head from his ass I will."

"That's my girl."

 Melissa grabbed her bags and gave Russell a big hug. They said their goodbyes and Melissa went into the airport. Russell headed back to Boothbay Harbor.

Anne saw Jack outside putting the plow back on his truck.

"What are you doing?" Anne asked the obvious to start a conversation.

"Gonna snow tonight. Just getting ready," Jack answered shortly.

"I don't mean that. I mean why are you here while your girlfriend is getting on a plane to fly home?"

Jack ignored his mother.

"What is the matter, she tell you 'no'?"

Jack paused a bit. "Is that what she told you?"

"No Jack, but I am smart, I can do math. You two not showing up at the New Year's party, then hardly talking to each other. You slugging around here. It all equals up to, you popped the question New Year's Eve and she said 'no'."

"She said she wasn't ready."

"And you think not talking to her and acting like this is going to make her ready sooner?"

"What am I supposed to do? I'm hurt."

"Oh, you're hurt… How do you think she is feeling? The one man she has ever truly been in love with. The one man that loved her for who she is just turned his back on her because she needed more time. Your father and I didn't raise you to be selfish. You are about to mess up a really good thing, Jack Finn. One of the best things that ever happened to you." Anne walked away.

Jack took in his mother's words. She was right. He took out his phone and tried to call her, but there was no signal. He left a voicemail asking her to call him as soon as she could. For the rest of the day he tried to keep himself busy, but kept checking his phone. All day long he thought about what Melissa had said and what his mother had said. How could he have been so selfish? Why couldn't he have just accepted her answer? It was seven o'clock when Melissa called.

"Hello."

"Hi, Jack."

"Melissa…. I am so sorry. I was hurt and acted like a fool…."

Melissa cut him off mid-sentence. "You hurt me. You ignored me….. you couldn't even say goodbye."

Jack could hardly breathe. What had he done? "Melissa, I am sorry. Please…." He stopped to think what to say.

"Jack…. I love you, but I need some time to think this through."

"Oh….okay."

"Love you, Jack, good night."

"Love you, too."

The phone went silent. Jack felt numb. "At least she said she loved me," he said out loud to himself.

For the next couple of weeks any conversation they had on the phone was short and awkward. She had sent the invitations to the Oscars to him, Anne and Russell, the Williams, and Lucy and Sam. She set up the travel arrangements with hotels for all of them. The limousines came to The Harbor to pick them up. From there they flew first class to Hollywood. Once they landed, they were taken to their hotels and Jack was taken to Melissa's.

The limo dropped him off at her front door and Maureen met him and helped him carry his things into the house. As he walked in the door, Melissa was walking down the steps talking on the phone. Jack didn't know what to do; he wanted to hold her but wasn't sure. She looked distracted and very busy. When she got off the phone she looked at Jack. She took him by the hand and led him out to the pool area. They sat down together on a bench. Jack started to speak, but Melissa cut him off.

"Jack…. I love you. I do want to spend the rest of my life with you, but I will not be pushed into something before I am ready. I have dealt with that my whole life. Can you wait for me to be ready?"

Without any thought or hesitation, "Yes. If I have to wait until we are 98 and all wrinkly. All that matters is we are together."

"Married or not, you cannot turn your back on me again."

"I won't Melissa. I had a picture in my head of what was going to happen that night. Even though I was nervous I was still confident you would say 'yes'. When you said 'no'… I didn't know what to do."

"I need to know if things get tough you are not going to turn and run away like you did that night. I need you to be the strong man that pulled me out of that water, I need you to do that for the rest of our lives."

"I will, Melissa, I will.

They hugged, kissed and cried, then sat there in each other's arms holding each other as the tension slowly faded away.

"So how did everybody like flying first class?" Melissa asked as a final move from the tension.

"Well, I am pretty sure Michael was a little drunk when we got off the plane. Abigail and the kids loved it. It was mom and dad's first time flying. They were a little anxious at first but then got used to it. The flight attendant got a kick out of dad."

"I wish I could have seen that. I hope they like the hotel I got them. I did go a little crazy. They should be here soon. Maureen is going to make pizza for lunch. After that they will all be getting fitted for tuxes and dresses. I hired a couple of stylists to help."

"What about you? When do we see your dress?"

"You will see it tomorrow night. You and I will leave from here. The stylist team will help them at the hotel and then a limo will bring them to the Oscars. Chris will be with them as a chaperone. We will all meet at the table at the Oscars. You guys will love who we are sitting by."

"Who?"

"It's a surprise."

Soon the limo showed up with the Finn and Williams clans. Everybody was awestruck as they looked at Melissa's mansion. She gave them the grand tour and when the tour was done, Maureen took orders for pizza. Anne started to get up and follow Maureen into the kitchen, then stopped and sat back down. She remembered this was Maureen's job and she wasn't supposed to intrude, but Maureen turned before heading into the kitchen.

"Mrs. Finn, would you like to help? I am afraid this is quite a big order for just myself," Maureen asked.

"Oh, definitely," said Anne as she sprung up to help.

Soon the pizzas were out, and everyone sat at the dining room table. Melissa paused for a moment to take in the sight of her family and friends in her house. She listened as everybody described the flight and the hotels. She was happy to spoil the people that had given her so much.

"Okay, now the limo will take you guys to get fitted for your tuxes and dresses. There are a couple of stylists to help. Please, you guys have given me so much, please let me spoil you with this. Don't hold back."

Russell made a grimacing sound and his face looked upset. Melissa had feared that some of the royal treatment might go too far.

"Well, you better hope you get one of them Oscars…. you are going to need to pawn it after I get done shopping."

The group shared a laugh, then were on their way. They arrived at the store and were immediately separated. The men went one way and the ladies another. Meanwhile, Melissa went with Jack to get his tux. After all were set up with an outfit to wear for the Oscars, they were also outfitted with some other designer clothes to go out to in. Melissa treated them all out to dinner. While they ate, they were greeted by celebrities. It seemed like everyone in Hollywood knew who they were. After dinner, they parted ways. Tomorrow was the Oscars, and they needed rest.

Melissa had planned for them to go on a tour of Hollywood during the day before the Oscars. She wanted something to take up the time before the big event.

Then it was time. The stylists met them at the hotel. They got into their tuxes and dresses and had their hair styled. Chris Pratt arrived ready to chaperone them.

"Hello, good people. As it is usually a tradition to have a date for the Oscars, I will ask Ms. Elizabeth Williams to be my date for the evening. That leaves you, Josh…." Chris paused as he glanced at the door. From around the corner came Taylor Swift.

"Melissa told me there would be a cute young man to be my date for the night." Taylor Swift stuck out her arm for Josh to take.

Josh turned red, smiled, and gracefully took Taylor's arm and started to introduce himself.

"Be careful, Josh…. you mess up and she will write a song about you," said Russell.

They arrived at the red carpet entering the Oscars. Elizabeth and Josh had to stop and pose a bit while reporters spoke to Taylor and Chris. After the walk on the red carpet, they were seated at their table. While they were talking about everything that was going on, Russell got a tap on his shoulder. It felt kind of hard so he turned around quickly. There looking at him with a grin was Clint Eastwood.

"If I come up to Maine, will you take me out lobstering?" Clint asked in his raspy voice.

"Well, if you want to, but not anybody gets to just hop on my boat," Russell said.

The two old men shared a laugh. In walked Melissa and Jack. Melissa seemed to glow with beauty and Jack looked as if he were getting an award. Soon the awards started. Actors and actresses all receiving different supporting awards. Then it came to Best actress in a motion picture. Melissa was obviously one of the nominees. The whole table went silent as the card was pulled from the envelope. Sure enough, Melissa's name was called. She went up on stage and thanked all the normal people that get thanked. She paused and looked down at the table. All the Finns and Williams proudly stared back at her.

"I do have an announcement to make. I have decided to retire."

The crowd stirred in their seats. There was whispering and comments being spoken softly. Melissa waited for everyone to settle.

"I have been an actress now for almost three decades. I know that some people in this room would call that a short tenure, but I found a life outside of acting and Hollywood. A life built on trust and integrity. Where you are not judged by one small moment, but by your day to day actions. I may come back, but not until I am ready. For now I am going…." She paused to think and to collect herself.

"I am going home."

Some may have been confused as to where home was, but not at the table where her new family sat. They knew where her home was.

It had been a busy couple of weeks. Melissa had been selling most of her estate. She had given Maureen a large severance package and her new contact information. Her mansion was already under contract. Her cars had been sold along, with a lot of her possessions. She wanted to keep her life as simple as possible. As for her wealth, she kept it tucked away, donating some to charities, but mostly to the Russell Finn Foundation. Maine was certainly cold in February but she had gotten used to it. She would start working down at The Harbor in the spring. She looked forward to working with Russell and Elizabeth. In the fall she would start working towards her teaching degree and start volunteering at the high school drama department. Tonight, she and Jack were going on a date. A simple nighttime cruise around Boothbay Harbor. The Red at Night had a cozy feel to it when all the winter backs were up and the cabin was heated. She loved looking back at the town, all covered in the white blanket of snow and how that blanket reflected light to make things seem lighter, even in the dark of night. Melissa had developed a love/hate relationship with the snow. She was in awe of its beauty, but hated its cold, and the difficulty it presented driving. She thought it was almost ironic that she had bought an old large full size SUV that was a virtual tank on Maine's winter roads. She had still managed to bounce off a few snowbanks here and there but it didn't seem to hurt the old K5 Blazer much. She laughed at herself in that memory. The laugh was needed. Her anxiety about tonight's date with Jack was growing. She had thought about it when he popped the question at New Year's and even more since the Oscars. She was ready now. Hollywood was her past. Jack Finn was her future. Would he say 'yes'? All her senses said, yes he would, but there was still a looming anxiety in her. Maybe he wouldn't like her proposing to him. Maybe that violation of tradition would be too much for him, from a family based on tradition. To her it was a final symbol of wanting to start a new life with him. A famous Oscar winning Hollywood actress humbly asking the Boothbay Harbor lobsterman that nobody knew, to be her husband. She liked the idea, it had meaning and purpose to her. It was modest and feminist at the same time, but that wasn't the agenda, just a point. She saw the headlights of Jack's truck bouncing off the side of the buildings and soon his boots could be heard coming down the ramp. Watching him approach only stirred the butterflies in her belly. He untied the lines and hopped into the cabin.

"Got her fired up I see. Did you check the oil before you started it?" Jack asked, challenging Melissa.

"No, but I watched the oil pressure gauge and checked for water coming out the exhaust," said Melissa, accepting the challenge.

"That's my girl," Jack said, as he pulled the boat away from the dock and idled out into the harbor. He kept a sharp eye out as he idled by boats on their moorings. When he got to the center of the harbor he turned the boat so they could sit and look back at the town. He turned to look at Melissa and give her a kiss. When he looked, she was crouched on her knees on the engine box.

"Jack Finn, will you marry me?"

"Wait…. what…aren't I supposed to ask that?" Jack stuttered.

Melissa took a breath and thought how to retain the moment without killing it with logistics and feminism.

"No, no rules, and if there are I want to break them. I am starting a new life Jack. I want you in it. Now and forever. Will you be my husband?"

There was pause as Jack processed what was happening. He drew a big smile. "Yes."

Melissa got up and kissed him. They held each other for a while.

"I am glad you said 'yes'. It makes the next thing much easier to say - I 'm pregnant."